WORTH
the
Trouble

NICOLE SHARP

The Simply Trouble Series:

Big Trouble in Little Italy
Simply Protocol
Worth The Trouble
A Simple Avalanche

Standalone Books

The Italian Holiday
La Bella Luna
Surviving Thirty

Novellas

Let It Snow
The Museum Guide

For my Grandma, Rose Marie,
the original smart, sassy, feisty, Italian woman.

WORTH the Trouble

"Look at this, look at what my people did!"
—My Grandma Rose sitting next to me in the Duomo
in Florence, gesturing around the impressive structure.

Chapter One

"Alex, sit down. Your pacing is giving me a headache."

Alessandra, Alex to her American doctor colleagues, abruptly stopped and knelt in the dirt next to her friend. "Is it getting worse, Maggie?" she asked in her thick Italian accent.

"Only when you pace." Maggie attempted a smile but it turned into a grimace; she touched her fingers to where her dishwater blonde hair was matted around the temple, where the blood had dried. She rested her head against the cave wall as Alessandra pulled the lantern they'd been left with closer to inspect the purple-black hematoma. She held up a finger in front of Maggie's eyes, and urged, "Follow the finger."

Maggie pushed Alessandra's hand away. "You and Sabrina have already done that. We all know it's not a concussion. It just aches, like I've been hit upside the head with the butt of a gun." Which she had been. "How is Sabrina?"

"Sabrina is fine," announced Sabrina, the other woman occupying the small cave with them. She was sitting across from them, several steps away, her back pressed against the opposite wall where she braced her left arm against her side, which she'd fallen on when being directed into the cave.

"Oddio." *Oh my God.* Alessandra stood and began pacing again as she ran her hands through her short, unruly black hair to get the mess away from her face.

"Alex ..." Maggie muttered.

"Everything is going to be okay. I'll get us out of this."

"We don't even know where we are," Maggie whispered.

"It will be okay. We'll be okay," Alessandra insisted.

"Yes, because we haven't done anything wrong," Sabrina hissed, changing her position in the hopes of somehow getting comfortable.

"And we're working under the international humanitarian law, they can't just ... keep us here," Maggie added. "Their attack is going to be seen as a war crime."

Sabrina caught a sob before it could manifest into something more, the weight of their situation thickening the air in the cave. "Maggie, you signed the same waiver we did. Just because we're doctors in Venezuela doesn't mean everyone is going to abide by the law. These men want cash. Simple as that."

"Basta." *Stop*, Alessandra said as she halted in place and took a deep breath. "I know for certain we are going to be okay."

"Then why are you pacing?" Maggie asked.

"Because his wife is pregnant. He cannot leave her *now*," she hissed.

Across the darkness, Maggie gave a questioning look to Sabrina.

"Are you having trouble with your English?" Sabrina asked. "You got hit pretty hard in the head as well."

"My English is very good. And my head is very hard." Alessandra gave a wave of her hand and a gruff laugh.

Sabrina sighed exasperatedly. "Well, my Italian dear, we are having trouble understanding who is pregnant and why it matters to us here in the middle of nowhere, in this cave, where we've been kidnapped."

Alessandra stopped pacing and crouched between her friends. "Mio fratello, my brother ..." she lowered her voice as she whispered, "he works for the CIA."

"CIA?" Sabrina breathed out, matching Alessandra's whispered tone.

"Yes. He will hear about our capture and he will save us ... perché lui è stupido." Alessandra took another lap around the cave, accompanied by Maggie's moan, a reminder that she needed Alex to sit down.

Alessandra sat next to Maggie, reached out and absently patted the woman's hand.

"What is stupid?" Maggie asked, referring to the Italian word she'd understood.

"My brother. His wife is four months pregnant. He will come save us, but it's going to upset her. And he shouldn't be leaving her upset."

"Don't you think she'll be upset enough if she finds out you've been kidnapped?" Sabrina asked.

"*When* ..." Maggie amended, her voice shaking, "when they find out."

Sabrina whispered, "Sure they'll find out, but that doesn't mean anyone's coming to help us any time soon."

Maggie contradicted, "We're doctors in the middle of a jungle. We're a pretty valuable commodity. Didn't you see how many sick people are in this camp? We're going to be put to work."

"It won't be as long as you think." Alessandra's smile could be heard in the dim light of the cave. "My brother will know very soon ..." She rolled her pant leg up, turning it inside out, and pulled on a small area of fabric that had a secret velcroed pocket. From that, she produced what looked like a flat battery, the size of a quarter.

"What the hell is that?" Sabrina crossed the small distance and picked up the lantern to get a better look at the device.

"When I told my brother I was coming to Venezuela for several months with Doctors Without Borders, we argued for days. Finally, he gave his consent, which I didn't need, and this tracking device, in case of an emergency." She held the device loosely in her hand.

Maggie's eyes widened as Sabrina blurted out in a loud whisper, "For Christ's sake Alex, I believe *this* is the damn emergency."

Alessandra pressed the button and held it for several seconds until a red light began to flash. She put the device back in the pocket. "He will come for us and leave his pregnant wife worried and alone." She shook her head. "Oddio, Jessica is going to want to talk about all of this. Because she's as stubborn as he is."

"Jessica being your brother's wife?" Sabrina asked, sitting back down, creating a triangle.

"My sister-in-law," Alessandra confirmed.

"You're older, aren't you?" Maggie guessed.

Alessandra frowned, but nodded her head. "Yes, why?"

"You act like the older sibling. Taking charge, worried about us, bossy ..." Maggie laughed but it turned into a groan.

Sabrina cleared her throat and gave a hopeful whisper. "But he'll come for us, your brother? He'll come?"

Alessandra gritted her teeth as she answered, "Yes. He'll come for us."

"How long do you think it will take?" Maggie asked.

Alessandra shrugged. "A couple of days?" A sob escaped Maggie's throat, Sabrina moved next to her and squeezed her shoulder.

"I'm just hurting." She tried to excuse her tears.

"Maggie is correct," Alessandra clutched her friend's hand, "we were brought here to work. We will just keep our heads clear and do what we have to, but we'll be ready to run when he shows up."

Maggie audibly swallowed, then let her whispered words tumble out. "Because in a few days your brother will be here to save us."

"Yes."

And for the first time, since they had been roughly excused from the hospital they were volunteering, by the militant men who now held them captive in the middle of the jungle, there was a glimmer of hope.

Chapter Two

I t had been four days since they'd been taken. And Maggie was right; the people who'd taken them weren't interested in holding them for ransom. Maybe they'd change their minds later, but for now, the women had obviously been abducted so that they could treat those who were living and hiding in the surrounding area.

And as convoluted as it was, the women saw to the patients, because their Hippocratic oath, as well as the humanitarian work they'd come to this country to do, bid them to treat all patients without discrimination.

A large canvas had been strung under the canopy of trees to form a roof and keep out the rain, while a collage of tarps created makeshift walls, fashioning the jungle hospital for the women to work. There were four pallet beds along one side of the cleared space, and two tables on the other that they used as examining surfaces.

There had been an inundation of patients with various ailments that afflict those living in the jungle without adequate care. The majority of problems were poor nutrition, gangrene, insect bites, and scurvy.

Sabrina, whose Spanish was better than everyone else's, tried to reason with one of the men who kept a steady eye, and gun, trained on them each day while they worked. She explained that the services they were being forced to provide in a very unhygienic area, were exactly why they'd come to work for Doctors Without Borders to begin with, and that the hospital they'd been working in had the proper medication and facilities available that would truly help these people. And if their captors would be willing to help the women return, they wouldn't press charges and they could, and *would*, help each person here.

The man informed Sabrina though, that the hospital was for people of Venezuela. The women had been brought across the border, to Colombia. The stunning information was followed by the insistence she get back to work, and was punctuated by the pointed tip of a gun.

When Sabrina shared with Alessandra and Maggie that they were no longer in Venezuela, Alessandra shrugged, reassuring, "It doesn't matter where we are. My brother will come."

But while they waited, they worked from dawn until the very last rays of light left the jungle. So far, their captors hadn't inflicted any more physical mistreatment, only threats uttered along with the continual watching of every move they made. They'd only been offered one meal each day. Sometime in the late afternoon, they were ushered to a small clearing, allowed to finally sit and given a few tortillas, rice, beans and some questionable water.

"We'll probably get giardia," Sabrina said as she sipped the water.

Maggie held up her cup and toasted the air. "To giardia."

"Cin cin." Alessandra grunted her "cheers" reply.

They were quiet as they ate; each too tired and too worried to do anything but focus on the food in front of them, eating slowly to make the most of the reprieve they were given.

Alessandra was most concerned about the paltry nutrition over the past few days. She had no idea what a rescue would look like exactly, or how long it would take to get it organized. She worried that if their captors continued to demand these unreasonably long hours from the women without providing proper sustenance, they might not be in very good shape by the time her brother finally *did* show up.

In an attempt to keep up their strength, she encouraged her colleagues to pocket the tortillas so they could nibble on them throughout the day.

As the last few patients disappeared into the forest and various homes beyond, the women were led back to the cave that had become their temporary cell. Alessandra looked directly up into the lush canopy, and where the sky tried to peek through, she saw a dark blue glow from the last light of the day. She lowered her gaze as the darkness fell around them, twisting the shapes and shadows of the jungle.

They were given no lamp tonight. The guard who ushered them back into the cave didn't seem to think they needed one. They stilled just inside the entrance, waiting for their eyes to adjust to the blackness, but all they could see were slight shapes where the walls were. Together, they walked to the spot in the cave farthest from the opening and exhaustedly sat down, huddling close. Alessandra didn't want to think about how each night they'd sat closer and closer together, a silent agreement to take solace where they could find it.

Alessandra stretched her aching back, twisting in each direction. After a satisfying pop on each side, she sat back and closed her eyes, trying to ignore the way her stomach groaned for food.

They would try to get what restless sleep they could. Unfortunately, with her eyes closed and the sounds of the evening jungle echoing outside the cave, the fears that stayed at bay during the day crept inside the darkness and settled on Alessandra's chest.

She tried to brush it away, focusing on how strangely grateful she'd been for the endless work. It helped numb the distress and worry and unanswered questions that circled. Could her brother really find her just because she pushed a button? What if it didn't work? What had become of the hospital and staff after the attack? Was anyone even left who could notify the proper authorities that they'd been abducted? And if there were, how long would it take them to get help and track them down?

The numbness wore off in the still, dark cave and invited the 'what ifs' closer. The weight of the past four days chose that moment to catch up to her. She felt the tears slip down her cheeks and wiped angrily at them. She would have been embarrassed if she didn't hear the silent sobs from her friends joining her own in the damp cave.

"We're not going to feel sorry for ourselves," Alessandra demanded.

"It's just exhaustion," muttered Maggie.

"Alex, not everyone's as strong as you are. Let us have our pity party. Tomorrow we'll rally," Sabrina said quietly, her words dissolving into a sob.

Alessandra reached out her hands and found her friends'. They squeezed when the connection was made, an anchor in the darkness from which they could take comfort.

Eventually, when her tears had been shed, she closed her eyes and even though uncomfortable, took solace in exhausted sleep.

A hand closed over Alessandra's mouth, waking her out of her fitful sleep. Her immediate reaction was to thrash and attempt a scream. Even though movement and sound, other than grunting, seemed futile; she still tried. And as awareness pushed the fog out of her brain, she heard similar muted abduction sounds coming from her friends, and one thought caught hold of her– they could not be separated. She could *not* lose Sabrina or Maggie. They needed each other. *She* needed them.

So she fought harder.

"Ma'am. I need you to calm down." The harshly whispered demand penetrated the rational part of her mind and stilled her struggling. "We've come to take you home," the voice insisted.

Alessandra froze as another wave of emotion took over: relief. It flooded through her whole body, causing a release of tears as she began to shake.

"Do you understand?" the voice asked.

Alessandra nodded in reply.

The quiet voice continued. "I'm going to let go, but no screaming, okay? I'm on your side, do you understand?"

Another nod of her head and the hand covering her mouth slowly released.

The same message must have sunk in for Sabrina and Maggie as well, as they had also stilled.

"Parker?" Alessandra whispered the name.

The man, still crouched in front of her, responded, "He sent us." Then he asked, "Can you confirm your names?"

They each gave their name and there was a crackle of a radio as another man called in, "Checkpoint Rome complete, headed to checkpoint Naples."

The man who woke Alessandra stood. "Ladies, we're wheels up in thirty minutes. Is anyone hurt?"

"We aren't in the best of shape," Sabrina offered, "malnutrition and exhaustion ..."

"Understood," he responded.

"But we're okay," Maggie added.

A dull green light lit up the cave as three men in full combat gear stood in front of the women. They were a menacing, lethal and daunting presence. Alessandra had never seen anything so wonderful in her whole life.

"No conversation, no sound," continued the man who'd been talking directly to them. He leveled his gaze on each woman until they'd each given him a physical nod of agreement. "Move when we move, stop when we stop." Again, he waited for nods of understanding.

"Twenty-nine minutes," came the whispered reminder to stay on task from the man standing closest to the opening of the cave.

That was the end of the conversation and directions. The women stood and with Sabrina first, lined up in single file to follow two men who took the lead. Alessandra was behind Maggie, and the man who had done all the talking brought up the rear.

Alessandra wondered how they were going to get past the guards, but that question was quickly answered when the slight light from the moon shone just inside the cave and she saw the motionless body of their guard. Any question of his health was clarified when she noticed the way his neck lay at an unnatural angle. She swallowed a lump in her throat and turned her attention to Maggie's back.

Once the whole group was out of the cave and in formation, they paused for a long moment; then one nod was all it took to begin their slow, methodical movements away from the cave and in the opposite direction of the makeshift hospital.

Alessandra tried to tamp down her worries. These men looked capable. Her brother wouldn't send someone who wasn't capable.

But no matter how skilled these men were, what if someone heard them? Their footsteps, their breathing ... hell, how could anyone *not* hear her heartbeat drumming so loudly in her ears? Surely it echoed throughout the jungle.

She was worried about the number of guards and the seeming vastness of the jungle, not to mention the number of patients they'd seen the past four days. Who knew where they had all gone or where they lived? And the undertaking of getting to safety seemed a daunting task.

She had no idea how the men knew where they were going, or how they were keeping them away from any of the people who'd abducted them, but did she really care? Just as long as they were proficient enough to do it.

The men moved in calculated steps, so slow it caused Alessandra's fear to escalate. Shouldn't they be running? She'd been privy to a glimpse of ammunition and fire power in the camp. It was no match for just three men, even with their guns and intimidating appearance.

They don't seem concerned, she reasoned silently. She needed to trust them. Trust their decisions and process. She didn't have any other choice but to follow the slow pace even though the adrenaline pumping through her veins screamed for her to give into primal fears and run.

She tripped over a protruding root, and beginning to fall, she slapped her hand over her mouth in an attempt to keep her cry of surprise from reverberating off the surrounding foliage. Before her knees touched the ground, the man behind her caught her around the waist. She steadied herself, then nodded and patted the man's hand to let him know she was okay. He released her and they began to move once more, easily catching up to the group.

The reality and actual distance of how far they'd gone was distorted by the darkness of the night and the careful pace. But the feeling that it was taking too long was a difficult fear to push aside. Hadn't one of them said something about wheels up in thirty minutes? If that were the case, they were going to be left behind. It felt like hours since this journey had begun.

As much as Alessandra thought about escaping and being saved, she feared this wasn't going to work, and now, they had run out of time and they would be left, lost in this dangerous jungle once again. She shook her head in an attempt to clear the fear, and tried to take as many deep breaths as she could. Being left behind with three well-trained, armed, military men seemed like a better prospect than the position they'd been in.

As if the jungle heard her silent pleas for help, their surroundings opened up. The foliage was suddenly less intrusive and the ground cover became more manageable, allowing the men to pick up the pace for several long minutes, until a hand sign was thrust in the air by the lead man, causing everyone to come to a silent halt and crouch down in the underbrush.

Alessandra strained to hear or see what could have possibly caught the man's attention. Maggie's hand crept into hers and she squeezed. When she turned to look at Alessandra, they exchanged weak smiles, the same thought running through their minds: *at least we're out of the cave.*

A rumble of the earth clarified the reason for their sudden stopping. A vehicle was coming. They were near a road. That was good, wasn't it? Or maybe it wasn't.

Alessandra's heart threatened to explode the moment they left the cave, but now, with the unknown danger they faced, she thought her ribs might not be a match for her erratic heartbeat.

She covered her mouth once again to hold back threatening, fear-induced sounds that came from the massive amounts of adrenaline pumping through her bloodstream.

The vehicle roaring down the road skidded to a stop, its tires crunching the dirt while spewing it up against branches and vegetation of the encroaching jungle.

The squeal of a door opening in the darkness reverberated against the humid air. Then, there was nothing but silence. After a moment the call of a bird brought lightning fast movements from the frozen men. Alessandra jumped as she and her friends were propelled into action.

They broke through the brush by the side of the road and found a warped black van waiting. The right side of the back double doors swung open, revealing another armed man with a gun leveled.

The moment he saw the women, he released the gun, slung it over his back and opened the other side. He jumped to the ground and held out his hand to help the women inside the gutted van while the other men used the side door. Alessandra waited for Sabrina and Maggie to climb in before she followed, but her legs were not cooperating as the exhaustion and adrenaline thundered through her veins. Thankfully, the man who helped them in was behind her. He steadied her, his arm around her waist as he pulled the doors closed with his free hand.

When she felt her legs would hold her up, she tapped the man's arm to let him know he could release her. Sabrina and Maggie had sat down in the only place available, behind the driver's seat, while the men each grabbed onto a belt loop that hung from the roof of the van, much like straps in a bus that helped keep a standing passenger in place.

The man had yet to release Alessandra, so she patted his hand again and whispered her thanks. "Grazie."

He still didn't relinquish his hold, and she wasn't sure, but she thought he might have actually pulled her closer.

She pushed against his arm just as he bent toward her and whispered in her ear, "Prego, amore." *You're welcome.*

Her head jerked away and she pushed out of his hold so she could make eye contact. When his smiling brown eyes came into view, she frowned. "No."

"Are you okay?" Even though his eyes were smiling, his gruff voice was thick with emotion.

Someone pounded a fist against the side of the van three times to alert the driver to go. The vehicle was slammed into action, causing Alessandra's feet to slip, allowing *him* to take her in his arms and steady her once again.

One of the men who'd extracted them began to call in a report to an invisible source while another made his way to the driver to relay information.

Alessandra steadied herself once again and was slapping at the man's hands as she continued to frown at him, stunned.

"Alex, do you know him?" Sabrina asked over the din of noise that was much different from the silent hike they'd just finished.

"Yes," Alessandra breathed out.

She hadn't found her bearings and with so many emotions flooding her system, she was having difficulty talking. She reached up and traced the line of his jaw, but then retrieved her hand as if she'd been burned.

"Is that your brother?" Maggie asked, since Alessandra hadn't expanded on Sabrina's question.

Alessandra shook herself free and slapped at his hands again as they attempted to wrap themselves around her waist once more. "No, he is not my brother. He ..." she cleared her throat as she finally broke free from him, "come si dice ... what is the word ...?"

"I'm Carlo," the man turned a wide smile toward the two women as he introduced himself, "her ex–fiancé."

Chapter Three

"Oh my ..." Cassie Dodd ran a hand through her short golden-brown hair, licked her lips and smoothed out her clothes in an attempt to rid herself of the long plane ride to Rome that had wrinkled them in the first place. She aimed an exaggerated smile at the hulking man walking toward her.

"He's not that great." Cassie's boyfriend of several months, Benjamin Stills, (mostly known as 'Stills') nodded amusedly at Carlo Moretti, the Italian intelligence officer that stood about six one with a broad build. He'd become a solid friend, and was almost now a roundabout relative. Stills liked to tell people if they had five minutes and a whiteboard, he could explain exactly how they were almost 'relatives'.

Carlo wore a short sleeve, white button-down – the sleeves of which strained against his muscles. His sunglasses were pushed atop his short, sleek dark hair, and a very slight grin became apparent as he made his way across the arrival area toward them.

"He's a shock," Cassie admitted. "Every time I see him, it's a shock. Of course, the sexy Italian accent doesn't hurt either."

Just then, Jessica, Cassie's younger sister, had caught up. She grunted her agreement as she tripped over her feet, causing the luggage she was pulling to swerve perfectly over Cassie's toes. "Ow, Jesus Jess."

"It's Mom's bag," Jessica said in defense as she dropped the handle of the rolling bag their mother had packed to the fifty pound limit, and watched as it unceremoniously thumped to the ground. "She handed it off to me when she saw Carlo." Jessica pointed to their mother, Barbara Dodd, now crossing the distance and pulling Carlo's large frame down to her five-five so she could hug the beast.

His smile grew as she slapped his back then pushed him away just enough so she could make eye contact. Cassie could hear the familiar words her mother spouted so often: "Let me look at you." Barbara Dodd was checking after his well-being and any secrets he might try to hide from a mother figure.

Cassie's father had caught up with his girls and muttered, "That's the weirdest friendship in the world." Though he was smiling as he dragged two more suitcases that were laden with gifts for the coming weeklong meet and greet.

He readjusted his hold on the luggage and continued to where his wife was, nodding at Carlo in greeting.

Jessica tilted her head toward her sister. "Five bucks he's asking about the soccer game Carlo promised to take him to."

"Most likely." Cassie sighed then turned her attention to her boyfriend. "You know Benji," she leaned toward him, "I had this idea of coming to Italy with my boyfriend and being taken to some really romantic places and making out everywhere. But as I stand here, I realize that I might have just come all this way with my parents, my sister and our boyfriends, only to find that the family dynamics are the same whether we're in California or Rome." She pursed her lips. "And that alone time now seems compromised."

"Well Dodd," Stills gave Cassie a sideways glance, "if you and I put our heads together, I'm sure we can figure out some trouble to get into. Besides, I know a few places I plan to take you to."

"Your favorite corners for surveillance?" Cassie joked, referring to her boyfriend's CIA job she wasn't supposed to know about.

Just then, Jessica's boyfriend, Parker - the reason they were in Italy in the first place – walked by. He overheard Stills' comment and gave a gruff reminder, "You've never been here before, Stills." Parker was referring to the clandestine part of their job, as he too worked for the agency.

"Ah yes, Dodd," Stills corrected, "I've never been to Rome before. However, I would still like to take you to a few local haunts that I might have fallen in love with *had* I ever been here before." He elbowed Parker; was that a better way of putting his intentions?

Parker grunted in reply, his attention no longer on Cassie and Benji.

Cassie followed Parker's frowning gaze and watched the way Jessica lit up as Carlo hugged her in greeting.

Cassie was about to soothe Parker when it became clear why his frown was growing. Another woman had joined the group. She had short, curly brown hair, olive skin, a knowing grin, and was radiating confidence. After giving Jessica the traditional Italian cheek kiss, she stepped into Carlo's side as he slipped his arm around her shoulders. Cassie nodded in the couple's direction. "So *that's* Alessandra."

"My sister." Parker grunted the affirmation.

"He's snarling," she whispered loudly to Stills.

The snarl intensified as he watched Carlo possessively pull Alessandra closer to him.

Cassie continued, "Parker, I thought you gave him your blessing to marry her. You know, just a few months ago, when he showed up at my apartment. Unannounced. Looking for you." She elbowed Stills, a sort of 'watch this' move because she was an older sister and antagonizing was one of her specialties. "Remember Parker? Because Carlo proposed and your sister insisted he fly all the way to California to get your blessing?"

Stills answered for his colleague turned friend. "I don't think he's ever seen Carlo with his sister. In real life. With his big, Italian Foreign Intelligence Service hands all over her."

A growl erupted from deep in Parker's chest.

Cassie shot a wide-eyed grin at Stills. He winked at her in reply as Parker stomped away. They watched with glee the agitated beeline Parker made toward Carlo.

"Did we say too much?" Cassie asked.

"Nah." Stills raised an eyebrow. "Maybe. I just hope they don't fight again." He glanced around as if he were assessing the logistics required for stopping a fight between them.

"They won't fight in front of my mom," Cassie said confidently.

"Parker!"

The name was happily called from a slight distance to the right of the gathered group; and hearing his name, Parker changed his trajectory. Cassie and Stills watched Gianna and Antonio Salvatore, Parker's parents, make their way across the crowded arrival area.

"Mamma, Papà," Parker called. His whole demeanor changed as the tension slipped immediately out of his shoulders, and his hands that had been tightened into fists, relaxed.

"The gang's all here," Stills stated.

The last time she saw the Salvatores had been the previous Thanksgiving, when they'd flown to California to 'meet the family'.

Cassie picked up the handle of the bag Jessica had left at her feet as Stills took their shared bag. They walked into the middle of the whirlwind of hugging and reintroductions.

Cassie interjected herself in front of Alessandra, "It's nice to finally meet you, Alex."

"Piacere, Cassandra." *Nice to meet you,* Alessandra greeted.

Everyone talked at the same time and it was Alessandra who finally spoke above the animated din, giving instructions in English and then Italian. "We have two vans, we'll head to the villa we've rented, then you can have a shower and maybe a glass of wine while we get dinner ready and we'll visit more there, yes?"

"I'll drive," Carlo offered.

She waved. "I'm fine. I can drive."

He pulled her hand to his lips and brushed a kiss across her knuckles before saying, "I know you can drive, I was offering to drive so you can visit."

"I can visit and drive at the same time," she affirmed.

Carlo took a breath to begin arguing with Alessandra when Gianna and Barbara stepped in; Carlo could ride with them, it would be good to catch up with him.

As they all headed to the vans, Cassie thought they resembled a tornado of hand gestures, baggage, and sound and fury, clearing a path through the arrival area.

Barbara and Gianna led the way, each having linked an arm through Carlo's as they began to excitedly talk over each other. His attention bobbed back and forth between the women as he attempted to listen and translate simultaneously.

The parents climbed in one van with Carlo, and Alessandra ushered the rest into the van she was driving. Cassie sat in the front next to Alessandra, Stills in the back row, Jessica and Parker in the second. Once they'd pulled out of the airport parking and stopped at the first red light, Cassie said to Alessandra, "So, here we are, two oldest sisters stuck in the middle of the meeting of the parents. The Roman edition."

Alessandra gave a gruff laugh. "This morning I was thinking of the way *Romeo and Juliet* starts, two households both alike in dignity … only this time, the families are divided by language."

Parker leaned forward, stating, "And we're already married."

Jessica shook her head. "We're just dating right now. I'm trying to figure out if I want to be married."

Cassie rolled her eyes. "Jess, you married him eleven years ago as a joke, but you kinda love the guy and neither of you got divorced, so guess what kid? You're married."

"But not the right way," Alessandra said, then continued with the pertinent parental information. "Cassandra, you know as well as I do, those two women in that van don't speak the same language, but they are both on the same mission."

Cassie slapped her knee and turned a mocking grin at Jessica. "I *told* you by the end of this trip you two were going to have to promise a proper wedding."

Jessica snarled in reply. She had fought against the planning of a wedding when Parker's parents came to California, and she knew she wouldn't be able to hold out too much longer.

Cassie laughed and sat back in her seat. "What about you and Carlo? He came all the way to California to talk to Parker face to face. When is your big day?"

"I also heard you and Benjamin were engaged?" Alessandra rebuffed the comment.

Cassie nodded her head approvingly at the blatant change of subject. "We are *not*," she emphasized. "Benji keeps threatening an engagement, but no ring yet." She held up her left hand and gave it a wiggle. "And thankfully, he hasn't made any definitive comments in front of my mother."

A sly smile pulled at Alessandra's lips and she glanced over at Cassie. "You and I both know, the reason we brought our boyfriends to this week of family vacation is because our parents will shine all the light on Jessica and Parker."

"And yet, we're still gonna get credit for bringing our boyfriends." Cassie barked out a laugh. "I *knew* I was going to like you, Alex."

"We older sisters need to stick together, no?"

Another rumble of a groan from Jessica erupted in the backseat. "Alex, pull over anywhere and drop me off."

Cassie worried that coming on this family vacation might be too much. On the plane ride, with everyone in the same row, her mother handed out gallon size baggies filled with candy, granola bars, wet wipes, printed copies of the itinerary and a euro coin for a pay phone (just in case anyone got lost and the battery on their phones died).

Cassie asked her mother to recall what Stills and Parker did for a living. To which her mother waved a hand and excused, it's never a bad thing to be prepared. And prepared was what Barbara Dodd excelled at. She had downloaded a talk to text translator on her phone and purchased almost every tourist travel gadget she could find.

As Alessandra pointed out how the two older sisters could appease their mothers and put all the attention on their siblings, Cassie was beginning to think she was going to have a lot of fun on this vacation.

"So, you met Carlo and my sister the same night." Cassie directed the conversation. "Tell me everything."

"Cass, you've heard this story," Jessica said, exasperated.

Cassie waved a hand, dismissing Jessica's comment. "I haven't heard it from Alex's point of view. And she was the first one to find out you two had been married in Vegas years ago."

"Actually, Carlo was the first one to find out." Parker said.

"Cass," Jessica pointed, "you don't want to know about when Alessandra and I met, you want to know about Carlo. You're being nosy."

"I have so many questions," Cassie said animatedly, then turned toward Jessica. "Of course I want to know everything about their relationship."

Jessica rolled her eyes. "But you just said you were going to put the spotlight on me, this is putting the spotlight on Alessandra."

"That's when we're around the parents, right now is the perfect time to find out everything about them," Cassie admitted, and angled toward

Alessandra again. "What was it like when you first saw him? He still shocks me. Is he romantic? Or is he ... I don't know, like a barbarian?"

"Cassandra!" Jessica reprimanded then called, "Benji, do something about your girlfriend."

Stills laughed. "I'm staying out of this one."

"Leave Alex alone," Jessica tried.

"Why? I'm fascinated by the woman who could tame Carlo Moretti."

Alessandra pursed her lips in reply.

Cassie begged Alessandra, "Please. Tell me everything."

"He's a big ox." She tried to sound contrite, but couldn't hold back a smile.

Cassie nodded approvingly. "Oh really? I think I'm gonna love this story."

Chapter Four

Alessandra yawned, stretched her arms over her head and did a backbend in her ergonomic chair, releasing a long drawn-out groan; her muscles longed for movement. But she had to get the monotonous updates on her patient files finished. It had, thankfully, been a slow night in the ER at the Ospedale San Raffaele. There had also been a scheduling mistake, resulting in two more trauma surgeons on hand, which meant Alessandra could take a much needed respite in her office and get caught up on work; an office all her own because it was the size of a custodial closet. But at least it had a window with a view of the alley.

She closed her eyes for a moment, then with a deep sigh opened them and let her gaze fall back on the surrounding décor of the office– sterile gray and brown walls, a flimsy wooden chair on the other side of her desk, and a dusty bookcase.

The office was trying to bore her to death, in a very unimaginative way.

"That's what you get when you volunteer to take over for another doctor's maternity leave," she muttered as she saved the file she was working on. She still had too much to do. "Cazzo." *Fuck.*

Her cell phone rang. It was an unknown number at 5 a.m., but she welcomed the interruption. Her shift was almost over and she'd done as much work as she could.

"Pronto?" *Hello,* she answered.

"Sono io, Parker." *It's me, Parker.* Her younger brother's voice brought a smile to her face. He was only younger by two years, but still, younger was younger. She often held fast to the age difference, of her being older and wiser, because when they stood next to each other, Parker's height eclipsed her more traditional Italian height.

She sat back in her chair, happy to chat. "Parker, come va?" *What's going on?*

They didn't get to talk or visit as often as she'd like. Not only did they both have demanding jobs, but add to that the long distance separating them, him living in California, and her in Rome, quick jaunts between the two locales weren't conducive for dropping in for a visit.

"I need help." The desperation in his voice brought an abrupt halt to the idea that this was a catch-up conversation.

She straightened in her chair. "What happened? What's wrong?"

"Are you home?" he asked.

"No, I'm at work."

"I can't explain now, but I need you to get to your apartment as quickly as you can. There's a woman who is hurt and I'm having her taken to your place. She's on her way and I'm right behind her, about twenty minutes."

"Twenty minutes? Are you in Rome?"

"Not officially."

Parker worked for the Central Intelligence Agency in the states. Other than that fact, there wasn't much more she or her parents knew about his job. She did get the idea that oftentimes, his job kept him *in* harm's way more than it did out of it.

But who was she to make a fuss about putting oneself in danger? She had voluntarily gone into war-torn, third world countries to help the less fortunate.

She swallowed the fear that tried to rise up from his announcement. "Are you okay?" She held the phone against her ear with her shoulder as she hurriedly grabbed her purse and began walking as she fished out her keys.

"I'm okay, but Aless, this woman is hurt and I'm not sure how badly, and we can't take her to a hospital. It's part of an operation I'm in the middle of and some bad people are going to be looking for her. The first place they'll try is a hospital. Hell, it's where I'd look first." He was breathless as he explained.

Alessandra took a detour to the nurse's station. She grabbed one of the extra emergency medical kits kept there, thankful no one was around to ask her a million questions. She hastily signed the checkout form for the kit, slung the large bag onto her shoulder, then continued to the exit.

"Aless?"

"On my way." She navigated a straight line to her car.

"How fast can you get there?" He sounded desperate.

"Ten minutes. There's no traffic yet." The sky had just started to lighten with the glow of the early morning. She threw everything into the passenger side of her car, then started it.

"I'll be there in twenty." Parker's voice became muffled as he yelled an order to someone.

"What's her name?" Alessandra asked.

"Jessica ..." His voice broke as he said the name, and he had to clear his throat to continue. "I'll be there soon." Several other voices in the background began yelling information just as Parker ended the call.

Alessandra tossed the phone on top of the rest of her stuff and took a deep breath. One thing she'd learned in the past twelve years as a trauma surgeon, was that rushing didn't do anyone any good. If she hurried she could cause another accident, and the last thing Parker or this woman needed was for Alessandra to be unavailable.

She'd learned to work through these high-tension moments with a calm urgency. Car started, deep breath, and with a steady, brisk speed, she headed to her apartment.

As she drove, she began to list the obstacles she might face in the next few minutes. The first would be parking in front of her building; if she couldn't find a spot, she'd double-park and deal with the consequences later. Next, she needed to prop open the main front door for when Parker arrived. When she got into her apartment, she needed to pull all the bedding off the spare bed and cover it with clean sheets from the armoire.

Fortune was on her side as she pulled onto her street and found an open parking spot directly across from her building. She threw the car into park and grabbed the bags as a taxi pulled up. Alessandra squinted at the woman in the backseat as the driver nervously climbed out.

"Scusi," *excuse me*, the driver called to Alessandra.

"Sì?"

"Are you the doctor?" His voice was apprehensive as he pointed to the black bag she had hoisted over her shoulder with the bright orange medical cross on it.

"I am."

As the words left her mouth, she witnessed an invisible weight slipping from the man's shoulders as he let out a breath she was certain he'd been holding for a long while. He pointed to his cab. "I was told by Signore Salvatore to bring her to a doctor at this address. He said you'd be waiting. This woman is in trouble." He pointed to the back window.

Alessandra nodded as he talked, opened the door to her apartment building and propped it open with a nearby doorstop, then made her way to Jessica's side of the cab. The driver hurriedly opened the door, giving Alessandra space to lean in and do a quick assessment: one bruised eye – swollen shut, broken arm that had been casted, oversize t-shirt, sweatpants and bare feet.

"Signora." She caught Jessica's attention.

"Am I late?" she asked.

"Jessica?"

"Yes." The woman nodded excitedly and then looked out the front of the taxi and began rubbing her hands together. "I'm Jessica," she whispered.

"Jessica," Alessandra said, bringing the woman's attention back to her, "I'm Alessandra Salvatore. I'm a doctor. My brother is Parker and he had the driver bring you to me. And now, we're going to go into my apartment, okay?"

"Parker." Jessica repeated the name, then fell sideways in the seat and began to cry.

"Jessica," Alessandra said her name harshly, "we need to move you. Can you walk?"

Jessica sat up and swung her legs out of the cab. "Only a little time left," she mumbled as she tried to stand, faltering.

Alessandra motioned for the taxi driver to help. They both put one of Jessica's arms around their shoulders and hoisted her onto her feet.

The driver began to explain, "She said she took something and it'll wear off in three hours." The trio awkwardly made their way into the building. "But I don't know how long it's been. She's only been with me for about an hour."

"Did she say what she took?" Alessandra nodded to the elevator.

"No. She just said someone gave her something. The man I talked to, Signore Salvatore, he said to bring her here. That you could help her."

Alessandra nodded.

"Parker is in trouble," Jessica slurred.

"Parker is fine. He is on his way," Alessandra responded.

The elevator arrived at the top floor and exiting to the right, it was just a few short steps to her apartment. But as they moved, Jessica was losing all ability to keep herself standing. She was crumbling under the weight of her own body.

They angled themselves so Alessandra could open her front door with a free hand, then turned sideways so they could all shuffle through the small opening the door provided.

"We'll put her in the room on the right," Alessandra instructed the driver. When they entered the room she asked, "Can you take all her weight for a moment?"

Alessandra dropped the bags, stripped the bed of the comforter, grabbed a single sheet out of the armoire and quickly covered the bed.

She aided the driver to gently lay Jessica down.

"I'll be right back." Alessandra left to retrieved her personal medical bag.

When she returned the driver was staring wide-eyed at Jessica, worrying his hands. "Signore Salvatore, he told me to wait for him. He wants me to show him where I picked her up."

Alessandra pulled out her stethoscope.

He continued his nervous dialogue. "She looked crazy on the street, but now ... she looks worse," he whispered as he made the sign of the cross.

"Non ti preoccupare." *Don't worry*. Alessandra reassured. "Signore Salvatore will be here any minute, could you wait for him downstairs and please close the front door? I hate to leave it propped open."

"Oh, yes. Okay." He was glad for the chore, and she thought he would be happier to be away from a situation he hadn't expected to get himself into.

Alessandra settled into her training. She started by taking vitals first. The woman's heart rate was raised, her breathing shallow, she had a slight temperature and her pupils were dilated.

"Begin at the top," she muttered to herself and slowly began to use her fingers to prod the skull. There was a raised welt on the back of Jessica's head, a possible head wound. The eye was swollen shut and a deep gash across her eyebrow had been expertly sutured. Someone had already doctored her, but since Alessandra had no history, she needed to be thorough.

The neck and shoulders were okay. The right arm was fractured, but the cast was serving its purpose. The other arm had a long gash that had been sutured as well.

Alessandra pulled up the oversized shirt and found a large bruised area on the left side. Another sutured area. She studied the work and nodded. The woman had been through hell, but she'd also had good treatment.

As Alessandra examined the ribs, she knew several of them were bruised. No fractures, but not comfortable.

"No!" Jessica sat up and screamed at the pain the action caused.

"It's okay. You're okay," Alessandra said softly. She gently stroked the woman's blonde hair that was falling over her eyes, out of the way.

"No!" Jessica sat up abruptly, swatting at Alessandra and grimacing in pain as she tried to escape the attention.

"Jessica." Alessandra called her name loudly, attempting to dislodge the fog the woman was tumbling through. It cleared a bit, so Alessandra continued sternly, "Jessica. Look at me. You're okay. I am a doctor. You are safe." She tried to lock eyes with her. "Do you understand?"

Jessica gave a jerky nod and furrowed her brows as she made an effort to focus on Alessandra, but the moment waned.

"Now. Your ribs hurt, yes?" Alessandra asked.

Jessica nodded.

Alessandra took her hand gently and patted it, using a firm voice as she explained, "I need you to lay down. You are safe. You are in my apartment. I need to examine you to make sure you are okay."

Jessica slowly lowered herself and nodded as she hissed through her teeth in pain. "He said I have bruised ribs. Deep gash in my side. Concussion. Swollen eye. Broken wrist and stupid Thomas hit me on the head again."

Alessandra nodded. She wasn't certain who 'he' was, but the report Jessica gave her was beyond helpful though the concussion part was worrisome.

"If you have a concussion Jessica, then I need you to stay awake. What is your last name?" Alessandra asked.

"Dodd. I'm Jessica Dodd," she said as her good eye fluttered closed.

"Jessica," Alessandra demanded, "you're going to stay awake for me, remember? Now, where do you live?"

"California," she muttered.

"Do you surf?" Alessandra asked the question as she pushed the shirt up once again. When Jessica stilled for that part of the exam, Alessandra continued, "Jessica, I'm going to pull the sweatpants down slightly over your hips."

Jessica nodded as if she understood so Alessandra pulled the pants down, proceeding with her examination. "Do you surf?" she asked again.

Jessica frowned. "What? No."

"I thought everyone who lives in California is always surfing," Alessandra said loudly, to keep her patient awake.

"No. Well, none of my friends surf. We used to boogie board when we were younger."

"Aless!" The booming voice of Parker erupted from the door of the apartment.

"Here," she called out.

He rushed into the room and she turned just in time to see his knees buckle taking in the sight of the woman on the bed. Her brother took two large steps and knelt next to Jessica, all but pushing Alessandra out of the way. He gently took the woman's hand. "Jess …" he breathed out as he brought her hand to his lips. She blinked her good eye and a smile pulled at the side of her mouth.

"Parker." His name happily slipped out of her mouth.

Alessandra was speechless.

She was about to yell at him for pushing her out of the way while she was trying to work, but now, she was very *very* curious about who this woman really was. So many questions begged to be asked.

"I'm sorry," Jessica croaked as tears began to fall.

"It's okay, tesoro. It's okay."

Tesoro? *Treasure*? Alessandra's curiosity was piqued even more. She'd only been introduced to two of Parker's girlfriends when he was younger, but she'd never heard him use any terms of endearments then. She knew he wasn't seeing anyone seriously, always stating that it was difficult with work, but something had definitely changed now.

She tilted her head and looked at Jessica with more interest. She should be angry that she was so out of the loop on her brother's life, but it would seem the current situation and Alessandra's convenient location would bring this story to light.

As much as she wanted to know everything, there were more pressing issues now. Once she was convinced this woman was not in any real danger, she'd get around to the bottom of this mystery.

"Parker, we need to be quiet. Thomas is coming." Jessica glanced around worriedly and began to try and get up again.

Alessandra was back at the bedside. "Jessica, you need to lay down. You're safe, remember?"

She stopped trying to sit up but her head was still on a swivel around the room.

"Aless?" Parker's voice was strained as he watched Jessica's eyes glaze over.

"She's been given something and she has a concussion. She's not in her right mind. Keep talking to her, though. I need her to stay awake."

"I'm sorry. Jesus, I'm so sorry." He kissed Jessica's hand again. "I'm going to kill him. I swear to God if I ever get my hands on Thomas Adler I'm going to kill him."

"Not that kind of talk," she tisked. "Here, help me turn her." She explained that she needed to assess Jessica's back now. Together, they gently helped her move, but Jessica hissed in pain and Alessandra glanced at her brother, his gnashing teeth visible as the muscles in his jaw angrily tightened.

"Stai calmo ..." *Calm down*, she cooed to her brother. He met her gaze and gave a nod, then stood and got out of her way.

In the end, the only thing left needing attention turned out to be several cuts on the bottom of Jessica's feet; a side effect of walking without shoes.

Just to be on the safe side, Alessandra did a blood draw so she could order cultures to try and find out what drugs Jessica had been administered. She called a trusted colleague who agreed to pick up the cultures within a few minutes and test them herself in the lab at the hospital.

Alessandra bandaged Jessica's feet and gave her a dose of Tylenol. "Until I am certain of what you were given, I can't take the chance of giving you more pain medication," Alessandra explained. "I know you want to sleep right now, but you said something about a concussion. I need you to stay awake." She patted Jessica's hand and then gestured for her brother across the room.

"Parker, what happened?"

"Is she going to be okay?" he asked quietly.

"Yes."

"I need to go." The admission was obviously tearing him up. "The driver's waiting for me. I need to study the area where she was picked up. Maybe ..." He shook his head. "I have a friend coming to watch you two."

"What?"

"He's working with me, his name is Moretti. Carlo Moretti. He's going to stay and make sure you two are safe."

"I can take care of us." Alessandra frowned.

"No. She's been through too much. I need to know she'll be safe. I need to know you'll *both* be safe." He aimed a tense smile at his sister.

Alessandra nodded, he was unraveling and would only unravel more if she argued. "Okay," she patted his arm, "that's a good idea."

He reached out and ruffled Alessandra's hair. She slapped his hand away. "I love you too. Now go. Let me see after my patient."

He knelt once more next to Jessica, whispered something in her ear that made her smile, brushed a kiss on her lips and after pulling away, studied her face for several seconds before he turned to leave.

Alessandra followed him to her door. "I have questions about all of this."

"I'm sure you do," he muttered.

She grunted, letting all but one question dissipate. "How will I know this Carlo?"

"He's with the Agenzia Informazioni e Sicurezza Esterna and has a badge to prove it." Parker stopped for a moment at the door and a wry smile appeared on his lips. "He's ... just trust me. You'll know it's the man I sent when you see him." With that he turned the handle and was gone.

Alessandra pulled the chair that sat in the corner of the room next to the bed and sat down. She began asking the woman a litany of nonsensical questions. It was something she'd learned over the years. When dealing with a possible concussion, strange questions that make the patient think about the answers were best at keeping them alert.

A buzz came from the intercom and Alessandra quickly went to deal with her co-worker who was going to test the blood.

"Did they find us?" Jessica was trying to sit up when Alessandra returned.

"No. We're safe. *You* are safe," she insisted, gently helping Jessica to lie back down. "It was just a friend from the hospital. I need to have your blood tested so I can find out what drugs you've been given."

Jessica nodded her head, the apparent fog in her eyes continuing its ebb and flow. "Where is Parker?"

"He'll be back soon." She hoped she'd made it sound like her brother was doing nothing more than going to the store.

But the shadow that crossed Jessica's face brought a new realization to Alessandra.

She knew Parker's job might often be dangerous. But coming face to face with the consequences rattled her. She'd seen a lot of pain and suffering in her line of work, but seeing what happened to this woman, knowing that Parker's job put him in the center of this storm, and that he was currently trying to find the man, or men, responsible ... tension began creeping up the base of her spine.

She straightened in her chair and attempted to force the fear away by stating, "Parker will be back soon, his skull is too thick not to follow through with the promises he makes."

Jessica smiled weakly and shook her head gently from side to side, her one opened eye unable to focus. "My head hurts."

"I know, bella." Alessandra reached out and stilled her head. "Just try to stay still. I'll get you something to help."

Alessandra returned with a cold washcloth which she placed at the back of Jessica's neck. "This will help pull the headache away," she claimed.

"Do you speak Italian?" Jessica asked. "Or am I speaking Italian?" She breathed in a wide-eyed excitement at the idea.

"No, you are speaking English." Alessandra gave a soft laugh. "But yes, I speak Italian. It's my first language."

"Your English is really good."

"I took English in school and then did internships in both Chicago and California."

"I'm from California," Jessica said as she glanced around the room. When her eye focused on Alessandra, she began to shake, then swallowed and whispered, "Did I get away?"

"Yes. You got away. I'm Alessandra Salvatore, Parker's sister. You are in my apartment."

"Has Parker been here?" She took another look around the room as if he were hiding somewhere.

"Yes." Alessandra pressed her hand against the woman's forehead.

"I can't keep any of it straight." A tear slipped down over her cheek just as Alessandra's apartment intercom system buzzed, echoing in the hallway. Jessica's voice hitched, "They found us."

"No. No one found us," Alessandra said firmly. "It's the man Parker sent to watch over us." She waited for Jessica to nod her head in understanding. The intercom screamed again. "I'm going to go answer the door. You are safe. Just keep repeating those words while I'm gone, okay?"

Another hesitant nod and Jessica whispered, "I am safe. I am safe. I am safe ..."

Alessandra answered the intercom. "Pronto?"

"Sono io, agente Moretti." *It's Agent Moretti.* The deep voice was a shock, though she wasn't sure what she expected; definitely not such a deep, robust voice.

She took a deep breath; a lot of trust was going into this moment. She gave the apartment number and pressed the buttons on the intercom that would unlock the front door of the building.

She went back to check on Jessica. The woman's good eye was heavy with sleep but she was muttering, "Safe safe safe."

Alessandra called across the room, "Jessica, you're doing really good. Keep concentrating on staying awake for a few moments longer."

"I'm tired."

"I know. But you can do this."

"I can do this."

Alessandra went to stand in front of her locked door. She looked through the peephole and as the shadow of a true monster of a man came into view, she took a step back. Is that what her brother meant when he said she'd 'know' it was Carlo when she saw him?

He knocked once and she jumped, even though she saw the knock coming.

"Identification," she called, and looked out the peephole again.

He frowned but pulled out a badge and held it up to the peephole.

'Carlo Moretti,' it read.

She unlocked the door and swallowed audibly as she opened it all the way.

Holy hell.

Carlo Moretti wore a light blue, long sleeve, starched dress shirt with the top button undone, light gray slacks, and shiny black loafers. Carrying a duffle bag over his shoulder, he created quite the picture. He was an intense specimen. A broad, tall, dark, and lethal specimen of a man.

She tripped backwards two steps. She had not anticipated him. Though, how could she? She imagined a copy of her brother, but this muscular beast of a man gave off pure power. With a no-nonsense frown in place, his eagle eyes attempted to take in the entire situation and digest the information in a nanosecond.

Alessandra cleared her throat of the shock and tried to grow another inch or two as she faced him down.

"I'm Carlo." He stepped inside the foyer and closed the door behind him.

"I'm Alessandra Salvatore. Doctor Salvatore. Parker's sister."

He nodded, and his eyes having taken her in, he glanced around her confirming, "Jessica is here?"

Alessandra gave a curt nod and led him to the room, shaken not only at how very aware she was of him and his large presence in her home, but also by the sudden heated temperature change throughout her body.

She stood aside when they entered the room and watched as he took in Jessica's appearance. If it upset him in any way, it didn't register. And Alessandra was closely studying his face. He was handsome. Provocative, powerful and handsome.

He pursed his lips disappointedly and announced, "Fine mess you've gotten yourself into."

Surprised at the tender harshness, Alessandra watched as Jessica's eye focused and a broad smile lit up her face. "I missed you too, Carlo."

At least Jessica knew the man, there was a relief in that.

A tear formed and slipped down Jessica's cheek. Carlo shook his head as he dropped his bag and sat on the chair next to the bed; then leaned forward and wiped the tear away. "None of that," he ordered, with even more gentleness now.

"Sorry." Jessica reached up her hand toward him.

As Carlo took Jessica's hand in his, Alessandra could feel the utter tenderness of the touch and she balled her hands into fists to keep hold of the feeling.

"It's okay," Carlo told Jessica. "Everything is okay now."

She nodded. "I'm tired."

He turned his attention toward Alessandra then and she had to weld her feet to the ground to not be knocked back a few steps from his gaze.

She cleared her throat until she could find her voice. "She has a concussion. I need to keep her awake."

He didn't give any indication he heard her, just allowed his study of her to intensify.

Alessandra's spine straightened into a marble column the longer he assessed her. She tried to hold her own, but finally crossed her arms across her chest and asked, "Posso aiutarti?" *Can I help you?*

"Voglio un caffè." *I want a coffee*, he said. It wasn't a request or a statement, it was more of an order.

"Me too," she scoffed. "But I'm not a waitress, I'm a doctor and she's my patient."

"I can watch her for a few moments."

"So can I. And if you want a coffee, I have faith you can see your way around the espresso maker," Alessandra shot back.

"I've been known to make good coffee."

"Then you'll go make yourself a coffee if you want one so badly." Alessandra was the one who gave orders, she did not take them.

"I'm your guest," he countered.

"You are a colleague of my brother. I didn't ask you to come here."

"It's okay." Jessica's voice wavered. "We can trust him."

Carlo had yet to take his eyes off of Alessandra. She in turn stood her ground, not about to be the first to break eye contact.

"Per favore." *Please.* His face softened, a slight smile pulling at the corner of his mouth; distracting and shockingly sexy. "Could you make me a coffee? I'm exhausted."

Alessandra took a step backward, off-kilter from that smile, off-kilter from this man.

She shook her head and made an awkward circle before she gave a huff and left the room.

What the hell had just happened?

She was dazed as she went about making the damn oaf a coffee. How dare he come into her house, upend her emotions and demand she cook for him?

It's not cooking, she told herself, *it's just coffee.*

Yes, but wasn't making coffee for this Neanderthal one step closer to cooking?

"Barbaro," *Barbarian,* she barked as she stood in front of the stovetop espresso maker, two cups and saucers ready at her elbow, watching the blue flame and trying to figure out how the snake had hypnotized her.

Chapter Five

Carlo wished he was a caveman.

He found the small bossy doctor quite intriguing. She had stared him down, waiting for him to blink first, daring him. And he liked it. Hell, he wanted to drown in it.

So he didn't look away, but instead, while taking in her curves, her dark curls that covered too much of her face, her challenging eyes, and her very backbone; he did the only thing that came to mind to break them out of the game of chicken- he demanded a coffee.

Because the other choice was to give into a very sudden need to pick her up, throw her over his shoulder, and find a deep, dark cave somewhere so he could take his time ...

"Carlo?" Jessica slurred his name.

"Jessica." He nodded, bringing his attention back to the task at hand. He didn't want to give another thought to the strange feelings catching him off guard. It was probably exhaustion causing them anyway.

"Did I get away?" she asked.

"Of course you did. You weren't going to let Thomas Adler get the better of you." He spoke of the man who abducted her matter-of-factly.

A tear slid out and she squeezed Carlo's hand that was still holding hers.

"It's okay," he said.

"Is Parker mad at me?"

"No, bella. No one is mad at you. In fact, we're pretty impressed."

She nodded her head and let her eye close.

Carlo said her name roughly. "Jessica."

She blinked open. "Carlo? Are you a dream? I can't keep anything straight."

"I know."

"Are you really here?"

"I am."

She glanced around the room. "What have you been doing?"

"Oh, nothing of consequence. I had a gelato and took a tour of the Vatican museum this morning, then decided I should help look for you."

"Really?" She furrowed her brows.

"Yes."

"Where are we?"

"Rome. And tonight, I thought I'd take you out for pizza and we could go see the Colosseum."

"I'm in Rome." Jessica breathed out. "I remember, I'm in Rome!"

"We are."

She sucked in a breath and attempted to move. "We have to get away, Carlo. Hurry."

He stopped her. "It's okay. I won't let anything happen to you."

The fog cleared and she stopped moving, narrowing her gaze. "Carlo?"

"Sì, bella."

"I can't keep anything straight."

Alessandra's cell phone rang in the other room, Carlo listened closely to her clipped greeting followed shortly by a relief filled "Grazie."

Alessandra came into the room and frowned momentarily at Carlo as she told him, "Your coffee is on the table in the kitchen." She then turned. "Jessica, I just received the results for the blood tests." She rummaged around in the emergency bag and took out a syringe and bottle of medicine. "I'm going to give you something for the pain, so you can sleep."

Jessica nodded, letting her eye close once more. "Carlo," she mumbled and he squeezed her hand as she continued, "you should take her out for pizza and to the Colosseum. I think you'd like her."

He let a deep laugh rumble through his chest, then let go of her hand as he stood out of Alessandra's way and watched her practiced movements. Oh, he thought he would like the good doctor too. But liking her enough to take her out on a date was a veritable landmine of problems. He was set in his ways. He had a job to do. He didn't have time, and she was the sister of his colleague.

Landmines.

And he was not happy at all by the unexpected heat that flooded his veins when he first laid eyes on the woman. Heat like that could get in the way of a man's life. He watched her give the shot and after a second, gave a grunt and left for his coffee.

Alessandra thankfully stayed in the room, allowing Carlo time to slowly sip his coffee and ignore how it tasted better than anything he'd had in a while. Which was ridiculous. He located the Lavazza coffee bag on the counter, it was the same espresso he used. It was the same espresso most people used. So why the hell did it taste better?

The phone for the front door buzzed and he was grateful for the interruption. He found he wouldn't mind if it was one of the goons that Adler had convinced to help kidnap Jessica. If Carlo couldn't throw Alessandra over his shoulder, then at least he could throw a few therapeutic punches.

Alessandra preceded him into the hallway.

"I'll answer it," he said.

"It's my apartment."

"Yes, but if it's someone looking for Jessica, they'll think twice when they hear a man's voice."

"And if they hear an annoyed female, they will think twice." She picked up the receiver and he pulled it out of her hand and grunted, "Pronto."

She looked up at him incredulously, then stomped on his foot. His eyes darkened with interest and annoyance. "Are you kidding me?" he scoffed as he watched her walk back into Jessica's room.

"What's going on?" Parker called into the receiver.

"Your sister ..." Carlo said while pushing the buttons to open the front door of the building. He hung up the receiver, then opened the door to the apartment and waited until Parker appeared.

The men exchanged a quiet greeting as Parker entered the apartment. Carlo watched him struggle with his emotions as he knelt next to the bed, his hand shaking as he gently touched Jessica's cheek.

"Parker ..." Alessandra was about to tell her brother to leave the poor woman alone so she could get some sleep, but he began a litany of questions about Jessica's health.

Alessandra was pragmatic and calm as she answered them, but when Parker began to repeat the questions, she pointed out the door, "Both of you. Living room. Now," she demanded.

When they were all in the living room, she faced them with her hands on her hips and asked two questions: "Am I in danger?" and "What else can I do to help?"

Carlo deferred to Parker as he was the man in charge of the current operation. Carlo's agency was working in partnership with the CIA.

Parker gathered himself with a long breath, then running a hand through his short, unkempt hair, he explained, "Jessica is...my informant. For an important case I've been working on. Carlo's agency has been working with us on this, he knows everything that's going on. You're safe, but I need to go before the trail gets cold."

She filled in his unspoken request. "You need Jessica to stay here."

"I want Carlo to stay as well." Parker glanced at the man next to him who gave a slight nod in agreement.

A nod he didn't mean.

For the first time in a long while, this job assignment gave him pause. He frowned and tried to shake the feeling off. He'd been in the thick of more difficult situations with some pretty dangerous men; what harm was one tiny doctor?

Alessandra fumed at the suggestion. "I can take care of her and watch after us both." She didn't care if her clipped comment offended anyone. She waved a hand toward Carlo. "If he would be of better use–"

"I'll stay," Carlo interrupted.

Alessandra glared at him and finished her sentence, "... if he would be of better use to you elsewhere."

"He stays," Parker insisted.

"So, there *is* a threat." She leveled a gaze at her brother.

He shrugged his shoulders tiredly as he shook his head. "Aless ... I don't think so, but I can't be sure."

"Okay." She crossed the short distance and pulled her brother's shoulders so she could look him in the eye. After a second, she gave him a hug, then slapped at his back while instructing, "Well hurry up." It was the older sister version of agreeing to his terms.

"I will."

"I need to call the hospital." She pulled out her cell phone and went to the kitchen to make the call.

Carlo followed Parker into the hallway.

"Do you mind?" Parker asked when they were out of earshot of Alessandra.

"It's been arranged." Carlo had called the director of operations on his way to Rome, explained the situation and that his current status would need to be shifted. "Do you have any leads?"

"Possibly," Parker blew out a breath, "but not much."

"Any threats?" He repeated the question Alessandra had asked, thinking there might be something Parker hadn't wanted to mention in front of his sister.

"Not sure. As I drove back here, I think I saw two familiar men trying to look nonchalant around the corner."

"Okay."

"I need to go." Parker seemed reluctant to leave.

"Don't you trust me Salvatore?"

"That's my sister and my ... Jessica in there," he said softly.

Carlo held his hand out to Parker and promised, "I won't let anything happen to them."

After a nod and shake of the large man's hand, Parker left.

Chapter Six

Carlo stood in the doorway listening to Parker's retreating footsteps. What the hell was he supposed to do now? Maybe he'd do some reconnaissance of the surrounding area and see if he could find the unsavory characters Parker thought he saw.

He closed the door and turned to find her standing in the small hallway, hands on her hips.

"I think you have a story to tell me," she said.

"I should go check out the area first."

"You should talk first," she insisted and headed toward the kitchen. When he didn't follow, she turned and raised an eyebrow. "Coming?"

He didn't want to.

But he relented with a grunt and followed, careful to keep his eyes focused above her head, even though they had already caught a glimpse of how her hips moved and hair bounced as she walked.

He let another growl escape as the walls of the two-bedroom apartment closed in on him.

She gestured to the small square table in the kitchen, where his coffee cup still sat. The kitchen was a bit larger than a traditional Italian kitchen. The dining table, with room for four, fit comfortably in the space. The stovetop, sink, pantry and fridge formed a u-shape around the square room.

Alessandra started another pot of espresso, then moved to the pantry and pulled out a box of plastic wrapped sweet croissants. She also grabbed the fruit bowl that sat on the counter next to the sink before placing everything on the table. "I haven't eaten yet and you probably haven't either." She retrieved his cup, rinsed it out and sat it next to hers as the coffee heated.

Carlo opened one of the sweets and finished it in two bites. By the time Alessandra set the coffees on the table, he'd eaten two croissants, a banana and an apple.

"Grazie," he said, then took a sip and sat back with a sigh.

"So." She nodded, crossing her arms over her chest, the only indication he was given that it was time for him to 'tell her a story.'

Damn, her blunt directness was an aphrodisiac.

He made her wait, unwrapping another croissant, taking his time. She took one as well, and patiently sat back in her seat as if she had all the time in the world for him to figure out how to explain what was going on.

And he was tempted to test her patience, but this really wasn't the time.

"This is all confidential," he finally began. "I can't tell you everything." He raised an eyebrow, did she understand? A slight nod was all the acknowledgement he got. Carlo cleared his throat. "Parker contacted our agency several months ago about a group he was keeping an eye on here in Italy and in America. I started working with him then."

"Do the CIA usually work with the AISE?"

"When it's highly beneficial to both agencies, yes." He took a sip then continued. "It was a typical job, typical situation. Powerful men who want more power and money trying to impress men who hold most of the power and money.

"I'd been undercover for a few weeks when Jessica accidentally tripped into the middle of the entire operation."

"Tripped?" she asked suspiciously.

"The organization we've been looking into is large. While the AISE has different offices looking into various areas and working several angles, Parker found a man that had a lot to prove to the organization and was just focusing on him."

"Organization." She snorted. "You realize I understand what *organization* you're talking about."

He shrugged nonchalantly. "The man Parker was following is Thomas Adler. He's no one really, but he was doing a lot of legal work for a lot of *members* and suddenly came into enough money to buy a large villa, some cars, and a small yacht.

"I was assigned to obtain a job as Adler's bodyguard so I could keep an eye on things from the inside and Parker was on the outside doing ... well, his job."

"And then Jessica tripped into all this?"

"She was engaged to Adler."

"*Was ...*"

He nodded. "It seems Jessica found out Adler had been lying to her about a few things, so she came to Italy to confront him and break off the engagement."

"Ah."

"When she showed up, the CIA approached her and convinced her to help them. In a strictly information gathering position."

"Wasn't that dangerous for her?"

Carlo cleared his throat. "We were prepared to keep a close eye on her." This was the reason he promised Parker he'd watch Jessica and Alessandra. It was his job to watch Jessica in the first place; to keep her safe. He'd promised her he would.

And he'd failed.

"So my brother met her, convinced her to gather information and then developed feelings for her?"

This was the part of the story Carlo wasn't so sure he should share. Parker's feelings for Jessica didn't *just* develop. Because Parker and Jessica hadn't *just* met.

The way Carlo understood it, the two met ten years earlier at the wedding of mutual friends. As the drunken weekend progressed, and being young and impulsive, Parker and Jessica got married. Then, they never saw each other again until the fates decided to push them back into each other's orbit.

Carlo gave a hesitant answer. "Something like that." The finer details were going to have to come from Parker. He picked up the story again. "We had Jessica wear a bracelet with a listening and tracking device. Everything was fine, until one night, Adler gave me a phony errand. While I was gone, he and Jessica had a fight that turned physical. By the time I arrived back at the house, Adler had beaten Jessica pretty badly, kidnapped her and killed the head of the *organization*."

Alessandra blew out a breath. "Oddio."

"The bracelet was destroyed. We had no idea where she was– until several days ago, when Adler contacted Parker and demanded protection in return for Jessica's life."

Alessandra nodded, and Carlo hoped that now she understood why her brother might have been so insistent on keeping her safe.

"We were working on trying to locate Jessica when she called Parker this morning. She'd figured out a way to escape."

"She's strong," Alessandra asserted.

"She is." Carlo couldn't wait to hear the minute details of Jessica's escape; as having gotten to know her rather well the past month, he was overflowing with pride at the accomplishment. He didn't take her as the kind of woman who would wait around for someone to save her.

"Okay. I see why my brother feels the need to keep us safe." Alessandra nodded and drummed the table with her fingers. "I am going to check on Jessica and then go take a nap. I haven't slept in twenty-four hours and it seems I need to be at my best, just in case."

Carlo raised an eyebrow. "Just in case?"

She shrugged. "We'll be prepared for whatever disaster might befall us, but hope for the best." She took both cups and deposited them in the sink. "If you leave, I have an extra set of keys hanging by the front door on an elephant keychain. And maybe you could pick up some milk and spinach. I'll make a frittata for dinner."

Carlo sat back in his chair, and again, was careful to not watch her walk away.

Chapter Seven

Alessandra stood in the doorway that led to the kitchen of the rented villa. She'd researched several in the countryside surrounding Rome, close enough to the city but far enough away to enhance the feeling of being on a relaxing retreat. And this updated farmhouse with its heavenly offerings had won her over. It offered six bedrooms – all of which looked like they'd been prepped for the cover of a magazine spread– three full baths, and two living rooms. There were also plenty of views to go around. Each room had large windows offering vistas of overgrown palm trees, ivy, and rolling vineyards that surrounded the house.

The true gathering place was the large kitchen which had a sturdy, cloth covered table that could seat sixteen comfortably. In one corner was a triangular fireplace with a loveseat and two armchairs.

On the opposite corner from the fireplace were two stoves, a dishwasher, sink, two fridges, and a kitchen island topped with well-used, dark wood.

At the far end of the room were large French doors that led to a covered veranda with a glorious view of rolling vineyards.

All of this and they were still fifteen minutes from the city.

"You did good kid," Parker said behind her as he put her in a headlock and knuckled the top of her head, creating a static mess.

She twisted out of the hold as her childhood defensiveness kicked in and she threw a playful punch toward his chest; only Parker caught her hand in his and began to twist.

"I make a living with my hands!" she yelled, trying to hide the laugh.

He stopped twisting, but didn't let go of her hand. "Can't hurt the money makers."

She brought up her knee, but he sidestepped that too and winked. "I know all your moves, Salvatore."

She jerked her hand away and took a step back, running her hands through her hair in an attempt to smooth it. "And I know all yours. Be careful or …" she lowered her voice, "I'll tell Mom about that ring you bought last month."

He quickly glanced around the room before he begged, "Don't."

"Be nice to me." She grinned.

"I'm always nice to you," he muttered. "Just … don't."

She playfully swatted his shoulder. "You know I'd never ruin something that monumental."

Parker had video called her, asking her opinion on the ring. He said he wanted to have it ready for the right time, whether it was next week or three years from now.

"Go help your boyfriend." Parker nodded to where Carlo was sitting at the far end of the table, with Gianna Salvatore on his left and Barbara Dodd on his right. The women were still laughing and talking over each other, taking turns slapping at Carlo's arm as he translated for them. "He looks miserable." Parker grinned.

"He's really good with them."

"The women love Carlo," he said dryly.

"Yes, we do." Alessandra watched the man and her fingers began to ache. He was a delectable specimen, and she enjoyed studying every inch of him. "You know, *you* could go help him."

"I was the one who did all the translating when they came at Thanksgiving. I need a break," Parker defended.

"Well, *I* need to start dinner."

"Sounds like an excuse."

"It is." She faced him, taking several backward steps into the room before loudly calling out, "Aiuta tua mamma." *Help your mom.*

Parker ignored the instructions and made his way to the other end of the table where Stills, Walter Dodd, and his father Antonio were sitting.

Alessandra watched with a raised eyebrow and mouthed the word 'coward.' He nodded happily as he sat down.

She shook her head as she headed to the stove, stopping to brush a kiss on her mom's cheek; she didn't get to see her parents as much as she'd like. And she couldn't remember the last time they'd taken a trip together, even if it was only just outside the city limits of Rome.

Cassie and Jessica, looking freshly showered, joined the group. They were halfway into the kitchen when Barbara Dodd's comment about grandchildren caused Cassie to roll her eyes. "Mom, you told Jess and me that we didn't need to have kids or even get married. As long as we're happy."

Barbara shrugged. "You don't have to do any of those things, but it doesn't mean *I* have to stop wanting grandbabies or planning weddings."

Cassie grinned at Gianna. "You know, my parents had to get married because they got pregnant with me."

Barbara laughed. "Cassandra, she's not shocked at all by that. In fact, they were pregnant with Alessandra when she and Antonio got married."

Carlo continued to translate, bringing nods and smiles from Gianna.

Cassie patted Alessandra on the back. "This place is gorgeous. It's something out of a dream."

"I thought so too."

"Can I help with anything?"

"Tomorrow I'll need help, don't worry about tonight."

"You got it." Cassie pulled open the fridge and took out a bottle of San Pellegrino, then held it up in offering. "Anyone want some?" She collected the number of glasses requested and joined the group.

Another playful slap on Carlo's arm by Gianna caused Alessandra to tent her fingers together and shake her hands. "Mamma, be nice to him."

"I am being nice to him. He's a good man."

It was Alessandra's turn to roll her eyes while she put a dish towel over her shoulder and opened the fridge, pulling out items she'd need to make dinner.

"Alessandra needs my help," Carlo said. She glanced at him in time to watch him shoot Parker a knowing grin. "I'm sure Parker can take it from here."

The mothers quickly repositioned themselves at the other end of the table with the rest of the group then continued their current conversation, causing Parker to exasperatedly utter, "Mamma ..." several times.

"Let me help," Carlo whispered, slipping his hands around Alessandra's waist and pulling her body back against his. The heat from his body and the need in his voice ripped through her stomach, resulting in an automatic tilt of her head to the side as his lips brushed a kiss on her neck.

"I'm just making pesto pasta and a salad. It's pretty easy."

"Please," he pleaded, "give me something to do."

She glanced over her shoulder at the table and laughed, then wiggled out of his arms, and when he reached out to pull her back, she took the towel from her shoulder and laughingly slapped it at him.

He caught the rag and raised an eyebrow; Alessandra's whole body fluttered with the action and she smiled as the heated memory floated between them.

Chapter Eight

Carlo was on edge. And frustrated. Which made him angry.

It had been twenty-four hours since he'd arrived at this damn apartment. This warm, bright, comfortable two-bedroom apartment of the curvy Roman doctor. He stood in the doorway of the kitchen and watched her; and never, in a million years, would he have thought coming here would force him to face some primal existential crisis - because his internal caveman paced nearby, urging Carlo to give in to his base urges and screw everything polite society had ever taught him. But his job and training sternly insisted he tamp down any confusing emotions and stay focused on the assignment.

He wished he could blame the unwelcome emotions on exhaustion and the disappointment he felt in himself for letting Jessica down.

But as frustrated as it made him, he was man enough to admit the disturbance could be solely placed at the feet of a fiery, short woman standing in the kitchen making homemade pasta while soft music drifted around him from the living room.

Alessandra.

She was just a woman.

Okay, an intelligent woman who had worked hard to become a doctor. But he'd met doctors before.

He'd met women before.

But he'd never met anyone like Alessandra.

The damn woman had a sense of history to her. Carlo knew instinctively that she came from a long line of hard working, innovative people.

When it came to her frame, his mind brimmed over with adjectives. Curvy, voluptuous, lush. She probably didn't mean to flaunt her chest, but she didn't have a choice with how prominent it was. Her short hair curled around her face in a way that made his throat swell when it caught the sunlight, sparkling hints of light brown, not to mention how it bounced as she walked.

She was pure Italian in all her actions. Carlo imagined her waving men's attention away with the handkerchief she kept tucked in her bra strap, laughing at them, but secretly appreciative of the attention all the same.

Fine wrinkle lines formed at the corner of her eyes and mouth, proving she was a woman who liked to laugh. But the same lines were ingrained in her forehead, undoubtedly from years of concentration. It was her career, Carlo thought, that brought the lines. It was also that same career that caused her olive complexion to be a bit sallow from all the time spent working inside under fluorescent lighting.

He should turn and walk away, but he didn't want to. He clasped his hands behind his back and let out a breath he wasn't aware he was holding. Watching Alessandra make pasta was too normal and domestic and no one had made him homemade pasta in years.

"This isn't the time to make pasta," he growled.

"Why not?"

"Because ... there are possible mafia related threats lurking and Jessica is unconscious in the other room."

"Jessica is fine. She is healing."

Unable to think of a retort, he uttered another grunt.

Alessandra glanced at him while she pushed a strand of stray hair out of her face with a clean spot on the back of her hand. "There is nothing to do and we're going to be hungry. And I am usually working at the hospital, so I haven't had a chance to spend this many consecutive hours in my own home in a long time." She went back to work. "I miss making pasta and since I have time now, I'm making pasta."

"But Jessica–"

"Is fine," she interrupted. "When the body is healing, the most natural thing for it to do is sleep. She just needs to sleep."

Carlo gave in to the urge to growl again; it made him feel better.

"Why don't you go ... scan the perimeter again?" She picked up the dough and slapped it angrily against the counter.

"It's better if no one knows I'm here."

She laughed and pointed a dusty finger at him. "How can no one *not* know you're here? You stick out like a sore thumb." She went back to kneading the dough, muttering, "Especially in those clothes."

"I was in a hurry." Carlo pulled at the cuffs of the dress shirt he had rolled up his forearms. When Parker contacted him about Jessica's appearance in Rome, he'd been in Florence. In a matter of minutes, he'd climbed aboard a waiting helicopter to head to the apartment. All he had was the suit he wore and his go bag, which had plenty of items to keep Jessica and Alessandra safe, but very little alternative clothing – just a few toiletries and change of cotton briefs. "I ordered some clothes, they should be here later today."

Alessandra finished kneading the dough, covered it with a towel to rest and went to wash her hands.

The truth of the matter was that Carlo didn't really know what to do. He'd already checked the apartment building, the perimeter and alley three times today. He needed movement so he could concentrate on something *other* than the woman in front of him, the smells coming from the apartment and those damn hips. He was an animal caged by a promise he made to fucking Parker Salvatore.

"Could I have a coffee?" He blurted the question.

Alessandra turned her head to snarl at him, full lips pursed, eyes glaring.

"Or I can make it myself."

She nodded her head to the table and ordered, "Sit down." She finished washing, then pulled the espresso maker from the dish drainer and began filling it with water.

Carlo allowed himself a few moments to appreciate the view. What the hell was happening to him? He'd worked for years around gorgeous women who were, more times than not, actual models. All of them draped in name brand attire, strutting around in slinky, sparkling sex.

But not one of those women had held themselves with the quiet pride Alessandra Salvatore did.

He thought perhaps those kinds of women wrinkled their noses in jealousy and confusion at the attention men lavished on Alessandra.

Hell, he found himself wanting to lavish her with attention. Which increased his feelings of frustration.

Maybe it was because this was one of his colleague's family members. Maybe that's why he was reacting so differently.

Because being around those women had been part of his job. When he'd been alone with any of them, he was normally driving them or lingering behind in the employ as bodyguard. None of those women had taken the time to make eye contact, much less talk to him; or talk back to him as Alessandra had done around each turn the past few hours.

So what if she talked back? She was just a strong Italian woman. When he laid this out on paper, it was just another job. A simple babysitting job. And babysitting jobs were supposed to be easy.

So why were every one of his emotions misfiring?

Why did the way her hands move so deftly at making a simple coffee cause him to adjust himself as he sat down?

Alessandra slid the cup and saucer in front of him, her hand lingering, her frown piercing him. Those big hazel eyes, filled with secrets he was desperate to uncover, held his gaze. She was so close, he could easily slip his arm around her and pull her onto his lap.

And here was the Neanderthal who was one hundred percent behind the decision of picking the pixie up and carrying her into a secret hideaway where he could spend days, weeks, months ... running his fingers through that mess of dark curly hair while tasting every damn inch of the curves hiding under the leggings and oversized t-shirt she wore.

"Grazie." His deep voice was hoarse.

She laughed and shook her head, releasing the cup and him as she went back to the counter and began the next phase of her pasta making.

Carlo lied about wanting a coffee. He just didn't want to leave this room or this moment. Familiar smells of his childhood were wrapped up in the flour and olive oil. And the temptation of the woman was intoxicating, no matter how frustrated it made him. But she also made him feel like a teenager; awkward and unsure of himself.

Stirrings of emotion fogged his rationale, which was probably the most dangerous thing that could happen to a man who needed his wits about him at all times. Just in case danger showed up at the door.

Alessandra opened a top cupboard and rising on her toes, used the tips of her fingers to pull out a pasta roller. He should have helped, but he couldn't stand up– watching her strain and flex continued to affect the tightness of his pants.

She slung a towel over her shoulder, attached the roller to the counter, picked up a piece of the dough and began to manually turn the crank to lengthen the dough, lost in thought as she worked, a soft smile pulled at the corner of her mouth.

"Why aren't you married?" The question burst forth, too rough, too loud. He cleared his throat and sipped at the espresso while they both recovered from the fumbling query.

Alessandra adjusted the setting on the side of the pasta maker and lifted the sheet so she could put it back through the center of the machine. "Well ... being a doctor takes years of school. When school was over, I did my residencies. Then I volunteered twice with the Doctors Without Borders program. There was never time for a relationship." She adjusted the machine again and began to feed the dough through once more. "I guess I really never made time for a relationship either."

He nodded, understanding how life happened that way all too well. His own job was not conducive to love or relationships.

"What kind of doctor are you?" he asked.

"I'm a trauma surgeon." She smiled then asked, "What kind of spy are you?"

"I'm not a spy."

It was her turn to grunt a reply.

"My official job title is Intelligence Officer."

"So ... a spy," she ribbed. "The very definition of which is a person who does work they can't talk about for an agency they can't admit to working for."

"Your brother does the same work."

She blew out a breath. "That certainly has come to mean a lot more the past two days than it did before."

"How old are you?" He bit out another awkward question.

Alessandra laughed. "How old are *you*?"

"Thirty-six."

"Me too." She grinned. "So, since we're getting the basics out, where do you live? Or do you live out of a suitcase?"

"A lot of the time I do, but I have an apartment in Pisa."

"Where your mail lives." She made the comment and chuckled to herself. "That's what my roommates and I used to say. When we were in school, we didn't spend much time in our apartment, so we liked to say we paid for our mail to have a place to live."

"Ah, then yes. I pay for my mail to live in Pisa."

They fell silent, the only noise the squeaking crank of the pasta maker as Alessandra turned the handle. After a few moments she glanced at Carlo –who hadn't been able to take his eyes off of her– and said, "You're hungry again."

His stomach clenched at the observation. It wasn't that he was hungry, it was that she was aware of his needs. How long *had* it been since someone saw to his needs?

She wiped her hands on the towel and replaced it on her shoulder. She opened the slim pantry and pulled out a bag with half a loaf of bread and a plate that had dried salami and aged cheese wrapped in a mesh casing.

She took the bread out and put it on a cutting board along with the meat, cheese and a knife, then set it in front of Carlo. She retrieved two smaller plates. "My mom made the salami and cheese."

"Where do they live?"

"South of Naples."

"Do they own a farm?"

"No, but they have a small plot of land. My dad sold insurance and my mother was a teacher. They're both retired now." She went back and began rolling out another sheet of pasta. "What about you, do your parents live in Pisa?"

No one had asked about him, or his life, or his family in such a long time ... "They passed away."

The comment stopped her and she turned her body toward him. "I'm sorry. Truly." In that moment he saw the humanity that she must meet her patients with. And the death that she understood.

He began slicing the cheese, meat and bread. "I grew up outside of Genoa."

She raised her eyebrows. "Oh, well then you won't like the salami. You'll think it's inferior."

"Because it's not Genoa salami."

She winked at him and he had to adjust himself again and clear his throat. "I'll struggle through. For my stomach."

"Thank you for the effort." She went back to the pasta. Having the sheets prepared, she switched the attachments on the pasta machine, lightly sprinkled the dough with flour on one side, slid it off the counter, and flipped it so she could flour the opposite side as well. She placed one end of the pasta sheet into the center of the machine and began turning the crank, producing long strands of fettuccine noodles. The light of the early afternoon streamed into the warm kitchen, and flour dust all but sparkled in the rays.

Carlo watched, enthralled, entranced. He slipped a bite of salami over his lips; the only release his inner caveman would get today was using his teeth to masticate the salty, spicy meat.

He shook his head. *Jesus,* he must need a break if all it took to lose focus was a woman from the 'south of Naples.'

Alessandra broke the silence. "Why aren't *you* married?"

Shrugging, he echoed her sentiment. "Work isn't conducive to love and marriage."

She nodded her head and let a few more moments pass. "What's really going on between my brother and Jessica?"

Carlo quickly popped some cheese in his mouth to give himself a moment. "He's just concerned for her well-being."

"Well," Alessandra scoffed, "that's some pretty well thought out bull-shit."

A booming laugh rumbled in his chest before it exploded. Alessandra jumped at the sound. If she knew him better, she'd know that the sound caught him off guard just as much as it did her.

She joined him in laughter and as she crossed the kitchen to fetch something else, she playfully tried to hit his shoulder with the towel.

He caught it with a smile, and the sudden smiles and lightness in the room tensed. He tugged on the towel to bring Alessandra closer.

And she didn't let go.

And Carlo didn't care why.

When she was close enough, he pushed his chair back, dropped the towel, settled his hands on her waist and pulled her between his legs. His face tilted up toward her, the only invitation he gave, and she took it without hesitating, pressing her lips to his.

The unexpected moment electrified his body, thumped against his ribcage, and intensified the hunger for her.

She moaned into his mouth, meeting his pleasure with her own.

He twisted his hand into her hair as he continued the assault on her lips. He couldn't get enough and her hands, slipping around his neck to cling to him, followed by another moan, it was his undoing.

God, he wanted more. He wanted to touch her, to feel her naked body pressed against his. He wanted a lifetime in that one moment and he took as much as he could. As much as she was willing to give.

When the kiss burned through the moment and the flames dimmed, they loosened their hold on each other as they parted, but only for an instant. Alessandra hovered above him, studied him, and then brushed her lips against his. He framed her face, feeling the weight of those curls, softer than he thought they'd be, and was surprised to find that her hazel eyes had slight flecks of green just around the edge of the iris.

She sighed as she brushed her fingertips against the nape of his neck. "You are going to be trouble for me."

"I was just thinking the same thing."

"Men don't like me once they get to know me," she warned.

He shrugged. "I'm not like most men."

"I'm trying to explain, I'm not like most women."

"Good." He abruptly pulled her back to him for another kiss.

Chapter Nine

J essica Dodd groped in the darkness for her cell phone and checked the time: 4 a.m.

Parker gave a soft snort of a snore as she put the phone back on the bedside table. She closed her eyes in an attempt to fall asleep; counted to twenty, took the same number of deep inhales and exhales, but instead of making her sleepy, the increase of oxygen mixed with the jet lag woke her up completely.

She slipped out of bed, found a sweater and her slippers and quietly made her way through the cold two-story villa, heading toward the kitchen. At the bottom of the stairs, she smelled a fire and heard rustling. At least she'd have some company this early in the morning.

She peeked around the corner and found Carlo, silhouetted by the light from the fire. He was adding another log and stood with the poker to adjust it.

"Good morning," Jessica whispered loudly as she pulled her cardigan closed, hugging herself against the coolness, happy for the opportunity to sit in front of a warm fire.

"Buongiorno," he whispered back, sitting down in one of the chairs.

"This is so nice." Jessica curled her feet under her and snuggled into the small sofa. "What are you doing awake so early?"

"Habit." He smiled. "Why are you awake?"

"Jet lag." She watched the yellow-orange flames dance and lick around the wood, then glanced over at Carlo, studying the sturdy man who was so relaxed in a flowered armchair. "Did you ever think, when we first met ...?"

"When I was forced to be your bodyguard," he corrected with a smirk.

"When you threatened my life in a dark alley," she pointed.

He tisked. "I never threatened your life."

She gestured to his whole body. "It's your size, you don't have to threaten, you just *are* threatening."

"And you just *are* a handful," he countered.

"Thank you." She tilted her head. "You look good. Rested."

"Love will do that to a man."

"Love ..." Jessica shook her head. "It's been a strange journey from hired thug to bodyguard to friend to ... well, you're almost my brother-in-law, huh?"

Carlo gave a gruff laugh and agreed. "It has been a strange turn of events."

She nodded and let the crackle of the fire and early morning settle, then asked, "You're doing good? Things are going well with Alessandra?"

He winked at her in reply.

"You two are fun to watch. You both continually look across the room for each other. And I thought last night at dinner, she was going to give up sitting next to you and just climb on your lap."

Another tisk of disapproval.

"Carlo, you're hot for each other and it's literally scorching everyone around you."

"I'll try to tone it down," he offered.

"No," she said a little too loudly and glanced behind her as if the outcry would wake someone up. "Please don't. I kind of want you to ramp up the heat. It might make my mom and Gianna stop talking about me and Parker."

"That's not what they're really talking about, you know."

"I kinda figured."

"They have a lot in common."

"I guessed that from how excited they were to see each other. Although, I think my mom was just as excited to see you."

"Barbara is nice to me."

Jessica snorted. "Yeah, she is. She likes to take people under her wing, and I think you ..." She cleared her throat and let the thought float away.

"You think I ..." he led.

She scrunched up her face and admitted, "I think you like having a mother figure in your life. Two actually."

Carlo got a faraway look in his eye but instead of responding to her observations, said, "Just so you know, they're willing to give you and Parker a year before you set a wedding date, but they don't care when the babies come."

"Thanks for the heads-up." Jessica yawned and shook it off. "If I thought I could have slept some more, I would have stayed in bed."

"Are you hungry?"

"I'd rather have coffee. But maybe it's too early."

"Too early for who?"

He stood but Jessica stopped him. "I can make my own."

"You're a guest in my country, I'll do it. Enjoy the fire."

She did as he suggested. Once Carlo had made the coffee, he brought it over, along with a plate of bread and cheese, which he placed on the small table in front of the sofa. She made a few slices and took a bite. "Damn," she said with a mouthful, "it's just bread and cheese, it shouldn't be this good."

Coffee in hand, and settled once again, Jessica took a sip and asked the real question she had. "How is it really going? You love each other, that's evident, but you're both so strong-willed."

He shrugged, verifying her claim.

"Carlo, I can't imagine your schedules offer a lot of room for a relationship. I don't really know where you live, but I know it's not Rome."

"Are you asking where I live?"

"Kinda. Actually, I have *a lot* of questions."

He picked up a piece of cheese. "I have an apartment in Pisa."

"But it's not really your home, is it?"

Another shrug in answer.

"I forgot how talkative you get." Jessica smiled. "C'mon Carlo. We've got food, we've taken a bite, by Italian rules we can talk about the important stuff now." She referred to several earth-shattering announcements that had been shared with her the last time she'd been in Italy; only *after* she'd eaten.

"Has it been difficult for you? Being back in Italy?" He flipped the conversation.

"Well, it's only been a few hours, but so far, no one's tried to kidnap me, make me work for the CIA or lied to me; so all in all, I'm pretty good."

"Jessica."

"Fine, we'll talk about my thing first, but then we're gonna go back to your thing."

He nodded his agreement.

"I was nervous on the plane," Jessica admitted, "but when we landed, I was excited. I think I needed to come back, to fight any remaining fears I might have."

"It hasn't even been a full year since ... everything."

"Do you *want* me to be scared?"

"No, of course not. I still feel ..." He cleared his throat. "I still feel guilty."

"Why?"

"I was the one who was supposed to look out for you and I failed."

She pursed her lips and studied Carlo for a moment, then shook her head. "Bullshit."

"What?"

"*I* put myself in a situation I shouldn't have been in in the first place."

"Jessica."

"Carlo, replay that whole night back logically. It wasn't your fault," she insisted.

She watched as the memories played and finally he shrugged. "I still have guilt."

"Then ..." she made a sign of the cross in the air in his direction, "I absolve you."

He gave a deep chuckle and then shook his head. "Fine. I'll try to be absolved. Now, you still haven't answered my question, how are you really?"

"It helps having Parker with me, and my parents. And my big sister and her boyfriend." She mockingly listed.

"I don't help?"

"Well, of course you help the most, but I don't want to inflate your ego."

A subtle upward turn of his lips accompanied his thanks. "Grazie. My ego will stay intact. And I'm glad you're not scared and that you came back. Though, I know you, you aren't the kind of woman who would let one rough situation keep her away from a gorgeous country and all it has to offer."

"I am pretty amazing," she agreed.

They both studied the fire and a few long moments passed before Carlo softly confessed, "It's hard. On both of us. We want to see each other more, but you're right, our schedules are difficult to navigate."

Jessica had a lot more questions; like would Carlo and Alessandra make the relationship work? They'd been engaged for a few months now, but there was no talk of going further. At the very least, shouldn't they be talking about moving in together?

Instead, she thought to start with the question she'd had for a while now. "How did it all start? With Alessandra? I never heard the whole story."

"It just did." He shifted his gaze and sighed, resigning himself to allow his vulnerability to show. "It feels like I've known her my whole life. But I never knew I was waiting for her."

"When did that happen? Was it a specific moment, or ...?"

"When I walked into her apartment and she led me to the bed you were laying in, I was only finally able to calm down when I looked across the room at her and– there she was."

"Whoa."

"It's all your fault, by the way."

"So for three days, while I was sleeping, you just fell in love?"

"I think I fell under her spell. She caught me and I was hers."

"Jesus, Carlo." Jessica pressed her hand to her chest.

"It wasn't romantic though, it was chaotic and ... frustrating."

Chapter Ten

I f Carlo was going to pinpoint exactly what was aggravating him the most about being stuck in Alessandra's apartment, he would say it was the sideways glances.

And Alessandra just being around.

And that damned, explosive kiss; the memory of which still floated around him, suspending him in a fog.

Or maybe it was the flour.

When Alessandra made the pasta with soft music drifting through the apartment, the fine powder of the flour sparkled and floated about in the sunlight, fine filaments of dreamy dust, casting a spell over him.

Carlo shook his head in an attempt to displace the ridiculous musings.

He was back at the kitchen table; day three of waiting for Parker. Day three of sleeping on a warped sofa bed. Day three of needing a respite, away from this place, so he could logically filter through the reasons he was spending every free moment pretending he had *no* desire to kiss Alessandra again.

Alessandra was washing a few dishes, and he watched her every move as he sipped his espresso. Espresso that continued to be the best he'd ever had, even though there was absolutely nothing different about the brand or type of espresso maker or the process. It must be the water in Rome; because if it wasn't, then the only viable explanation was that it was the woman.

He growled his irritation and took another drink, which only elicited another growl.

Maybe Carlo was losing his mind; maybe it was that simple. Because little things –like the warmth of the kitchen and the smells of homemade food, or the way the light played across the large balcony throughout the day– caused him to have fanciful thoughts that would not be deterred as they tried to convince him that magic might be real and it lived in this unassuming apartment.

He muttered a curse and straightened in the chair.

All right, he could get to the bottom of this.

It was a woman who was intriguing and capable. He was stuck in a small space with Alessandra and the need to keep both her and Jessica safe had heightened the stakes.

That was why he was thrown so off-balance.

Add the attraction he hadn't felt in a while and of course he was feeling awkward and jagged. Attraction wasn't a weakness. Attraction happened.

And maybe he shouldn't have kissed her. Because the memory of the kiss lingered. And *that* was the reason he felt as if he'd been propelled back to his youth and a first crush.

They'd been cordial to each other since the kiss. Acting as if it hadn't happened. And he tried to be nonchalant. But when she was in his orbit, he wanted to watch her. He tried to be cool, only taking sideways glances, though when she caught him, neither of them looked away. And it was the sideways glances that were heating up the whole damn apartment while his lips burned from the memory of one, insignificant kiss that had him raging with urgency to either get out of the apartment or get into Alessandra.

He tilted his head to the side and cracked his neck, lecturing himself internally that the best thing would be to leave the damn kitchen.

Nothing he did to shake off these feelings was helping; so he regressed into the actions of a juvenile idiot and argued with Alessandra. *About everything*.

It didn't help, because she would tilt her head, put her hands on her hips, jut out her chin and argue right back. And her challenge lit him up. The strange aphrodisiac was a throwback to primal mating rituals.

But he should be better than this. (That's the speech he gave himself in the mirror after every cold shower- a running total of four at this point ...) Yet here he was. Back at the table trying to ignore the domestic comfort and the woman who, not only had him adjusting himself, *again*, but also sparked the overwhelming need for more than just sideways glances.

So maybe he didn't need to be better. Why was he fighting so hard? He'd learned how short life was, how fragile.

After she finished the dishes, Alessandra was heading out of the kitchen; when she was close enough, she brushed her hand against his, and whether it was a sign or a mistake, this time– he took what he wanted.

He caught her hand and as he stood, pulled her against his body and lowered his lips to hers ever so slowly, studying her eyes as he went. Whether it was a dare or he was just looking for her consent, he wasn't sure. But his answer came when she pressed herself against him and lifted up on her tiptoes to reach him. Maybe they were both curious if there was more than the anger and flirtation that radiated between them.

Immediate shockwaves exploded. And she didn't hold back an intoxicating moan as she wound her arms around his neck.

It was more than a simple flirtation.

Whatever this was, it was more than simple.

The sound of the front door opening was accompanied by Parker's booming call. "Aless? Moretti?"

They didn't jump apart, but sought one more lingering kiss before Alessandra slipped down his body, placing her feet flat on the floor once more. She held Carlo's gaze, a frown creasing her forehead. His arms loosely held her waist. Time stood still for just this moment, for just the two of them, as if there would be no interruption until they allowed it. They were frozen, held in place by the final ripples of electricity softening, loosening.

Alessandra stepped back, allowing her hands to slide from his neck, over his shoulders, down his biceps and forearms until she was holding his hands.

He needed to let go; he sure as hell wasn't in the mood for Parker to find him entangled with Alessandra.

He didn't even know what this was. All he knew was what she *did* to him. She turned his world on end and he had no idea what to do about any of it.

"Here," Alessandra called out to her brother, starting time once more.

Her hands slid across his, so there was still a slight entwining of fingers as they slipped out of each other's grasp, dropping completely a mere second before Parker entered the kitchen.

"Is everything okay?" Parker asked.

Carlo studied the man, his hair disheveled, dark circles around his eye, some of the franticness still hovering around the edges. Carlo knew that meant he'd found no trace of Jessica's ex, Thomas Adler.

"Everything is fine." Alessandra hugged her brother. "Jessica is healing and still sleeping. I'll make you a coffee and we can all talk."

Chapter Eleven

Alessandra was happy for the excuse to gather herself with no one watching. Well, almost no one. She could feel Carlo's gaze on her back. She knew he was paying close enough attention to her brother to be able to talk about the current situation at hand, but in between, she could feel his sideways glances, as if they had the ability to caress her skin.

Her hands shook as she rinsed the espresso maker and readied it once again.

What was happening to her? And what was that kiss? She figured the first kiss was a fluke, at best. But this time, pressed against him, the heat, the electricity … what the hell was going on?

Lord knew she was attracted to the man, she wasn't the type of woman to play games and pretend she didn't find him quite attractive.

And she was single, so why not take advantage of a moment and kiss an attractive man? And he was the one who initiated contact, his big strong hands pulling her to him, causing her knees to quake, her heartbeat to quicken … so of course she gave into the curiosity to test the waters once more of being kissed by those full lips, and held against that broad, solid chest.

What she didn't expect was the way her breath left her. The way the world stood on its side. The way she disappeared into a feeling of being whole. And the need for so much more.

When they parted and she looked into the shining, confidence of his light brown eyes, she was taken aback at what she saw– a reflection of herself.

She knew, without a shadow of a doubt, Carlo was seeing her for who she truly was. And it was both invigorating and crushingly terrifying.

Parker interrupted her thoughts. "Alessandra, did you get the rest of your shifts covered?"

"What?" She took out two demitasse cups and poured the coffee. She handed him a cup and sat down.

"I called you yesterday and asked you to get your shifts covered for the rest of the week. Until I can figure out how to make sure you're safe."

"Oh. No," she said matter-of-factly.

"What do you mean no?" her brother asked.

"She thinks she'll be safe at the hospital," Carlo supplied, eyes sparkling as he sat back.

The kiss and its power dissipated in his knowing grin. This was one of the many arguments they'd had since Carlo had been put in 'charge'. He fought her on everything, from her walking to the corner store, talking to colleagues at work on the phone, and taking groceries to a neighbor.

"I'll be safe there," she reasoned, then gestured toward Carlo. "He can watch over Jessica here and we have security at the hospital. I need to get back to work." And the less time she had to spend around this man arguing and wanting to kiss him again, the better.

"Aless, please, I need you to stay here," Parker stated. Carlo winked at her, and she frowned as Parker validated his request. "I told you, the man who did that to Jessica is still out there. We don't know where he is, and for all we know, he might know where we are."

"So you'll stay," Carlo added definitively.

"I will do what I feel is the right thing to do," Alessandra snarled.

Carlo might be so good-looking it was causing her physical problems, but so far they had three speeds; the electricity when they touched, her need to feed him, and arguing. And one thing the well-formed brute hadn't seemed to understand in these past few days was that she didn't like being told what to do.

"I need you to stay with Jessica," her brother pleaded, a slight shake in his voice.

Alessandra narrowed her gaze on Parker. "Do you love her?"

"I'm *worried* about her. I want the men who did that to her to pay." It wasn't an answer.

Alessandra tried to soothe him. "She's on the mend."

"She's been sleeping for three days," Carlo added.

"Three days?!" Parker yelled.

"Yes," Alessandra straightened, "and she's fine. Her body is healing."

"Mi dispiace." *I'm sorry.* Parker ran a hand through his hair. "It's been a rough few days."

Alessandra glanced over at Carlo- he had thick brown hair, there might even be a bit of natural curl there; but he kept it short.

She shook her head, what the hell was wrong with her, thinking about running her hands through his hair again.

Clearing her throat in an attempt to dislodge the images, she flexed her hands under the table. "Parker, when was the last time you slept?"

He rubbed the back of his neck. "I don't know. I'm running on anger and adrenaline and caffeine at this point ..." Then with a glance toward the hallway, he muttered, "I just wish she would wake up."

"I've been monitoring her vitals, she's doing well. I've also been giving her something to help her sleep."

"What?" Parker bit.

"Is that safe?" Carlo asked.

Alessandra looked incredulously between the two men and gave a shake of disbelief. "Please, if you could *both* show me your medical degrees, I'd love to talk about my patient at length and how you might know better than me what should or should not be done."

Carlo grinned as Parker held up his hands in surrender. "Alessandra, please. While I'm combing the streets of Rome, I need to know you're safe. I can't worry about you too."

"Fine," she reluctantly agreed.

"Part of not worrying about you is leaving Carlo in charge while I'm gone."

"I don't need a babysitter," she muttered.

Carlo raised an eyebrow. "She went to the supermercato, il panificio e il fruttivendolo while you were gone. She didn't wait for me to accompany her. Just does as she pleases."

"All three of those stores are on the corner. Less than two minutes away, and most of that time is waiting for the elevator," Alessandra defended.

"And like your brother said, we don't know if the men we're looking for know where we are. They could be watching us."

"Isn't that why you continue to do your 'rounds' outside? Ten, twelve times a day, you walk around the whole block. So if someone knew where we were, it would be because of your ..." she gestured to his whole body, "all of you is bringing attention to us."

"She doesn't listen." Carlo rolled his eyes.

"I've been to the store three days in a row, where are these phantoms? I am not a child. I don't need a babysitter," she insisted.

Parker put his hands up. "Please Alessandra. Stay in the apartment. Let Carlo take care of the security and go to the store for you. He knows what he's doing."

She slapped her hands on the table and stood up, snarling down at her brother.

"Alessandra, you aren't going to intimidate me. I'm your brother, I know all your tricks." He stood and took a step closer to her, towering over her, purposefully looking down his nose. She jammed her fists against her hips and tilted her chin up at him.

They stood that way for a few moments before a slight smile pulled at the corner of Parker's lips, and he relaxed, reached out and rubbed her head.

She slapped at his hands as he announced, "I'm exhausted and I'm sure I smell. I'm going to take a shower and maybe have something to eat?"

"I have cheese and salami from Mom."

"Oh, I haven't had that in so long."

She watched him shuffle down the hall, fully aware that she'd lost the argument.

But she wasn't about to tell him the reason she needed to go to work, or why she'd gone to the store three days in a row. Because then she'd be admitting to her brother how fiercely Carlo was affecting her.

When she was working, she could get into a rhythm, drown out the noise and figure out solutions to the kinds of problems brought on by tempting men. But here, there was no rhythm, just a man whose body dared her to explore every enticing inch. A man who was always in the way.

"Ale ..." Carlo called. The nickname, new and lovely, slipped over her; his rich voice, as smooth as the dreamy brown of his eyes, swirled around her.

She didn't dare look at him, but instead began to wash the cups. Taking her time as she tried to catch her breath and waited for the tell-tale sound of the chair, signifying that he was leaving the room.

It never came.

The repeat of her name did come, however. "Ale."

She took as deep a breath as she could and attempted indifference as she turned and asked, "Yes?"

"You're a strong woman."

"Yes. I know."

"I like that."

"I don't care what you like." She decided her words would put an end to whatever this conversation was going to be, then thought better of it, and pointed at Carlo. "You're arrogant."

"I think you like a dash of arrogance in a man." The small, slight beginning of a smile pulled at the corner of his mouth.

"Not particularly."

Carlo changed the subject. "Should I get your hospital on the phone for you?"

"I'll contact them myself. When *I* am ready. Like I told my brother, I don't need a babysitter."

He stood up and the scrape of his chair excited her in a way she most certainly was not prepared for. "I think you do."

"Scusa?"

"A woman like you needs to be looked after."

She wasn't sure if he was trying to anger her or come on to her. She threw the towel she'd been holding at him and demanded, "You need to get out of my kitchen."

"Your brother told me to watch after you." His voice dropped an octave as he whispered the words, his meaning quite evident.

His hooded eyes scanned the length of her body, causing her neurons to hijack her everyday body functions and send shivers throughout.

She crossed her arms over her chest. "Stop it."

"No."

She angrily raised her voice. "Get out of my kitchen."

He growled and matched her tone. "Salvatore's in charge here. I'll do what Salvatore tells me."

"Yes, Salvatore. And I'm a Salvatore!" Alessandra yelled.

"Why are you yelling?" Carlo returned, matching her volume.

She clenched her jaw and shook her head in disbelief. *Why was she yelling?* Because in one breath he wanted her and in the next, he was telling her what to do and picking a fight.

Wasn't he?

"You are infuriating!" she yelled for good measure.

"You're going to wake Jessica up." Carlo gave the lame excuse and left the kitchen.

Alessandra blinked wildly at his retreating back.

What the hell was this all about? She marched after him; he did *not* get to say her name in that husky voice and look at her that way and start an argument and then just ... walk away. "You just said that you think she's sleeping too much. Now you're worried we're going to wake her up? Make up your mind."

He stopped in the hallway by Jessica's door. When he turned to face her, she ran into him, and instead of stepping back, tried to stand her ground. But it wasn't easy because she could feel the heat coming off his body.

He took a step back and Alessandra felt a hint of vindication.

With nowhere else to go, he pushed open the door to Jessica's room; whether to escape or to reignite the argument, Alessandra didn't know, and she wouldn't find out because what neither of them had been ready for was Jessica, eyes wide open, blinking with a frown at the strange interruption.

"I told you so!" Carlo yelled before the reality of what he was seeing sunk in.

"Jessica?" He crossed the room and took her hand in his.

"You were yelling?" she asked hoarsely.

He picked up a glass sitting on the bedside table and helped her take a sip. But when she started to cough, Alessandra shook her head and brushed past Carlo. "Idiota." She tried to dislodge the glass from his hands. He tugged once, but she was insistent and he let go, throwing his hands up in the air muttering a very Italian curse. "Minchia."

Jessica began to laugh and cough at the same time, moaning in pain. Alessandra pushed at Carlo. "You're making more problems. Go away," she demanded.

"I make problems? *You* make problems." He frowned.

She pushed him once more, not meaning to be so physical with him, but the release of her pent-up emotions felt so damn good she pushed and yelled at him again. "Vai via!" *Go away.*

He grunted but followed her directions, though she could have sworn a sparkle of a smile lay underneath.

Needing to have the last word, she added, "And stay out of my kitchen."

He slammed the door – *his* last word; and Alessandra looked down at Jessica while she pressed her palm to her chest. "Oddio! He is too handsome."

Chapter Twelve

Walter Dodd sat back in the kitchen chair and studied the label on the cold beer Parker handed him: Ichnusa.

Parker held up his own beer as he sat down, explaining, "This is a pretty popular beer, it's made in Sardinia."

Walter took a sip and nodded. "Not bad."

Antonio patted his son's back as he sat down at the table and held his beer toward Walter in a toast.

Walter copied the action and took another long sip then let out a satisfied sigh. It had been a remarkable few days in Rome.

The Salvatores had taken everyone to some unbelievable restaurants, a vineyard owned by a friend of their family, and last night he, Parker, Antonio, Carlo, Benjamin and Cassie went to a soccer game at the Stadio Olimpico, the largest sports facility in Rome.

Walter had been to Europe before, he and Barbara had gone on a tour and visited friends in Sweden. He'd also been on plenty of vacations with his daughters and wife; always there was bickering and moodiness and a litany of problems that came when traveling with family. So he was ready for whatever headaches might come from locking ten strangers –who were basically becoming family– in a villa in a country where only half of them spoke the language.

But it had been remarkable. Other than the ribbing for Jessica and Parker to get married, each day surpassed the last, and he was downright delighted.

It was also a revelation, seeing his kids in this new light, with two young men who went out of their way to show him and his wife respect; as well as his daughters.

He glanced at Jessica and Cassie showing Carlo the photos they'd taken that day. His girls gave Parker and Benjamin a run for their money, but he liked that too. He was one of those fathers who often thought that no man would ever be good enough for his girls; but after the past few days, he was willing to admit that these men came pretty close.

They'd make good in-laws.

Sons-in-law.

The idea was strange, but he found the trip was also allowing him to get used to that probability as well.

"This has been such a great trip," he mused, then smiled and turned his attention out the large French doors of the kitchen that gave an unobstructed view of the vineyard dipping slowly beyond the grassy backyard. It was hard to believe they were a fifteen-minute drive from the busy city.

Almost out of sight of the doors, he saw his wife and Gianna Salvatore laughing and talking with their hands. He and Barbara had taken a community Italian Language class, though they didn't tell the girls they were taking the class (as they wanted to surprise them as well), but the moment they landed, they forgot everything they'd worked so hard to learn. Granted, the little things still stuck: please, thank you, I don't like this idea, can you tell me the exchange rate of the euro today?

The continued usage of some of the phrases had helped him. Still, he was sure his wife hadn't learned fluent Italian in the past four days, but she and Gianna seemed to get along without a common tongue. It had been the same when the Salvatores stayed at their house over Thanksgiving.

The setting sun on the horizon began to bathe the surrounding trees and vines in golden light, turning the green branches nearest the house a dusty sage. He squinted his eyes, applying a bit more abstraction to the moment.

So it was with a squint, out of the corner of his eye that he thought he saw Gianna Salvatore begin to flip his wife over her shoulder. "Fuck!" he yelled, bolting up and blinking wildly. Had his eyes played a trick on him?

"What?" Cassie asked following her father's gaze, and caught the moment her mother landed on her back, Gianna standing over her. "Holy shit!" She joined in the shock as everyone else followed their gaze, stared disbelievingly for a moment, then began to run as a group outside.

They arrived and stood mouths agape to find Gianna bent at the waist laughing as uproariously as Barbara, who was laying in the grass on her back clapping.

"Mom, what the hell is going on?" Jessica asked at the same time Alessandra repeated a similar question in Italian.

"Barbara?" Walter said his wife's name, frowning as both women tried to control their laughter, but when they made eye contact, they started up again.

Conversation erupted in Italian and English, both parties trying to get a proper explanation.

Finally, Barbara was able to laugh out, "I was teaching her some of the stuff we learned in our self-defense class."

Cassie frowned. "What?"

"Gianna," Barbara held up her hands to her husband who hoisted her back into a standing position, "is a very quick study."

Alessandra pointed to her mother declaring, "You just threw her over your shoulder on the ground!"

"I know, isn't it amazing?" Gianna beamed.

Barbara hugged Gianna and then patted her on the shoulder. "Way to go."

Barbara glanced around at the open-mouthed, stunned, incredulous glances.

Gianna became animated just then, speaking a fast streak. Jessica and Cassie glanced at Alessandra for the translation, which was given with a laugh. "My mamma loved that so much, she's looking for volunteers to throw."

Barbara barked out a laugh.

"Jessica," Carlo caught her attention, "self-defense classes?" He looked between Parker and Benjamin, the silent question 'is everything okay?' passing between them.

Cassie slapped Carlo on the back. "Mom decided the best way to handle the job these two have, was to take self-defense classes. Just in case. We did so well and liked it so much, we started taking a martial arts class."

"We all just got our blue belts," Jessica offered.

Carlo pursed his lips. "Interesting."

Cassie took over the explanation. "Two weeks ago, we learned how to get an attacker off-balance and throw them over our shoulder."

Walter sighed. "Yes Babs, you learned to throw an *attacker*, not our in-laws."

"In-laws," Cassie repeated with a snort just as Jessica snarled, "Dad."

Gianna began to wave her hands at her son, no one needed to understand Italian to know she was volunteering him to be her attacker. Parker took his time walking over to stand directly in front of her. When she offered her wrist, he grabbed it lightly. She slapped at his arm and with a roll of his eyes, he tightened his grip. She turned her attention to the group. Alessandra interpreted, "Guardate questo." *Watch this.*

She stepped the way Barbara taught her, turned her wrist and yanked it out of the tight hold. Parker's eyes went wide with appreciation.

Barbara began to clap. "Isn't it fun?! You know, even Walter took some of the classes with us and has started going to the gym. We lift weights together. I'm so strong now," she bragged. Then leaning toward Gianna she whispered theatrically, "I could even carry two babies at once if I had to."

Jessica and Cassie exchanged eye rolls as Carlo translated.

Jessica pointed a warning finger. "Hey Carlo, maybe no more translating. If they want to be such good friends and plan weddings and babies, then they should have to learn each other's language first."

Walter was standing next to Cassie when Alessandra approached her and asked, "Can you teach me something?"

Cassie nodded. "Sure. But if you want to toss someone over your shoulder, it's not gonna be me."

Walter Dodd watched as the twilight activities became an impromptu lesson in self-defense. He was proud of his girls, but now that he knew no one was in any mortal danger, he left the group with Antonio joining him. They retrieved their beers and sat down on the patio. Walter held the beer aloft toward Antonio and with a smile nodded. "It's a good beer."

Chapter Thirteen

"Signore ..." An airport police officer was approaching Carlo. Probably because he'd been parked in the loading zone for fifteen minutes and was casually leaning against the passenger side of the rented car he was driving.

Carlo held up his left hand and slowly reached into his front pocket, pulling out his wallet and flipping to his credentials. The officer studied the identification and raised an eyebrow.

"It shouldn't be too much longer," Carlo informed.

The officer paused for a moment and then gave a tired shake of his head. "Okay, but not too much longer, eh?"

Carlo ended up waiting another twenty minutes.

Finally, Parker exited the sliding doors that lead to the departure area. He slipped the sunglasses that were atop his head over his eyes but not before Carlo caught a glimpse of the strained look and the telltale redness around them.

They climbed into the car, and with Carlo behind the wheel, pulled into traffic.

The tension wafting off of Parker made Carlo feel he needed to say something. Parker had just sent Jessica home, even though they still hadn't caught Adler. She would be looked after by the CIA, Benjamin Stills being the agent flying back with her and assigned to her detail. Parker felt personally responsible to find the man who caused Jessica so much pain. Carlo understood the reasoning because he'd be glad to finally join Parker in tracking the man down.

"Stills is a good agent," Carlo assured. "He'll look after Jessica …" He gritted his teeth as he finished the thought internally, *Stills would do a far better job than Carlo had.*

"I trust him with my life," Parker confirmed.

Carlo had driven the trio to the airport. Stills in the front seat, Jessica and Parker in the back. The couple had held hands, but they barely spoke or looked at each other. It was as if the amount of what needed to be said and the diminishing time left, tied their tongues into a multitude of knots.

Add the pressure Parker placed on his own shoulders and the fact that the CIA and AISE weren't any closer to finding the smallest trace of Adler, it all made for a somber ride.

"Alright," Parker began, giving a shake of his head as they pulled onto the autostrada, "we found the doctor that Adler kidnapped and forced to tend Jessica."

"But he doesn't have any information to help," Carlo verified.

Parker ran a hand through his hair. "No. But I'm going to talk to him again. Maybe …"

"Take a breath," Carlo encouraged. "We need to go back to Florence, where we started this. Retrace the steps. We'll find something."

"*I'll* find something," Parker corrected, then cleared his throat several times before he admitted, "I need you to do me a favor."

Alessandra's face hovered before Carlo's eyes, he knew what the favor was and grasped at any reason to leave Rome. "I was the inside man with Adler. I'm an asset."

"You've been gone for a week. How are you going to explain where you were? At this point, all fingers point to you as helping Adler. Best case scenario, you talk your way back in, but you'd be given menial assignments. Worst case, you'll be shot on the spot."

Carlo knew the moment he'd left Florence and headed to Rome, he'd blown his cover completely.

But he would rather try to get back in the good graces of the rats that remained in the employ of the crime family they'd been investigating, than be asked to do this 'favor' for Salvatore.

He scoffed at himself, *are you really scared of a little woman?*

The simple answer: Hell yeah.

"She won't like it," Carlo stated.

Parker laughed. "Alessandra doesn't like anything that isn't her idea."

Carlo grunted.

"I've already cleared this assignment with both our agencies," Parker said.

Carlo wasn't going to be able to get out of this one.

So he repeated the same promise he'd given a few days earlier. "I'll keep her safe."

Parker gave a wry laugh. "Yeah, but who will keep you safe?"

Carlo tightened his grip on the steering wheel, if only Parker knew the weight *that* statement held.

"Where am I dropping you off?" Carlo asked.

"We actually have a meeting to go to first."

Carlo understood the hidden innuendo that this meeting would be with a group of CIA as well as his own operatives. "Thanks for telling me."

"Did you have somewhere else to be?"

"I thought I did?"

"She's at work," Parker offered.

"Salvatore, have you told your sister yet that I'll be *looking out* for her?"

Parker's silence was answer enough. Carlo gave a hollow laugh. "You're letting me do that too?"

"I didn't want you to feel useless."

Carlo wouldn't mind feeling useless, it was all of the other emotions lately that had become more worrisome. And as he drove away from her apartment today, he'd felt better because he thought he was putting all of that behind him.

After a trying meeting that involved two different agencies attempting to dominate a spotty video conference and crappy connection, Carlo and Parker left together with a tentative eight-day assignment. That's how long the CIA was willing to give Parker to find any trace of Thomas

Adler. If he didn't accomplish anything by then, the whole operation would be scrapped; as the head of the organization was dead, and therefore didn't need any more attention. If nothing came from Parker's search, he and his operatives would return to the states and Carlo would be reassigned.

Carlo pulled up in front of the hospital and tossed the key fob on the dashboard. "This rental is your problem now, Salvatore. I think it'll be better if I let Alessandra drive me around. She might feel more in control or ... something."

"And she might feel bad if she left you on the side of the road?" Parker asked.

Carlo laughed. "I don't think she'd feel too bad about ditching me."

"No, she wouldn't," Parker agreed. As they both climbed out of the car, Parker's parting words were, "I'll be in touch."

Carlo watched him pull away. He made his way to the entrance of the hospital, stood for several long seconds, then stepped aside for an elderly couple making their way in. Entering after them, he found a map of the hospital and took his time studying the building's interior floor plan. Then he gave himself a pep talk and finally approached the front desk, showed his badge and asked after Alessandra's schedule.

She would be off in an hour.

He decided the best place to wait for her was outside. He wouldn't feel so confined there. And an hour gave him time to practice several different explanations.

If he was feeling this trapped by the situation, it was because he knew Alessandra was going to unleash her angry, assertive prowess.

Of course, he liked that part of her.

He checked his watch- only a few more minutes now, and none of the speeches he came up with were going to work. He cursed Parker several times.

When she walked out of the hospital, he did the only thing that really made sense. He called out, "Doctor Salvatore."

She glanced over her shoulder, shifting the large bag she was carrying, and frowned the moment she spied him.

He shrugged. "It's your brother's idea."

Fury ignited, she flared her nostrils and stormed toward her car. Carlo followed and when they arrived at her car, he stood by the passenger door.

She clicked the key to open her side, glancing across the roof of the small white Peugot. He didn't move while she came to terms with the situation, but he was *truly* interested in what she was going to do.

Leaving him standing in the employee parking lot was a definite possibility at this point.

She pulled out her cell phone, dialed a number and then clicked the fob, opening his door. As they got in, Alessandra released an impressive litany of foul wishes upon her brother's head, and he hadn't even answered the phone yet. But when he did, she growled his name. "Parker."

She started the car, and Carlo was genuinely glad Bluetooth picked up the conversation; he could hear both sides as they drove and Alessandra yelled at her brother –rather than him– while Parker attempted to defend his decisions by raising his voice and matching her tone.

Out of the corner of his eye, he caught a few of her angry glances; verifying the fact that he wasn't off the hook either. But all things aside, he enjoyed the ride more than he thought he would.

Chapter Fourteen

W hen Alessandra's breathing returned to somewhat normal; and her heart stopped trying to escape her chest; and the walls of her bedroom formed into a solid state once again; and feeling returned to her toes and fingers; she opened her eyes and thought perhaps there was more color and light and sound in her room than there'd ever been before.

She shivered and smiled as the naked man next to her released a deep sigh that reached her very core. His large wandering hand slipped across her stomach, turning her smile to a frown.

Damnit.

"I told you we couldn't let this happen," she muttered.

"Did you?"

"How did this happen?" she muttered, still stunned.

In reply he pulled her body against his and whispered, "You told me you don't like me," then captured her lips with his and she melted against the intoxicating power of him.

Alessandra didn't say anything to Carlo on the way to her apartment. She didn't say anything when they exited the car. And she didn't say anything when they walked into her building. When the elevator arrived on the first floor, she walked in, then turned and stood in his way, denying him entrance and staring him down as the doors closed.

When she opened the door of her apartment, she dropped all her things in the hallway, grabbed clean clothes from her room and locked herself in her bathroom.

The soft click of the front door closing seemed to echo into the bathroom. Alessandra angrily turned on the water for the shower and stood staring at the white tile while the water heated.

What was she going to do?

Eight days!?

She'd kept herself in check for almost a week while that man was in her house, and she was overly grateful for Jessica and Parker's presence, even if Parker was gone and Jessica was asleep. At least Alessandra was able to work within the parameters that she wouldn't 'do' anything, just in case someone returned or woke up.

And after the two times Carlo kissed her, she wanted to do so, *so* much more. But she knew it wasn't conducive to ... anything. They weren't the type to have relationships, she already had a life partner, and it was her work. Hell, Carlo Moretti wasn't even her type.

Yeah, right.

She scrubbed her face with her hands, frustrated that no amount of calling her brother names had made him renege on this arrangement. It would seem Carlo was here to stay for the next eight days.

EIGHT DAYS.

What the hell was she going to do now? Work, obviously. Thank God she'd be able to work. She could trade some shifts and if she scheduled it right, she could spend the majority of the next eight days at the hospital.

That was good, she nodded as the idea grounded her. That would work.

After her shower and formatting a plan, she tried not to make eye contact with herself in the mirror as she dried her hair, put on a light layer of eight in one foundation and concealer, then pinched her cheeks.

"I'm doing this for me," she lied to her reflection.

Her trepidation about the current situation was long gone when she walked out and found her TV on in the living room, the patio French doors open and Carlo in the kitchen, smoke spilling out of a frying pan.

"What the hell are you doing?"

"Making dinner," he told the pan.

Several sausages had been halved and were sputtering and burning on high heat in one pan, while another pot held a science experiment of thick, yellow polenta bubbling, ready to release the building air pocket and its contents onto the stove.

"Jesus ..." She drew out the word as she edged him out of the way and turned off both burners.

"What are *you* doing?" Carlo asked.

"I'm saving my pans." An eruption of dense cornmeal hopped out, a multidirectional attack on the backsplash and burner. "And my stove."

"I'll clean up after. I've been cooking for myself for years."

"Successfully?"

"I was trying to help." He turned the stove back on. But the moment he pulled his hand away, she turned the knobs off.

"*I'll* finish this."

"I can cook, let me help," he seethed.

Alessandra reached over the stove, to the back and turned off the main gas line. "It's my kitchen." She crossed her arms over her chest and glared up at him triumphantly.

He threw his hands up. "I was trying to help. I know Salvatore put us in this awkward situation and I was trying to make it easier on you." He turned away.

"You want to make it easy? Leave."

He'd made it to the center of the kitchen when her words stopped him. He turned slowly, mirrored her crossing arms and eyed her for a long, quiet, uncomfortable moment then gave a definitive shake of his head and said, "I'm not going anywhere."

"You could easily watch from the street," she reasoned. "Go stay in my car, do surveillance down there. I'll be at work for much of the time and you can sleep then. The way I see it, you'll have done your due diligence."

"It's not that easy."

Oddio, she needed it to be that easy.

Alessandra wasn't so naïve as to not understand that there truly was a viable threat. She was the one who'd treated Jessica and understood the man her brother was searching for was a force to be reckoned with. But Alessandra was a force herself. She agreed to being babysat the first time around because her brother's face was drawn, distraught with stress, anger and exhaustion.

But this new turn of events was not helping her at all. Carlo was a handsome brute who tried to see into the very depths of her soul when he made eye contact, and at the moment, *he* was a lot more dangerous than the ghost Parker was looking for.

Carlo Moretti threatened everything Alessandra had built. She'd married her work a long time ago, she didn't just want to be a doctor; being a doctor was a finite vocation for her. And when she started school, and the hours and years it would take to work toward her end goal were laid out before her, she recognized there would be no room for kids and a husband. But that was something she never wanted anyway, so there was never any feeling of sacrifice.

"This is only temporary. I'll try to stay out of your way," Carlo muttered.

She shook her head. "You can't stay out of anyone's way, look at you. You take up all the space, wherever you go." She'd meant for it to be an angry comment, but the admission caught in her throat because she wasn't deterred by his size, she was enthralled by it.

"I'll cook something for myself later." He started to head out of the room.

"Stop!" Alessandra snapped. "Don't be stupid, we're not cooking at two separate times, and if this is how you cook," she waved to the stove, "*I'm* doing the cooking."

He stopped at her words and turned back around, shaking his head. "Do you let anyone help you?"

"Sit down," she ordered.

He snarled, but followed directions, doing the only thing they'd perfected over the past few days: sitting and watching her cook.

"I can cook," he said, sounding like a pout to Alessandra. "At least let me clean up after."

She took a deep breath. "Thank you, but I'm just ... particular about ..."

When she didn't continue he prodded, "About?"

"My things," she finished quietly.

Carlo laughed. "You don't like sharing your toys, huh?"

She didn't answer as she turned the gas back on, then the burners, but on low this time. She covered the sausage with a lid and retrieved cheese and spinach from the fridge. If she shared her 'toys', she was opening herself up to more. And as much as her center quivered with wanting more from him –a few more hundred kisses; to feel those big hands on her naked skin; to study his broad chest and find out if his olive skin was covered with a thatch of dark black hair– he was only going to be here for eight days.

He would leave when his assignment was done and she needed boundaries to keep her on the path she'd chosen.

So he was damn right, she was not interested in sharing anything with him because she needed to be in complete and utter control to get through. And she didn't want to play house with him, even though that was exactly what they were doing.

"Wine?" he asked.

God, yes. She nodded. "But aren't you working?"

"I don't think one glass will be a problem."

He took out two glasses and retrieved the bottle they'd opened last evening to celebrate Jessica's final night in Rome. Though it was a dour affair and no one wanted more than a sip or two.

He poured them each a glass, set Alessandra's next to her on the counter before sitting back down.

After a few moments, she calmed down enough to ask, "Do you like your job?"

He nodded. "I do. Do you like yours?"

"It's my whole world. I worked hard to get where I am."

"I can't imagine doing anything else," he supplied, "and I'm good at it."

Alessandra looked over her shoulder at him, *was* he good at his job? Sure he was intimidating in size and how he presented himself, but so far, all she'd really seen him do was sit at her table, eat and argue.

"Is it dangerous?"

He shrugged. "Sometimes."

She was taken aback by the honest answer. "I think you like the danger."

Another shrug, but after a few moments he added, "I don't know anything else. I joined the military when I was seventeen and started working in this field soon after."

"As an intelligence officer?"

"As an intelligence officer," he verified.

She dished up the cooked spinach, cheesy polenta and sausages and delivered the plates to the table. They ate in silence, offering polite half-smiles when they made eye contact.

Awkwardness was good, Alessandra mused– she could do awkward for the next few days.

After he took his last bite, Carlo offered, "I'll do dishes. And clean the stove."

"You don't know how," she said.

Carlo sat back in his seat. "I don't know how to do dishes or clean a stove?"

She glanced up at him and nodded. She didn't want any level of domesticity with him. And she went about explaining that poorly. "There's a particular way I like things done."

"Well, maybe this one time, you accept the help and it gets clean, but not *your* way."

"I said don't worry about it."

"Let me help."

"You are helping, you're helping give my brother peace of mind. I can cook and do dishes." That's what she should have reasoned in the first place, to keep them each in their respective lanes.

"And I'll just sit around and do nothing?" he asked, irritated.

"No ... you'll keep me safe from a phantom."

"Jesus, do you argue with everyone about everything?"

"Yes," she said simply.

He shook his head in disbelief. "Well, you don't have to. And I know you don't want me here and I'm *in the way*, but I also know how to do my job and how to clean a damn stove." He tossed his fork onto his plate and pushed it away.

"I didn't say you were in the way, I said you take up a lot of space." This whole conversation was getting away from her.

Carlo rubbed his temples with his fingers. "No one has ever been this much of a pain in the ass before."

She ignored the comment. "You know what's going to help us? Ground rules."

"Ground rules."

"Yeah, for the next few days, I think we need to set up some ground rules so we don't fight all the time."

"And you can control everything."

She blew out a breath. "Yeah, so I can control everything. I'm thirty-six years old Carlo, I've lived alone for a long time, I know who I am, and I know how I like things done. So maybe rule number one, I'll cook for you and you stay out of my kitchen." She stood up and took her dishes to the sink, angrily tossing them in.

"Fine, your house, your *rules*." He followed her example and with plate in hand headed to the sink. Only Alessandra intercepted him. She tried to take the plate, but he tightened his grip. "I can clear my own goddam plate."

"Just give it to me." She managed to pull the plate out of his hand and he gave a frustrated roar, "Are you kidding me?"

Alessandra snarled and in one quick motion slammed the plate onto the tile floor.

The cracking sound echoed around the kitchen and she glanced down around her sock covered feet at the mess she'd created. *Oh, she liked that.* It felt good to shock him and get her frustrations out. When she glanced up to see how Carlo was reacting, he wasn't angry, he was entertained, and maybe a little impressed.

She didn't want him impressed. But his gaze narrowed and a small smile curved his lips, adding to the whole dangerous and attractive thing he had going on. Which reminded Alessandra, that was another ground rule. He wasn't allowed to kiss her or look at her like that. And if she could have, she would have tried to explain that she wasn't opposed to the amount of space he took up. It was just the *way* he took up space that affected her– those muscles, that gruff exterior, the way he wore a button-down shirt, and how he took in every damn detail of every moment ... that was what she objected to.

She opened her mouth to relay the next rule, but couldn't find her voice.

When she thought back to this moment at a later time, she couldn't recall who moved first or even what slight movement propelled them into action. But somehow, she launched herself over a broken plate into his arms as they sought each other's lips and their hands began a skillful, heated exploration– going against not the first rule, but the most vital rule she hadn't even explained yet.

"This was just a dalliance," Alessandra said, even as her hand reached out without her approval and touched the side of his face. "This isn't anything. It doesn't mean anything, and it can't turn into anything."

He nodded, his fingers lightly tracing her side.

"This was just a neurological reaction. We've been together in a small space and we both need to feel in charge and it's been a while since ..."

"We just needed to get it out of our systems." His deep, whispered agreement echoed and vibrated along the length of her body.

She whispered, "There's nothing really here. This was merely a one-time thing."

"Mmm hmm." His lips were a breath away from hers.

"Carlo," she begged, but she wasn't really sure what she was asking for.

A smile pulled at his lips as he gave voice to what she was asking for. "Just one more time..."

Chapter Fifteen

S he found him waiting for her in the hospital lobby. Sitting with his right ankle resting on his left knee, no newspaper or magazine in hand, just a bored and slightly menacing expression on his face.

An expression that sent shockwaves to her core.

She rolled her eyes, muttering, "That's enough," as his gaze that was slowly tracing the bland walls of the lobby, landed on her.

She dropped her purse, her hands forgetting how to work of their own accord. Because all they really wanted to do was examine more of the man whose hooded gaze held all the burning, tingling, elicit memories they'd shared each night so far.

She was thankful for her light schedule today that had her seeing admitted patients rather than helping in the ER. She'd been frustratingly sidetracked today. She walked in on a patient fumbling with the button of a sweater and she was instantly transported back to her hallway the previous evening.

Carlo, pulling at her shirt as he rumbled his frustration into her mouth. "I need to feel you ..." A declaration that was followed by those large hands grabbing her shirt front and ripping it open. The echo of displaced buttons in the hall, accompanied by her shocked gasp, which Carlo caught with his mouth as he deftly removed her bra.

She had likened Carlo to an ox on several occasions and it was meant to be a joke, but the reality was that this mountain of man truly was a warm, hot beast. And his sturdy power radiated and rippled off of him, singeing her fingers when she touched him. Alessandra thought on several occasions that his largess should probably make her feel ill at ease, but instead, she felt only appreciation and attraction. And in turn, Carlo made Alessandra feel delicate and wholly desirable.

"Ready?" Carlo asked, holding her purse. When had he crossed the room? She took the purse nodding, words difficult to form.

Once they'd exited the hospital he slipped his hand on her lower back and around to her hip. The heat from his hand spreading fiery memories.

After getting in the car first, she watched the way his shoulders stretched taut, as his muscles moved beneath the cotton fabric when he climbed in.

Last night, as they lay in bed, spent; Alessandra, draped over his body, was using her hands to measure the distance of his chest.

"I've always taken up space," he said.

"I like it."

He gave a dry laugh. "I thought you said I take up *too* much space."

"You do," she said, mesmerized.

"I always have," he muttered again.

She met his gaze. "I didn't mean to make you feel bad."

"I've been large my whole life. Big kid, big teenager."

There was a vulnerability in the confession.

"Does it bother you?"

"It used to, until I turned it into a power."

"A power?"

"Let me ask you a question, and I want your first gut reaction," he instructed and she nodded in agreement. "When you see a man walk down the street and he looks like he lifts weights every day, what do you think?"

"Weightlifter," she supplied.

"Is he smart or dumb?"

"Ah ..." She supposed her initial reaction would be that he was an unintelligent goon. "Big ox," she said softly and brushed a kiss on his chest.

"I was underestimated in intelligence because of my size. Not by my parents or family, it's just something that happens. My parents were older, so I helped with a lot of the physical labor and things around the house. I was smart, but introverted. So outside the family, in school and on the streets, I was treated a certain way." He shifted his weight and hugged her body against his, continuing his story.

"My parents both passed away by the time I turned twenty-four. They married late in life; my father was fifty and my mother forty-three. It was the first marriage for both of them." He gave a soft laugh. "My mother said they waited for love and were both shocked when they found it." He paused, and she wondered how long it had been since he'd told anyone this. "My mother had me when she was forty-five. She called me her miracle."

"You grew up around family?"

"My parents both had four siblings, and they all had kids and most everyone is still in the area. But after my parents passed away ..." He cleared his throat. "My mom had cancer and Dad held on for two more years, but he loved her so much, and missed her ... my family claim he died of a broken heart."

She pressed her hand to his chest as he continued. "I'd finished my military service and been recruited. I'm glad I found the path I did, I could never see myself continuing the family business, and with my parents gone ..."

"What's the family business?"

"Olive oil." The sadness of his story loosened.

She gave a mocking gasp of disbelief. "You gave up olive oil for being a spy?"

His laugh rumbled. "My size made me desirable when I first joined the military, but then my test scores came in and caught the attention of high-ranking officials."

Alessandra didn't know how to soothe the boy he exposed to her; the boy who lost his parents at a young age and found a world to fit into.

"When I began to work in the field, I found that since most people mistook me for brawn and no brains, they said a lot in front of me they normally wouldn't have. My intelligence was greatly underestimated so I used that to my advantage." A grin twitched. "And it's my superpower that has paid off in more ways than one."

She propped herself up. "You *do* take up a lot of space," she let her hand travel down his chest, "but even when I said it, I didn't mean it the way you might have taken it. The space you take up confuses me. You came into my apartment that first day and you took up too much space physically but also you took up a very sudden, very large amount of space in my thoughts."

"I'm in your thoughts?"

She pursed her lips. "Of course you are. All I can think about at work is getting back here."

"Here?" He grinned, patting the bed.

"Of course *here*. And you can't tell me you don't think about being *here* all day too."

"Ale ..." Carlo's voice echoed from the previous evening and the present moment, warping time. "Ale," he repeated and she blinked as the car formed around her. She was gripping the steering wheel but had yet to turn on the ignition.

"You okay?"

When she glanced at him, a knowing grin spread across his face. His hand slipped around the back of her neck and pulled gently. She melted toward him and when she was a breath away he growled, "Thinking about all the things we're going to be doing together?"

She didn't answer, just hungrily accepted what he was offering. Promising herself what she had decided to accept the second time they fell into bed together- that she'd just get this little 'itch' scratched for now.

Fully.

Enthusiastically.

Expertly.

Chapter Sixteen

With the vans parked in a local garage and the stomachs of the ten tourists full of a luxurious lunch, Alessandra had taken over the sightseeing itinerary for the day. She didn't explain what they were going to see, just that they would love it.

Now that they were tourists, they walked with stuttered steps. Walter Dodd continued to point out doors that fascinated him: large mahogany, warped, weatherworn, light wood with brass rivets. "I don't know what it is, I love these old doors."

Alessandra's mother went into every other linen shop, followed closely by Barbara Dodd. While the rest of the group waited for the women, her father would point out something interesting to Walter, and either Parker or Carlo would follow to help translate.

On their mothers' third stop, Alessandra and Jessica found a worn bench and sat down. While the main thoroughfare they were walking down had all sorts of tourist traps and shopping opportunities, there were just as many intersecting roads that created piazzas with benches, small fountains, and planters.

"Do your parents visit you often?" Jessica asked.

"Not as much as I'd like. My schedule is so busy and they don't like how large Rome is."

"Really?"

"They're from small towns, and when they got married, they stayed in a small town. It wasn't until Parker and I moved that they began to travel."

"You didn't spend summers exploring Italy or France ... or Austria?" Jessica was curious. "You're so close."

Alessandra laughed. "I miei genetori," *my parents*, "they're from a different generation. They don't have the urge to travel. I think I could count on my hand the number of times they've been to Rome."

"So when they came for Thanksgiving last year ..."

Alessandra gave a large nod of her head. "It was as if they were going to the moon. There were so many phone calls between all of us."

"Why didn't you tell me?"

"They're proud, and they didn't want to seem weak."

"Alex, your parents are far from weak."

She shook her head. "Maybe that's not the word I mean. They didn't want to seem ... ignorant," she amended.

"Well, they don't. How are they doing on this trip? Are we too much? My family can be too much at times." Jessica pursed her lips and corrected herself. "My family can be a lot *all* the time."

Alessandra pointed to their mothers coming out of the latest store, each holding a large handled paper bag, laughing with linked arms. "I think they're fine."

"Jesus, Barb. We're going to have to buy another suitcase to take all this crap home," Walter Dodd called out.

"Why do you think I brought a suitcase with gifts? So I had room for souvenirs."

At the same time, Alessandra's father began the same argument with her mother.

Jessica laughed with Alessandra. "Okay, they're fine." Jessica headed over to her parents to either bare witness or intervene in their argument.

Carlo was there, holding out his hand to Alessandra to help her up off the bench. Even though she didn't need it, she took his hand and felt the tingle of his touch rush up her arm and heat run through her. She grinned at him and tilted her head so he could kiss her. His hand slipped around her waist, his mouth claiming hers while two sets of parents mindlessly argued.

When they pulled away from each other, he brushed her hair away from her face. "Onward?"

"Maybe. But there are too many stores between here and there." She spoke in code about their final destination.

His voice was a whisper as he offered an alternative plan, "Or, you could just give them a map and we could go back to your apartment and you can help me with this desperate need I have that's been building."

Alessandra laughed and pushed him away, the temptation too much. "Okay," she called to the group as she took Carlo's hand, "andiamo."

They made it almost another block before they came to a pharmacy and almost the whole group erupted with reasons they needed to go in: Drops for her father's eyes; to see the differences between an American pharmacy and an Italian pharmacy; because the soap and perfume display in the window was darling; and since they were there, indigestion pills weren't a bad idea.

Alessandra laughed as she held the door for everyone. When she spied Cassie and Benjamin continuing to meander, she called out, "Hey, you two don't get to get out of the family fun."

Cassie barked out a laugh and turned her attention to Alessandra. "Come with us Alex! The three of us can outrun them if we go now." She pointed to a bench in the small piazza. "I'm going to go sit in front of that little fountain over there and make out with my boyfriend."

Regrouping after too long in the pharmacy and once again 'on the road', Alessandra realized why she was getting agitated. She knew what was coming and she wanted to get there sooner rather than later.

Out of the corner of her eye, she saw her brother move into 'attack' position. She stepped out of the way as he tried to put her in his patented headlock of brotherly love.

"Oh, the girl's got moves." He laughed and lunged again.

She sidestepped him. "We are too old for this." She tried hiding her own laughter.

"You'll be ninety years old and I'll still try to find ways to antagonize you." He swiped at her again and she twirled out of his way, bumping into Carlo. He steadied her and she glanced up at him with a smile.

"Careful, or I'll make my fiancé beat you up," joked Alessandra.

Carlo growled in reply as Cassie chimed in, "They tried that once already."

"And I won," Parker offered.

"Because I was trying to get you to like me," Carlo excused.

"I believe I was the winner," Barbara Dodd interjected. "I was the one who was able to stop the fight."

Cassie snorted as the translation of the fight that took place between Carlo and Parker was told, and how the whole altercation ended with Barbara Dodd yelling at the two men to behave themselves.

Alessandra was glad for the storytelling that kept everyone out of the shops and finally into the piazza they were headed. The view at the other end abruptly stopped the narrative and a round of 'oh's' filled the air.

The Pantheon stood opposite. Large marble Corinthian columns held up a triangle portico that had Latin letters carved into the precipice. The gray domed ceiling and the rest of the structure were only slightly visible beyond the front of the building that greeted them.

"It's amazing." Cassie gave an impressed shake of her head.

Alessandra felt like she was showing off her sense of place and home to her family. "Carlo?" She was asking him to translate for her and he nodded. "When I first moved to Rome, for school, it was a lot of hard work and adjustment." She nodded to Jessica. "I was a small-town girl, in the big city. But when I wasn't studying, it helped to walk. I walked far and got lost a lot."

Her mother gave a tisk at hearing this story, and Alessandra tented her fingers together and then shook them slightly, an Italian gesture for her mom to accept that it was a thing that happened and she wasn't stupid. "One day, I was really lost, and I turned a corner and found *her*." She turned and glanced at the structure for a moment. "I sat on the steps of that fountain for a long time that day." She gestured to the fountain in the middle of the piazza. A large bowl-shaped marble fountain, intricately designed with rounded dragon heads expelling water; and protruding from the middle, an obelisk where pigeons were perched on the base, cooing and fluttering their wings as if they knew the attention had just been brought to them.

"I overheard a tour guide that day. This Pantheon, built as a temple to the gods, is the most Roman structure in this city. It's aged and weathered, it has seen empires built up and then crumble. It has stood while lives were lived a hundred times over. This two-thousand-year-old building, it *is* ancient Rome. And yet it lives within the present. This very building is the antithesis of tangible legacy and memory." Alessandra cleared her throat.

"I was homesick," she admitted. "I was here for school and working so hard, I wanted to give up so many times. But I found my backbone and fortitude represented in this building."

"Aless ..." her mother called softly but didn't seem to know what to say.

Alessandra continued, "We come from powerful ancestors. I figured, I am a descendant of the people who built this, I can do anything."

Her mother, eyes sparkling with tears and pride, wrapped Alessandra in a hug.

Alessandra laughed. "Mamma, I just wanted to show everyone my favorite place in Rome."

"I love it." Gianna stepped back, linked her arm with Alessandra and after a moment of appreciation gestured to the Pantheon and said, "Look at this. Look at what my people did."

Antonio gave a guffaw. "*Your* people?"

"Do you know what the letters mean?" Barbara asked, referring to the inscription across the top of the portico.

"Basically that Marcus Agrippa built this." Alessandra motioned for everyone to follow her to the steps of the building. She pointed at the monolithic columns, and they all craned their necks to look up at the beasts. "Each column is made from one piece of marble and they were all imported from Egypt. They were symbolic of Rome's power and how far that power stretched."

"So that obelisk on the fountain is from Egypt too?" Jessica asked.

Alessandra nodded. "Ramses II."

"When was this built?" Stills asked.

"They say 25 BC, but the emperor Hadrian rebuilt it, or improved it, I'm not sure exactly how that all worked, but the final adjustments were made about 114 AD." Alessandra had to clear her throat, she hadn't anticipated getting this choked up. "So, if four of us held hands in a circle, we could span the base of one column."

They passed through the double bronze doors leading inside. "These are the original doors, these monumental Roman bronze creatures."

"Like me," Carlo whispered against her ear.

"You're Genoese, a different kind of creature," she replied softly. When he responded with a growl she felt it radiate between her legs.

"Oh, man ..." The words were drawn out by Cassie, interrupting them, "this place is amazing."

The group stood just inside, awash in rich colors that swirled around the massive rotunda. Deep burgundy, faded orange and gray granite floors crawling with black veins amid circle and square motifs.

The eye was drawn instantly up to admire the vast dome, a feat of Roman architecture and made of perforated concrete. In the center of the roof was a giant oculus, a circular opening, providing the only source of light in the whole building, meant to take away the barrier between heaven and earth.

"This was built as a place to worship ancient gods, where the earthly could meet the heavenly. It was meant to manifest the heavens on earth; the sun shining through the oculus moves across the floor and walls throughout the day, a reflection of movement from the heavens."

"Alessandra ..." Cassie gasped. "Are you always this poetic?"

Alessandra's own head had fallen back to admire the view. "No, I just love this building."

"What happens when it rains?" Walter asked.

"Then it gets wet," Alessandra answered as she walked them toward the center of the room, where she pointed at a velvet rope that made a square around a drain.

"Is this still a church?" Gianna asked, gesturing across the room at the largest alcove that held a tabernacle with candles.

"Actually, this building has been in continuous use since it was built. It was a temple, and then used as a senate meeting place for a while, and finally a Catholic Church."

"Affascinante." *Fascinating,* Antonio said and then elbowed his wife. "Look what my people did."

Jessica asked Carlo, "Has Alex brought you on this tour before?"

"She has."

The group was dissipating, cell phones in picture mode, necks careening.

"It's something else," Jessica said into the round air above her as she wandered away.

Carlo's arm wrapped around Alessandra. "She sure is," his rich voice caressed.

She leaned into him as the memory of the first time she brought Carlo here brushed past her.

Candlelight. Dinner. Steam. A warm, scented breeze. The city awash in a romantic glow. Bodies aching for each other, from the exertion of being with each other. The walk was supposed to be a cooling-off.

She showed him her Pantheon, her vulnerability that night.

After a lifetime passed without comment from him, she glanced up and saw that he wasn't looking at the building she was trying to describe, but rather his gaze was intent on her.

"I love you," he said simply.

Shock flooded her, turned her around, stepped her away from him as she waved away his words. "No you don't."

"Yes, I do." He didn't move, just kept that sexy, slight grin and declared, "And you love me too."

"I just met you, I can't love you," she whispered as the idea swirled around her, growing, enticing her.

"You lust after me," he said definitively.

She fought a laugh and nodded, her voice barely recognizable as she admitted, "I do lust after you."

A step forward; would she allow him to come near her? This moment could change everything.

The words changed everything.

"I love you," he repeated– another step.

She didn't move.

Another step closer, he bent and brushed a kiss across her lips, the swirl of lusty emotions picked up speed and the heat engulfed her. He pulled away and looked down into her eyes. "You love me too." He grinned.

The words *would* change everything.

She reached out and gently touched the side of his face.

She wanted to change everything.

"I love you too."

Chapter Seventeen

Alessandra took the deepest breath she could manage, tightened all the muscles in her body then released everything as she slowly exhaled.

The eight days Parker had been allotted was up. Carlo had walked Alessandra into the hospital and smiled as he explained he had a meeting at the Rome office where he, Parker, and a handful of operatives would bring this operation to an end.

She offered her car, but he claimed public transportation would be easy enough.

If these weren't the actions that signified the end of an affair, she didn't know what was.

And that's what this was. The end of an affair. A fun affair.

She agreed to meet Carlo here, at the café close to the hospital, during her lunch break.

They'd come here several times the past week. Because she wasn't in the mood to explain the large, handsome man who made her laugh and blush to any of her colleagues. The café had been an extension of the affair, a small vacation from reality. She and Carlo had spent a lot of time here talking about insignificant things; favorite foods, seasons, past pets. They never talked about what it was between them, or expectations, or the future.

Which was the way it should have been. Sure it got a bit convoluted, but it was over now. It wouldn't be that hard to move on. All she'd done was take advantage of good sex with a very motivated, highly proficient man.

And it hadn't been some romantic dream. They'd also argued. *A lot.* About the proper time of day to water the plants on her patio; the exact amount of ragu sauce that should be added to pappardelle; and which region of Italy produced the best olive oil. (A debate that ended with Carlo stomping out of the apartment.)

On the third day he pointed out spaces between cars she should be moving into as she drove. The fifth day, he corrected the route she should take home, stating "It would be quicker if–"

She made a hard turn in the opposite direction from where she was going, throwing his weight against the car door and making sure to take an extra hour to get back to her apartment.

Of course, when she pulled onto her street, there was no parking and Carlo didn't hide his grin of validation at the outcome.

So Alessandra had put the car in park, left the engine on, gotten out, retrieved all her things, then said in frustration, "I'll see you upstairs."

It was good that this was the end.

Another deep breath.

It was definitely time to get back to her real life. Alessandra couldn't continue to survive on the adrenaline and excitement, a result of her body releasing endless amounts of endorphins and oxytocin.

For the sake of her job, she couldn't maintain a life burning the candle at both ends like this. She needed to be at her best, and her best required concentration, control and rest; none of which she had when Carlo was around.

"We aren't compatible beyond the bedroom," she'd acknowledged quietly the night before, after yet another ridiculous disagreement.

He'd pulled the broom away from her when she was trying to sweep and told her she was doing it wrong.

She stood dumbfounded, thinking he was joking, until he gripped the broom and gave a dissertation on how to properly sweep.

"Vaffanculo." *Fuck you,* she'd snarled at him and tossed the dustpan across the room.

"I'm just trying to help you be more efficient," he'd argued back.

"I need to be efficient when I'm performing a lumbar puncture, not when I'm sweeping the floor."

"But you can work smarter, not harder ... in all areas of your life," he mansplained.

Alessandra was incredulous. "What are you talking about?"

"You don't do everything right," he'd said pointedly.

She pushed him, physically pushed him, but he caught her arms and of course, the anger flared into passion; creating intoxicating flames that continued to devour them.

But passion burned out, that was its nature. And their passion seemed spared only for evenings and daydreams, the rest of the time was for arguing.

Carlo said they fought because of their situation, but Alessandra knew it was because neither had room for more than work in their lives, and coming to terms with that was difficult.

She tensed her muscles again, held in a deep breath and then blew it all out and relaxed herself.

"Ale ..." His voice caressed her name.

Damnit.

It wasn't real, the way she was drawn to his deep voice when he said her name, it was pheromones and neurons and lack of sleep.

She turned and gave him a tight-lipped smile. His sunglasses were pushed atop his short brown hair and he wore dark slacks, a tucked white button-down with the sleeves rolled up. (And he needed to *stop* rolling up his shirt sleeves.)

She stayed seated, glued to the wooden chair, and when a part of her tried to stand, she gripped the table, forcing herself to stay put.

It was easier if she couldn't press her body against him.

She shook her head no when he asked if she wanted another coffee. He then brushed a kiss on her temple and went to order for himself, giving her a few more moments to steel her spine against the coming goodbye. She watched his every movement, memorizing him.

When Carlo was seated across from her she decided on a neutral conversation starter. "Did you see Parker?"

"Video conference. I cannot confirm that he may or may not be in Florence." He winked. "But he did say he'll call you later and try to visit you this weekend."

She nodded. "So ... it's over." The whispered declaration held a substantial heft of truth.

"For our organization," he tilted his head, "but *this* doesn't have to be." He gestured between them.

"Where will you go now?" The question did what she knew it would; remind him that anything between them really couldn't work. His gaze darted over her shoulder and she nodded in understanding. "You can't tell me."

"Ale–" he started again.

"This was fun," she interrupted. "Not all of it," she gave a stiff smile, "but we had some fun."

"Just like that? It's over?"

"Carlo you live in Pisa, that's not close. And since I no longer need a babysitter ..."

"Bodyguard."

"Hmph," she tried to shrug off the moment. "At any rate, wherever you're headed next, I don't think you get nights and weekends off to try and make a relationship work."

"But we could try."

"I'm being reasonable. I have to be. You're right, we *could* try, but be honest with yourself for a moment, Carlo. It won't work."

"So you want to just walk away?"

She stood then, because lingering any longer was going to break her. She leaned over and brushed a kiss against his cheek. "Yes," she whispered and pulled away. He reached for her but she was unwrapping his hands from around her waist the moment they touched her. She cleared her throat and took a step back. "Be safe."

"Alessandra."

"Carlo." They could argue about it and try to work it out, but she wasn't going to make room for him, and his career wasn't conducive to a real relationship. "It's better this way."

He stood and she took a step back.

"I need to get my things," he said dully.

She pulled out the extra set of keys from her purse. "I won't be home until late. If you could leave these on the table, then just pull the door shut behind you ..."

He put his hands in his pockets. "Okay."

They stood awkwardly for a moment until the urge to leave or change her mind was too much. Alessandra reached up on her tiptoes, and he bent down, allowing her to brush another kiss on his cheek.

When they pulled away from each other, he gazed down at her face, smiling. "Take care of yourself Dotoressa."

"You too."

Chapter Eighteen

"What can I do for you, Moretti?" Carlo's boss, the director of covert affairs, asked the question but his attention was glued to his computer screen rather than the man standing in front of his desk.

Carlo gripped his hands behind his back. "I need to take some time off."

That got the director's attention. A slight smile pulled at his lips as he sat back, shooting Carlo an amused look. "Really?"

"Yes, sir."

"This isn't a joke? Matteo and Piero didn't put you up to this, did they?"

"No, sir." Carlo raised an eyebrow. "When was the last time I was part of a prank?"

"How much time?"

"Two weeks?"

Carlo had returned to Pisa and gone into the satellite office where he spent two days being debriefed. He'd then filled his fridge with food and slept like crap for a week before he decided this was bullshit.

He wasn't going to just walk away from Alessandra Salvatore. And he sure as hell wasn't going to let her walk away from him.

"Personal reasons?" the director asked.

"Yes, sir."

"How long have you been working with us, Moretti?"

"A little over nine years, sir."

"I don't think you've ever asked for time off." He squinted, trying to recall.

"No, sir."

"Does this time off have anything to do with a doctor in Rome?"

Carlo shifted his weight. "Yes, sir." It had *everything* to do with a doctor in Rome and an apartment on the fifth floor of a nondescript building in the middle of the city.

"You know, we're putting together an operation in Rome. All the known players are in that city or close by." He shrugged. "Right now we're gathering intel, but in about a month or two, the operation will be up and running. It'll be a simple surveillance job." The unspoken perks of the offer swayed between them. The director continued, "I think the timing is interesting."

Carlo nodded slowly. It was quite interesting. To be that close to her. But would he tell her if he took the job? *Should* he tell her?

First things first, maybe he should just go see what it would take to get the woman out of his system; if that was even a possibility. Because it had only been a handful of days without her, but he spent his long nights staring up at the ceiling, longing for her, imagining her under him; hell, he was even having imaginary arguments with her in his head.

"I'm in," he finally said.

A nod from the director accompanied the simple announcement. "Take your vacation days and then report to the office in Rome."

"Don't you need to give me a speech on *not* mixing my job with the reason I asked for time off?"

The director sized Carlo up. "I don't think that's necessary." He stood and held out his hand to shake Carlo's. "Best of luck son."

Chapter Nineteen

Barbara Dodd waved to the group standing in an alcove that overlooked the deteriorated arena of the Roman Colosseum. She had excused herself to go to the restroom when they entered, and now was returning with a man in tow.

"Dad," Jessica sighed, bringing her father's attention to the scene coming their way.

He shrugged, giving the eternal excuse he'd always given, "Your mother's never met a stranger."

"Oh, I'm sorry I took so long. This is Giovanni and I forgot his last name." She flourished her hand to the good-looking, tall, late thirties specimen with short dark hair, a slight stubble of beard growth and hands politely clasped behind his back. Around his neck hung a lanyard with his credentials.

"Donato," he finished his introduction, "Giovanni Donato."

Barbara squeezed his arm. "I got turned around after I came out of the restroom, but then I overheard this young man talking and it was so fascinating. When he was finished, I told him I was lost and that you said to meet you in front of the Emperor's Cross and he said he'd help me."

"The cross *in front* of the emperor's box," Jessica clarified as the muttering of introductions were made and thanks given.

Cassie asked Giovanni, "Are you a tour guide?"

"Well, no."

Cassie gave Jessica a sideways glance; of course the man their mother had abducted wasn't a tour guide.

Giovanni continued, "I actually work for Rome's Archeological Ruin and Excavation Team."

"You do!" Barbara declared as Carlo translated for the Salvatores. Upon hearing the Italian, Giovanni reintroduced himself, repeating the information.

Giovanni's easy smile lit up his face as he went on. "Today, I'm working with a class of archeological students who came to Rome to study in a sort of internship. Your mother caught the end of an introductory class I was giving."

"Mom," Jessica sighed.

"That's so cool." Cassie smiled.

Walter Dodd nodded his thanks. "Thank you for helping my wife." He'd long ago stopped apologizing for his wife's idiosyncrasies, because truth be told, he liked that the most about her.

"Oh, not at all." Giovanni nodded toward the arena. "I have some time, the class has taken an extended lunch break. So if you'd like, I'd love to tell you a little about the Colosseum. And if you have time, I've got these credentials that would get us onto the re-created wooden floor section of the arena."

As Giovanni repeated his offer in Italian, Alessandra linked her arm through Carlo's saying, "And you wouldn't have to translate for a few minutes."

The group happily agreed and Walter leaned toward Jessica and whispered, "You have to admit, she finds some pretty interesting people at times." And that was what made his life continually exciting.

Giovanni began with information he must have given on more than one occasion. "The Roman Colosseum is over two thousand years old. While we know that this amphitheater saw some brutal games, it also stands as a symbol of Rome's genius and their power." He gestured for everyone to follow him as he began the impromptu tour.

Alessandra patted Carlo's arm before joining her parents in the front of the group. Behind them, Walter Dodd and Parker overheard Barbara as she linked arms with her daughters and whispered, "This is why you talk to strangers."

Cassie and Jessica exchanged horrified looks, because *this* advice was the polar opposite of what they'd been given for the past thirty years.

Carlo and Stills brought up the rear.

"It's strange being on vacation," Stills admitted as he casually scanned the crowd of tourists crawling through the Colosseum.

Carlo nodded. "It takes some getting used to. I haven't been off a job or around a family in a long time."

"And the Dodd family is ..." Stills drifted off, as the number of adjectives he could use were suddenly too abundant.

"Sassy," Carlo supplied, deadpan.

Stills barked out a laugh and nodded in agreement.

Carlo explained, "When I first met Jessica, she was so scared she talked nervously, but she had a sass about her."

"They're just like their mother," Stills chuckled, "but God forbid we tell them that. How about Alessandra, is she like her mother?"

Carlo thought for a moment. "Signora Salvatore is very strong. Ale is the same. But her mother has more patience. Ale ... she doesn't put up with too much."

"It's hard to imagine you engaged, even after seeing it firsthand the past few days," Stills said.

"The thug and the intelligent doctor?" Carlo muttered.

"No. It's not like that." Stills frowned. "You know, you and I never talked during the Adler case, but I read your file and of course, I was the guy on the other end of all the bugged equipment."

"I never said much."

"You are a man of few words," Stills agreed. "But you loved the work. I could tell that. Now something is different."

"Alessandra."

Stills nodded. "That's part of it." But he couldn't quite put a finger on the rest of it.

Carlo understood what Stills was trying to say. He *was* different, where he was considered a robot at work, and maybe he was - all sharp, jagged edges; Alessandra had smoothed him out.

"Something *is* different," Carlo admitted.

"Have you set a date?" Stills asked.

"For the wedding?"

"No man, for your colonoscopy. Yes, your wedding. Last time I saw you, we had a very strange dinner at the Dodds after I tried to stop you and Salvatore from killing each other."

Carlo smiled at the memory. "Anyone ever told you, Stills, that you have a pretty good right hook?"

"Changing the subject." Stills raised an eyebrow. "Cold feet?"

Carlo's jaw clenched a few times, and he did another scan of the area around them. "We need to figure out how to live together in the same city before we can set a date," he acknowledged. "Besides, in Italy, a long engagement period is normal."

"How long?"

Carlo shrugged. "Most people date for a few years before they get engaged."

"But you jumped the gun?"

"Something like that." He cleared his throat. "Have you been able to relax on this vacation?"

Stills noticed the second change of subject and gave it the respect it required. "A bit. It was nice the other night when I was able to take Cassie to my favorite restaurant, just to have some alone time. But when we come to these crowded places, I'm a bit more wary. But having three of us split the work helps." He was speaking of the training that he couldn't always get away from, and the fact that Carlo and Parker were in the same boat.

Carlo admitted, "My current job is actually here in Rome."

Stills gave a slow nod; that would explain the slight tension, and extended scans Carlo gave of the crowds when they'd gone on all the normal 'family' outings.

"I wish you would've told us earlier," Stills said.

"There's no danger. It's purely surveillance."

"Does everyone know?" Stills asked the leading question.

"No." Carlo's answer was accompanied by another clench of his jaw.

Stills nodded. "How's your stomach?"

"My stomach?" Carlo frowned.

"Yeah. You're on surveillance which means you're sitting and watching. I was on a *business trip* in Paris a few years ago and spent a lot of time sitting, drinking coffee, and pondering the horizon. All that acid tore my stomach up."

Carlo laughed. "You have a weak American stomach, I'm Italian."

"Whatever." Stills shook his head, grinning.

They were silent for a moment before Carlo asked, "You changed positions at the agency, didn't you?"

Stills nodded. "I did."

"Do you miss the field?"

Stills glanced at Cassie who had just been pushed off-balance by her sister, and without missing a beat, pushed Jessica back. She was laughing and turned to catch Stills' eye, winking at him as if he was in on the joke. His grin grew. "Nope. That one there is adventure enough."

A grunt was all the reply Carlo gave, and Stills knew the big man was trying to figure out how to make things work with Alessandra.

Stills slapped him on the back. "You'll figure it out."

When Giovanni stopped to point out some more fascinating details, Parker gazed over at Stills and Carlo who were both calmly scanning the area.

Parker waited until the group was moving before heading over to the men to ask, "Everything okay?"

"Yeah," Stills said, "Carlo was just telling me the story of how he proposed to your sister."

"I've already heard this story," Parker grumbled. "They went to some villa in Tuscany and the light and summer or some bullshit made him do it."

"And the wine," Carlo smirked, "don't forget about the wine."

Chapter Twenty

The sun yawned as it dipped into the horizon, giving a burst of final golden rays and transforming the sparse clouds that had gathered to watch, into a pallet of pastel pink, orange, and yellow, all the colors blending together against a surrealist blue sky.

The Tuscan countryside rolled out in a carpet of everything that was expected of it. Cypress tree lined hills, tan bales of rolled hay, lush green plots of olive groves and orange roofed villas dotted various plots of land here and there.

Carlo and Alessandra had waded through their schedules to find five corresponding days so they could get out of town together. The final five days of September, the official end of summer, won the scheduling roulette. Carlo found the perfect agriturismo twenty minutes south of Siena. A one-bedroom farmhouse complete with fireplace, garden, grill, covered patio and the perfect view of the rolling hills planted with rows of grapevines and olive trees.

Just beyond the patio was a gazebo with two large outdoor armchairs where Alessandra sat, soaking up the last blushes of the day's heat. Carlo watched her– relaxed, satisfied, beautiful.

She belonged here, he thought. From this slight distance, in the light blue dress she wore, she looked like a mythical faerie, a fate. Awe-inspiring, otherworldly and powerful. She was the goddess who blessed the harvest and helped the flowers bloom.

He shook his head and let a smile escape, what was happening to him? He wasn't given to flights of fancy when it came to women, or even thinking overly much about them. He'd never philosophized about his own life's defining moments, but there was something about his goddess, Alessandra, seated just so, that in that moment, he understood why men painted and wrote songs. He understood poetry.

He blew out a laugh.

The words of his boss, when he'd asked for these days off, rang in his head. "You know Moretti, there comes a time in a man's life, when he realizes the adventure and adrenaline rushes just don't cut it anymore. And those are difficult days. You have to decide if you want to build a life with someone, or continue working in the field. The two have rarely gone hand in hand. Not in this line of work."

And in this moment, Carlo felt he could give it all up and be a content man. The only reason he itched to move at all was to be closer to the woman he couldn't stop staring at.

The faint sound of imagined music drifted past and he pushed himself away from the doorjamb, in search of the old record player he spied in the living room when they first explored the house.

He shuffled through the sparse collection of albums, found one by Nilla Pizzi, and sharp childhood memories washed over him as he lazily drew a finger across the well-loved cover. Nilla, a singer from the late fifties, had been considered the 'Queen of the Italian song'. She had also been one of his grandfather's favorites. He hadn't thought of her or his grandfather in a long time. Carlo was nine when his grandfather passed away, but he had fond memories of the strong, stoic man. This was one of them.

He put the album on, turned the volume as loud as it would go without distorting the sound, then opened several windows in the living room so the music could spill outside.

For a moment, he was transported back to his childhood as Nilla's soft, sultry voice filled the air. The tell-tale fifties' big band orchestra mingled with the slow whine of a trumpet, the arrangement a pedestal for Nilla's enchanting vocals.

"Bella," he whispered.

Between the woman and the music and the land that stretched before them; poetry was taking hold along with memories of his youth. He hadn't foreseen that this trip might become a journey into his past, but here he was. One sweet memory after another appeared before him, surrounding him like welcomed ghosts.

He wondered if he shouldn't take Alessandra north. They were only three hours from where he grew up. He could show her his past. When his parents passed away, he'd sold the house he inherited to a cousin, but still ... he could take her.

He didn't go back often, never really felt a pull to return. There were a mess of cousins, uncles and aunts still there, but he'd excused himself from visits, reasoning that it would keep his family safe. And his schedule kept him too busy anyway.

At least once a year, a cousin would reach out and ask if Carlo was sure he didn't want to come back and take his proper place as partner in the family business. He always politely refused, he wasn't a farmer at heart. He'd go through the obligatory 'catching up' with the cousin tasked with calling him, and when there was nothing left to say, he'd wish everyone well and end the call.

There was no animosity or longing for him to go back, he loved his life. He'd even spent some time in the region of his youth for work but he'd never had an inkling of homesickness when he visited. But lately, Alessandra had him thinking of roots, and he was feeling moved to show her where his had begun.

With many years as an agent, Carlo had developed certain special skill sets. They included wearing Armani and Gucci and knowing the difference between the two. He was well adept at handling 'difficult situations' for highly important, mostly corrupt men. He knew how to size up a woman with just a look and provide her a wardrobe from the finest Haute Couture stores in Milan. But his ultimate specialty was gathering intel with absolutely no one catching on to what he was doing.

Except when it came to the woman sitting before him. He'd been surrounded for so long by men and women whose every move was a well-plotted chess game in order to gain power and money -- all the while stabbing each other in the back and climbing some invisible ladder to be top tyrant – that he had lost touch with...well, with a part of himself.

Now, spending as much time as he could with Alessandra, who cared about other people and was not trying to use them as fodder to rise to the top; she was bringing his humanity back to him.

It was just one of the things, in a long laundry list, that drew him to her.

Not to mention those eyes with flecks of green that twinkled when she was angry. Or the way her hair curled and bounced as she walked. Or those hips that swayed just as tantalizing to their own rhythm, but somehow kept time with her hair. And her breasts ...*Jesus* ... when she wore V-neck sweaters or button-down blouses, the top button always seemed to pop open against the strain of her ample cleavage. One glance during a conversation at the glorious rise of her chest, and he could scarcely remember his name.

And Lord, when she wore her favorite black and white patterned housedress that should have made her look matronly and shapeless, he was undone. The light would often hit the sheer covering just right and reveal the shadows of all her curvy beauty, causing him to become single-minded, focused only on getting his hands on her.

He loved the ruffled look of her first thing in the morning, he liked it even better when he'd been the cause of that look. He loved her appearance at the end of the day, when she sat on the sofa, in that black and white housedress, her legs tucked under her as she finished paperwork.

Hell, he just loved her.

"Then what the hell are you doing in here?" He chided himself into movement, picked up two wine glasses, a bottle opener, the wine and headed outside.

As he made his way to Alessandra's side, he let himself be overtaken with the waking dream he seemed to be walking through. The music, the breeze that smelled of olive trees and the dying heat of the day. The sunset, the landscape, and the woman.

"Who is this?" Alessandra asked as he handed her a glass and opened the bottle.

"Nilla Pizzi."

"Oh," the relaxed smile broadened, "I thought I recognized it. My grandmother loved Nilla Pizzi."

"So did my grandfather." He poured the wine, then sat down putting the bottle on the small table in front of them.

"Is this the wine they left for us?" A complimentary bottle of wine and olive oil met them upon arrival.

He gave a nod in answer and took a sip.

The villa they had chosen was part of the Agritourism movement happening throughout Italy. So many vineyards, olive groves, and working farms had villas on their property where no one lived. So farmhouses were refurbished and rented out to tourists who'd come to the countryside to live out their Italian fantasies; while locals came to escape the heat of the summer.

Alessandra held her glass toward his. "Salute," she toasted and he touched his glass to hers.

They sat in silence, watching the final glow of the day disappear. The lazy sounds of cicadas became an orchestra once the record ended. A few birds readying themselves for the evening chimed in along with the warbled hoots from nocturnal creatures just waking.

Alessandra reached her hand and traced a finger along Carlo's forearm. His jaw clenched and his muscles tightened. He glanced over at her and saw her eyes clouded with desire. That was all it took to stir the need for her within him.

He turned his arm so she could trace the inside of his forearm. God, just her touch excited him. He wondered if there would ever be a time when a slight brush of her against him, even an innocent one, wouldn't ignite a longing.

She watched his eyes as she touched him. He often wondered if that was something she did because she was a doctor, or if that was how she was with men.

Men. The idea punched at his gut. His Neanderthal was kicking in once more; *he* wanted to be the only man. Carlo wasn't naïve. Alessandra had a life before they met, the same as him. He didn't expect her to be some cloistered virginal nun. He was no saint himself. But what he wanted was to be the first to explore the lines of her waist. He wanted to be the first man who spanned a hand over her breast. He wanted to be the first man to watch the light in her eyes as she threw her head back in delight as she climaxed.

"You are so ..." she breathed out, bringing him out of his thoughts.

"No, amore, it's you who are so ..." He gave a Cheshire grin.

Alessandra stood and moved to stand between his legs. He slipped his hands around her waist. She lowered her lips to his for a soft kiss. But one touch between them was never enough and one touch was all it took for the desperation and urgency to set in.

Alessandra tilted her head so she could deepen the kiss. She ran her hands into his short hair. His tongue twirled with hers and he would have sworn she tasted as intricate as the wine they'd shared. Bold, with hints of chocolate, vanilla, sunshine and rolling hills. She soaked up the life around her and he could taste it on her lips.

She kissed a line to his neck and he tilted his head, giving her better access.

"Carlo." She whispered his name. He knew what she wanted just by her moan of frustration and excitement.

He picked her up, her legs wrapped around his waist, her lips still teasing his neck. He started toward the house, but Alessandra protested.

"Here. Out here." Her whispered request weakened his legs.

He lowered her to the ground and knelt next to her, making quick work of discarding their clothing, grateful they'd decided to find a private villa. When he sat back to look at her, laying in the dusk, her arms reaching for him, her body twisted with need for him, he was lost.

He held his breath, then reached out a trembling hand and rested his palm on her stomach. She was real, still real and still part of his life, still in his world. And he would take it, for as long as he could have her.

"Carlo ..." She moved his hand lower and he went dizzy with his desire for her. He lowered his mouth and caught her moans as his tongue imitated his fingers. She held his strong wrist, wanting more and wanting him to stop at the same time.

"Not yet," he whispered against her neck. Good lord he loved the feel of her, how uninhibited and wanton she became when he touched her.

He was aching with need, desperate to slip inside her as badly as she wanted, but he held onto his last reigns of control for her. Seeing her writhe under his hand should have been a selfless act of pleasure for her, but he thought perhaps he derived more from it than she did.

She screamed out his name as her body convulsed. That was his cue, he moved over her and slipped inside. She wrapped herself around his large body with a groan of delight.

He hissed out his appreciation into the shadowy night as they fell into each other and the rest of the world disappeared.

He always thought he would try and take his time, but she urged him to quicken his pace, and he became dutiful in following the demands of Alessandra's body.

They grunted and she cried out in his arms, Carlo quickened the pace and finished mere seconds after she did. Together they collapsed into the grass.

The song of the nighttime creatures swelled as the pounding of their heartbeats receded and their heavy breathing slowed.

A soft breeze cooled their sweat-stained skin. Carlo rolled onto his back and brought Alessandra with him. She snuggled atop his chest and kissed his neck.

He couldn't imagine life ever got better than this. Alessandra was still a mystery to him, one he wanted to spend the rest of his life unraveling. In this very moment, he only had one thought that swirled within his chest. He wanted Alessandra for his own. Forever.

"Marry me," he whispered into the darkness. It seemed the right time, the perfect place, and he knew, *she* was the only woman.

Alessandra sighed her whispered agreement. "Yes."

Chapter Twenty-One

"And here's your receipt." The clerk behind the rental car desk handed over a long slip of paper to Alessandra. Carlo watched her fold it and nod her thanks. It was the last bit of business to finish from the Dodds' visit.

Goodbyes were given, wild waves of gratitude gushed, cheeks kissed, and promises to write, call, message or facetime were firmly in place. The Dodd Family, Stills, and Parker were winging their way back to California while Gianna and Antonio had been dropped off earlier at the train station, headed for their home south of Naples.

Carlo fell into step with Alessandra as they exited the airport car rental kiosk and headed to the taxi stand.

"That was a whirlwind," he commented.

"The Dodds are ... lively." She smiled, taking his hand.

Carlo laughed his agreement, but then fell silent. He was exhausted from the long week. From the residual glow of being surrounded by so much love, conversation and sightseeing. He hadn't been considered part of a family in so, *so* long. And the way the Dodds and Salvatores had so readily accepted him as one of their own, threw him off-balance. So much so, in order to steady himself, he often stood apart from the group.

Exhaustion was one reason behind his and Alessandra's quietness, but there was a growing layer of discomfort as well.

After the silent ride to the apartment, and going through the dance of arriving at her front door and turning the key in the lock, she stopped and sighed. "You're leaving in the morning."

"I've taken a lot of time off over the past few months." He meant to state it as a simple fact, but knew the second the words were out, they sounded as if he were blaming her.

"I told you this wasn't going to work." She didn't look at him, just pushed into her apartment then dropped her bag by the bedroom door before continuing to the kitchen.

He followed, watching as she opened the pantry, closed it then moved to the fridge.

He still hadn't told her he had an apartment on the other side of the city where he was staying; it seemed like such a good idea when he took the job. The pull to be close to his siren was impossible to resist. But now as the operation progressed, he realized the danger it put her in. What would happen if any of the men he'd been watching saw him with Alessandra?

He had made a difficult situation more complicated.

"Amore."

"I'll be drowning when I get back to work as well." She shut the fridge, then stared at the closed door.

"Don't do this," he said gently.

"Do what?" She turned.

"This," he gestured toward her, "you pick a fight so it doesn't hurt when I leave."

"It doesn't hurt." She jutted out her chin in defiance of the truth.

"It does," he hissed, and she took a step back, as if his words had stung. He sighed and scrubbed his face with his hands. "Ale, this is a mess and we need to figure it out, but I don't know how."

"What is there to figure out?"

Was poking at him to make him angry part of her coping mechanism? To protect her own feelings? He wouldn't let her do that and answered, "Us. Our future."

"Our future," she scoffed.

"Goddammit Alessandra, we had an amazing week and you want to end it this way? With a fight?"

"I'm not fighting," she insisted and took a step toward him, her ire up. "I was thinking about why we were so quiet in the taxi and it dawned on me the moment I turned the key in my lock; we don't know what to say when we have to leave each other. Because we never know how long it's going to be. Because we have to fight schedules and so much bullshit just to see each other and it's creating too much pressure and ..." she shook her head, "too much distance between us."

"So what?"

"Aren't you exhausted Carlo?"

"What if I am?" He frowned.

"Is it really worth it?"

His voice was dangerously calm when he admitted, "I think it is. But do *you* think it's worth it?"

"I don't know."

He pointed to her ring finger. "I think you do know, but you're just scared."

"What am I scared of?"

"That everything you planned for your life that you could control is being challenged. So while you want to be with me, the part of you that doesn't like the change continues to push me away every chance it gets."

"It's not hard to push you away, you're rarely here," she said.

"And that's what we have to figure out," he insisted.

She snarled, "So I'll stop pushing you away."

"Yes."

She poked him in the chest. "When have I done that? When?"

He took a step toward her so her finger pressed harder into his chest. "When I asked you to marry me. You said yes. I had the best weekend of my life and on the drive home you declared that if I *really* loved you, I would go ask your brother, in person, for his permission."

"So?"

"So? What was that Alessandra? I do everything you want me to. I bend over backwards for you."

"Do you?" she snapped.

"Ale–"

"Because we don't even live together yet. You're right, we need to figure this out, and maybe I *am* scared; but you aren't some sparkling hero, Carlo. Every time we try to talk this through, something gets in the way. Your supervisor is out of town, then he's busy and can't take a meeting or some other crap gets in the way. How hard is it to send an email that says I'm going to move to Rome?"

"Because it's not that simple."

She shook her head and held out her hands. "See? Nothing is easy about this but the sex."

"It isn't just my work that gets in the way," he bit, angry at how out of control she could make him feel. "You do your fair share of changing the subject when we try to talk about us."

"Fine. I'm here now, let's talk about it." She put her hands on her hips.

"I'll move in with you!" He yelled out the sentiment; this was not how he ever saw this conversation going.

"No." Alessandra shook her head and blew out a frustrated laugh.

"What? Why not? Isn't this what you want? It makes the most sense."

"You would never be *here*, Carlo. Not in this apartment." She waved her hand around. "You say you'll move in, but all that would happen is I'd be surrounded by your things, not you."

"Do you want me to quit my job?"

"I *never* asked you to do that. I would never ask you to throw away what you've worked so hard for, and you'd never ask that of me."

"Ale." He said her name with all the frustration that had been building between them since they met, since they'd decided to see where this relationship could go.

"Carlo." She matched his tone.

They stood facing each other, their uneven, frustrated breathing echoing off the tiled floors. This was the standstill. This was why they were stuck in the middle of the idea of an engagement.

"Can we at least try?" he asked.

"I thought that was what we were doing," she said incredulously.

"Alessandra I just said I wanted to move in with you and you said no. So I don't think that's trying."

She licked her lips and opened her mouth, but no words came out. She took a deep breath and began to laugh.

Carlo tilted his head to the side as the mood in the whole house abruptly changed, as if all the windows had been opened and a gust of air swept out the tension.

"Carlo." Her face broke into a smile. She splayed her hands on his chest and he put his hands atop hers as he looked down into her bright eyes. "I don't know how, but we'll figure this out," she finished.

"We'll figure this out," he repeated.

"I'm scared," she admitted.

"I know."

"You use your job as a crutch though, because you're scared too."

He shrugged, maybe he was.

"You try and I'll try," she promised.

He nodded his head in agreement. "What else can I do?" he asked.

She raised an eyebrow. "Work on communicating better with me between visits. And right now, I think you need to make sure walking is difficult for me tomorrow."

He gave a deep, aroused growl in answer as he swept her up in his arms; her laughter rang through the apartment as he carried her to bed.

Chapter Twenty-Two

Alessandra smiled as she listened to the message from Carlo. He'd made good on his promise to make sure her legs were jelly today, causing her to inadvertently squeeze her legs together as his deep voice tried to caress her over voicemail.

All their frustrations melted away between the sheets, and this morning they walked hand in hand to the café on the corner to have coffee and pastries before parting with a heated kiss and promises of how they'd do better.

Ciao bella. I know you said you'd be busy, but I called just in case. I put the request in for a transfer, and it was approved. We'll talk about how we can make this work, so it's not just my things that take up space in your apartment, but me as well. I love you. I hope you know that, amore. I'm going to be unavailable for a few days. I'll call you as soon as I can.

Unavailable for a few days.

He repeated the phrase often, and the number of days varied. It was never a problem until the days turned into weeks and she was alone at night, in the quiet, with her imagination that had time to play out awful scenarios.

And working in the ER gave her plenty of awful scenarios to choose from.

When it got to be too much, she'd call or text, but the calls went immediately to voicemail and texts went unanswered.

This was what scared her the most; beyond the normal relationship trust and honesty, it was the constant worrying about him that was seeping into her subconscious and affecting a lot of her day to day life.

Twice now when an emergency vehicle called in the arriving trauma, announcing: 'Male in his late thirties with a gunshot wound,' her stomach had twisted in knots and Carlo's face flashed. Alessandra was unable to settle down until she verified the patient wasn't him.

She opened a text message and wrote: *I love you too. Text me in two days, so I don't spend all my time worrying about you. I'd like to be able to focus at work and get some sleep.*

Chapter Twenty-Three

The intercom of Alessandra's building rang from her foyer, waking her. She struggled to sit up, grabbing her cell to check the time, shaking her head and blinking in an attempt to focus her eyes: 4:54 a.m.

Again the intercom buzzer screamed.

She frowned as she shuffled to the phone, picked up the receiver and angrily yelled, "Whoever this is better have a good reason for bothering me!"

"Ale," came the unmistakable voice of Carlo on the other end.

"Is this part of you working on our relationship and trying to be better at communicating?" she joked, but it fell flat when he said, "I need help." The no-nonsense, brusque exclamation heightened her blood pressure and instantaneously put her head in a vice.

She pressed the buttons that would unlock the building, then grabbed her slippers and a robe. She turned on lights, propped open her door, then waited by the elevator. What had happened? Why was he in Rome? Was he okay? Was this a booty call? Did the kids still call it a booty call?

The elevator door opened revealing Carlo, with a bloodied polo shirt and dirty khaki pants, half carrying, half dragging a semi-conscious man next to him.

"What the hell?" she asked, taking the man's other arm.

"Stab wound," Carlo said quickly.

They took the moaning man to the guest room, Carlo shouldering all the weight once again as Alessandra ripped the comforter and sheets off the bed, leaving only the fitted sheet in place.

"Lay him down."

She opened the armoire, pulled out her medical bag and put on a pair of disposable gloves as Carlo explained, "They would look for him in the hospital."

Where had she heard that before?

The man's face was covered with abrasions from a fight and he was pale, shivering as he held his hand against his side.

"I need some pillows," she instructed Carlo as she pulled out scissors and began to cut away the shirt while explaining to the hurt man, "We need to get your legs up, your body is in shock. I need to look at this wound."

The stranger released his hand.

Carlo returned with the pillows. "Put them under his feet," she instructed while she pulled the shirt away from the skin, eliciting a hissed reaction.

The blood had begun to clot, so the wound wasn't new. She scrubbed the area with iodine and pulled out a large gauze pad and applied it to his side, then told the man to "Hold this gauze here."

Once he did as she instructed, she began a complete assessment of him.

"I didn't know you were in Rome," she said to Carlo as she worked.

He grunted in answer. They both knew what that meant; she wasn't *supposed* to know he was in Rome.

"What happened?" she asked instead of pressing him on why he was in the city.

"He was mistreated," Carlo responded.

"No shit." She palpated the bruises on the man's face. "These are superficial, nothing broken ..." though they'd turn a nasty shade of purplish yellow.

His eyes were glazed over with pain, but she was still able to check for signs of a concussion. "Definitely a concussion. What's his name?"

When Carlo didn't answer, she turned to see if he'd even heard her. "His name?"

"It's better if you don't know," he muttered.

"Of course." She angrily sighed as she placed her stethoscope against the man's chest, palpated his ribs where he was bruised, which released a groan and wheezing sound in reaction. "They don't seem to be broken, but maybe fractured."

She pointed for Carlo to help her roll him to his side, a task done with a cry of pain from the man. She listened to his lungs, and when she was satisfied they weren't filled with liquid, nodded for him to be rolled over again.

She pulled the gauze away from the stab wound and studied it for a moment before she frowned up at Carlo. "Do you know what kind of knife it was?"

He stared at her for a long moment before finally reaching into his back pocket and producing a switchblade. He opened it for her.

Alessandra stared wide-eyed at the offending weapon. "Did you stab him?"

"No, of course not."

She gazed back at the man as another thought passed her. "Did you beat him up?"

"Ale …"

"Did you bring him here so I could patch him up because you're *going* to hurt him?"

He muttered a curse and rolled his eyes at her accusation.

She took the knife, it was a small one, the blade just eight centimeters long. "I can't know for sure if any major organs or nerves were damaged, but it's a small knife and if you insist on not going to a hospital, the best I can do is suture the wound and then he'll have to keep an eye out for infection."

"Do it."

She frowned at Carlo and pursed her lips as he widened his eyes; a silent urge for her to get to work.

She removed her gloves, rummaged around in her bag and pulled out the supplies she needed, then put on another pair of gloves and began cleaning the wound this time.

She sprayed the skin with a topical numbing agent then quickly applied the surgical glue. She pinched the skin together and waited. "Are there any other wounds I should know about? I haven't checked his legs yet."

"It was all upper body."

She released her fingers, checked to make sure the skin would hold, then ripped off her gloves, threw them on the ground and turned her anger at Carlo.

"What the hell is going on Carlo? How long have you been in Rome?"

He cleared his throat, she raised an eyebrow and jutted out her chin in challenge.

"He's one of my confidential informants. He called with information, but refused to give it to me over the phone. When I finally made it to the rendezvous we'd agreed on, I found him already in the middle of an altercation …"

"What happened to the man who was doing this to him?" She waved to the man on the bed.

"Dead."

The honesty backed Alessandra up a step.

"Alessandra…" He held out his hands, begging for her to understand, but her attention was suddenly drawn to the dried blood on his arms. She assumed it was from the other man, but now she saw the patterns and long welts.

"Are you hurt?" She pointed.

He glanced down. "It's nothing."

She covered the space between them, gently grabbed his arm and began to study the deep, bloodied defensive wounds on the back of his arms. After a moment she quietly asked, "He would have killed you? This other man?"

"Yes."

She tried to process the tangible evidence of how dangerous his job was.

Carlo gently tugged at his arm until she released him. "Don't worry about me." He could try to sluff off this altercation, but his strain and stress was palpable.

He leaned forward and brushed a kiss on her lips– soft, gentle and not nearly long enough. But as he pulled away, he hovered over her lips, his eyes drinking her in. "I missed you."

"I missed you too." She took a step back, breaking their connection. "I'll finish here. But then I'm going to clean and bandage your arms."

"When do you have to be at work?"

"Nine, I was going to sleep in this morning."

"Will he live?" he asked and she turned her attention back to the man.

"He'll live," she confirmed.

"I'll go make us a coffee."

Carlo backed out of the room and she shook her head, calling, "I still have time to bandage your wounds and talk about all this."

"I realize that," he called back.

"You know, you're the second person to show up on my front doorstep needing a doctor," she muttered to the wide-eyed, pale man staring up at her. "You're going to be fine. I just need you to stay awake for a few hours. Until then," she pulled a bottle of Tylenol and a prescription bottle with two pills in it, "this is for the pain, and this is an antibiotic. Hopefully that big ox in the other room has connections to get you a refill in the next twenty-four hours. Because I might be the new emergency off-site doctor, but I'm not going to be prescribing illegal antibiotics."

She handed him the pills. "I'll go get you a glass of water."

"Thank you," he said.

"Are you really his confidential informant?"

He nodded.

She studied him for a moment, then pointed. "Your stab wound isn't bad. They usually heal within a week, you'll be able to walk in a few hours." She left to get him water.

Chapter Twenty-Four

"Doctor Salvatore?"

Alessandra looked up from her computer to find Maria, the secretary that worked for the whole trauma surgeon team, standing in her doorway grinning.

"Yes?"

"There is a man here to see you."

"Okay."

"A *man*." The secretary elongated the word and gave an appreciative raise of her eyebrows.

"Okay." Alessandra repeated with a frown.

"Doctor, you don't understand. This man is ..." She licked her lips looking for the right adjective to use. Alessandra frowned, she knew what the man was. He was trying to smooth things over with her after showing up this morning with a wounded stranger and a hollow explanation.

Of course, Carlo hadn't said much or made time for them to talk about what was going on as she was bandaging the total of seven deep cuts on his arm. Instead, he promised he'd come see her later.

She left in a foul mood, slamming the door, but then went back into her apartment and gave the final instructions of what the mystery man should look for to make sure his wound wasn't infected. She handed the extra set of keys on the elephant keychain to Carlo, her hand lingering for a moment before she released them. Then she slammed out a second time, which had been so therapeutic, she toyed with the idea of going back for a third.

"What do you want me to do? Do you know him?" the secretary asked.

"Just send him in."

"He's so manly." She shook her head in disbelief. "Is he your ..." She wiggled her eyebrows at the question.

"Maria," Alessandra sighed.

The secretary almost skipped off to get Carlo.

Alessandra sat back in her chair. Maybe she should have told Maria to give her apologies and ignore him. But if Alessandra didn't let him in her office, he would be stupid and patient and wait for her all day.

And she'd find him in the lobby at the end of her shift, and he'd grin at her, causing her whole body to ignite with longing for his hands and lips and tongue ...

Not that being cornered in her tiny office by him would keep such want at bay.

He appeared then, just as he had this morning. An apparition. Dressed in a pair of dark slacks, a blue button-down shirt, the long sleeves covering his recent altercation, and sunglasses pushed onto his head.

His face softened when he saw her, he propped his hip against the doorjamb and softly greeted, "Ciao, bella."

At least she was sitting down as the feverish yearning for him washed over her.

"So you're in town," she stated.

"It was last minute."

She tilted her head in answer.

"You look good." He smiled.

How did his voice continue to deepen and caress her from all the way across the damn room?

"How long will you be here?"

"Long enough to take you to dinner tonight to make up for this morning?"

She nodded. "Are you okay? Really?"

He held up one of his arms. "I have a good doctor."

"You have a *damn* good doctor."

"I'm okay. Tired, but okay." He answered her question. "How are you?"

"Today, I'm a bit tired because I was up so early."

"Sorry."

She tisked, he wasn't really sorry.

"Did you miss me?" he asked.

She sat back and studied him; his powerful, sculpted body resting so easily against the door, taking up too much room and sucking the air out of it, while at the same heating up the space. "Nope, not really," she lied.

"I think about you all the time. Even more at night." He winked.

She felt that wink between her legs. She squeezed her thighs together and shrugged. "I'm too tired to think about you."

"Are you really mad at me?" he asked.

"I'm not mad." She exhaled.

"Then come here."

"I'm frustrated," she admitted.

"Ale, come here." His velvet-soft, rich voice electrified her cells, a Pavlovian response to the voice he reserved for the bedroom.

"I have work to do."

He moved toward her, and she watched his progress, excitement pouring through her. He turned her chair, kept his hands on the armrests and lowered his mouth to within a fraction of an inch. "I'm sorry I put you in such an awkward position this morning, but now that it's over, I'd like to take you to dinner tonight. Then maybe later, I can put you in a few more awkward positions that you might enjoy a lot more."

"You–"

He stopped her with a kiss before she could call him names, argue with him, or make excuses.

When he pulled away she sighed with her eyes still closed. "I'm off in about an hour."

"So, what is it you're not telling me?" Alessandra glanced sideways at Carlo as they walked back to her apartment after dinner.

He grunted in reply, she mocked him with the same grunt.

"Am I safe?" she asked finally.

Carlo stopped and turned his full attention to her. "Of course."

"Because you and my brother thought it was important to linger on my doorstep for weeks after you brought Jessica to my apartment. And now, one stab wound victim has come and gone and everything's fine?"

"Everything *is* fine."

She gave a laugh and put her hands on her hips. "Is it?"

"Amore."

She grinned. "Amore." She aped his deep voice and then said, "Don't amore me. I'm tired, but I don't have to go in until nine tomorrow. Are you spending the night?"

"I'd like to."

"When do you have to leave?"

"Early."

"So I sew up your CI and in return I get dinner and a booty call?"

His eyes darkened and he reached, slipping his hands around her. She tried to wiggle away but he tightened his hold, pressing his obvious arousal against her. "I mean, since things went sideways as it was, why not make the most of a mistake?"

"You didn't stab him just to see me, did you?" *It wasn't completely out of the realm of possibility.* She pulled her upper body away to study his face.

"Of course not," he scoffed, then tilted his head in a mocking deep thought, "although, if that's what it would take to see you again ..."

She pushed against him and finally freed herself, rearranging her clothes and looking around to make sure their impropriety hadn't been too blatant. "Did you clean up all the blood before you left?" she asked taking his hand.

"I did."

She sighed. "So is this what we've been reduced to?"

"We're not reduced to anything Alessandra, we're trying to figure things out. That's what humans do when they want to be together."

"I'd like to talk to you more," she admitted.

"I'll work on that."

"That's what you say ..."

"And it's getting better."

"I suppose, but maybe when you show up with stab wound victims and people who need help, you could call first."

"I'll call at least five minutes before I arrive."

She laughed, shaking her head.

"That rule goes for your brother too, right?" Carlo asked.

"I'll be sure to text him about it soon."

"Any other demands, amore?"

She stopped and considered him for a moment. "I think you need to follow through on the promise you made me."

"Which promise is that?"

"Something about awkward positions and being very, very attentive tonight." She shrugged and batted her eyelashes. "You know, to make up for everything."

"Oh, I plan on it."

She picked up her speed, with Carlo matching her pace as she walked faster and faster. Then when she broke into a slight jog, laughing as she turned the corner of her street, he happily chased her until they reached her front door, out of breath with excitement and exertion.

He pulled out the keys and opened the front door, then handed the key ring back to her.

She stared at his hand for a moment then gave a soft laugh as she folded his fingers around the elephant. "I suppose you should hang onto these now." She glanced up at him; his eyes had narrowed intently. He was searching her face, silently asking her if she was sure.

She shrugged her left shoulder and pursed her lips. "We have to start somewhere, right?"

He grabbed her around the waist and hoisted her body against his, crushing her to him with a kiss.

Chapter Twenty-Five

"How was your slumber party?" Matteo Arcuri, one of the agents Carlo had been working with, and living with, the past few months, wiggled his eyebrows suggestively as he walked to the espresso maker.

Carlo grunted from his computer in reply.

"You got home pretty early?" Matteo said. "You didn't have to rush back."

"I need you to read through this report."

Matteo yawned as he sat down at the table across from Carlo. "I mean, it's only eight fifteen. In the morning. Did the doctor kick you out?"

Another grunt.

"Fine, give me the report." Carlo turned the computer toward him. Matteo scanned it and said, "You know, Moretti, I can't figure out if bringing your CI to your doctor girlfriend was a stroke of genius or the stupidest thing you could have done."

Carlo sat back and frustratedly untucked his shirt.

"Whoa," Matteo pointed with a chuckle, "this must be rough. *That* is the most human, upset thing I think I've ever seen you do."

Carlo glared, he wasn't in the mood for the ribbing he often received from his co-workers that compared him to a robot.

Matteo continued, "Alright look, it was a good idea," he turned the computer back around to Carlo, "and as you assessed, no danger to the good doctor."

"That's all I wanted verified."

"You kept her safe." Matteo tapped the table to end that part of the conversation. "And I'm glad you didn't bring your CI back to our little home away from home after he got patched up." He was referring to their Roman three-bedroom apartment they'd been sharing with another agent for the past few months now.

"I figured it would be better to put him up at a safehouse than with us and all the information around here." Carlo reached his arms above his head and stretched his torso out.

He was worn out; from lack of sleep, from attempting to work out all his aggression and need with Alessandra's receptive body, and from the stress of keeping so many damn secrets from her.

While he thought it was going to be easy to be in the same city as the woman he was trying to build a relationship with, he never took into consideration the fact that not being able to tell her how close he was, would eat away at his consciousness.

Matteo pulled out his own computer and turned it so they could both see the screen, then pulled up the most recent photos of the associates of a drug smuggler known as Il Serpente, *The Snake*. While his associates had been logged and surveilled, the man who called himself Il Serpente had been near impossible to find.

"Okay, here's the latest," Matteo began, "the man who was beating up your CI was Il Serpente's number two. So that's bound to bring him out of hiding."

"Hopefully."

"We still don't have a photo of Il Serpente, but in the next few days we'll get your CI to a sketch artist and then we might finally have something to work with."

"Wouldn't that be nice, to get this whole thing put to bed sooner than later?"

"Worried about the doctor? I'm telling you, she's safe."

"I'm worried about a lot of things," Carlo muttered.

Matteo sat back heavily in his chair. "Che cazzo ..." *What the fuck ...* he breathed, "when you go human, you go all the way."

Carlo ignored the dig. "So we'll have a sketch to finally work from. What do we know about the shipments rumored to be coming in?"

Matteo slowly nodded his head, getting the hint to stay away from Carlo's emotional side. "Well, hopefully we find something this time.

Last time we followed all the leads and opened up crates of dog food. And there was nothing inside the cans except actual dog food."

Carlo raised an eyebrow. "That was one day I was glad to be gathering intel. I would have hated to be one of the poor bastards that had to open all those cans."

Matteo laughed in agreement, then continued, "So, we'll just keep watching and waiting and hope that either the death of his number two or this magic sketch will produce some sort of lead."

Chapter Twenty-Six

"Now, tell us all about that ring on your finger." Lara, an old friend from her early days of medical school, pointed at Alessandra's hand.

"Oh, yes. Please," added Francesca, Alessandra's former roommate and also a doctor.

The three longtime friends tried to get together every few months to catch up. There was always a lot of scouring through difficult schedules in an attempt to find a time and day they all had free.

Finally, their schedules aligned, so they met for dinner in the Piazza Navona, an ancient oblong circus maximus that once held chariot races but had since been cemented over. Where the viewing area had once been, now there were a large number of restaurants that offered the newest spectator sport- tourist watching.

Dinner, reminiscing and her share of the bottle of wine, had relaxed Alessandra into the lovely, balmy evening spent outside with the clatter of dishes, conversation and the splashing of nearby fountains.

Alessandra smiled dreamily. "It means what you think, I'm engaged."

"Holy saints!" Lara screamed. "I never thought I'd see the day."

Alessandra shrugged and tried to look properly secretive but these friends knew her better than that.

They pressed her for details until she gave in. She shook her head as she began, "He's frustrating, he argues with me too much, he could plough a field in a day, he's smart, he's underestimated, he's funny, he smells good, he's handsome ... like a gladiator." She sighed as her friends' eyes widened at the long-winded description. "But what I really love are his eyes, when he looks at me and sees *me*." She picked up the wine bottle and poured the last swallow into her glass so she could quickly drink it.

"Oh, *my*!" Lara shook her head in wonder.

"And the sex?" Francesca asked with a suggestive wiggle of her eyebrows.

Alessandra rolled her eyes in reply.

Lara gushed, "Oh my God, that good? Look at Aless, her face is turning red."

"Yes, it is. And yes," Alessandra blushed, "it's *that* good."

"Where is he, what does he do for a living and when can we meet him?" Francesca asked.

Alessandra wasn't sure how to give these answers. It had been another three days since he took her to dinner and attentively apologized. "He lives in Pisa and was just transferred to Rome. As soon as all our schedules align again, I'll introduce you."

They dissolved into stories of 'remember when' sprinkled with new details of their lives as the night wore on.

Finally, Francesca glanced at her watch and moaned. They all had busy schedules and needed what sleep they could get, which promptly drew the evening to a close.

Hugs and promises to meet again soon were exchanged. Lara offered Alessandra a ride, but as she was only a twenty-minute walk from her apartment, she declined the offer. "It will be nice to stretch my legs."

Alessandra glanced around at the busy piazza after the women left. She smiled and decided to toss a coin in her favorite fountain here, slowly crossing to the Fontana dei Quattro Fiumi, *Fountain of the Four Rivers*, where the white marble and crystal blue water were illuminated against the dark evening. She could never remember all of the rivers it was supposed to represent. The Nile and the Danube, she recalled, the other two she'd forgotten. She could easily look it up, but she didn't mind the mystery or that the same thought crossed her mind each time she viewed the fountain.

She pulled out a coin, gave a slight glance around her before she tossed it in. Not that it was illegal, she just wanted a bit of privacy for the superstitious act.

She took a deep cleansing breath and began to meander, allowing the loveliness of the evening, as much a balm as the wine, to slow her normal haste.

Music and conversation twirled around her as she crossed the piazza, maneuvering around people taking pictures and walking hand in hand. This would be a lively place until late in the evening, as several of the restaurants didn't close until two in the morning.

She smiled as her gaze scanned the outdoor seating of the restaurants; it was a colorful display of romance, laughter, and whining children; with women in date night attire, tourists in wrinkled clothes, and men in button-down shirts with the sleeves rolled up.

She saw a man looking particularly laid back at a table with a friend as they seemed to be catching up, neither with a care in the world.

Her feet changed course, carrying her to the table of two such men, and when she arrived, she crossed her arms across her chest as a frown heated her face.

The man who appeared so relaxed glanced up at her, but his smile became strained as he questioned her presence. "Yes?" he asked, as if he'd never seen her before.

"Carlo," she growled.

"I'm sorry, do we know each other?" He let his gaze calmly scan the area beyond her.

And that was when the anger that was quick to ignite when she saw him sitting so nonchalantly in the middle of a restaurant in Rome, gave way to dread. Her back went rigid as she realized that she might have just walked into the middle of something.

"I ..." She swallowed and took a step back. "I'm sorry, I thought you were someone else?"

His eyes were apologetic as he gave a shrug of indifference.

The other man stood up then. "Perhaps I can help," he said in English. He pointed to the tables that designated the edge of the restaurant, then gently touched her elbow, guiding her away from Carlo. When they were free of being overheard by anyone, he lowered his voice and continued speaking in English. "I'm Matteo, and I assume *you* are the good doctor. I'm sure you have a lot of questions." He pointed across the piazza as if he were giving her directions.

She gave a simple nod of her head.

"As you've probably guessed, we are indeed working."

She answered in English, thinking there was a reason he wasn't speaking in Italian at the moment. "I'm sorry." Her voice was thick with emotion. What had she done? It was the shock of seeing Carlo so casual. And in Rome. And twenty minutes from her apartment. And was he still here, or was he here again?

"It's okay. No one knows who you are or that you're with us." He pointed again, a friendly Italian giving directions. "Now, you'll go out the south end of the piazza, because if you go the other way, a man whose wounds you may or may not have recently treated, might recognize you."

She swallowed and glued her eyes on the path Matteo laid out before her.

"It was lovely meeting you, dottoressa."

She nodded, too many emotions rushing through her system to find any words.

"One last request," he said softly, "you might be tempted to look back at some point in our direction, but if you could try not to."

Another nod of agreement.

"We're going to be about two more hours, and then there should be a time when he can call you."

She realized even in this ruse, the only name Matteo had used was his own. She gave another nod and without looking back, without a goodbye, she put her chin up and tried to control her breathing as she shakily headed out of the crowded piazza.

The feelings she'd had all evening had been doused by the reality of seeing Carlo on the job. But what did she really see?

He was eating dinner in a very crowded public place and watching. There was nothing wrong with that. He couldn't be in danger, she couldn't imagine he would be required to do anything that would hurt the number of people he was surrounded by.

But as the time passed and she waited for him to call or stop by, the threatening 'what ifs' gathered force.

What if she'd gone the other direction, the way she was originally headed? What if she hadn't seen Carlo? What if the man she'd glued back together saw her at the moment he was doing ... whatever it was he was being watched for?

She couldn't make up her mind if this situation was more difficult because she suddenly knew how close Carlo was, *or*, because of the continued dangerous scenarios her imagination placed before her.

She checked the volume on her phone several times, made sure the intercom was working and tried to find something to help her pass the time. She paced through the apartment, dusting, reorganizing her bookshelves and obsessively changing TV stations.

She would sit down, reposition herself, but unable to sit still, would jump up to pace once more.

"Worrying doesn't help anything," she tried to remind herself.

It was 1 a.m. when her cell finally rang. She'd been holding it, and even though she was waiting for the notification, she yelled and fumbled the phone as she tried to answer.

"I'm sorry," she said.

"No, Amo. I'm sorry."

She started to explain, "I was having dinner in the piazza tonight with some friends–"

"It's okay."

"Did I ruin anything?"

"No, it's fine," he soothed.

"So, you're in Rome still?" She felt the alignment coming back to her body putting her in a little more control.

"I am."

"And you were going to tell me ..." She led what she wanted to hear from him next as way of explanation.

"Alessandra." He took an audible drink of air. "The current operation I've been working ... I've been in Rome this whole time."

She felt like she'd been punched in the gut.

"I didn't know how to tell you."

"So is there really a transfer?"

"Yes," he insisted, "it was approved. I swear. I have the paperwork to prove it."

"Carlo." She didn't know what to say or what she wanted to hear from him.

"As soon as this operation is wrapped up, we can move forward," he vehemently promised.

"And how long is this operation?"

"It's already been a few months, and now we're hoping that there's an actual end in sight."

It was more than he'd given her to date when it came to his job, but the new information felt like an anvil.

"Maybe I should try to run into you more often if it means you'll be this honest with me." She tried to shake off the weight of his confession.

"I shouldn't even be telling you this much."

"I realize that." She sat down heavily on her sofa. "So ..." What could she really say? She was at least grateful that her blood pressure was finally falling back into place. "Matteo seemed nice."

"He's my roommate. While I'm in Rome."

"I see. Do you always have roommates when you're working?"

"Sometimes."

"Well, he seems nice. Capable."

He gave a grunt, then said, "Being here, in Rome it's why I've been able to show up a bit more than usual lately."

"I don't know how I feel about having you here in Rome," she admitted.

"I understand."

"Do you?"

"I think so." He cleared his throat. "I thought it would make me feel better being closer to you, but I couldn't really tell you. And then the weeks became months ..."

"You worried you'd bump into me one night when you were trying to work? And I might take it all the wrong way and get my feelings hurt and be utterly pissed off at you?"

Carlo gave a grunt of confirmation.

"Okay. Well, it happened, I went through all those emotions, but now I think I've settled on understanding."

"Really?"

She yawned then as the buildup of stress eased out of her bones and exhaustion took over. "Or I'm really tired. And now that I've talked to you and we have some more honesty on the table, I'm willing to put this conversation on hold. But you're okay, right?"

"I'm okay," he insisted.

"You aren't going anywhere tonight? To meet any stab wound victims on darkened street corners?"

"I'm staying in."

"Okay."

"I'll make it up to you when I can. I'll cook for you and explain as much as I can."

"And clean the stove when you're done cooking?" She made the joke she wasn't feeling.

"I promise to clean the stove if I make a mess, which I won't."

It was her turn to grunt in response. "When–" She bit off the rest of the question she was getting tired of asking: When will I see you again?

"A few days, I promise."

They fell silent, having nothing else to say. Another yawn claimed Alessandra and she nodded to herself. She'd take these next few hours knowing all was well and get some sleep. "Good night, Carlo mio." Her voice cracked slightly on the endearment that she had thought so many times in her mind, but never been able to say.

"Amore, I'm safe." His voice lowered, "Buonanotte."

She hung up and his words, "I'm safe," rang of empty promises. A chill ran over her as she recalled their time together in those first days, tracing the sinewy lines of his body, and the scars he carried of the life he'd led.

Chapter Twenty-Seven

Alessandra wasn't sure how much of the mandatory eight days of 'babysitting' had passed or how much was left. And at that moment, she didn't even care.

"I told you this couldn't happen again." She panted, stretching her body, tensing all her muscles and loosening them; she was melting into the center of her mattress, supple and satisfied.

Every time Carlo touched her, her body craved more; demanded more. And he fed her need by giving her what she needed and continually taking her to new heights.

"If you didn't want this to happen again, why did you pick a fight with me?"

"I didn't pick a fight," she muttered. She had simply explained to him that the eggplant he picked up at the grocery store had been inferior to the ones they could have bought at the corner fruit vendor.

Five minutes later, fuming, they threw themselves at each other and ended up in bed, *again*.

He rolled onto his side and began sliding his hand down her stomach, his final destination apparent.

She picked up his hand and pushed it away, turned and pushed his whole body back, then straddled him.

"Mmm," he grunted approvingly. His hands started slipping up her waist, but she cut them off and put them back down by his side.

She let go, and when she was sure his hands would stay put, she spread her hands out wide and ran them through the hair on his chest, across his collar bone, shaking her head.

"What?" he asked.

"You're like a gladiator," she whispered. "When I first saw you, I liked that you looked like a man who worked hard, with his hands."

He held up his hands. "I *want* to work hard with these hands, you won't let me."

"That's right, it's my turn." She continued her examination as if his body were braille and she yearned to read all of him.

He wriggled slightly. "I don't know how much I can take."

"Carlo ... this is an important prerequisite for a woman who's dedicated her whole life to examining bodies."

His olive skin tempted her lips, and she brushed a kiss along his collarbone. Her hands were unable to stop measuring the distance of his broad chest, causing the muscles on his stomach to react to her ministrations as he pressed his hips up.

She laughed and rearranged herself so his access to her wasn't that easy. She licked her lips and began to kiss a trail from his stomach downward, he hissed in a breath. But her playfulness faltered when she pulled away and ran her fingers gently over a long scar on his left side, just above his waist. She was aware of what a poorly healed wound looked like, because it hadn't received the proper care at the time.

She moved up his body, not lips and flirtation, but curiosity. A scar on his shoulder, knife wound probably. His left bicep had scar tissue from a gunshot wound. She worked her way down the left side of his body, a welt on the side of his hip, a scar just above his knee, another bullet wound in his leg. Up the right side, there was a staggering scar on the inside of his thigh, poorly stitched up. Just below his ribs on the right side, the third gunshot wound.

She sat up and glanced at him, he had gone rigid. His eyes gave off no account of what he was thinking. "Do they bother you?" he asked.

"You really are a gladiator," she whispered.

He raised an eyebrow and she reached out and touched a welted scar near his collarbone. "Scars don't bother me. It's the pain that I know came with them."

"It's not that bad."

"Really?" she scoffed.

"Okay," he took her hand to stop her and kissed her fingers, "some of them were bad."

"This is the kind of danger your job puts you in."

"Some of these are from growing up on a farm," he tried to excuse.

"And some of them aren't." She traced her finger around the scar tissue of a bullet wound.

He sighed and propped himself up to meet her gaze. "I'm not going to pretend that my job doesn't sometimes put me in danger. But I am going to say that I am very well trained, I am very good at my job, I am very strong and I'm resilient as hell." He raised an eyebrow in question, did she believe him?

"Fine," she huffed, "then you need to do me a favor."

"Anything."

She whispered in his ear, "Show me how resilient you can be."

Chapter Twenty-Eight

Carlo hung up the phone and tossed it unceremoniously on the table then scrubbed his face with his hands.

"It's okay man. We're fine."

"Someone could have seen. Someone might know who we are and that we were watching and if they saw her ..."

"I'm telling you, she recovered like a champ and so did we. It's fine."

The last time Carlo felt even the slightest pang of concern like this was when he'd been pulled off watching Jessica the night she was kidnapped.

"It's fine," Carlo said, more in an attempt to convince himself.

"She's cute," Matteo verified. When Carlo glanced at his partner, the man wiggled his eyebrows and made an hourglass shape with his hands. "Short little thing, but she looks like she's full of spirit."

"Watch it," Carlo warned.

Matteo laughed and slapped his knee. "Oh my God. I'm going to win so many bets. We seriously thought you were a robot for so many years, and a few of us had bets on any romantic entanglements you might get yourself in the middle of, and I always said you needed a strong brunette from–" He drew out the word, but Carlo narrowed his gaze, he would not be answering. "Somewhere," Matteo supplied.

"Okay." Carlo pulled the computer toward him and began to run down what they'd found out that evening. "Il Serpente isn't in Rome. But there's been an awful lot of activity lately."

Matteo pulled out a few sheets of paper and laid them on top of the stack they were studying. "And thanks to your CI and the work he did tonight, we know that everyone is getting ready for something big."

"You ever feel like we're chasing our tails with this one?" Carlo asked.

"How did you meet Alessandra?"

Carlo gave Matteo another warning look.

"Hey man, this is all news to me and I can't stop trying to figure out how a man like you meets a woman in the first place. I mean, you're just so starchy and serious, and she's so smart, sexy ... and you're not a man of many words."

"I was doing a favor for her brother," Carlo said in an attempt to stop Matteo.

"Oh, picking off the friendship tree?"

"It wasn't like that," he clipped, then stood and started pacing through the small living room turned office.

"Look," Matteo changed his tune, "I didn't mean it like that. Sorry."

Carlo shrugged off the comment. Seeing her tonight, appearing like a vision, with angry, heated cheeks and all that disappointment; a piece of him broke as he said the words, 'do I know you?' and the flicker of hurt that crossed her face scared him.

He had growing concern for her safety after taking his deadbeat CI to her apartment. Luckily, the guy was so loaded up on painkillers, he wouldn't be able to recall where he'd been or even if what had happened had been a dream.

But still, he never should have involved her.

Now, she was more involved than he ever intended. And while the city felt wide open when he first arrived on this operation, it was now closing in on him, tightening like a noose around his neck. How much longer did he have before he would be recognized? What if he were with Alessandra when it happened?

He was willing to protect Alessandra with his life, but he was now the reason her life would need to be protected in the first place.

"Maybe you need a break," Matteo said as he watched Carlo pace like a caged animal.

"I'm fine."

"Are you?"

Neither of them was sure the answer to that question was a positive one.

"I'm fine," Carlo insisted once again.

"Okay, Okay. I know you're 'the robot'. You'll do what you have to in order to get the job done," Matteo said in an attempt to comfort.

But it didn't help.

He wasn't 'the robot' anymore. His concentration was misfiring. If he were being honest with himself, the reason he felt so caged at the moment, was because now there was a lot more to his life than just the job. And he had no idea how to compartmentalize Alessandra Salvatore.

Chapter Twenty-Nine

"Doctor?" A nurse got Alessandra's attention. "We have a GSW currently en route. Patient is male, late thirties, unconscious. ETA, two minutes."

Alessandra nodded. "Prep the OR."

"Done," the nurse replied.

Alessandra pulled on a disposable surgical gown, then went to the nearest wash station while another nurse tied the back. The ER team came together like a well-oiled machine, prepping the emergency room the patient would be brought into. Alessandra was helped into a pair of gloves seconds before they heard the ambulance siren cut off as it pulled into the hospital bay.

She walked behind the gurney the patient would be transferred onto, the sliding doors opened and the paramedics began to give their report: "GSW to the left shoulder area, exit wound is apparent. Unresponsive. Labored breathing, no sign of collapsed lungs or pooling of blood in the lungs. Loss of blood. BP eighty over sixty."

The group quickly arrived in the trauma area, Alessandra nodding in understanding at the vitals. The blood loss would account for the precipitous drop in blood pressure; they were racing against time to make sure proper blood flow could continue, otherwise vital organs would start to shut down.

One nurse began to remove the shirt that had already been halfway cut off at the scene. Alessandra called out, "I want labs, chest x-ray, and a stat EKG. Get me vitals for lungs, heart, esophagus and tracheobronchial." Blood was drawn by one nurse while another helped switch the monitors from the ambulance over to the ER's equipment. A third nurse placed an IV with antibiotics beside the one the paramedics had already started which was pushing fluids.

"What are my vitals?" Alessandra asked, once the machines had been switched over. Numbers were called out and she nodded.

"Was he lucid at all?" She began a litany of questions for the paramedics who had followed the team.

"Only for a moment."

"Is he on any drugs?"

"There was no sign of anything where we found him."

"Where are my labs?" she asked.

"Five minutes," came a reply.

"Name?" Alessandra asked.

"No ID, passed out before we could get an answer."

"Any other wounds?" Alessandra asked as she scanned the patient for other wounds, now that she had the information she needed.

"None."

Her eyes focused on the patient as her head whispered her calming mantra, '*start at the top,*' but her hands froze in mid-air.

The air left the room and an invisible force slammed into her chest and robbed her of her balance.

"Matteo?" she whispered, gripping the edge of the gurney, as everything around her darkened; slipped, twisted and choked her. Numbing her hands, warping her concentration.

"Doctor?" A nurse attempted to pull Alessandra back from the void she was falling into.

"I know him." Alessandra forced the words and then shook her head and demanded her feet find their placement. "Matteo." The name cracked in the back of her throat but she was pushing past the shock and fear that was attempting to wrap her in its strangling embrace. "His name is Matteo," she repeated. "Find out if there was anyone else at the scene," she demanded more loudly, knowing someone would do her bidding.

"Do we need another doctor?" the nurse asked.

"No." Alessandra pulled herself together. "Matteo." She said his name emphatically as she bent over and began palpating his head and neck as stats continued to be relayed to her. "Matteo." She said his name again, this time even more forcefully. His eyes moved, trying to blink open. She nodded and continued, "No muffled heart tone, no distended neck veins." That was good, it meant no fluids were collecting in the sac around his heart.

A nurse pulled off the gauze she was holding against the wound on his shoulder and replaced it with a new one.

Alessandra yelled, "We're still bleeding here! Has he been typed and crossed? Get me some blood people!"

"Here," came the call as the bag was hung and the transfusion began.

Her team finished the overall assessment and it was time to focus on the gunshot wound.

"Doctor, there was no one else at the scene." The voice drifted into the room and she tried to push thoughts of what that meant out of the way so she could focus on the new task at hand, treating the gunshot wound and determining how much damage it had caused.

Matteo's eyes blinked open slightly, a frown creasing his forehead.

Alessandra leaned over so he could see her. "Matteo, remember me? I'm Alessandra. Doctor Salvatore?" He gave a half nod and she smiled reassuringly. "You're okay. We're going to take good care of you."

She thought he was trying to give her a smile in return but his eyes fluttered closed.

"BP rising," someone called out.

"Let's move," Alessandra instructed. Her team completed the transfer from trauma up to the OR with practiced precision.

The anesthesiologist began their diligent work and Alessandra affixed her mask then was helped into clean gloves and gown.

She was relieved that the shock had worn off and been replaced with the focus and steady breathing she was used to in these situations. All worries and thoughts dissipated with the rest of the chaotic surroundings as she floated into a world of simple muscles and ligaments, nerves and bones and how they connected to each other and the glorious way they all worked together. She disappeared into repairing the damage to the shoulder.

"Doctor?" The voice came from far away.

Alessandra hadn't moved since Matteo had been stabilized and rolled out of the room to be transferred to the ICU.

"Doctor?"

The room came back into view, the aftermath of the trauma was a story in itself. Discarded equipment, bloodstained gauze, castoff wrappers, various surgical implements haphazardly piled on a moveable instrument table, and empty blood and IV bags littered in a tornado.

"I need you to sign this." The nurse tried a third time to get her attention. Alessandra took the pen and clipboard, signed and handed it back.

"Has any family or friends come for him?" she asked, nervous about the answer.

"There were two men in the waiting room, but when they were told he would recover, they left."

Alessandra swallowed. "Was one of the men about six feet tall, muscular build, dark brown hair, brown eyes?"

The nurse shook her head. "No, these were shorter men, pretty average looking."

Alessandra blinked several times, who could they have been? Why had Matteo been shot? Did Carlo know? Had he been there? Or had Matteo gone alone to meet up with his own CI and been double-crossed?

"Is there anything else, Doctor?"

"I'll be in my office, I need to make a call." She turned on her heel, walked quickly, and fumbled for her phone when she reached her desk.

There were four missed calls from a number she didn't recognize, but a text message blinked gloriously:

I'm safe. I'm not hurt. Will contact you as soon as I can.

She sat down heavily in her chair as everything she'd been holding in overwhelmed her. Washing over her was the anger at finding Carlo in Rome, the constant ache of worry, and the fear she'd experienced today, unlike anything else she'd ever felt, when she recognized Matteo.

She wiped fiercely at a tear and after a deep breath picked up her phone and went to find who had been in contact with the men that asked after Matteo. Once she had the nurse who could identify the men in tow, they went to the security desk.

"Doctor." The man sitting at the monitors greeted her.

"There was a GSW male brought in a few hours ago, and two men were asking after him. When they found out he would pull through the surgery, they left. It isn't sitting well with me, so I thought, just in case …"

"Send a reference photo to the police?" the man filled in for her.

She nodded and glanced at the nurse who was trying not to look so shocked.

On a separate computer screen, he pulled up the waiting room and began to scroll through the time frame that the nurse indicated.

"There," she pointed, "those are the men."

The security guard clicked frame by frame until he had a clear image and then copied the screen. "I'll send this over to the police," he said.

Alessandra took out her phone, focused her camera and took a picture. She thanked the nurse and guard, then made her way back to her office, texting Carlo as she went.

These two men came and asked if 'he' was okay, when they found out he was, they left. Not sure if this is important or not.

A call then came in that she was needed for a consult. She put her phone on silent, slipped it in her lab coat and tried to shake off the past few hours.

Chapter Thirty

Alessandra checked one last time on Matteo, extremely pleased with his vitals. She instructed the staff to alert her if there were any negative changes in his recovery.

She changed, then with her purse slung over her shoulder, stood with her hand on one of the back exit doors of the hospital. She glanced at the message from Carlo once more.

They are a known problem. When your shift is over, leave out the back, east door. Leave your car. Take a cab to the restaurant we've gone to the most.

She straightened her spine, pushed open the door and quickly made her way down the block to where she would find a taxi, her head on a continual swivel as she studied her surroundings.

She was grateful her shift ended at a normal time today, 6 p.m. The cafés that surrounded the hospital were overflowing with customers, and the grocery store on the corner had evening shoppers congregating at the entrance and exits. The crowds made her feel safe.

She studied the photos of the men until their faces were seared into her mind. She gripped her phone tight, her lifeline at the moment.

As she walked she tried to piece together a story she wasn't privy to. The question that came again and again was the two men; were they the ones who shot Matteo? Had they been watching him when he walked her away from their table in the Piazza Navona? Did they know who she was? She asked the nurse who identified the men if they inquired about her or asked the name of the doctor taking care of Matteo? They hadn't, not that they would have been given the protected information. But she still worried.

It was a short cab ride from the hospital to a local trattoria that sat on a piazza, just a few blocks from her apartment. She had become friends with the owner over the years and the food was wonderful.

It was a simple establishment. The name, Trattoria Rosa, was etched on the glass of the double doors that were propped open. Light from the large windows on either side of the doors poured onto the patio. Large umbrellas bumped into each other, covering eight tables arranged within a makeshift border of wrought iron and planters growing crawling ivy.

The taxi dropped her off, she scanned the area until she found him. In the shadows of the doorway to the right of the restaurant, she saw Carlo's unmistakable silhouette.

Relief flooding through her made walking difficult, but the need to touch him propelled her forward. She didn't stop until she had her arms wrapped around his waist and he was engulfing her. She pressed herself closer into him so he'd tighten his hold. She didn't cry, there were no threatening tears, just overwhelming relief.

He pulled away and framed her face in his hands. His expression drawn; there were dark circles under his eyes and a general disheveled look about him that Alessandra had never seen before.

Had it really only been three days since she'd last seen him looking so comfortable and relaxed?

"What's going on?" She touched the side of his face. "Are you okay?"

He took her hands in his and brushed a kiss across her knuckles. "Let's get something to eat. I'll explain." He swallowed and asked, "Matteo?"

"He'll be fine. He'll need a little physical therapy, but he had a great doctor."

Carlo nodded several times, his gaze scanning their surroundings.

"Carlo."

He gave her hands a squeeze. "Let's eat."

They were greeted with a flourish given to locals. Carlo requested a table in the back of the dining room, lit dimly with candles illuminating the red tablecloths.

The waiter strongly suggested the evening menu, insisting that today, they should begin with artichokes braised with garlic, parsley and olive oil. A first course of pasta; rigatoni in a rich tomato sauce with prosciutto, wine and a dash of cream; followed by a second course of oven roasted lamb cooked with olive oil, rosemary, lemon, salt and pepper.

Alessandra wasn't hungry when she arrived, but upon hearing the menu and smelling the decadence waft in from the back of the kitchen, her stomach decided she wasn't allowed to argue with perfection like that.

A small carafe of wine delivered and poured, Carlo took a deep drink then sat back in his chair.

"Were you there?" she asked.

"No." He sighed deeply. "If I had been, it would have been different."

"Who were those men in the picture? Were they the ones who shot him?"

"They work for the man we've been following." He took another drink, studying the front of the restaurant.

"Carlo, I'm not going to try and pull all the information from you. Just tell me what you can. And, what I need to do to stay safe."

"You are safe," he insisted.

"Am I?" She tilted her head. "Because the way you're constantly scanning our surroundings says otherwise."

He ran a hand through his hair. "This job has been such a nightmare. Normally, there is a commonality, these assholes follow a veritable playlist, but not this time. Everything that is happening seems amateur, or cleverly orchestrated. I'm not sure."

She had never seen him this off-balance before.

"Amo, I'm going to request surveillance for you."

She raised an eyebrow; so things weren't okay.

He continued, "Just from afar. It won't interfere with your day to day life."

"So, the kind of surveillance *you* should have done in the first place?"

His demeanor softened. "There was no way I was going to do anything from afar when it came to you, I was desperate to get into your pants."

They both laughed and she reached over and ran her hand through his hair. "I'm worried about you."

"Thank you." He took her hand and kissed the palm, before returning it to her side of the table.

Alessandra frowned. "Carlo."

"There is a suspect we've been attempting to find." He lowered his voice. "We've found a lot of his associates, but no sign of him."

She nodded, not daring to interrupt.

"The patient I brought to your place? He had intel, two locations that needed to be surveilled at the same time. We split up, other teams were en route, but it all went to shit. Like they knew we were coming."

Alessandra was surprised by the amount of information he was imparting.

"So what do we do now?"

"*We* have a nice dinner, and I walk you home."

"And what do I do on the nights when I can't sleep because I'm worried about you?"

"Ale–"

She held up her hand to stop him. "I know that you don't have a traditional job and that you're in harm's way more times than others. I understand the stress of a job like that, I can sympathize with that part. However, I didn't know the danger would affect me the way it has."

"I understand."

She shook her head and gave him a sad smile. "I don't think you do. I get all the worry and you get all the reward."

He raised an eyebrow. "You don't think I worry about you?"

"What is there to worry about? I don't put myself in danger on a daily basis."

He exhaled heavily; Alessandra felt that exhaustion in her own bones.

She took a sip of her wine before saying, "We keep going around and around with the same bullshit. You'll ask if I want you to quit your job, and I'll explain that I would *never* ask you to make a choice like that. I couldn't make that choice either. And you'll ask me to try, and of course I will, but then you'll leave for 'a few days' and I'll worry and lose sleep."

"Alessandra."

"Carlo, I'm just ... I'm just ... angry."

"It feels like you're always angry."

Even though it was the truth, she hated that he voiced it.

"I'm angry at the situation," she bit and before he could speak, continued, "and now, I'm always worried too."

"I don't want to fight," Carlo said.

"We've had worse fights."

The first course was delivered and they came to a silent agreement not to talk about work or worries or their current fears, and instead, allow the food and canned music and wine to take the edge off.

The owner came over and slapped Carlo on the shoulder. "You'll have dessert."

"I couldn't." Alessandra gave a terse smile.

The owner waved his hand at her words as one of the waiters brought out two slices of millefoglie, a cake made up of several layers of puff pastry, creamy custard, and a mix of berries on top.

"You would break my heart if you didn't have a piece." He pulled up a seat and asked Alessandra about work and the latest improvements he'd read about in the paper that the Ospedale San Raffaele was undertaking.

Alessandra was caught off guard as an unforeseen glimpse of a parallel life she and Carlo could have vividly presented itself in her mind: visiting with the owner of her neighborhood trattoria about nothing in particular, on a normal date night. Groceries to be picked up on the way home. The nightly news, brushing of teeth, and setting alarms for generic nine to five job with weekends off. The month of August spent between his family's farm and her parents' house or the beach; and absolutely no life-threatening situations to be had.

But that wasn't the life she wanted.

Maybe she wanted the part with no threats, and Carlo ... but the rest of it, that didn't sound like any fun.

The owner left, moving to another family who 'needed' dessert. They paid the check and as they walked out, Carlo kept Alessandra behind him, slowly scanning the area outside the door.

He gestured for her to walk so she was near the buildings, with him on the street side, shielding her. He didn't reach for her hand, didn't slip his arm around her shoulders. They turned a corner and were almost to her street when Carlo cursed under his breath.

Alessandra glanced anxiously at him but he looked calm and collected, his attention on nothing in particular. He edged ever so slightly to her as he pulled out his cell phone and made a call.

"Assistance, location Echo."

The hair on the back of Alessandra's neck stood on end.

"Turn right," he instructed, "we're just taking a slow walk."

She swallowed the lump forming in her throat, but gave no indication she heard him and didn't change what direction she was looking.

There was no sign Carlo was concerned other than the phone call. Though her own worry wanted to manifest in a set of jokes about how none of this was going to help her sleep any better. Not to mention the questions she had; like, when did he have time to name locations near her apartment and who the hell had he just called?

They walked three more blocks, in the opposite direction from her home, when Carlo edged her into a darkened doorway with his body and turned so he was shielding her.

She looked up at him, wide-eyed, but he smiled down at her, though it didn't necessarily reach his eyes.

"We're okay," he said quietly.

She didn't feel like they were okay. "What's going on?"

"I thought I saw someone."

She tilted her head and scrutinized his face. "No, you *did* see someone."

"I did."

"And you're shielding me."

"I am."

Caught in an awkward staring game, she reached to touch his face, but he gave a barely perceptible shake of his head just as his phone rang. Her hand dropped like a lead weight to her side as he answered without a word, and after a second, hung up and slipped the phone back in his pocket.

He looked down at Alessandra. "A car is going to pull up, you're going to calmly get in. He'll introduce himself and explain what he can." He pulled away from her; blatantly making sure to not touch her.

"Are you coming?" she asked.

His tense smile meant no.

"Are we safe?" She felt like a parrot, asking the same question again and again. But she had yet to receive an answer that quelled her fears.

"I'll call as soon as I can. It might be one or two days."

A car pulled up and there wasn't time to say anything else as he took the two steps to the passenger side and pulled the door open. She climbed in and didn't look at him, she couldn't.

She'd no sooner settled herself than the door closed and the car took off simultaneously.

"Doctor Salvatore, I'm Luca. I've been assigned to watch you." A thin, young man, dressed in a black t-shirt and baseball hat introduced himself.

She nodded as they drove away, finally allowing her gaze to fall on the rearview mirror; Carlo walking in the opposite direction was all she saw before they turned a corner.

"We'd like you to just go about your normal routine, I'll be watching. But do you have any questions?"

She cleared her throat. "I've been through this before. I think I know what to expect."

Chapter Thirty-One

Carlo didn't look back, but he knew the man that was following them, was more intent on him than Alessandra.

It was Il Serpente, at least he looked like the man whose description his CI had given. But how the hell had the man found Carlo? It didn't make sense; then again not one damn thing in this whole fucking operation made sense.

Carlo was beginning to think maybe the man wasn't a cagey drug smuggler, but a damned magician. Before his CI had helped a sketch artist, no one knew what the man looked like. Those who did recognize him had their loyalty bought by said smuggler, and those that turned against him ended up dead. Il Serpente brought bad omens and illness to everyone he or his product interacted with– no wonder the nickname had stuck.

Carlo and Matteo had done a lot of café sitting and newspaper reading while watching some of the lower-level goons, hoping to catch wind of Il Serpente.

Carlo had been in this field long enough to know that unscrupulous men often knew someone was watching; but they never knew who. Only this time, Matteo was in the hospital with a gunshot wound, Carlo's CI had vanished without a trace, and Il Serpente –who was reportedly in a small coastal town an hour north of Rome– was across the damn street from him.

And he'd seen Alessandra.

Hopefully not too well, when Carlo spotted the man as they exited the restaurant, he immediately shielded her. He just wasn't sure it had been enough.

Hell, the last thing he'd wanted was for Alessandra to be in the middle of all this. No matter how much he longed for a life with her, this was a blatant, bright sign that being together really wouldn't work. Maybe he *should* let her push him away, maybe it was the best for both of them.

Though, plenty of other agents had wives, children, families. They figured it out. But how? And at what cost? How the hell could he live with the selfishness of keeping her in danger, just to have a warm body to wrap around when he had a little time to spare?

And now Il Serpente would be made aware of *something* because, even though Carlo hadn't touched her, shielding her from the criminal would be enough of a hint that she meant something to him.

He cursed himself and tried to shake off the thoughts, now wasn't the time. Now was the time to focus on facts; the first being the only explanation that made any sense in this whole operation was that the AISE had a mole.

When he'd walked far enough, finding himself at a busy intersection, he turned his attention to the man on the opposite side of the street. Even though most of his features were covered by a black hoodie, Carlo caught a glimpse of Il Serpente as he lifted his head in greeting, a crooked, greasy smile stretching across his face.

Carlo took out his phone, aimed the camera at the man and snapped a picture. Il Serpente didn't move and they stayed locked in the staring game of chicken as cars and pedestrians hurried past. When a large bus wobbled down the street, Carlo didn't move, but he wasn't surprised that when the bus was finally clear, the man was gone.

Carlo cursed under his breath. He should have made a move, but they needed to catch the snake red-handed, otherwise none of the allegations would stick.

Chapter Thirty-Two

"Ciao Bella." The deep voice on the phone robbed Alessandra of her balance, so she sat down heavily on her sofa and blew out, "Carlo."

Saying his name and hearing his confirming grunt on the other end of the phone calmed her.

"You're okay?" she asked.

"I'm fine. Are you?"

"I've been in worse situations." She tried to ease the tension.

"Really?" He sounded genuinely curious.

"I was once on the streets of downtown Chicago on Saint Patrick's Day." The release of worry and the ridiculous comparison caused her to bark out a laugh. She slapped her free hand over her mouth, but Carlo's unexpected chuckle matched hers and they allowed themselves to dissolve into the shared amusement.

"Is it safe to talk ... this way?" she asked.

"It's fine."

But what was there to say? Alessandra had a thousand questions, and they were all bumping into each other along with the emotions of missing him, wanting him, and being angry at how he'd put her in this unfamiliar, dangerous situation. But what questions *could* he answer; *would* he answer?

"You can't tell me where you are, can you?"

"I know where I *wish* I was."

It wasn't enough.

"You know what the problem is? I want everything from you, all your time and attention and to see you when it's on my schedule."

He gave a grunt of frustration.

"But that isn't fair," she continued quickly, "I'm not about to wave ultimatums around. And every time we talk about how to make this work–"

"After this is over, I'll have time."

"But there is always going to be another job, and a next one and a next one," she said with a sad smile.

"I don't want to fight."

"I'm not trying to fight. I'm just trying to be a voice of reason." And the voice of reason needed him to understand why they needed to call this what it was, a failed experiment.

"Amo," he begged.

She opened her mouth to speak, but everything had become overly complicated and more difficult.

"Maybe you're right," Carlo said softly.

"I'm always right," she muttered, then thought about hanging up. Because this time she didn't want to be right. She wanted him in her life and she wanted him gone, and it was agonizing. She wanted to really start a fight that would break them up or go back on her word and insist on ultimatums. She settled on saying, "I should go."

"Alessandra."

"I assume my new babysitter will make sure I don't accidentally run into you. Here. In Rome. Where I live and work." This was the fight she wasn't going to start.

"I need to keep you safe." His voice was gruff. "In a few weeks we should be able to see each other."

"What's the point?"

"What do you mean?" His voice was almost a whisper.

"Are we even *in* a relationship anymore? The way this feels, is that I've somehow become a convenient safehouse doctor for the AISE."

"That's not what this is," he argued.

"Isn't it?"

He didn't answer, and Alessandra felt the distance between them growing in the number of days they'd been apart, the new threat she didn't truly understand, and their matched abilities to be unbending.

There was too much to say and not enough time. The result was a wall of silence.

"Alessandra," he began, but whatever he wanted to say died somewhere among the Roman streets that separated them.

She pulled the phone away from her ear and looked at the face of it, the red 'end call' button tempting. Because this was too hard. Even though she wasn't against working on difficult things, this difficulty had to do with her heart.

Carlo's voice echoed from the phone as he called her name again.

She put the phone back in place.

His misery was palpable. "I'm sorry, but–"

"*But.*" Alessandra punctuated the word. "But this is your job. But it's just for a while. But we'll figure this out. But this won't be forever." But if he really loved her and wanted to be part of her life as much as he claimed he did, he would have made different decisions.

"I'll quit," he said quietly.

"Then you'd hate me. For the late hours *I* work, for the unexpected calls in the middle of the night when I'm needed at the hospital. You'd hate me because I was allowed to be happy and you weren't."

"It would be worth it to be with you."

"We both know it's not enough." God, how many times would they have to talk themselves in circles over this topic? She just wanted to reach out and touch him, be touched by him whenever she needed him. "No matter how noble your intentions, eventually, the boredom and resentment would creep in."

"I can't live without you." He rumbled his need.

"But you *are* living without me. You've been living without me since we met." The threatening tears began to burn the back of her throat.

"One week. I promise," he said vehemently.

"You can't make that sort of promise, we both know that."

"Alessandra ... I still want you to be my wife."

The declaration floated across the room to where she'd put the engagement ring he'd given her. The sheen of promise it once held had dulled amid empty promises and arguments that had no resolution.

"I don't think we can make any decisions right now. We'll let this current situation play out. And then see."

"I will find a way to see you soon. I promise."

She closed her eyes and rubbed her face with her free hand. After a moment, she nodded and agreed. "Fine." She didn't wait for his reply and ended the call.

Chapter Thirty-Three

Alessandra was listening to Matteo's lungs when the assisting nurse interrupted. "Doctor?"

Alessandra glanced up at the young man with a frown, but he nodded toward her hand with steady eyes; it was shaking.

Alessandra slipped the stethoscope around her neck and shook her hands, then splayed her fingers, stretching them several times as she said, "Things are looking really good."

Matteo gingerly sat back against his bed. "Thanks to you."

"Well, I had help." She smiled.

"I haven't had any visitors. So, it's nice to see you," he said nonchalantly, a silent question as to what had been happening.

"Well, that's because only family is allowed in the intensive care rooms. It's not like your old roommate Luca could come hang out with you."

He gave a slow nod of his head in understanding. "I suppose not. But he was always a good guy. Never caused much of a scene, overly protective and great at his job." Matteo winked.

"What does he do?" asked the nurse, who was cleaning up the wrappers of the gauze he'd just replaced on Matteo's shoulder, as if he were just being polite and helpful.

"He works in insurance." Matteo's easy grin widened.

Alessandra cleared her throat and nodded to the nurse, excusing him with a clipped "Thank you."

When he left, she took a step closer to Matteo and crossed her arms over her chest. "Insurance?"

"It's not too far from the truth." He shrugged and then winced at the pain.

She frowned. "How are you really feeling?"

"Like I got shot. And I'm pissed. I let that asshole get the jump on me and I should be working." He sighed. "So, is Luca hanging around for me or you?"

"Me."

"I see."

"Your other friend," she leveled her gaze, to make sure they both knew which *friend* she was talking about, "told me enough about the current situation. And he even took me to dinner the other night. However, afterwards, he saw something that required obtaining Luca's *insurance*."

"Looks like we put you in a sticky situation, Doc."

"Well, you aren't the first, and probably won't be the last," she muttered.

"Are *you* okay?"

She gave a snort of a laugh. "Not really."

"I hope you don't mind me saying, but you look rough."

"So do you," she leveled.

He wiggled his eyebrows. "Ah, but I have a reason."

"I've got my reasons too."

He pursed his lips. "He's crazy about you, you know."

"That isn't the problem."

Matteo tilted his head. "I can't imagine it's easy; but if there's anything I can do for you Doc, just let me know."

"Rest. Get better." She patted the bed, ending their conversation.

In the hallway she stopped and took several deep breaths while she stretched her fingers.

The nurse who helped her change the gauze on Matteo's shoulder was headed her way. He handed her a chart to be signed asking, "Are you okay?"

"I'm fine." She was getting sick of that damn question. "My blood sugar is a little low."

"Did you eat anything today?"

"I had a coffee and pastry this morning." She signed the appropriate places.

"Doctor Salvatore, it's past dinner," he stated.

Alessandra nodded, returning the chart. "That would be why my blood sugar is low. I'll go get something."

"Doctor," the young man began, and when Alessandra looked at him he gave her a soft smile and said, "take care of yourself." Only it wasn't a lighthearted suggestion, it was more of a plea.

Alessandra knew everyone had noticed her growing anxiety over the past several months. Of course, no one had approached her to talk about it. Alessandra was not the sort of person to sit down and have heartfelt conversations with her colleagues. Unless it was a heated debate over proper care for a patient, she tended to keep her emotions firmly in check.

But the dark rings under her eyes were growing along with her irritability. She knew it was only a matter of time before someone took their concerns to the Chief Medical Director. Then Alessandra would be made to take mandatory time off, which would require her to stay home and rest. And home was the last place she wanted to be.

Alessandra saw Luca at the end of the hallway, lurking. He'd been cleared by security and now spent his days skulking. An unwanted shadow.

She ducked into the bathroom, splashed water on her face and rested her exhausted head against the mirror. Drops of water slipped down the collar of her shirt, onto her lab coat.

It wasn't low blood sugar causing her to shake, it was the three days since she'd seen Carlo last. It was the continual, overwhelming worry. It was the shadow of Luca, the knowing glances of Matteo and the waiting all hours of the quiet night for her phone or intercom to ring.

She angrily ripped paper towels out of the dispenser and patted her face dry. When she reached her office, she retrieved her cell phone from her desk, where she'd taken to keeping it so she wouldn't obsessively check it. No messages, no missed calls.

Her shift was over, and she didn't want to go home. She hated it there now. She was surrounded by memories of his laughter, of sitting on the sofa wrapped in his arms while they watched nonsense on TV, of cooking for him, and talking late into the night.

As the distance between them grew, the memories gained more power.

Alessandra would have hid in her office longer, but that would add another element for the Chief of Medicine to scrutinize and declare problematic. The irony was that work was the only thing keeping her sane.

She gathered her things and made sure to smile and wave at the nurses as she left.

As she shuffled to her car, the aching smile slipped away. She turned and found her ever-present shadow standing by the car next to hers. Luca didn't ask any questions, just waited.

"I don't want to go home," she said heavily. "I just need a little break." She licked her lips. "I want to go for a drive."

He gave a slight nod, closed his car door and came to stand by hers.

She didn't mean she wanted him to ride with her, but if she didn't want to go home, this was the price she'd have to pay.

She drove and was grateful for Luca's silence. As she twisted around streets, she was soothed by the impatient honking of local traffic amid the dusky neon evening. She wound around the neighborhood she'd lived when she was going to medical school. She slowed in front of her old apartment building, it hadn't changed. Same six-story building, yellowed from age and dust. The little, street level fruit vendor shop was still in business; its small door propped open with an old chair that held a chalkboard with the day's available fruits.

She drove up the street and turned the corner, where the café she used to frequent was located. She slowed the car once again, then clicked on the hazard lights, since she was double-parked and told Luca, "I just want a quick coffee."

He climbed out of the car and didn't follow her, but instead leaned against the car watching her walk inside.

Claudio, the proprietor who was ancient when she used to come here years ago, hadn't changed a bit. He waved away the group of friends he was talking to and rushed over to plant kisses on Alessandra's cheeks and tell her how good it was to see her.

There was a solace in the memories of the life she'd lived when she was a new doctor, new to Rome.

"Dottoressa!" Claudio shook his head and grinned. "How are you?"

"Better now." She found her first real smile of the day and eased herself into the momentary memories of when life had been simple.

He waved to his barista, calling out Alessandra's order, a macchiato: a shot of espresso with a dash of steamed milk and a mark of foam. She thanked him and asked about his family.

He leaned his hip against the bar as her coffee was slid in front of her. She took a sip and fell back into the shades of her old life as Claudio filled her in on his wife, children, grandchildren and business in record time. But that was Claudio; in the time it took to drink one caffé, he was able to share his life story, his opinions on the state of the world, and the recipe for a happy existence. Alessandra opened her mouth to ask him what a person did exactly to have a happy life, but her courage faltered and thankfully, another customer arrived, calling out a greeting.

Coffee finished, she made her apologies as Claudio leaned in to kiss her on the cheek. "Don't forget about us, huh? Come back to visit me again."

"I will," she promised.

Before leaving she tried to pay her bill, but he waved her out the door. "One day, I'll need some medical advice. We'll trade then. It will be an uneven trade, but still ..."

"Not if I get to talk with you and have your famous pastries." She smiled then called "Buonasera" as she left.

She thought driving would ease her mind somehow; that she'd find a touchstone, a person, a memory, something to connect with, something that would help fight the loneliness and the worry.

But if she were so interested in connecting with another human, she wouldn't have double-parked.

She drove around for another hour, thought about getting a hotel room for the night, but in the end, she was drawn to the miserable ghosts in her apartment. She would go home, where there was no peace. She would stumble to her bed and lay down, only to be taunted by the quiet. The unsettling isolation would seep into her bones, and the shadows on her walls would play out cold memories in shades of black and light.

She took Luca back to the hospital so he could get his car and follow her home.

She found parking right away in front of her building, and as she walked in, made eye contact with Luca who gave her a nod of good night.

In the lobby, she collected her mail and forced another smile when one of her elderly neighbors from the first floor caught her attention, droning on about her arthritis.

"Maybe try a heat pad or hot water bottle on the affected areas before bedtime." She gave the placebo prescription.

It was something she did often, when people found out she was a doctor and wanted quick, free medical advice; what they were really after was common sense verbalized.

"Grazie," the woman said, brightening. "I'll try it tonight."

Alessandra thought about taking the elevator, but she preferred the stairs; for the thin hope that the exertion would help her sleep.

At the top of the stairs, she turned the corner toward her door and abruptly stopped.

"Eccola." *Here she is,* a deep voice announced.

Alessandra's heart stopped as she looked at the man leaning against her door. She had a moment to take a breath before her legs gave out and she crumbled to the floor, along with her purse, keys and mail. She let her head fall into her hands; her body overcome with wracking sobs.

He was there, by her side, lifting her into his arms. Alessandra turned her head into his chest, clutching his shirt.

Somehow, he gathered her things, found her keys and she heard the loud click of the lock on her front door as it opened. He dropped her belongings on the table in the small foyer, and his feet shuffled across her floor, but it was all soft, white noise because the sound of his heartbeat, strong and powerful against her ear, was keeping time with her sobs, a melancholy symphony.

He was safe.

He was *here*.

Chapter Thirty-Four

Carlo was sure his own legs might give out any moment. Alessandra's reaction caught him off guard. He thought to surprise her by waiting outside her door. He could have used the keys she gave him, but after their last conversation, he wasn't so sure. He notified Luca of his intentions, having done a recon of the apartment building himself, and saving Luca some work.

As he waited, he fantasized about her running into his arms. He thought maybe they would argue, she'd put her hands on her hips and admonish him for showing up again without calling first. But among all the scenarios he imagined, his strong, gorgeous Alessandra, crumbling before him with soul-wrenching sobs as she broke into a million pieces before his eyes ... he hadn't been prepared for this.

He wasn't sure where to go, but her room was the closest. He sat on the edge of her bed and hugged her tighter. He shushed her and whispered into her hair, "I'm here, it's okay amo, I'm here now."

Little by little, Alessandra gained control of her senses. She took deep breaths and tried to slow the sobbing. Carlo kissed the top of her head, he pulled her hand up to his mouth and brushed kisses along her knuckles. "I'm here. It's okay," he repeated softly.

She nuzzled her face into the crook of his neck.

"Amo." He put his hand under her chin and tilted her head so he could look at her face. In the dim light coming from the hallway, he could just make out the shimmer of her eyes. "I'm sorry."

She leaned forward slightly and it was all the invitation he needed. He lowered his lips to hers. He meant to be gentle with her. To go slowly. He had spent so many nights dreaming about the little things; holding her hand, the feel of her hair on his chest, the way his palm splayed across her stomach.

But whatever had come over Alessandra to cause such an emotional outburst, had changed his intentions. And now the fierce relief that overwhelmed her when she first saw him, had mutated into desperation. Desperation to be one with him. And he was more than ready to meet the silent challenge she issued.

She kissed him with such unbridled passion, Carlo was quickly, completely, and utterly undone. Just because of the way her lips fit against his.

Passion had always been their strength, and now, after being absent from each other, all it took was one touch for the flame to detonate and burn; an explosion of desire.

Alessandra pulled away and her fingers trembled as she attempted to unbutton his shirt. He pushed her arms aside in his own attempt to rid her of her shirt at the same time. Their hands argued over who would remove what clothing, until they were finally reunited, only heat between them.

Alessandra slid her hands up his broad chest and he caught the low moan of appreciation from her in his mouth.

Her touch scorched his skin, she moved her lips to follow the path her hands were making. He wanted to let her explore, but the need for her overrode his intentions. He wound his hand in her hair and pulled her back to him where his lips captured hers in another searing promise.

He treasured the way her hands crept up to his shoulders, around his back, and under those hands, his muscles pulsed and jumped of their own excitement.

Carlo's anguish was just as impassioned as wave after wave of desire and craving shocked him. He wanted all she was willing to give and more, so much more. He wanted to leave her satiated and exhausted, as much as he wanted the same for himself. At the heart of the need, he wanted to be inside her. Just kissing and feeling her pressed against him brought him too close to release.

He wanted to taste every inch of her, had planned on bending her body to the will of his hands and lips as he extracted moan after moan from her, but now, he wanted to be buried in her heat for the rest of his life.

He picked her up and laid her down in the middle of the bed. When he pulled away to adjust himself, she fought him, a desperate moan of "no" rushed out as she linked her hands behind his neck, an attempt to pull him back into place.

After quickly readjusting their bodies, Alessandra pressed her hips up to meet him at the same moment she strained her neck to reach his lips once more, her whole body demonstrating the desperate message that she was not in the mood for anything other than frenzied, feverish joined passion.

He pulled away, to adjust himself for her once more, and when he glanced down, he froze. The slight light from the street lamps illuminated the room in a soft yellowed glow. His siren, his Alessandra, eyes shimmering with passion and need. Need for *him*.

And God knew his desperate carnal need for her was equally matched.

"Carlo." She reached between their bodies encouraging him.

He moved and let her guide him, grunting as she raised her hips and wrapped her legs around his waist, and finally, he buried himself deep.

Alessandra moaned and urged him to work. He sank deeper inside her and his head snapped back from being gripped in such silk.

He gripped her hips in his hands, thinking he'd attempt restraint, but the ravenous hunger expanded until Carlo was lost in the fire.

Alessandra gripped Carlo around the neck and held on as her own voracious craving for more seem to untangled her soul from her body. She worked frantically to meet each of his thrusts, to keep the wild rhythm.

They muttered encouragements to one another, but heavy breathing and pounding heartbeats drowned out their voices. Alessandra moaned her release and as her body tensed around Carlo, and he was encompassed in an erotic vice, he picked up his pace until finally, he was able to hiss out his own release between his teeth, crumbling into the warmth of the woman beneath him.

It took a while for their breathing to steady and when it finally did, Carlo rolled off Alessandra, pulling her to him so they were facing each other and he could press as much of her naked skin as was possible against him.

"I missed you." His deep whisper reverberated in his chest. She closed her eyes and rested her forehead against his.

A sob caught in her throat. "I can't do this anymore."

Chapter Thirty-Five

The van in front of Carlo made a harrowing swerve across three lanes, clipping two cars and leaving a trail of honks and screeching brakes in its wake. He blew out a litany of curses as he accelerated, attempting to follow the agitated path.

None of this made sense.

After his CI was stabbed, Matteo was shot, and he found Il Serpente waiting for him outside the restaurant; the very next day it was as if every rat associated with this damn drug dealer went underground. There had been absolutely no suspicious activity. Anywhere.

Which was a large neon arrow that pointed to the fact that there *must* be a mole somewhere in the AISE.

Carlo trusted Luca and Matteo. The three men had a conference call in order to exchange theories, but other than an agreement that it was most likely someone on the inside, they didn't have anything more substantial to go on.

Matteo was told to watch his back while Luca looked out for Alessandra, and Carlo would continue to surveil and sift through intel. Once they knew what was going on, or who was at the helm of this fuck-up, they'd make their move.

With the silence and non-existent activity, Carlo made the calculated attempt to see Alessandra. Now he wasn't sure if that had been the right thing to do or not. He'd broken her. The stoic woman who he considered near unbreakable...well, he'd pushed her over the edge. And when he held her in his arms and she began to cry after the heart-wrenching announcement that she couldn't do it anymore, his goddamn phone had rung, it was time to get back to work.

He left her apartment, unable to utter more empty words or promises. He didn't plead for her to wait for him. He couldn't. He was at a loss of what to do.

She walked him to the door and kissed him. And as she closed the door behind him, he wasn't sure where their relationship stood.

Carlo made his way to a warehouse used by Il Serpente; once a hotbed of activity, it had been abandoned for months now. Until an anonymous tip called in information about two known colleagues of the drug smuggler entering the building in the middle of the night, requiring Carlo's immediate attention.

He had been instructed to watch from cover, so he settled in, trying not to think about Alessandra. And he had plenty of time to *not* think, because nothing happened until the next afternoon at three, when a black van pulled up to the building. The two men inside exited carrying two large black duffle bags each– accompanied by agitated yells as they hurried into the van.

The van made a crooked turnabout, making sure to pass Carlo's car, and when he saw the gun appear out the window, he ducked as the tinny sound of several bullets bounced off.

He followed the van, calling in the details as he swerved and was assured the local polizia would be informed to help, clearing what streets they could and creating a roadblock.

Just then the van honked and barreled through a red light, causing cars to stack up in minor accidents. Carlo tried to follow, but was waylaid by the angry traffic. But the van didn't continue, it swerved to the right and stopped across the intersection, idling.

As Carlo maneuvered the car through the stopped traffic, the passenger side door of the van opened, and one of the men jumped out, shooting at Carlo's car, the shots ricocheting off his bumper.

He slammed on the brakes, ducked down, called in "shots fired" just as his earpiece erupted with reports from two other agents who had both been watching separate buildings, and were also taking fire.

"What the fuck is going on?" came the angry question from Command.

Carlo opened the car door and slid out of the seat, squatting behind the makeshift barrier just as a report came in of a fourth agent under fire.

"They're trying to divide us," he muttered as he watched bystanders get out of their cars, not aware of what was going on just yet because of the noise and honking from the rest of the traffic.

Carlo pulled out his gun and shot into the air once, causing the exact effect he wanted; people running away, and diving behind or back into their vehicles.

He aimed at the tire of the van and successfully shot it out, but ducked as another round of bullets came his way.

Over his com came another announcement: "Shots fired in front of Ospedale San Raffaele."

"What?" Carlo's vision blurred, he didn't understand what was being said. "Say again!" He couldn't make sense of the words or the escalating fear, and he wasn't given any time, as the back door of the van opened and another gunman got out.

Carlo jumped behind the back end of the car next to him as the men opened fire. He called in the new information and waited until the men were reloading to poke his head around the car and take aim. He was able to put them both down and as the second man fell, the tires of the van screeched to life and took off awkwardly given the now flat tire. Carlo climbed back in his car and continued the pursuit as he listened to the sirens in the distance and the updates of other agents over his coms. And amidst all this urgency, he tried to convince himself that Alessandra was alright.

Chapter Thirty-Six

"It's fine. Everything is fine," Alessandra muttered to herself. This was the mantra she spent the whole day chanting to over and over and over again.

She'd told Carlo she was done and his damn phone rang; and he jumped to do its bidding, proving that parting ways was for the best.

It was what had to be done.

Now she could finally patch her life back together. She could shake this off and focus once again on work. And most importantly, she would finally be able to get some sleep. The exhaustion had begun to manifest itself in physical ways; stomach problems, shortness of breath and headaches.

Today at work, when breathing became difficult and an unsettling wave of nausea covered her, she decided to verify her theory that it was emotions causing all these problems and not something else. She took a pregnancy test. Just in case. Of course, the test was negative. But as she stared at the results, the life she never wanted before she met Carlo materialized and dissipated in a wave of relief and disappointment. They never even talked about if either of them wanted kids. But they never seemed to be able to talk about any of the 'important' relationship things.

She packed away her emotions along with the negative results of the pregnancy test, wrapping the stick in toilet paper and placing it all back in the box it came. She threw the box in the small plastic lined trash bin under her desk, then knotting the bag, marched it to a larger garbage can by the janitorial closet.

With her shift over, Alessandra walked exhaustedly to her car. She tried not to look in Luca's direction, where he hovered several cars away, but she could still see him out of the corner of her eye. She snarled her annoyance as she fished her keys out of her purse.

"Excuse me, Doctor Salvatore?" She glanced up at a man walking toward her.

"Yes?" She frowned.

Alessandra was taken aback by the snarl on his face and his hand that moved lightning fast; she had just enough time to catch a glint of the knife he was holding and drop everything as the knife was thrust into her stomach.

Eyes wide, she let out a silent scream. He tried to pull the knife out but she bent over her waist, her short stature causing him to crouch slightly, and she held the knife in place as a sick fight or flight reaction took over.

Keep the knife in, a frantic voice yelled inside her head. *It will do less damage if it's left in place.*

She held her attacker's hands in place and he growled in her ear, attempting to pull it out.

Another voice screamed in her head then: *whoever has the power of the hips wins.*

Bent over, her hip was already against his groin, he was already scrambling. She moved her foot, wrapping it around the outside of his, then gave voice to a powerful scream as she twisted and successfully tripped him. The motion shocked the man, causing him to release his hand and fall with a thwack and thud. She stumbled forward, her hands releasing the knife to catch herself as she fell to her knees. Someone was yelling her name just as gunshots erupted. She looked up, but the world tilted; *don't fall on the knife*, another invisible directive. She pressed against the car tire nearest her and thankfully fell onto her side.

In front of her now, was the body of her attacker, his head at a strange angle, his eyes staring in shock at nothing. She thought she glimpsed a dark puddle forming under his head and she held up her arm in the air, attempting to call for help, but the light was moving into a pinpoint, the edges growing darker and darker.

Chapter Thirty-Seven

Someone was calling Alessandra's name.

But it was coming from inside a tin can.

She needed to open her eyes, but they were so heavy. The exhaustion must have finally taken its toll. The last thing she recalled was how tired she was.

She tried to open her eyes, but they weren't cooperating. She tried to lift her hand, to physically open her eyes, but someone held it. Sensation shivered up her arm as she identified a strong warm hand holding hers. It was nice, but she needed her hand. She tried to pull away, but it wasn't possible.

"C'mon, Doc," a deep voice urged her.

Doc.

She didn't like the shortened monogram; didn't this person know how long she worked to obtain the right to be called Doctor?

She reached up with her other hand to her eyes, but stopped when her fingers came in contact with a plastic tube attached to her nose. What was happening?

"Alessandra." It was her name, but she didn't recognize the voice.

Curiosity forced her to find the strength to part her weighted eyelids. Light blinded her and as her vision focused, she realized she was in the hospital. Her hospital, Ospedale San Raffaele.

The memories of what happened swept over her.

A man in the parking lot, stabbing her. Gunshots.

Another squeeze of her hand brought her attention to Matteo sitting next to her.

He smiled. "Eccola." *There she is.*

"Carlo?" she asked, her voice scratchy.

"He's safe," Matteo offered.

"What time is it?"

"It's about six in the morning. Do you remember what happened?"

She nodded and tried to move, but was thwarted by a searing pain in her stomach. "Stabbed," she moaned. "I was coming out of work, done with my shift." She frowned at Matteo. "Six in the morning?"

"You were taken immediately into surgery, it took a while, and then it took some time for the anesthesia to wear off." He winked at her. "And for me to convince security to let me see you."

"Why isn't Carlo here?"

"Alessandra, he'll be here soon. But I need to ask you about the man who attacked you. I'm sorry to have to do this, but do you think you can describe him?" Matteo tried to ask the question nonchalantly, but the edge in his voice was rough with concern.

She shook her head as she relived the moment again, as the darkened shadow of a man lunged at her with a knife. She trailed her free hand to her stomach and slightly palpated the area. She'd been in surgery. That would account for the feelings of wanting to cry and being so confused. It was the after effects of the anesthesia.

"Alessandra?"

"So fast ..." A shadow, lunging, then they were both on the ground. "He smiled, happy to attack me," She swallowed, her throat sore from being intubated. "He had a hood, dark beard, dark hair."

Matteo pulled out his cell phone. "I'm going to scroll through a few pictures. Tell me if you recognize anyone."

He swiped through several photos before she pointed. "That's one of the men from the lobby that asked about you."

He went on to the next picture, which was the other man that had been looking for Matteo as well. When he came to the last photo she shrugged. "I didn't get a good look at him."

Matteo sat back and nodded.

"Isn't he here? In the hospital? I tripped him, he got hurt."

Matteo shook his head. "You did some damage, but he wasn't down for long. By the time Luca was able to get to you, there was no trace of your attacker."

She frowned. "But ..."

Matteo squeezed her hand. "You got a good shot in Doc, Luca said there was a decent puddle of blood left behind."

Alessandra squinted as she tried to remember everything that had happened. She thought she killed him; she could see the man, head tilted awkwardly to the side, eyes staring up at nothing, growing pool of blood ... he couldn't have walked away from that.

"But you did good, kept the knife in place, kept your wits about you. You're damn good under pressure, Doc."

"I remember gunshots."

"That's why it took so long to get to you. It was mayhem."

"Was anyone hurt?"

"Thankfully no. A car with two men shot up the front of the hospital. They didn't target people, just cameras and windows, the whole thing was more like a distraction."

"Is this connected to your work?"

"Everything points to that, but there are so many questions still left unanswered."

"Carlo?"

Matteo shifted in his seat as he said, "He's fine."

"Did that man know about me and Carlo?"

Matteo shrugged. "I don't know, but I think this was a sort of threat."

"Threat?"

"If someone really wanted to hurt you, to kill you, the attack would have been something else, something different. So this, and the gunfire at the front of the hospital, I think it was a message."

"What kind of message?"

"Don't fuck with me." Matteo didn't sugarcoat the threat.

"Who?"

"If I had to guess, my money would be on Il Serpente."

She couldn't hold back the tears and didn't try. It was a result of the medications and all the intricacies of the situation she found herself in.

"It's okay." Matteo gently patted her hand.

A nurse came into the room and frowned. "What are you doing in here?"

"I'm a friend of Doctor Salvatore." Matteo smiled. "I was just leaving."

"Doctor Salvatore needs her rest," the nurse scolded.

He gave one more pat on her hand. "I'll let you know if I hear anything. But everything is going to be okay. You just look after yourself, okay Doc?"

"Tell him ..." She bit her lip as she wiped at the tears.

Matteo brushed a concerned kiss on her forehead. "I'll see you soon."

Chapter Thirty-Eight

Matteo scanned the waiting room; the chaotic sea of stunned patients who had bumps and scrapes from the manic attacks carried out in several areas of town had thinned. There were a handful of patients still left, but the heightened police presence remained to aid security.

Matteo knew all the intelligence organizations in the city were scrambling to figure out what the hell was going on. The only ray of hope Matteo had, was information that came through a few hours before all hell broke loose. A database search on Interpol, using the photo Carlo took, had finally resulted in the true identity of Il Serpente. A man by the name of Paolo Costa.

He made his way to a taxi, tossing his phone in the trash on the way. He gave his request to the cab driver, "Piazza di Spagna." The piazza near the Spanish Steps. There was a café near there that he and Carlo agreed would be their final fallback location if things went bad.

And things had gone bad.

Matteo hadn't heard from Carlo. He lied when Alessandra asked how the man was. Truth was, Matteo had no idea. He figured he'd wait until Alessandra was out of surgery to see if she could ID her attacker before he made his way to the piazza. The owner of the café was a friend and would open the door if either man needed a place to hide, but it was the café's hours, 5 a.m. to midnight, that also made it ideal.

The Piazza di Spagna was quietly waking up. Not too many tourists yet, but there was an increase of police walking around. Matteo snorted a laugh, normally he would make a comment about security that lounged in police cars, but not today.

He arrived at the café and when he opened the front door, was met with the heavenly aroma of freshly baked goods. His stomach reminded him that he hadn't eaten in a while. He ordered two pastries, an espresso and a sandwich of mozzarella, basil and tomato. With goods in hand, he made his way to the back room.

The café boasted several rooms; the main lobby with a bar, the pastry cases, and ten tables; two more rooms with a variety of tables and chairs; and a back room, where he found Carlo sitting near the exit door.

"So, you're okay." Matteo sighed as he heavily sat down. "And you're in our emergency location. And I ditched my phone, which means neither of us knows what the hell is going on."

"Did you find out what happened at the hospital?"

"Don't you know?"

"Ditched my phone and coms then came here to wait."

Matteo pursed his lips as he studied his friend. The man looked like he'd spent some time dodging bullets and rolling around on the ground. The weight of the world was on his shoulders given how this operation had gone to hell.

Matteo took a sip and a big bite of the sandwich, then brushing crumbs from his hands said, "Okay look, as far as I can make out, the attacks yesterday weren't meant to harm anyone other than agents. There were only two bystanders who were hit with a stray bullet, they're alive. There are a ton of scrapes and bruises that have more to do with car crashes and people running and pushing each other."

Carlo's jaw clenched, he must know Matteo was working his way up to delivering information he wasn't going to like.

"The gunshots at the hospital were a distraction because at the same time ..." Matteo cleared his throat, "Alessandra was just leaving work and a man approached her in the parking lot and stabbed her."

Matteo could practically see the big man's whole body shutting down from the announcement. "She's fine," Matteo hurried. "Luca was shadowing. When he saw a stranger approach, he started heading over to help her, but then a car pulled up and opened fire. It all happened within a split second. But she tripped the attacker and got herself out of a bad situation."

Carlo's voice was a bare whisper. "She shouldn't have been in the situation in the first place."

"Luca and the doctors got to her in time and she was in surgery in a flash. She's out. The surgeon promised everything was fine. They're going to keep her for observation and Luca is directly outside her room this time."

Carlo gave a curt nod, but didn't say anything.

Matteo sighed, it wasn't time for the man to shut down, but he didn't know if that was really what was happening. So he continued, "I waited until she woke up to see if she could ID the attacker. Luca told me she had tripped him, and he'd looked like he was dead. He assumed other staff took care of the man. Luca stayed with Alessandra until they got her into surgery. But if they did, no one knew where the body went. It was chaos."

"So he lived."

Matteo shrugged. "Luca and Alessandra both say they thought the attacker was dead."

"Dead men don't walk away on their own," Carlo said.

"I realize that, but in this particular situation, it seems like they fucking do."

Carlo was silent for a long while, and Matteo took several more quick bites, then felt compelled to break the silence. "The good doctor is one hell of a strong woman."

"I made a call to a friend at the Guardia di Finanza." Carlo promptly changed the subject by referring to the militarized police force that dealt with financial crime and smuggling.

"We've been working with them." Matteo frowned.

"This is a friend who isn't working with *us*."

"Ah."

"I think my friend found the leak."

Matteo leaned forward, eyebrow raised. "Do we get to help plug this damn leak?"

Carlo grunted, "Unknown."

"Okay, tell me."

"Well, it seems our snake friend had someone who could supply him with the Guardaia schedules, so as to do a lot of business and never get caught. This man on the inside felt he deserved a bigger cut for all the information he was providing."

"Il Serpente did not agree with this?" Matteo asked.

"No. And coincidently, this agent was found dead in his apartment late last night."

"Drugs and money," Matteo said. "It's always the simplest explanations. Speaking of breakthroughs; did you get the information that we now have the true identity of Il Sperente?"

"Paolo Costa."

Matteo nodded and stretched. "Okay, where do you want to start?"

"We still need to follow up and make sure the agent was actually the mole. Then we go back to the beginning." Carlo sighed heavily.

They fell back into silence, and finally Matteo figured he owed it to the good doctor who saved his life to bring her back up. "Are you going to go see Alessandra?"

Carlo glanced across the room.

"Are you going to call her at least?"

Still no answer.

"Are we leaving Luca in place?"

"For now."

Matteo shook his head. He was shit at relationships himself, so he had no idea how to help this big robot and his tender heart. But he knew Alessandra deserved better than being ghosted; which was the road it seemed his partner was taking.

Chapter Thirty-Nine

"Excuse me." Matteo interrupted the nurse at the front desk, then pulled out his credentials and smiled at the young woman. "I came to see Doctor Salvatore, however she isn't in her office and the secretary who the nurse told me to talk to is at lunch."

The woman scrutinized his credentials and then looked at him. After a moment she made a call and suggested he take a seat and wait.

After the shooting and stabbing, the hospital had intensified their security. Matteo had meant to come back and check on Alessandra, but he'd been busy. Carlo's friend had identified the mole and it looked like the simultaneous attacks on all the agents had indeed been a message to not fuck with Il Serpente. Using the distraction of the multiple strikes, the drug smuggler had ordered a cleanup of his own trash- six of his men along with two dirty detectives had also been killed.

So Carlo and Matteo were once again scouring the intel in an attempt to find Il Serpente. They'd arrested six known associates, but the questioning all led to nothing.

It seemed Il Serpente had blown up his operation and gone into hiding. And having his real identity now, didn't seem to help.

Luca kept Matteo and Carlo updated on Alessandra's recovery, which had been a two-day stint in the hospital and three days at home before she returned to work. Of course, Luca never reported how the good doctor was doing emotionally. Just her superficial movements.

After ten days, the threat on Alessandra's life had been considered nominal, and Luca had been taken off the watch detail.

Carlo continued to keep his distance, fighting some strange demons, so Matteo felt it was only right that he stopped by and checked on Alessandra.

"Are you the man inquiring about Doctor Salvatore?" asked a woman with dark hair in a bun, sensible shoes, and hands tucked into the pockets of her crisp lab coat with a name tag that boasted Chief of Medicine.

"Yes."

"The nurse says you're an agent?"

"Yes." He handed over his identification.

The woman studied it for several minutes and after a deep sigh, she nodded and explained, "Doctor Salvatore has taken a leave of absence. I understand she left early this morning to go work with the Doctors Without Borders program for a few months."

"Oh. I didn't realize ..." Matteo was shocked.

"If you would like to leave a message, she has a service that she'll check occasionally while she's gone."

"No, no. I'm just a friend. It's okay." He put his ID away. "Thank you so much for your time."

As he walked away he ran a hand through his hair; how the hell was he going to tell Carlo this bit of information? Or should he tell him at all?

Chapter Forty

Carlo had a strange feeling of déjà vu as he walked off the plane and followed the signs through customs, finally arriving at the exit of the Los Angeles International Airport.

He didn't rush through the crowd of people like he had the last time he was here; acting like a lunatic, coming to California to do Alessandra's bidding and getting the ridiculous 'blessing' of her brother.

That time in his life seemed like a dream now. Two years ago he'd dreamt of a life with a self-assured, feisty, smart, sexy doctor. But that was the thing about dreams, easy to come up with, difficult to put into action.

He rolled his shoulders, then adjusted the garment bag that carried his suits, slipped on his sunglasses and once again began walking with his small carry-on pulled behind him as the sliding doors opened, welcoming him into the warm L.A. sunshine.

Damn if the familiarity of the smells and warmth, and the fact that he was now looking for the same asshole he'd been looking for then, didn't deepen his frown.

As if on cue, a loud whistle caught his attention, he turned toward the sound to find Parker Salvatore, said asshole, lounging against his car. Only now, because karma thought she was hilarious, Carlo was here for a Salvatore wedding, just not the one that would make his life complete.

Parker, wearing sunglasses, a fitted gray t-shirt, and jeans, looked as non-descript as the car. If Carlo didn't know better, he would have thought they were about to go on a stakeout.

"Eccolo." *Here he is,* Parker said, holding out his hand in greeting when Carlo reached the car.

"You finally ready to marry your wife?" Carlo asked.

"Thirteen years later? Maybe."

As Parker pulled into late afternoon traffic he said, "Alessandra and my parents arrived last night." As if he was trying to rip a band-aid off first thing.

"I didn't ask."

"I realize that."

"I also figured she'd show up to her brother's wedding."

"I didn't know how long it'd been since ..." Parker shrugged.

"She broke things off?" Carlo turned his attention out the window. "A little over ten months."

"I didn't know until I called her to tell her we'd set a date," Parker offered.

"She went to Kyrgyzstan to work with Doctors Without Borders," Carlo supplied.

Parker nodded. "Are you okay?"

"It's a nice day." Carlo grumbled.

"It is," Parker conceded, allowing the subject change.

Carlo glanced at the man he'd worked with so closely a few years ago. That Parker Salvatore had been rough around the edges and driven, exhausted and unkempt. Willing to go the distance for the job, but now, after being reunited in a very strange way with a girl he married as a joke when he was young and stupid, he was more at ease.

"Your desk job has made you soft," Carlo announced.

Parker laughed and nodded his head. "Probably."

"Was it worth it?" The question came out angrier than he'd meant.

"Was what worth it?"

"Waiting all those years to reconnect with Jessica."

Parker shrugged. "Yes. No. I know what I was missing now, but that's hindsight. I wouldn't have accomplished as much as I had in my career if I'd pursued her instead of my job when we first met." He glanced over at Carlo. "There's no easy answer. I think it played out the way it was supposed to."

Thirteen years in the making, Jessica and Parker's story was still developing, growing. In front of family and friends, they were tying the knot once again, but clearly not as a joke this time and probably a lot more sober than they'd been the first time around.

When Parker called and asked Carlo to be his best man, he politely turned down the offer. Mere seconds after he hung up, Jessica called. And since he respected the hell out of her and she still held a soft spot in his heart, he didn't have it in him to tell her no.

So here he was, angry and nervous.

Carlo hadn't expected the nerves. And if he were being honest with himself –which he hadn't been for months now– he would admit he was nervous about seeing the woman who still haunted his dreams and whom he hadn't had the balls to call when he found out she was in the hospital. Stabbed because of him.

Of course, that was also why he didn't want to face her brother. He was sure Alessandra hadn't told Parker of the incident, and he had no desire opening that can of worms either.

"Logistics," Parker interrupted Carlo's thoughts, "might as well cover those first."

This was good, maybe if Carlo treated this week as another job, he could easily navigate things.

"Tonight is the rehearsal dinner, close family and friends. A total of forty-three people will be in attendance."

"Forty-three people are close family and friends?"

"Don't get me started," Parker muttered then continued. "Tomorrow, at three, wedding; followed by pictures, reception, drinking and dancing. Pretty straight forward."

"Straight forward."

"Sunday, midmorning, hangover brunch for closer family and friends."

Carlo grunted.

"Jessica is excited to see you," Parker said.

At least there was one woman who would be happy to see him. "Hey, is her sister still dating Stills?"

Parker gave a gruff laugh. "Yup."

"Have they gotten married yet?"

"Engaged."

"So, there's still a chance there." It was a joke of course, but Carlo knew the relationship between Cassie and Stills had become irrevocably tied together after some incident in Colorado.

Parker changed lanes. "You going to be okay seeing my sister?"

"We're both adults, Salvatore. It's fine," Carlo stated.

"Okay, how's work?" Parker sighed, changing the subject.

"A mess."

"So, nothing new."

Carlo raised an eyebrow and growled. "I suppose not. Internal affairs got involved after we found a mole in the last operation. Almost a year's work imploded from the inside. After I was interrogated and cleared, I became part of a skeleton group trying to tape the whole mess back together."

"I've had a few operations like that."

"Everything's been at a standstill. I'm wading through paper while everyone gets their shit together."

"And you are not a man to patiently sit in an office," Parker joked, but all Carlo heard was the phantom words of Alessandra, *you'd be miserable if all you did was work behind a desk.*

"It's not so bad," he lied.

"Well, we're almost to Cassie's place. Are you sure you don't want to stay with me and Jess?"

"I don't want to intrude."

Thankfully, Cassie had understood the undercurrents of drama the wedding might bring up for Carlo and Alessandra, so she contacted Carlo on the sly and demanded he stay with her and Stills.

"My family is staying with the Dodds," Parker said. "I can let you know when Alessandra is about to arrive and give you the keys to the car so you can escape. We really wouldn't mind if you stayed with us."

"Salvatore." Carlo's voice didn't hold any room for argument.

Chapter Forty-One

"**Y**ou look like you're headed to a funeral." Cassie turned in her seat and glanced at Carlo who wore a gray suit and a frown. "I was serious when I said you didn't have to come to the rehearsal dinner if you didn't want to. I would have made an excuse for you. Jet lag. Food poisoning. Strip club ..."

A smile pulled at the corner of his mouth. "It's just dinner, I'll be fine."

Cassie glanced at Stills who winked at her and reiterated, "It's just dinner Dodd, he's fine."

Carlo fidgeted with his sleeves and shifted in his seat. He wanted to see Alessandra. But the part of him that was still standing at her door in Rome, note in hand, heart crumbling ... that part wanted to turn tail and run.

They arrived at the restaurant, but as they were headed across the parking lot, Carlo stopped. Cassie faced him, tilted her head to the side and sized him up. She brushed a stray speck of lint off his lapel, then squeezed his shoulder and nodded. "Take your time. You got this."

A slight smile broke through. "What is it about the Dodd sisters?"

"It's the challenge," Stills said.

Cassie rolled her eyes. "We'll see you in there." She took Stills' offered hand and Carlo watched as they fell into companionable sync.

He paced back to the car and caught a glimpse of his reflection in the window, tugged on his tie to pull it into perfect place, then muttered, "Che cazzo fai?" *What the fuck are you doing*? "Vai, idiota." *Go, you idiot.*

Jessica and Parker were standing near the entrance, greeting guests. When she saw Carlo, Jessica detached herself from Parker's side and happily threw herself into his arms.

"I'm so glad you're here."

This was why he came. For Jessica. The fact helped ease his tension and refocus.

As she dislodged herself, he kissed both of her cheeks in his preferred Italian greeting and offered, "You look beautiful."

She ran her hands down the lapels of his suit. "You don't look so bad yourself." She gave an approving nod of her head as she took in his tailored gray suit.

"You know, you're already married," Parker said.

"Really? No one's mentioned that at least once a day for the past two years," she muttered.

"Isn't this ceremony considered a vow renewal?" Carlo asked.

Jessica started, "We wanted to go back to Vegas and renew our vows in the same little White Chapel we got married in before–"

"But the moment Jess agreed to marry me–"

"*Again*," she said.

Parker smiled. "Well, our mothers got involved ..."

Carlo laughed, knowing full well that the culmination of this day was brought on by the love of two people, and a barrage of Catholic guilt from an Italian mother and the unstoppable, overbearing insistence of the other.

Jessica continued, "So now we're having the wedding our mothers always dreamed of, which feels like a modern day shotgun wedding."

"Shotgun wedding?" Carlo wasn't familiar with the term.

"In the old days, if a girl got pregnant, in a time when girls weren't supposed to get pregnant before they got married, when the girl's father found out, he offered the boy who'd done 'the deed' two choices: marriage, or the ripe end of a shotgun barrel."

A smile spread across Carlo's face. "Are you pregnant?"

Parker's attention whipped to Jessica as a bark of laughter rushed out of her. "I am *not* pregnant," she said assuredly.

Parker raised an eyebrow. "You sure?"

"Jesus, I'm sure."

Carlo winked at Jessica and moved on as a new group of arrivals took his place.

He eased his way into the restaurant's bar where everyone was gathering first and did what he'd always done in these situations; melted into the background, disappearing into the surroundings of the restaurant.

Alessandra entered with her parents twenty minutes later. Thanks to his vantage point, he could see her, but she couldn't see him. He hadn't seen her face yet, just her back.

And even that caused his whole body to react. He scanned her from top to bottom, hungry for the sight. His hands itched to slip around the black fabric of the wrap dress she was wearing and take ownership of her body. His mouth was dry from the need to taste her again. And at the core of it all, was a desperation to just sit with her; cuddled on a sofa, or across from her in her kitchen. To be in a conversation with her, enjoying her sense of humor and intellect; he even missed the fighting.

Damn, but she looked good tonight. He knew seeing her again would feel intense, but he never anticipated this. In an attempt to end his visceral reaction, he fisted his hands, as if he could cut it off; then she turned and he saw her face.

He took a step forward before he knew what he was doing, and it wasn't until he was halfway across the room he realized what he really wanted was to pick her up in his arms, leave this restaurant, and find the nearest bed.

Carlo was overwhelmed by his instinctual urges, but they didn't stop his stride. He wanted to be closer to her, to hear her voice, to touch her. Even if it was only for a moment.

She knew he was there, he'd watched her eyes search the crowd and when they found him, a frown furrowed her brow.

His stomach punched, what was she feeling?

He watched her excuse herself from her family, turn toward him and square her shoulders.

She didn't look mad. That was something. But she looked a little thinner, and, he thought, there was something missing in her eyes. She was worn out, more so than the last time he saw her, but she'd expertly covered it with makeup.

A thousand questions ran through his mind as his heart quickened with each step he took toward her

Maybe he should have taken Jessica and Parker up on their offer to stay with them, it might have been better to run into Alessandra earlier. Not now, with all these people around. All this family.

Maybe he could feign the need for privacy. That could get them closer to the front door. Closer to a taxi. Closer to a hotel room. He licked his lips and tried to dislodge the thought of how good that dress would look on the floor next to his suit.

"Ale ... Alessandra." He nodded the greeting.

"Carlo." The sterile way his name dripped off her lips cooled his nerves as well as his need.

She stuck out her hand before he could lean forward to brush a kiss on her cheek.

He shook the offered hand but she pulled away as quickly as he'd put his hand in hers, as if she'd been burned.

"You look nice," he said, hating the sterilized compliment.

"You as well," she returned.

Maybe there really wasn't anything left. Maybe it really had all been a dream.

"How was your plane ride?" she asked.

"Fine. Yours?"

"Very nice," she answered. "What airline did you fly?"

He tilted his head and wondered if she had practiced this nonsense before, knowing she was going to run into him. "Do you really want to know?"

"It was good seeing you, Carlo. If you'll excuse me. My parents need me. As you'll recall, they don't speak English." Again, she stuck out her hand.

She *had* practiced it. So maybe there was still something here.

Carlo accepted her hand; only, when she tried to pull away this time, he tightened his hold, and stepped closer to her, pulling her arm so that he had the leverage.

She frowned up at him as she tried to pull out of his grasp. "Let go," she hissed between her teeth.

"It was good seeing you Alessandra." He whispered her name, as if he were praying for forgiveness or for just one more moment with her.

He brushed a kiss on her cheek, lingering as he inhaled her scent. He didn't remember the name of the perfume she was partial to, but he remembered how she smelled when she wore it; flowers and spice.

"Have a good night," he said and then finally let go of her hand.

She turned on her heel and marched away from him as quickly as she could.

He sighed and muttered, "I'm sorry," to her retreating form.

Chapter Forty-Two

Alessandra wished the priest would pick up the pace. She tried to concentrate on what he was saying and the way her brother's eyes were misting over with tears, but all she could truly do was press the bouquet she was carrying against her chest as the top of her strapless dress attempted to creep down.

"Do you, Parker Salvatore, take this woman ..." The priest was methodical, making the most of the important vows. Normally, Alessandra would love the attention to detail. Now, she just wanted the man to hurry up.

She didn't even dare breathe deeply for fear that the expansion of her lungs followed by the deflation would encourage more slippage.

She dared a glance down at her chest.

Mamma mia!

The need to hoist the bodice of the ridiculous dress up or make the sign of the cross were currently tied in level of importance.

She gritted her teeth as she offered up a silent prayer that she didn't look too much like the prow of a ship. Or that it wasn't as distracting as she thought it was.

She attempted another slight adjustment using the heels of her hands, but the dress moved another agonizing fraction downward.

It's fine, no one is looking at you. It's all about the bride and groom.

She gripped the flowers tighter, pressed harder and willed everyone to keep their eyes glued on the happy couple. She casually glanced around to make sure everyone was following through with her telepathic instructions.

Her mother was clutching her father's arm, crying into a handkerchief– very Italian.

Barbara and Walter Dodd were beaming and wiping at their own tears. Smiling faces were radiating rapt attention and the priest was finally getting to the important stuff. "Jessica Dodd, do you take this man ..."

This was good. Almost done.

Then she went ahead and glanced at the one man she'd now spent the better part of twenty-four hours trying to avoid.

And his slight smile was not aimed at the couple, but at her.

That damn man aiming his passionate, strong, intent stare at her.

She frowned.

He winked.

Her stomach churned.

She looked away and tried to convince herself his fitted tux and sexy grin weren't sending a warming trend straight downward, causing her to press her thighs together and clutch the flowers tighter.

Jessica worried about the two being in the same room. Granted, Alessandra never told anyone until a few months ago they'd broken up, or that she'd run away and left him a note because he never showed up or called her when she was in the hospital. When she needed him the most.

She swallowed.

None of that.

She was over it all. This was fine.

She promised everyone it was all water under the bridge and she planned to spend the whole wedding weekend proving it.

Hell, last night hadn't she shook the man's hand and said hello? She didn't make a scene, he didn't make a scene. It wasn't weird for anyone.

She let her eyes dart once more.

Carlo, standing next to her brother, looked more like a bodyguard than a best man. But wasn't that what ancient best men were? Bodyguards?

And what a body it was.

She chided herself, her mouth forming a slight frown while a widening smile pulled at his lips.

She hoped the blush creeping up her cheeks wasn't evident and straightened her spine in response, which wasn't helpful; she felt another slip of the bodice. So what would a small blush matter when the top of her dress slipped down to reveal her cleavage?

"Ladies and Gentlemen, I am happy to introduce to you, for the second time," the priest joked as a chuckle ran through the audience, "Mr. and Mrs. Parker and Jessica Salvatore."

Finally!

The collection of family and friends stood and began to riotously clap and whistle. Parker took Jessica in his arms and bent her back slightly and affixed his lips to hers.

Alessandra added a whoop of congratulations, as clapping was not accessible at the moment.

"Get it, girl!" one of the other bridesmaids yelled. She'd forgotten these women's names, but genuinely liked all of Jessica's friends, who constantly talked over each other, but were also protective, opinionated and fiercely loyal.

And over the past few days, they'd seamlessly taken Alessandra under their collective wing. She turned toward the woman next to her. "My dress is about to fall down."

The information was quietly passed along and with pit stop precision, a barrier was made, flowers were taken away, and Alessandra was able to pull and wiggle the dress back into place. She felt a divine relief as another bridesmaid checked the back of the dress.

"Grazie," she sighed.

"I would have thought *those* would keep the dress up," the woman behind her commented. "The top two hooks aren't done. No wonder you were about to fall out." Then after a few quick ministrations and a pat on the back, she said, "That should help."

And it did.

The women repositioned in time for the procession that would follow the beaming couple.

On the front steps of the church, everyone congregated, visiting with swirling declarations of "What a beautiful wedding." "They were glowing." "Didn't the bride look gorgeous?"

Alessandra found her parents talking with friends of the Dodd family who spoke broken Italian.

"Mamma, Papà! Come state?" *How are you?* Alessandra asked.

"Bellissimo. Everything was so beautiful." Her mother smiled.

"Are we going to the reception now?" her father asked.

"Sì," Alessandra glanced at the street and the line of cars, "the car that brought us here will drive us to the reception."

Gianna nodded to where Carlo was standing among the bridal party. "Carlo looks handsome today."

"Gianna ..." Her father's voice gave the kind of warning that it wasn't time to talk about this.

"What? I'm just saying he looks nice. And he still looks at Aless with want in his eyes."

"Jesus, Mamma."

Gianna did a sign of the cross. "Aless, we're in front of a church."

Alessandra growled as her mother laughed then changed the subject. "I left my shawl in the church. Can you go get it, Aless?"

Alessandra found the shawl, but instead of rushing back, sat down and took a deep breath in the silence. She couldn't remember the last time she'd gone to church. She was raised Catholic and had gone through all the motions, but her sights had always been on science, things that could be proven or tested.

God was a turn of phrase in her life, not someone she spent much time thinking about.

Her eyes strayed to a statue of Mary, and she smiled. Now, the Mother Mary had evolved into something different as her medical career had developed. The idea of an intangible spirit of a saint she could carry on an internal dialogue with, had become a sort of meditation. More like a friend.

"You look beautiful." The deep voice seeped into her bones from just over her shoulder.

She closed her eyes and steadied herself. When she opened her eyes, the vibrant statue of Mary had lost the soft ethereal smile, and instead was winking a knowing smile.

Some friend.

She stood, turned her attention in Carlo's direction, and was only able to give a nod of greeting as he made his way up the aisle toward her.

"Ale." His voice was a whisper, but the want in the endearment weakened her legs as well as her resolve. She gripped the pew to hold her up.

"You do look beautiful," he repeated, standing at the end of the pew, and blocking her exit from this direction.

She was adult enough to admit he looked good, but that would be the end of it. "Anche tu." *You too*, she said, then took a breath so she could tell him goodbye. But in a flash, she was exhaling her shock into Carlo's mouth.

He moved so swiftly, all thoughts of leaving were abandoned as one hand crept into the hair at the base of her neck, curling it around his fingers. The other was making its way toward her posterior. She welcomed the familiarity, each cell easing into the memories she'd tried so desperately to forget for so many months now.

He growled, tilted his head and deepened the kiss. She pressed herself against him and pushed her hands through his thick hair as their bodies took over.

It was the priest clearing his throat that stopped them from losing themselves even more in the moment. A loud, obvious clearing of a throat echoed, and they pulled back from each other slightly.

Alessandra blinked as Carlo's clouded gaze focused. He still held her, and she still clung to him when the priest let out another dramatic noise that finally separated them.

"Excuse us, Father." Carlo recovered with a smile. "It was a beautiful ceremony. Will we see you at the reception?"

"Yes, as soon as I clear the church and change." He nodded toward them.

Alessandra used the excuse to push past Carlo and put space between them.

He followed her at a distance but when they arrived at the door that would lead them back to the steps, he stopped her, his hand on her shoulder.

She shrugged away but faced him.

"I'm sorry," he said.

She shook her head sadly and pursed her lips. "You know how this ends. It's always going to end the same way. We don't work."

"Alessandra."

"My parents are waiting." She pushed through the door, not wanting to hear anything else he might have to say.

Chapter Forty-Three

It took Jessica twenty minutes to dislodged herself from her wedding guests so she could go to the restroom.

Once she arrived, she stood in front of the stall, regretting that she told Cassie she didn't need help. She decided to start outside the stall, hoisting as much material around her waist as she could, then she stepped into the small space, slowly turning around so she could shuffle backwards, waiting for the back of her knees to hit the front of the toilet seat. Then she did the most unladylike squat until bare ass hit cold seat, and smiled in triumph.

She used the toe of her shoe to close the stall door and didn't care that it sagged open slightly.

The bathroom door slammed open then, followed by Italian cursing and a loud thump of something being thrown across the room.

"Alex?"

"Jessica?"

"Yeah. Is everything okay?"

More Italian was the answer.

Finished, Jessica somehow managed to wipe then decided she'd wait until she was out of the stall to pull up her undies.

"Alex, come open this door for me and help me out, please."

Alessandra was a doctor and her sister-in-law after all.

"What happened?" Alessandra asked as she opened the door.

"I thought I could do this alone. Thank God for automatic flush toilets, huh?" Jessica put herself back together, smoothed the front of her dress then held her hands out to the side. "Ta da," she sang.

Alessandra smiled. "I haven't had time to tell you, *sei bellissima.*" *You are beautiful.*

"Grazie." Jessica washed her hands, watching Alessandra out of the corner of her eye as she retrieved her purse from across the room.

"You wanna talk about it?"

"No," Alessandra answered firmly.

Jessica raised an eyebrow as Alessandra slapped the small clutch on the counter.

"Carlo?" Jessica made the assumption.

Alessandra frustratedly pushed her hair away from her face in reply.

Jessica sighed. "I knew it would be too weird."

"It's fine. Va tutto bene." *Everything is fine,* Alessandra bit with a wave of her hand, as if that could make it all better.

Jessica snorted and pointed to Alessandra. "That doesn't look like everything is fine."

"I don't want to talk about it." Alessandra jerked open her purse and pulled out her lipstick, hastily reapplied a coat and threw the tube back. "He kissed me." She pursed her lips.

"What? When?!" Jessica screamed, slapping Alessandra's arm, then righting herself. "Sorry, I didn't mean to scream."

"In the church, Mom forgot her shawl, so I went back to get it. He followed me."

"And what, he just ... kissed you?"

Alessandra pulled at the top of the dress. "I hate this dress."

"I didn't pick it out, I let the girls do it." She casually threw her bridesmaids under the bus. "What did he say? What did you say?" Jessica pinched her lips together with a finger, then leaned closer to Alessandra. "How was it?"

"He was there, said I looked nice, and then he just kissed me. But it didn't mean anything. Old habits. That's all it was."

Old habits.

Jessica fought to restrain her eyes from offering a dramatic roll. Carlo and Alessandra burned for each other, but they were also both pigheaded and made everything more difficult than it needed to be. They could figure their shit out, if only they'd each give in and bend a bit.

"What happened?" Jessica asked, more curious than concerned. "When we were all in Rome everything seemed fine."

Alessandra shrugged. "It was all new then. There was passion, a lot of it. But in the end, the passion burned everything down." She cleared her throat. "Some people are lucky, they find that after the fire burns, they're left with a foundation. All we found was ash."

Jessica watched Alessandra for a few moments before she shook her head and bit out, "Bullshit."

Alessandra's eyes widened. "What?"

"I said, bullshit. You two didn't find ash. You're too scared of the fire. You haven't even gotten that far yet."

Jessica could hear the phantom voice of Parker in her head, telling her to leave it alone, that his sister's relationship was none of their business. She grinned, when had she ever listened to Parker?

"We fought all the time," Alessandra countered.

"Because you're both pigheaded. That's just temperament. Have you *seen* how he *still* looks at you?"

"Lascialo." *Leave it*, Alessandra warned.

"Alessandra, I know you. You have the same faults as your brother. You and Parker are so sure you were put on this earth to *save* everyone. The only problem is, when you think that way, you don't leave much room for someone to be there for you."

"I don't need to be saved."

"I didn't say you needed to be saved. I'm saying that you're so busy trying to save the world, that when true love comes and slaps you in the face, you can't see it."

Alessandra crossed her arms over her chest. "He wasn't willing to change for me and I wasn't willing to change for him."

"Stai zitta!" *Shut up*, Jessica said frustrated.

"Scusa?" Alessandra narrowed her gaze on the Italian insult.

Jessica elongated the words for impact. "Ho detto, stai zitta, Alessandra." *I said shut up*.

"Aspetta, parli italiano?" *Wait, you speak Italian?*

Jessica sighed and continued, slowly, in Italian. "I've been taking lessons for two years. But that's not important. I'm trying to talk to you about the man you love and how angry you two are making me."

Alessandra grinned. "Why didn't you tell anyone?"

"Because ..." she couldn't hold back a smile, "you'll see. I wanted to surprise Parker and your family when the toasts start."

"It *is* a surprise." Alessandra pulled Jessica into a hug. "A big surprise."

Jessica switched back to English. "I'm glad you think so. But stop hugging me, I'm trying to lecture you," Jessica muttered into Alessandra's hair.

"Your guests will miss you." Alessandra changed the subject as she pulled away and touched Jessica's cheek.

Jessica laughingly pushed the hand away. "Don't change the subject. And it's my wedding day, I was told I get whatever I want today."

"I don't want to talk about Carlo."

"Then why did you tell me he kissed you?" Jessica argued.

Alessandra threw up her hands. "I had to tell someone."

"Then it *does* mean something!" Jessica yelled.

"I don't want to talk about it!" Alessandra matched her tone.

A gaggle of cousins entered the bathroom along with Jessica's sister, Cassie. The group swarmed Jessica and began a barrage of compliments and questions. Jessica tried to keep her focus on Alessandra calling, "This isn't over!"

But Alessandra gave a cheeky wave, knowing it was.

Jessica watched a quick interaction between Alessandra and Cassie that left a confused look on her sister's face. When Cassie was close enough, Jessica asked, "What did she say to you?"

Cassie shrugged. "She thanked me for the self-defense lessons; said they made a difference."

Jessica's interest was now truly peaked.

Chapter Forty-Four

"We have never danced together." The voice came from behind her, from one of the unoccupied tables that were set up between the reception area and the entrance for people who wanted to talk without having to compete with the music once it started.

She slowed her steps, not sure what to do. She hadn't anticipated the visceral reaction she was having to him this weekend. He could still make her blood heat with just a word.

She should keep walking. It would be easier to walk away from him again if she didn't talk to him.

But Alessandra was apparently a glutton for punishment. She took a deep breath to settle her nerves, pulled her shoulder blades together, clasped her hands in front of her, pressing her clutch to her abdomen then turned her full attention to him. "What do you want, Carlo?"

She thought she had steeled herself, but it didn't work. It never worked.

"You." The deep tremble of his voice vibrated under all the noise spilling out of the reception, and slipped into her ribcage.

"It's not that simple."

"It used to be."

He didn't move, staying several feet away, slouched against one of the tall tables that had been set up. He'd removed his tuxedo jacket, and seeing the fabric of his white shirt pulled against the muscles in his shoulders, caused a twirl of traitorous heat between her legs.

The group from the restroom came whirling back into the hallway with the bride in tow. Jessica headed for Alessandra. Maybe she could use Jessica as her excuse to leave. But he was tempting her, his muscles strained, ready to pounce if needed. And Alessandra was stupid enough to stand for the sweet torture.

Jessica narrowed her gaze and followed Alessandra's gaze to see what she was so intently looking at, "Oh, I see ..." the humor in Jessica's voice was apparent, and she didn't give Alessandra a chance to use her as an escape, quickly changing route and walking away from them both.

"Would you dance with me?" Carlo asked.

Alessandra should have gone with Jessica. "I can't."

"Sì, puoi." *Yes, you can.*

No, she *definitely* couldn't.

If she felt his warm hands on her naked skin (which there was plenty of because of this stupid dress) her resolve wouldn't stand a chance.

"One dance," he urged.

Alessandra gave an almost undetectable shake of her head, and took a step away, finally breaking the tension.

Carlo didn't move but continued to wear her down, pinning her in place as his eyes drank her in and his deep voice joined in the temptation. "Alessandra. It's a wedding. One dance. To celebrate your brother and Jessica."

It was never just *one* of anything. One kiss, one dinner, one more try ... they'd all lead to the same outcome.

"No."

"I promise—"

"Carlo, please don't make another promise you can't keep."

He clenched his jaw. "You're my siren. I can't help it."

She huffed, "Siren," waving the compliment way. It was enough to break the spell.

She turned, making her way into the large hall, but Carlo was at her side, taking advantage of their proximity by slipping his arm around her shoulder. His warm hand purposefully grazed as much of her skin as it could, leaving a heated trail.

The DJ was conspiring against Alessandra as well; as if he had been looking for her to enter the room, he began to play Frank Sinatra. (Part of her parent's request for the wedding was for the DJ to play songs that encouraged people to glide across the dance floor in each other's arms.)

She tried to stop their progress to the edge of the dimly lit floor, but Carlo ushered her forward. When they arrived and he held out his hand, she had a decision to make. She could stay or walk away. She decided to lean into the ridiculously flimsy excuse that she didn't want to make a scene.

She put her hand in his, allowed him to drape her left hand on his shoulder, and held her right hand aloft, then had the audacity to smile.

"One dance," Alessandra negotiated her terms, "then you leave. Go to the other side of the room and stay there."

Carlo leaned forward and brushed a kiss against her cheek, she tried to pull her hand out of his grasp, but he tightened his grip. "Whatever you want."

As he waited for a space among the surprising number of couples traveling across the floor in a foxtrot, Alessandra's stomach twirled excitedly at the feel of his body pressed against hers once more, taking up the empty space.

But it was the space he took up that caused the biggest problems. He was always in the way. In the way of her thoughts, in the way of her life, in the way.

He moved then, beginning the simple steps; one, two, three, four; one, two, three, four; expertly leading her around the floor.

They fit so well. Always had. From that first moment he pulled her to him and kissed her, they fit. Though it seemed like they shouldn't; with his bulging muscles, strong spine, and height; compared to Alessandra's short stature, abundant chest, small waist and curvy hips that her mother liked to sigh was the 'perfect body for babies.'

The rest of the 'fit'– emotionally, career wise, the need to always be right was akin to forcing a square peg in a round hole.

As they drifted across the dance floor and Sinatra crooned about the way they looked tonight, all those problems slipped away. They were a centrifuge of movement, allowing the residue of their past to stick to the edges, as the center of their momentum was clarified and it was just the two of them. Basking in the heat and light of each other, the rest of the world tilted and slid off of both of them. The soft lighting soothed, the music baptized, and the feel of him so close made her feel whole.

She was just a woman being held by the one man in the world who had ever made her feel whole. Made her feel safe. Made her feel sexy. And made her feel like she was home.

A man who couldn't compromise for her.

She tripped at the thought and was finally free of his embrace.

"Alessandra?" Carlo reached for her.

She gave a sad shake of her head and backed away. "I danced with you. We're done here," she muttered and when she was a safe distance away from him, turned and tried to make her way out of the reception hall as quickly as she could without drawing attention to herself.

What was she thinking? She ended the relationship once, and it was the hardest thing she'd ever done.

Jessica was wrong, Alessandra knew what was left after they burned each other up. Consequences.

She'd made it to the door of the reception hall when the first tear fell.

Chapter Forty-Five

"Moretti. Where are you?"

Carlo blinked several times as the voice penetrated, bringing his field of vision back into focus; the focus being a warehouse spied through the scope of his gun from the vantage point of a nearby rooftop. He growled his answer. "Same place I've been for the past four hours." *Back at work. Back in Rome. And back to being a robot.*

"I've called you five times," stated ALPHA Leader, the voice on the other end of his earpiece.

"There must have been some interference." He wasn't about to admit that he'd been lost in a memory of an apartment in Rome, surrounded by the smell of home-cooked food and the tantalizing perfume of a woman. Or that he was losing his breath as he thought of how it felt to run his hand along her warm, naked skin. Or what it was like in the early morning hours to study the subtle highlighted auburn in a mass of dark brown, curly hair that lay provocatively on a pillow. Not to mention the feeling of being lost in a tangle of arms and legs and passion that could energize and fuel him, and scare the shit out of him at the same time.

"Wonder what kind of interference," Matteo's unmistakable voice on the other end joked. "Maybe the brunette variety?"

"Moretti's a machine," another voice chimed in, "he doesn't get hard for that kind of interference, what gets him going is a volatile operation."

Carlo laughed with the ribbing. "And this one isn't doing much for my libido."

He stretched his head from side to side and gave a quick shake; whether he wanted to admit it or not, it was an attempt to put some space between himself and the visions of Alessandra that danced before him. It had been three months since the wedding, and he needed to find a way to put her behind him.

"He's not all machine. Are you Moretti? I heard a rumor about how he loved Rome like a teenager in heat." Another agent said.

"What happened?" someone asked.

"No one knows, and Moretti ain't talking."

"Well, since we're back in Rome, maybe someone should see if they could shake some information out of him."

Carlo grunted in reply and fixed his position again as a few raindrops began to fall. He adjusted the hat he wore so it didn't interfere with his sight.

Carlo was helping keep an eye on the warehouse where rumor of a meeting between the long absent Il Serpente and some interested investors was to take place. Since it had been such a long time since the notorious drug runner and his people had gone to ground, no one knew what to make of this evening's meeting.

"Do you miss your suits, Moretti?" Matteo changed the direction of the taunting Carlo was receiving. "Or do you like not having such a high dry-cleaning bill and slumming it with us in your street clothes?"

As the sounds of respective laughs and curses erupted, Carlo replied, "You know, I used to wonder what took the intel team so long on the ground, and now I think it's all the chatter that keeps you from doing your jobs properly."

"Radio silence," ALPHA called when headlights were seen from a car pulling into the abandoned lot that butted up to an entrance being guarded by two armed men.

Carlo's attention was brought back with pinpoint focus.

Months ago, after Il Serpente's trail went cold, there'd been several lucky arrests by local law enforcement. Upon interrogation of these low-level criminals, the same confusing information was given. No one actually knew where Il Serpente was or why his supply chain was crumbling.

With not even a whisper of the drug smuggler's whereabouts, several agents were reassigned and Carlo was granted leave for Parker and Jessica's wedding.

Finally, a few weeks ago, an informant relayed the time and place of this meeting.

A second set of headlights pulled into the lot, followed by a third, fourth and then a fifth.

Carlo looked through the sight of his gun as various men exited the cars. They were all known players in the drug game, no strangers here. But this was a lot more men than intel suggested, and so far, not one sign of the goddamn snake.

"Where is he?" one of the voices asked frustratedly.

"Something's wrong," Carlo muttered.

Whatever they'd been told had been a lie, but something *was* going on tonight and whatever it was, was bigger than what they'd been briefed.

"Orders?" another voice asked.

"Intel," ALPHA answered.

Everyone on the coms confirmed their acquiescence. The bugs that had been placed inside the building began to transmit. Carlo shifted, readying himself for a boring evening until the first round of gunfire erupted.

Two vans flew into the parking lot, doors open, firing on the guards who stood watch in front.

Two giant garage doors opened and in the shock of headlights, Carlo watched as men took cover and muscle men opened fire.

"Orders?" someone asked.

"Let 'em kill each other," Matteo muttered.

"Hold your positions."

Carlo watched the chaos. It was the kind of thing that happened when an entire hierarchy was falling apart.

"Fall back to checkpoint Delta," came the order. "Now."

Carlo began to systematically shimmy his way out of his current position. The rain had begun to increase, and was joined by a flash of lightning and thunder. He slowly made his way down the stairwell and around the corner, heading quickly and quietly back to Delta location.

What he hadn't counted on were the men waiting for him when he opened the door of the building. He reacted instinctively as flashes of lightning and gunshots lit up the darkened corner he was on and voices erupted in his ear– "Delta has been compromised," and several "Taking fire," joined with "They know where we are."

Chapter Forty-Six

Alessandra's attention was interrupted by a crack of thunder. She looked out the window just as another flash of lightning illuminated the rooftops of Rome beyond her balcony. The rain was in a frenzy to escape the violent whipping of the wind, which only led to a strange wicked dance between raindrops as they twirled to the booming sound, and took turns posing dramatically during flashes of light.

Alessandra returned to her book when the buzzer for her apartment began to scream impatiently. She frowned and glanced at the clock, it was well after midnight. Not a time for visitors and not the kind of weather anyone should be out in.

And with the kinds of visitors she'd had at these odd hours the past few years, her stomach churned with worry.

A second screaming buzz and she set aside the book, shuffled in her stocking feet to the intercom and pushed the button to answer: "Pronto?" *Hello?*

She waited for an answer, but just heard the rain and another crack of thunder. Maybe it was a prank, some teenage kids. Though, she thought she heard breathing, and was about to hang up when the impatient visitor at the front of her building gruffly replied, "Sono io." *It's me.*

The floor fell away and she gripped the receiver held against her ear until her knuckles turned white. She hadn't seen him since the wedding. After she walked away from him on the dance floor, she'd made sure to keep her distance for the rest of the trip.

"Per favore." *Please*, the voice weakly muttered.

She pointed a finger at the button that would open the door, hovering over it. Her emotions raged as wildly as the storm outside. She shouldn't answer. It had been too long and what the hell was he doing here anyway?

"Alessandra, please ..." his deep voice repeated.

Her finger pushed the button then she hung up and let her forehead fall against the phone as she tried to take a deep breath, steeling herself against her midnight visitor.

She unlocked her door, opened it a crack and listened to the echo of the elevator humming its way up. Unable to stand still, she paced several laps back and forth in the small hallway until she heard the arrival of the elevator, followed by the parting doors and shuffle of feet.

She glanced at her reflection in the mirror by the front door, ran a hand through her hair, nodding, as she straightened her shoulders, all while slow footsteps drew near.

When she was sure he was close enough, she swung the door all the way open and angrily shoved her balled fists against hips. "What the hell are you doing here?"

"I didn't know where else to go." He gave an exhausted, lopsided smile.

She took a deep breath to fill her lungs so she could properly admonish him, when she noticed that something wasn't quite right. All the years of medical practice kicked in and her anger left, replaced with a frown as she began to take in his entire form.

"Carlo? What happened?"

"I've been shot."

She narrowed her gaze on his face, saw a grimace firmly in place, and watched him pale as they stood there. He was dripping from the rain, and his tired arms hung by his sides, the sleeves covered with blood. His belt had been used as a tourniquet on his upper thigh and the dripping water gathering around his feet was taking on a pink hue.

"Jesu! In. Now." She stood aside so he could pass her. "To the guest room."

"I know you want me, but do you really think this is the time?" The words fizzled out with a hiss of pain as he finished.

"Bastardo," she mumbled.

She retrieved her medical bag and found him standing in the middle of the room, trying to shrug out of his shirt, his face contorted in pain.

She waved his hands away, quickly put on a pair of gloves then pulled out her trauma scissors, deftly cutting his shirt off. His chest and stomach were fine, but there were, what she could only describe as defensive cut wounds on the outside of his arms. (Again.)

She ripped open large sheets of sterile gauze, applied them, hastily taping them into place, anxious to attend to the reason he'd applied a tourniquet.

She once again grabbed the scissors, knelt in front of him and cut the pants away until she could study the wound on his thigh. "Luckily, it went through and looks like it penetrated the fleshy part." She gently prodded the area. "When?"

"Hour and a half, maybe two," he answered.

"I didn't even know you were in Rome," she said as she pulled the bedspread off the bed and began to help position him on his side so she could clean and suture the wound.

"I'm not here." He grimaced in his discomfort.

"Of course you're not here. Even if you were 'here' ..." She cleared her throat. Even if he was here she wouldn't have known about it. Which was normal, and nothing to get upset about. They weren't together anymore.

"I can go." He tried to sit up.

Alessandra pushed him back onto the bed; he needed help first, once he was stitched up then she could yell at him. She studied the wound. "Don't be ridiculous, you big ox."

"I thought you liked how big I was."

She might have pushed a little harder around the area of the bullet wound, causing Carlo to suck in a deep breath against the pain. She began to pull out several items from her bag.

"How much blood do you think you lost?" she asked.

"Enough that I'm dizzy."

"Damn you." She pulled out the blood pressure cuff and stethoscope, quickly applied both and began to pump it up. "What's your normal bp?"

He gave her the numbers and she nodded, listening. After a moment she let out the breath she was holding. "Your blood pressure hasn't dropped."

"Is that good?"

"It means you haven't lost enough blood to go into hemorrhagic shock."

"Oh good."

"It means you aren't going to die from blood loss and not seeking medical attention at a hospital. Which there are plenty of in Rome, you know."

"Can't go to a hospital."

"Of course you can't go to the hospital," she murmured, helping him adjust his leg so she could properly clean and treat the wound.

He laid back and sighed. "I think we still have someone who's infiltrated our agency."

"Still?"

"Thought we had the right guy, now I don't know. Everything went to hell tonight. When I left the area I'd been posted in, they were waiting for me. They were waiting for all of us. This whole operation is fucked up." He yawned.

"So help me, Carlo. If you showing up means I'm going to have to spend even more time with another shadowy babysitter …"

"It won't."

She grunted. "Roll over." She worked on the exit wound and when she was finished, she sat on the bed, took his right arm, uncovered the gauze and nodded. "It's good, the blood clotted." She began to clean the wounds. "A few deep ones, they'll have to be sutured. Lucky for you, last time you showed up with similar wounds and a stabbed patient, I replaced the liquid stitches."

"Amore …" His deep voice vibrated with exhaustion.

She shot him a frown at the endearment.

"You look good, amore."

"You look awful, Carlo."

He smiled and yawned again. "I don't know why I'm yawning."

"The adrenaline is wearing off." She took his other arm and repeated the removal of the gauze. There was just one long slash, superficial. "You'll live."

He closed his eyes and muttered, "Without you, it's not much of a life."

Chapter Forty-Seven

Carlo grunted as he rearranged himself. He was sore all over, he felt like he'd been in a knife fight and shot.

The chair on the balcony wasn't very comfortable, but he couldn't spend another moment inside the apartment that haunted him.

He'd finally gotten a call through to Matteo from a burner phone he made Alessandra keep on hand in case of emergencies. Matteo had escaped unscathed and returned to the Rome office; which was in an understandable frenzied state.

Turns out the original seller of agency information, the officer who had been killed for his greed, had a partner.

"Jesus, are we sure that's all of them?" Carlo asked.

"Well, chances are we're going to be spending the next few months repeating another internal investigation and hanging out in the office," Matteo muttered angrily.

"I'll get back to the office as soon as I can," Carlo promised.

He winced at the pain as he adjusted himself once again. Taking a deep breath he closed his eyes as the sun, peeking out from behind the clouds, warmed his face. From below the sound of the traffic swirled up the five stories to take flight on the wind.

The balcony, encircled by intricate wrought iron bars, had room for a large table, several planters and a large awning that he hadn't bothered to open. Bright maroon bougainvillea grew wildly where the wrought iron met the wall of the building, with planters completing the scene with yellow, purple and white flowers. Somewhere church bells began to clang the noon hour.

Rome.

He hadn't always been a fan. The city was too crowded; too busy. But he'd come to appreciate it, or rather, he'd come to appreciate the treasures Rome held. Notably, a treasure with soft curly brown hair and hazel eyes.

Jesus. He rubbed his face with his hands and tried to focus on the view.

As far as views went, it was pretty good. Aged terracotta roofs created a jagged puzzle. Slanted rooftops met yellowed flat tops. The drifting rain clouds obstructed the mountains that could be seen on a clear day beyond the city. But the storm from the night before had left a sheen on the rust color city.

There had been several sunsets seen from this balcony when the mountains were a postcard perfect background of the Eternal City. Not to mention the candlelit dinners; but he knew better than to reminisce about how those ended– with moaning and writhing.

Goddammit.

He shifted in the seat, adjusting himself and gave a brusque laugh. He was in too much pain to try and ignite more moaning and writhing. Alessandra didn't want him here. But if he really wanted to, he could put on the radio, convince her to sit next to him, hold her against his good side, and watch as the next storm washed over the city.

Maybe he should just go. He should be grateful she hadn't thrown out the few extra clothes he'd left behind; grateful she'd answered the door and patched him up.

He should just offer her a 'thank you' and a 'sorry' and go.

Only, he didn't *want* to go.

Music from a neighbor's open window rose into the air and he gritted his teeth.

Rome was almost as much a problem as the woman.

The damn city conspired against him, threatened his life one day, then tempted him with romantic ideas the next; produced the woman of his dreams, then denied him the ability to figure out how to be with her.

Rome.

Where the ancients met with tourists. Where technology intertwined itself with a heady bowl of pasta.

Rome.

Where women wore fashionable heels and clicked down roads that had long ago been smoothed by the sandaled feet of emperors, laborers and gladiators.

Rome.

Where no matter what Carlo tried, the intense system of roads built in antiquity, inevitably led him back to Alessandra.

He gave a grunt of laughter, what the hell was happening to him?

"Cosa stai pensando?" *What are you thinking?* Alessandra asked from the door to the balcony.

He shook his head free of the fanciful ideas. "Non importa." *It doesn't matter.* He made the mistake of glancing at her over his shoulder.

She was wearing the worn bathrobe that hid her figure; a bathrobe that was too easy to slip off her shoulders. How many times had he pulled her to him by the loose belt and unwrapped her like a damned gift?

She cinched the fabric belt tighter, and he allowed his gaze to move to her face. Another mistake. As much as coming here was. Her hair was a disheveled mess; and he was jealous the wild morning curls weren't his fault.

"Caffè?" she asked, bringing his attention to her eyes; bloodshot with dark circles. Now *that* was his fault.

"If my doctor thinks it's okay."

"You have a gunshot wound and a few abrasions on your arms. I can't imagine coffee is going to do too much more damage." She went to the kitchen.

He shifted, winced and stared once more out over the terracotta rooftop sea of Rome. The color was reminiscent of the hills in the fall where he grew up. He regretted not taking her. He should have taken her when the harvested land and the rolling hills was a reflection of this vision.

"Jesu," he hissed, stretching his neck and face up to the sky. He needed to ask Alessandra what drugs she'd given him. Or perhaps it was being shot again that was making him feel so nostalgic. No, not nostalgic; human maybe. Mortal. After all, he supposed a man could only get shot at for so long before he started to wonder what would happen if he didn't constantly put himself in danger.

When he returned to work he was going to be forced to take some paid time off to convalesce. That's when he would sift through these thoughts, not now. Not so close to her.

"Ecco qui." *Here you go.* Alessandra handed a cup and saucer to Carlo.

He nodded his thanks and glanced up into her eyes. He'd had forced time off before where he thought he would die of boredom, but this time, caught up with thoughts and memories of Alessandra, was going to be a nightmare.

"It's a beautiful day," he muttered then took a sip of the coffee, returning his gaze to the rooftops.

"How did you get shot?" she asked instead of agreeing with him.

He shrugged, "Can't a man show up with a gunshot wound and get patched up without being questioned?"

"Carlo," she said sternly, taking his wrist so she could take his pulse.

Her soft touch mixed with his name dripping from her lips would be his undoing.

"What did you give me?" he asked to distract his thoughts.

"Pain reliever."

"Good pain reliever," he muttered.

She ignored him as she finished taking his pulse, then she held up her finger. "Follow it with your eyes, not your head."

He did as instructed but held his breath when she leaned closer to study the dilation of his pupils; even though it was the concentration of a doctor in place, it was his Alessandra. The woman he loved.

Shit.

"Do you feel nauseous?" She frowned.

He shook his head, no.

"Are you feeling like you can't catch your breath or as if your heart is beating erratically?"

"Sì," he whispered.

She frowned and began to take his pulse again. "Really? What does it feel like?"

He didn't dare answer that question. Instead, he turned his hand and entwined his fingers in hers, bringing her hand slowly to his lips so he could brush a kiss across her knuckles.

"How did you get shot?" she asked again.

"I wasn't fast enough shooting the other guy."

She frowned.

"There was a team of six in various locations watching a meeting of major drug dealers. Things went wrong. The rendezvous was compromised, I needed medical attention and couldn't go to the hospital."

"So here you are."

"Here I am."

She pulled her hand away and took a step back.

He shifted his weight. "But you said I'll live."

"It was a clean wound. Best possible outcome. And you're healthy, so it will heal quickly. Of course, I suggest an x-ray as soon as you can. Just to be on the safe side."

"Well, it isn't the first time I've been shot and it probably won't be the last." He attempted a joke, it didn't work.

"Sorry." He shrugged. "I thought we could go one visit without ... well, without."

"Then you shouldn't have come here. Don't your people have someone you could have gone to for this? Or did you think it would be fun, while you were closing some new wounds, to open up some old ones?"

"Alessandra."

"If you hadn't been shot I never would have known you were in town." She raised an eyebrow, was she right?

"No, you wouldn't have," he agreed tiredly. "You were the one who made it perfectly clear how you feel about me." He scrubbed his face in his hands. "Please Alessandra, I don't want to fight."

"Then you shouldn't have shown up at an ex-girlfriend's doorstep in the middle of the night," she said in exasperation.

"Ex-fiancé."

Alessandra raised an eyebrow and crossed her arms over her chest.

"You said ex-girlfriend. Whatever we were went way beyond the boyfriend-girlfriend dynamic. We were engaged once, so the proper word would be ex-fiancé."

"You want to get into this now, Carlo?"

"No, I don't."

"Then don't."

"I'm hurting," he said.

She gestured to him. "I realize that."

"That's not what I'm talking about. I'm hurt by the way you left."

She huffed a laugh. "You're hurt? I was in the hospital Carlo, where the hell were you?" She shook her head and walked away. "I'm not doing this."

He grunted as he stood up and followed her. "It was work."

"It was *always* work, Carlo. It always *is* work." She pointed to his thigh.

He caught a glimpse of what he had put her through. Had he ever truly realized what he'd done to her?

He didn't mean to open old wounds, but he'd done it now, and maybe that was what they needed. To open them, clean them out and put them to rest.

"Why didn't you tell me to my face? Why leave me a letter taped to your door and run away to Kyrgyzstan?"

Alessandra went still. "You know what bothers me? The fact that you can find out where I went, but you couldn't figure out how to pick up a phone and ask if I was okay."

"We had a spy, we didn't know how deep–"

"Rest for a few more hours and take the pain pills I left on the kitchen counter."

"Ale–"

"The pills will get you through the next twelve hours. I'm leaving for work in fifteen minutes for a long shift, so you're welcome to stay here for the rest of the day." She turned her back on him and slammed the door of the bathroom.

He muttered a curse at himself under his breath. Was his ego so bruised that he couldn't apologize and work like hell to find another way to win her over?

The idea dazed him and he sat back down in the patio chair. He had a lot to think about.

Chapter Forty-Eight

A s full clouds rolled across the sky, brushes of deep blue dusk winked. The rain had cleaned the air and the streets, and the inviting cool evening air and promise of the coming fall months bid Alessandra to walk.

Even after her long shift, her body longed to shake off the day. Shake off the past twenty-four hours. And shake off Carlo. Again.

Her time would be better spent contemplating statues sculpted by great men that had stood the test of time rather than standing in her apartment where his memories had been released. Again.

She headed toward her favorite coffee shop. Not caring that she'd taken Carlo there several times, it was hers before they began seeing each other, and it would be hers again.

Again.

That damn word.

That damn man.

The last bit of sunlight disappeared, and strategically placed spotlights illuminated ancient buildings and ruins, painting Rome in a contemplative glow; of course, she was projecting. Most people claimed the city was romantic when it glowed like this.

"Romance is the last thing you need." She made the personal observation just as she passed a young man, late twenties maybe, who, overhearing her winked and offered, "That's too bad, bella."

The ridiculousness made her laugh, she waved him off with. "Buonasera." *Have a good evening.*

See, there was life outside of Carlo Moretti.

First things first, she was definitely going to rip out her intercom system and change her phone number.

She *should* have told him to go away. She didn't know he was hurt. And he was resourceful enough to find someone else to help him.

She pulled the light sweater she wore more securely around her, wishing the shiver that ran through her was from an invisible breeze, not the memory of Carlo.

When she saw him, standing once again in her doorway, regardless of his soaked and exhausted state, every damn cell in her body charged. The hair on her arms stood, her legs threatened to give out and her hands ached to touch him.

He still affected her. He'd done the same at the wedding, leaving her to spend the past three months reminding herself that her attraction was just a chemical reaction; her body experiencing high levels of dopamine and the hormone norepinephrine being released when he was around. It was a chemical high. She counterbalanced the feeling with memories of how he never showed up for her when she needed him the most.

The walking helped more than she thought. It cleared the confusion Carlo had brought when he showed up. Alessandra turned the corner and smiled as the road emptied out onto a piazza that held the Pantheon. It was like seeing an old friend.

Alessandra sat on the shallow steps built around the fountain that stood opposite the monument and tilted her head as she contemplated the way the amber lighting accented the ancient stones.

Near her, two American women excitedly pointed out architectural elements and reminded each other of the history in hushed tones, as if to not offend the gods.

She watched couples and families walk the piazza. She listened as music from surrounding restaurants fought and twirled into gibberish in the early evening. It was a wayward whiff of coffee that moved her to continue to her café.

It glowed neon and inviting. There were ten tables outside, surrounded by several large planters, strategically placed, that held tall palms and lemon trees. Vines of ivy planted in boxes on either side of the doorway, crawled up the walls, framing the entrance.

At the counter, she was greeted by the barista.

"Un caffè corretto, per favore." She requested an espresso with a shot of liquor in it.

The barista asked her preference of alcohol, she chose Sambuca– the anise flavor seemed apropos for this evening.

"So, you truly weren't planning on saying goodbye," the voice rasped in her ear.

While she outwardly remained calm, every atom she was made of condensed and expanded violently.

"The same, please." Carlo added his order.

Alessandra watched the barista pull the shot of espresso. The clink of the spoon, as it was placed on the saucer, followed by the clunk of the cup sounded like it was coming from inside a tin can.

She was frozen, unable to decide what to do or say, so she continued to stare intently at the counter, trying desperately to not use the hanging mirror behind the barista to glance at Carlo and make eye contact.

"I'm sorry." He stepped away from her as the coffees were placed on the bar. "If you don't mind, could we sit together? One last coffee together and I'll leave."

Alessandra gave a miniscule nod, picked up her coffee and headed outside to the farthest table so they could have some privacy. Although, truth was, she probably should have sat closer to the noise. She should have stayed standing at the bar, drank her coffee and left without a word. The way she left her apartment.

Instead, she swallowed the shock of seeing him, and their history, then applied her doctor voice inquiring, "How are you feeling?" She steadied herself as she finally allowed her eyes to take all of him in.

"Better," he answered.

"You should have a doctor check those wounds as soon as you can."

He opened his mouth and began to say something, thought better of it and instead agreed. "I will."

She took a sip and tried to look anywhere but at him.

The list of things she 'should' have done when it came to this man continued to grow. And saying goodbye was just prolonging more heartache. Everything about Carlo had been too difficult.

He cleared his voice. "Thank you. For helping me."

"How did you find me?" she asked.

"Can't you even look at me?"

She allowed her gaze to settle on his face. The same black rings, a dull sheen to his eyes. He was exhausted. But so was she; that was nothing new. He had a touch of jaundice, and she squinted, tilting her head, wondering if it was truly jaundice or the neon lighting. "You look jaundiced. I would ask the doctor you see to look into that as well."

"This is your favorite place," he stated. "Actually, this walk was your favorite. I figured if you didn't want to see me again, instead of going home after work, you'd come this way."

She raised an eyebrow.

He rolled his half empty cup between his hands. "I know I'm intruding. But I couldn't let it end like that."

"Let what end?" She gestured between them. "There's nothing here."

"I wanted to respect your wishes," he shrugged, "but I also wanted to see you one more time. I got to the piazza in front of the Pantheon this afternoon and just thought I'd wait. Then when I saw you ..."

"You followed me?"

"I followed you," he said dryly.

She grunted in reply and he continued, "I don't know what to say Ale ..." She shook her head at the endearment. "I just couldn't leave it like this." His voice faded on the feeble explanation.

She sat back and licked her lips. "We've said everything there is to say. We dated. We were engaged," she waved a hand at the past, "now, we're exes Carlo. It happens. Plenty of people have felt a kindred pull to another person, and then broke up." She gave him a sad smile, repeating quietly, "It happens."

He nodded as her words washed over him. After another sip he tilted his head and softly asked, "I wasn't crazy, was I? We did love each other, didn't we?"

Alessandra studied the contents of her cup. What the hell was she supposed to say to that? After a moment she finally said, "I need to get going."

"Thank you." His voice was thick with emotion. "For everything."

She glanced up then, bit the inside of her mouth as she tried to remind herself of the weeks turned months that she waited for this man. Of the sleep she lost, and of the worry that disintegrated her stomach lining.

Of the nights she thought she would go crazy because she feared he was dead. The way the anxiety drained out of her when she heard his voice on the other end of the phone. And the utter turmoil she was put through every time her phone rang and it wasn't him.

She stood. "Take care of yourself." She began walking away, and it was all she could do not to run.

Because the other option was to run back into his arms.

Because as much as her logical brain knew it must end, she still wanted this man. She wanted him in her life, and she wanted to be in his. She wanted to laugh with him and be touched by him.

But they'd tried and tried and tried to make something work, and all it brought in the end were agents watching over her and a bottomless pit of agonizing worry.

Her throat was closing with threatening tears, her vision fogging over as she walked. She was nearing the Pantheon when she heard him yell, "Aless, wait!"

She gave a growling sob and quickened her steps.

"Damnit, Alessandra!" He was gaining on her, which meant he was walking faster than he should on a wound that wasn't healed. "Talk to me."

She angrily stopped but didn't turn to watch him catch up to her.

"Alessandra." He was almost there.

"Why did you follow me?" she demanded, still not able to face him.

"I followed you because I'm still in love with you!" he yelled.

As if his confession was a punch to the gut, she bent at the waist as the sobs took control.

He splayed his warm hand on the center of her back. "Are you okay?"

"I'm not the moron who got shot," she said in between desperate gulps of air as she tried to pull herself together.

"Amo ..."

"No." That helped. She righted herself and finally faced him. "Carlo, I am not your love." She angrily wiped at her tears.

"You are," he insisted.

"Go away," she hissed.

"I'm going to figure this out," he hissed back.

A scoffing laugh burst out. "Another empty promise."

"No, it's not," he said vehemently.

"Carlo, there's nothing to figure out. Have a good life." She turned but he reached out and took her hand before she could get too far and placed himself in her way.

"This isn't over."

"Carlo, go away." She couldn't take any more.

"Amo, I'll go. But this *isn't* over."

"Yes. It is. Just let it go so we can both heal and move on with our lives," she begged.

"No."

"Yes!" she yelled.

"I'm going to figure this out." His face broke into a smile, but he let go of her hand.

Free now, Alessandra took a step away from him. Distraught and tangled by his words, she turned in confused circles, looking for an exit. Finally, she faced him. "Please. This needs to be goodbye."

His mouth was on hers before she could stop it. The kiss was possessive and hot and quick. When he pulled away his smile had grown. Alessandra's frown had deepened.

"No," he said.

She pushed at him and wiped her lips with a shaking hand. "Goodbye Carlo. Don't contact me again." She turned and walked away as he called out, "I love you."

"But I don't love you," she yelled over her shoulder.

"I'll make it right. You'll see."

She shook her head as she picked up speed. "Idiota," she muttered, taking a turn that would lead to a busy street where she could catch a taxi.

Chapter Forty-Nine

Carlo's grin grew as laughter beside him erupted.

He glanced to his left to find a short, older man hunched over a cane watching him.

"Buonasera," Carlo called.

"I don't know if you're really having a good night, young man." He pointed a shaking finger in Alessandra's direction.

"I'm going to marry her." Carlo watched as she turned the corner and disappeared. God he was a sorry ass excuse of a man. He had that woman waiting for him, and he'd chosen the job over her.

"I don't think she's too excited about it."

"It's going to be tough," Carlo agreed.

"It seems like you have your work cut out for you."

"I do. I never really worked at our relationship."

"And now you're going to work at it?"

"Yup." Carlo wasn't sure why he was being so open with a stranger, it was his mood, he figured. He'd spent the better part of the day thinking about Alessandra and making up his mind that if he wanted her in his life, things really did need to change. She was right, he couldn't just give her empty promises.

"Seems like a monumental decision," the old man said.

"Actually," Carlo felt light-headed, "it's the easiest decision in the world."

"Your young woman there seems to think it's over."

"Ah," Carlo winked at the old man, "but it's not."

"How can you tell?"

"She never returned the ring."

The old man frowned. "If I wasn't headed to meet some friends for dinner, I would make you sit down and tell me this whole story." He held out his weathered hand. "So I'll just say good luck, and tell you this; if she's the one, you fight for her. The ones you fight for make a man's life ..." His eyes squinted as his smile grew. "Well, they make a man's life."

Carlo watched him walk away and decided everything about the random interaction was a good omen.

He had a long road ahead of him and one hell of a task. But he also knew Alessandra. He knew what her anger and love looked like, he knew her challenging nature and her need to control everything. And the way she looked at him, the spark was still there and he could work with that. But any miracles that came about would have to be of his own making. He couldn't just hope for a miracle to fix things. *He* had to do the work.

First, he needed to apologize. Truly apologize to her. In a sense, he *had* mistreated her. He assumed she'd always wait for him. No matter what. He assumed he didn't need to cultivate their relationship. He had mistreated her by the simple act of leaving her for so long and not trying to change things.

He couldn't live without her. He knew that now. He thought he'd get over her, but his need for her had grown as time had passed.

He didn't mean to kiss her, but she had kissed him back. Even though she wiped her lips with the back of her hand for a show of disgust, the passion was still there and *she'd kissed him back*.

So he would apologize for his lack of action and make amends.

And secondly, he was going to have to find a job that would fulfill him and allow him to be in Alessandra's life every day. So they could walk to dinner hand in hand, to the small trattoria in the piazza near her home. And he would take her to Genoa and introduce her to his cousins and show her where he grew up. And he'd wake up next to her and know her tousled hair and the dreamy look she had in the morning was his doing.

Damn he felt like the weight of the world had lifted from his whole being.

This new phase of his life would be the biggest operation he'd ever faced. And he was going to work this problem from every angle until he achieved the ultimate goal. Even if it took the rest of his life.

"No, not that long," he muttered. He couldn't wait that long.

He plunged his hands in his pocket and limped down the street whistling.

Chapter Fifty

"Can't you just talk to her?" Parker whispered to Jessica, pointing to their closed kitchen door. He'd waylaid her in the hallway between their living room and kitchen.

Jessica gave a quiet laugh then matched his volume. "She's not my sister. *You* talk to her."

"She doesn't listen to me, *because* she's my sister, so it would be better if you talked to her," he reasoned.

"It won't be better," Jessica insisted. "She'll do that thing, where she tilts her head, makes really intense eye contact while she nods, until she can pick out something I say and the next thing you know; we're talking about *my* life and problems."

"What problems do you have?"

Jessica pressed a finger against Parker's chest. "I have a chickenshit husband who's scared to talk to his older sister about her broken heart."

"The older sister can hear you both," Alessandra called from the kitchen, "and there's nothing to talk about because she doesn't have a broken heart."

Jessica slapped her hand over her mouth to hold back the laughter as Parker rolled his eyes. He pointed to the kitchen and gave his wife his best pleading, puppy dog eyes. '*Please?*' he mouthed.

She shook her head and dramatically mouthed, 'No.'

He slipped his hand around her waist and pulled her against his body, dipping his mouth to her neck. "Tesoro mio." *My treasure,* he cooed. "For me?"

"No ..." she tilted her head, melting against his body, "this is how you get us in trouble, you know."

"I know."

"Well, since she doesn't want to talk, how about we take this to the bedroom."

"Jess, she needs to talk to someone," he pleaded as his attentive hands roamed, making their own plea.

Jessica sighed. "Then you go talk to your sister, and I'll be in the bedroom waiting for you."

He slouched to be eye level with her. "Please amore, you're our only hope."

She pushed him back. "I hate when you 'lower yourself to my level,'" she scoffed, "it's demeaning."

His voice dipped. "If we were in bed and I adjusted myself to your level, you wouldn't think it was demeaning."

"God, you're annoying."

Alessandra's voice again interrupted from beyond the kitchen door. "The sister can still hear you. She's glad the conversation is moving away from her, but she's not interested in your sex life."

Parker frowned at the door.

"First renovation we do is to get doors made out of thick ass wood," Jessica muttered.

"It doesn't help us much now." He took Jessica's hand and abruptly pulled her along into the kitchen.

She tried to pull away, causing them both to trip through the door.

Alessandra watched the show from where she was standing next to the stove, hands on her hips.

As Jessica righted herself and slapped Parker on the arm, she winked at Alessandra. "Your brother is worried about you and wants to talk to you."

"There's nothing to talk about," Alessandra said and then asked, "Caffè?"

"Sì." Parker sat down at the table.

"I suppose." Jessica sat down as well and they both watched Alessandra finish making coffee, while giving each other silent wide-eyed directions mixed with exaggerated nods and shakes of heads.

"The sister can see you." Alessandra laughed.

The cups delivered and a plate of baked goods Cassie brought over the day before placed in the middle of the table, Alessandra sat down and pointedly said, "There's nothing to talk about. I'm not heartbroken. Everything is fine."

"Yet here we are." Jessica smiled.

Alessandra took a biscotti and dipped it in her coffee, after a bite she sighed. "I'm fine."

"I didn't say anything." Jessica shrugged. "It's your brother who's jumping to all sorts of conclusions."

Parker playfully pinched Jessica's arm. "Ow," she said slapping his hand away.

Alessandra continued, "It's just that a doctor I worked with in Kyrgyzstan contacted me and thinks I would be a great help in Venezuela. And she's there, so it makes sense to go now."

"Okay, so you're doing another stint for Doctors Without Borders. That's great," Jessica offered.

"It's not safe." Parker frowned.

"It's safe enough," Alessandra bit.

"Safe enough?" Jessica glanced between the two.

Alessandra was quick to defend her position. "The political climate won't affect the work we're doing."

"What political climate?" Jessica asked.

Parker gave her a look that said he'd explain it all later.

"So," Jessica decided if she was forced to be in the middle of this, she'd take a straightforward approach, "I heard Carlo showed up at your apartment a few weeks ago with a gunshot wound."

Alessandra crossed her arms and raised her eyebrow.

Jessica met the arm cross with her own. "Your brother thinks it's an interesting coincidence that you're going without any notice to another country so soon after another run in with Carlo."

"A run in?" Alessandra scoffed. "A run in is what happens when you see someone al supermercato. My home is suddenly an emergency room for spies. Showing up at all hours ..."

"I had no other option," Parker defended.

"That's what you all say."

"Who's all? Carlo? Because he was in trouble?" Parker bit.

"Did you know he brought his confidential informant to my apartment? The man had a stab wound. I think it would actually be more productive if you all would just take sewing classes. Who do I write to about that? I'll teach it if I have to. Sewing for spies."

Jessica barked out a laugh. Parker's reaction was the opposite, a frown drew across his face. "What do you mean, he brought one of his CIs to your home? To your apartment?"

"No, he brought him to my hairdresser," Alessandra shot.

"I'm gonna kill him. Do you know what kind of danger he could have put you in?"

"Yes. I do. Because I ended up with a babysitter for a few weeks because of it. And then ..." she trailed off and waved her hand.

"Then what?" Jessica asked just as Parker yelled, "Why the hell didn't you tell me? I can't believe he put you in that kind of danger."

Jessica screwed up her face and turned her whole body toward Parker. "*You* put your sister in danger first. And *you* were the reason she even met Carlo."

Parker pointed at Jessica. "Because *you* had to confront your ex in person. If *you* weren't there, you wouldn't have gotten in a fight with him and ended up kidnapped in Rome."

"Are you seriously saying that it was my fault I was kidnapped?!" Jessica yelled.

"Yes."

"Asshole," Jessica hissed.

"Basta." *Stop.* Alessandra raised her voice and gestured to Jessica. "Fighting isn't good for the baby."

Parker's face fell as he turned toward his sister. "Really?"

Jessica snarled, "No." But she did rub her stomach as if she'd forgotten she was three months pregnant. "Your sister is full of old Italian wives' tales when it comes to this pregnancy."

"It's your fault for having the first grandchild." Alessandria shrugged.

"Oh, my God." Jessica stood and paced to the fridge, "What else is my fault?" She stopped and pointed across the room. "I didn't get pregnant on my own you know, and I didn't get myself kidnapped all by myself either." She ripped open the fridge, the condiment bottles in the door wiggling a strange chiming at the abrupt action. "And we are talking about how it's Parker's fault you met Carlo in the first place."

"Because I was working with him on a case you walked into," Parker muttered, his last attempt to win the argument.

Jessica returned to the table with a cheese stick and sparkling water. "Alex, I'm pregnant and I'm pissy. And we think you need to talk."

"Talking will only make you feel better, not me." Alessandra glowered.

Parker slowly began to stand as he said, "Maybe I should leave you two—"

Jessica's head spun whiplash fast to make eye contact with Parker. He had stopped in a squat position and held his breath for a beat before sitting back down.

Jessica took a drink and sat back in her chair. "We're not trying to blindside you Alex, we just thought you and Carlo were going to figure it out and make it work. I love you both and you seemed so good together."

Alessandra radiated confidence and empathy to the outside world, but when she was hurt, she was very good at hiding her pain. Only this time, Jessica could see the cracks appearing.

"Alex," Jessica said gently, "you look like shit. You've got dark rings under your eyes and I don't think you're sleeping. We don't know what really happened, you and Carlo are so stoic, neither of you is talking. We're not trying to fix anything, we just love you so much we want to help. And I don't think it's a coincidence you came to visit us before heading to Venezuela. And in my opinion, it looks like you're running away."

"I don't run," she muttered.

Jessica shook her head. "Alex, at some point you're going to have to let someone get close enough to help you. It's okay to have a friend. I'm your damn friend, you know."

"I'm fine."

"Jesus," Jessica sighed.

"Aless," Parker started, "Jess is right. You and I think we need to save everyone. We forget that there are people who love us and are there for us when we need them. And you did come all this way to visit us first."

"I'm not running," she insisted. "An opportunity presented itself to me ..." A tear slipped down her cheek then, and she swallowed the obvious lie.

Jessica was taken aback, she'd seen Alessandra angry, confident, laughing, but she had never witnessed the woman cry.

Alessandra quietly said, "I wanted it to work. We both did. It was just never going to. We were both so busy." She wiped at her eyes and cleared her throat. "My job is demanding. There are long hours, and sometimes there are difficult days, but I love my job. I love the challenge of it all."

"And you like saving people." Parker winked.

"I *love* saving people." Alessandra wiped the tears away and smiled. "I have been married to my job, to the idea of being a doctor my entire life. Una Dottoressa, it's who I am. It's all I wanted to be and I never made room for anything or anyone else. I never felt like anything was missing."

"Then Carlo came along." Jessica filled in the detail that was propelling Alessandra to run.

"Then that big ox of a man came into my life." Alessandra met her brother's eyes. "I don't think you want to really hear about this."

Parker gave a gruff laugh. "Probably not, but don't you think we're old enough to talk about things and be there for each other during the difficult times?"

After a nod and a long pause she aimed a soft smile at her brother. "I'll leave out all the sex talk."

"Thanks." He rolled his eyes.

Jessica elbowed him as Alessandra took a deep breath and began. "The passion between us was never the problem. It was everything else. He was gone all the time and I worried about him every moment. But I had work to do as well. I had to try and compartmentalize so I could give the best attention to my patients. And it took a toll on my health. And when he did show up ..." She shook her head. "His last job was in Rome. Did you know that? But he never told me."

She continued the story of her relationship, the parts she'd yet to tell anyone else.

Chapter Fifty-One

The early afternoon dragged itself into early evening as Alessandra came to the end of her story. The one thing she tiptoed around was Carlo's last operation and the events that ended with her stabbed in the hospital.

"Well, shit." Jessica sat back heavily in her chair.

Parker listened patiently, though she was aware of the many times he clenched out of protective anger.

She didn't want to admit how much she needed to talk about this. Before, she felt better packing it all away. 'Out of sight, out of mind' had been her coping mechanism of choice.

But there was a relief that came from sharing her story, and as she finished, she leveled her gaze at Parker and Jessica. "He breaks my heart. I can't live that life."

"I'm sorry," Parker said softly.

She smirked. "I said you wouldn't want to hear this story."

"But, he said he was going to fix it?" Jessica raised an eyebrow.

"I got home from the café and reached out to my contacts at Doctors Without Borders that night. The following day I signed up for the very next assignment I could and took a leave of absence." She swallowed and splayed her hands on the table before she gave the grumbled admission, "So yes, you're both right. I'm running away."

"And you needed to talk all this out," Jessica added.

Alessandra raised an eyebrow in Jessica's direction. "I did." She continued before Jessica could utter an 'I told you so'. "But Carlo and I are done. I don't care if he's going to try. He can't be in my life."

"I understand." Jessica nodded and reached out a hand to pat Alessandra's. "I really do. When I finally got home from my troubled Italian holiday, I couldn't stand to be alone," she admitted. "I stayed with Cassie and spent months on her sofa crying and licking my wounds. I think it's a much needed, healthy and *human* thing to do."

"You're going to tell me that eventually, you gave Parker a second chance and everything has worked out."

Jessica shook her head. "No. You're not me. I'm just trying to say that I understand how you're feeling. That I know what it's like to need to get away from all the memories."

Parker was having a different reaction. "You know I want to jump on a plane and go beat the shit out of him."

"He got shot," Alessandra shrugged, "it's enough for now."

"So," Jessica sat back in her chair, "Venezuela."

Alessandra nodded. "It's the only thing I can think to do, so that I can wake up one morning and finally feel like myself again." She pressed her hand to her chest as if to punctuate the point she was trying to make.

"And where Carlo won't find you," Jessica offered.

Alessandra gave a dry laugh. "At least he won't try to corner me there. These guys," she nodded toward her brother as an example, "if they wanted to find someone they could."

"I'm not telling the asshole," Parker said.

"Okay, team Alex from this point on. What do you need from us?" Jessica asked.

"Stop making me talk about things I don't want to talk about."

"Pass." Jessica smiled. "But seriously, please know we are always, *always* here for you. No matter what time of day. You aren't alone and nothing you are going through, or ever will go through, needs to be done alone."

Alessandra nodded as a few tears freed themselves. She didn't wipe them away. "Okay," she whispered.

"Okay," they agreed in unison and then Parker finally got down to business. "I still don't think Venezuela is a good idea but if you're still going through with it, there are some things you need to take with you."

"I've had all my shots."

"This is more ... specialized equipment."

Chapter Fifty-Two

Indigestion woke Jessica up. She groaned and rolled out of bed. Finding no medicine in the bathroom, she shuffled into the kitchen and found Alessandra sitting at the table in the glow of her computer's light.

"Are you okay?" Alessandra asked.

"Indigestion," Jessica said as she took an antacid and sat down. "It wakes me up in the middle of the night and in a few hours, the morning sickness will get me up again."

"It's nature's way of training you to get up every few hours for the baby."

Jessica grunted. "Nature sucks."

Alessandra laughed.

Jessica nodded. "I like having you here. You know, you could always come live here. Close to us. I'm sure you could find a job."

"I can't leave miei genitori." *My parents*.

Jessica shrugged. "Well, we'll move them here too."

Alessandra shook her head. "Do you really want to give up the three months a year you get to live in Italy?"

"I mean, we don't have to *sell* your parents' house, then we could all still go back every year."

"Ma vengo dall'Italia." *But I'm from Italy*, Alessandra said.

"But now you need to be somewhere else," Jessica supplied.

"Now, I need to be somewhere else," Alessandra confirmed.

"Do you remember when we first met?" Jessica asked.

"I remember, but do you?"

"Okay, I don't remember the first few days, but at one point, we were all sitting on your balcony eating lunch; me, Parker, you and Carlo." She cleared her throat at the way Alessandra's face blanched when *his* name was said, but Jessica barreled on. "I understand you're going to Venezuela in order to heal, but I also think ..." Alessandra's gaze was intensifying and Jessica was losing her nerve, so finished quickly." I think when you feel better, you need to go back and fight."

"For what? For him?"

"For *yourself*," Jessica pointed.

"I *am* fighting for myself. You don't know the whole of it. You don't know everything."

"Then tell me."

"I just need to get over him and figure out how to live my life when I'm invisible again."

"What do you mean invisible?"

Alessandra ran a frustrated hand through her hair. "I can name every bone in the human body. I can name all the skeletal muscles. If you went into cardiac arrest right now, and I had to, I could save your life in this very kitchen. I can do emergency surgery on a collapsed lung with machines beeping and nurses yelling. But I couldn't make a relationship work with the love of my life."

Jessica felt Alessandra's declaration of love in her bones but she knew this was not the time to smile or even point out that she was right. Instead, she reasoned, "That's the difference between work and your heart."

"Jessica, until you came into my life, I thought my work was my heart's desire."

Jessica frowned in confusion.

Alessandra waved her hand. "I met Carlo the same day I met you. I think it's why I can't come and live here anymore than I can stay in Italy right now because you and Parker remind me of him."

"Oh, Alex ..."

"His memory is tied to you and Parker. I see you, I remember the first night Carlo kissed me. I see Parker and I remember Carlo proposing. You have two pictures of your wedding in the living room and I know where he's standing and what the smile on his face looks like."

"I'm sorry, I never thought about that."

"Neither did I. Not until I got here. It's why I changed my plane ticket. I'm leaving the day after tomorrow."

"What? Did you *just* change it?"

"No, I changed it yesterday. But now you understand why I need to go?"

"I understand," Jessica said, her stomach churning again. She retrieved a can of seltzer water and held it up to Alessandra. "Do you want some?"

She nodded. "You know, they say if you have bad indigestion when you're pregnant it means your baby will be born with a lot of hair."

"Is there an old Italian wives' tale book that I can buy somewhere?"

"Maybe."

Jessica sat back down with a grunt, and while arranging herself said, "Okay, you said you were invisible again and that doesn't seem like something I should just let go."

"You know how he would look at me?" Alessandra muttered and watched Jessica nod. "It wasn't just how he looked at me. It was that he *saw* me. Really saw me. Into the depths of my whole person." She cleared her throat. "I never knew it was something that was missing before, but now it's like I've lost a limb."

Jessica didn't know what to say in reply to Alessandra's vulnerability.

"I've seen the way you and my brother look at each other. You understand. You see each other."

It was true. No one ever made Jessica feel the way Parker had. No one ever brought her to the very heights of being her best self the way he did. And if she could believe her husband, he was the man he was today because of her.

"But it hasn't been easy," Jessica started, "we had to figure out how to give and bend too. There's been a lot of fighting and a lot of compromise."

"You're going to say this is why I should fight for Carlo," Alessandra bit.

Jessica shrugged. "Yeah."

"Jessica, there was always so much arguing and fighting. And it was draining."

"You challenged each other," Jessica revised.

"No, we exhausted each other, and not in a good way," Alessandra said sadly. "I had to make decisions for my health and well-being."

"But–"

"Jessica, basta." *Stop it.*

"Okay. One more question then I'll leave it alone."

"No."

Jessica didn't stop. "How is he in bed? He looks like he'd be *real* adept."

Alessandra shook her head, the unexpected humor seemed to catch her off guard. "He was fine."

"Fine?"

Alessandra rolled her eyes. "More than fine."

"I knew it."

"Jessica, we liked each other. We were in love. It didn't work. I'm getting tired of insisting that it's over and you not listening to me. So believe me when I say, it's over."

"Bullshit." Jessica smiled. "In one breath you say you found a man who truly sees you for who you are and in the next you dismiss it with a wave of your hand because you are just ill-fated shooting stars." Jessica shook her head. "I call bullshit."

"My heart is breaking," Alessandra said passionately.

"Now *that* I believe. And I am so sorry you have to go through this. But Alex, I think there is so much more left between you two."

"There is nothing left."

"You know, you are two of the most obstinate, thick-skulled idiots that have possibly ever lived. You are both so serious, you forgot that at some point you need to let go and have some fucking fun in this life."

Alessandra looked like Jessica had slapped her face, she pursed her lips and slightly snarled, "It isn't that easy."

"I'm not saying it's easy. I'm saying that there is something big between you two and you don't just give up on it."

"The worry was killing me," Alessandra confessed.

"Did you ever actually ask him what he could do? If he was willing to meet you halfway?" Jessica asked.

"I didn't want him to resent me."

"Did you ever actually ask him? With words?" Jessica asked again.

Alessandra looked down at the table in answer. "I would resent him if he asked me to change jobs."

Jessica frowned. "But would you be willing to bend, just a little, in order to make things work?"

Alessandra looked away, and Jessica continued as an intriguing idea spilled forth. "Or, maybe you were looking for *any* excuse, because you scared each other too much."

"I am tired of fighting."

"But Alex, that's who you are. That's what you do. Maybe you should just embrace it and accept it and once in a while say fuck it and have a laugh."

"I'm leaving the day after tomorrow."

Jessica knew she'd pushed as much as she could. And she knew for Alessandra, opening up that much would probably take her a while to process. "Okay. I understand. I hope you know that."

They fell silent for a few moments before Alessandra said, "And don't worry about me in Venezuela."

"I won't. I was just as exhausted as you were from Parker's safety briefing."

"Yeah, if I get in trouble, I'll just push the button on the tracking device and he'll save me," she added dryly.

Jessica smiled. "You know the bracelet I wear? My tracking device is strategically placed in that."

"How often do you forget it?"

"Most of the time."

Alessandra laughed and they both heard a creak of Parker's arrival in the hallway.

"Everything okay?" he asked.

"No, your sister is leaving sooner because you're a pain in the ass," Jessica answered.

"And you give your wife heartburn," Alessandra shot.

He frowned, running a hand through his unkempt hair. "Whatever."

Jessica sighed. "Okay, but Alex, just promise me you'll at least be back in time for the baby?"

Alessandra looked blankly across the table at Jessica, her eyes shimmering with a buildup of new tears. Jessica frowned, she meant for the question to be lighthearted, something Alessandra could look forward to.

"Alex?"

Alessandra shook her head, as if to dislodge her thoughts. "I'll be back in time."

Chapter Fifty-Three

Carlo sighed and thought about taking another walk, to supplement his physical therapy and get the hell out of his apartment, and his head.

He'd been forced into taking some time off, which he knew would happen. But the therapist he'd been coerced into visiting, decided that his latest gunshot wound, which brought his lifelong total to four in all, was four too many. And it was strongly suggested that Carlo take at least two months off in order to regroup.

Which was the polite way of demanding Carlo go to therapy until the powers that be cleared him for active duty.

And really, the whole situation was fine with him. He wanted time to think. To figure out how to win Alessandra back, come to terms with what had gone wrong in the first place and figure out what other line of work he would like to be in.

The one thing he hadn't counted on was how the endless personal analysis mixed with absolutely nothing to do might make him stir-crazy.

He had his shoes on to go for a walk when his work phone rang.

Thank God.

He glanced at the international phone number, welcoming the distraction. "Pronto?" *Hello.*

"There's a problem."

Carlo sighed. "Hello to you too Salvatore." He should have been surprised by the call to his agency issued, unlisted number, but Parker Salvatore was probably using CIA favors to obtain it.

Carlo stood and crossed the living room to look out his apartment window, thinking he would be greeted by the sight of Parker standing in the shadows on the street below.

When he didn't see anyone lingering in front of his building, Carlo joked, "What's wrong Salvatore? Are you finished being behind a desk? Ready to come back into the field and play with the big boys?"

"Alessandra's been abducted." Parker's voice was hollow.

The blood in Carlo's veins froze. "Tell me."

"She went to Venezuela for another stint with Doctors Without Borders."

"Fuck, Salvatore. Why the hell didn't you talk her out of it? Don't you know what it's like down there?"

"Of course I do," Parker spat, "it's why I argued with her until I was blue in the face. But apparently, she just had to get out of Italy because she's so damn heartbroken that she didn't feel like she had any other choice," he finished angrily.

"Ah, so this is my fault." Carlo tried to be defensive, but he knew it was the truth.

"I'm just saying, if you would like to point a finger ..."

Carlo grunted. "There'll be time to deal out blame later. What are the parameters? Ransom note? Did she call?"

Parker took an audible deep breath. "When it was evident I couldn't change her mind, I tagged her and gave her a tracker."

"You tagged your own sister?" Carlo asked.

"You never have?" Parker asked.

Carlo didn't dare answer, because the truth was, he'd put one in the lining of her purse a day after Parker asked him to keep an eye on her. The tracker was still active, but it had been sitting in the same location in Rome for months now. Obviously, she didn't use that purse anymore.

"Tell me what you have," Carlo instructed.

"She never told me exactly where she was going, let me think it was Caracas."

"But it's not."

"No, the hospital is in a small town as far as you can get from Caracas, near the border of Colombia."

"Minchia." *Fuck.* Carlo drew out the curse.

"She activated her tracker about six hours ago."

"And you're just now calling?" Carlo asked angrily.

"I actually wasn't going to call you at all," Parker said evenly, "but I need help. And you know how this works. Step one, make sure the threat is credible."

"Alessandra would never cry wolf."

"Step two, gather intel," Parker continued. "I contacted the organization and they contacted the hospital she'd been working at; we now have verbal confirmation that she and two other doctors have been abducted."

"Who took her?"

"Local militia group. Into Colombia. I was able to get a flyover of the area where her location pinged, but a visual is problematic so far because of the jungle terrain. I ordered a LiDAR flyover, but we're a few hours away from those results."

"Safety concerns?" Carlo asked.

"All three of the women abducted were surgeons, it's believed they were possibly taken to treat impoverished locals fighting the current regime. No ransom request as of yet."

"It's only been a few hours," Carlo said. They both knew that when it came to war-torn countries, and militia trying to get their shit together enough to ransom someone after abduction, it took days.

Parker cleared his throat. "I wouldn't have called you ..."

"I get it, I'm the reason she's in South America and now in trouble," he seethed.

"No." Parker's voice was thick with emotion. "*I* get it, and she still loves you. And if I believe my wife, you still love her. You two just need to figure your shit out," he said with a rush. "I just need help on this one. I can't ... there's some complications with the pregnancy."

"Jesus." When it rained it poured. "How–"

"She's fine," Parker supplied quickly, "Jess is fine and the baby's fine. She just has high blood pressure and the doctors have been great. She's on bed rest and they're monitoring everything. They're completely positive that everything will be fine. But Jess is scared to death. And now Alessandra ... Carlo, I can't tell Jess and I can't leave her."

"I'm on my way," Carlo said. "You back me up from where you are, I'll do the rest." He ripped open his closet door, grabbed his 'go bag' and added a few more items.

"Okay." Parker blew the word out.

"She's strong," Carlo reminded them both.

Parker grunted an agreement. "I've already made contact with our field office in Pisa, they'll be expecting you."

Carlo zipped his bag, grabbed his jacket and was out the door as he said, "I can be wheels up in thirty."

"Unless you can get there sooner. I've got you through to the capital of Venezuela. It's going to be touchy at customs there, but I'm calling in every favor I can to clear your way," Parker said.

Carlo threw his bag in the back seat of his car before climbing in. "I have a contact south of Puerto La Cruz, might be helpful," he said, talking about a port city just outside of Barcelona. "He can get me the firepower I might need and a few mercenaries hanging around who need some work. Is this on the books or off?"

"It's whatever we need it to be in order to get Alessandra," Parker insisted.

"That's a lot of gray area," Carlo stated as he pulled his door closed and started the car.

"As much as you need," Parker offered.

"I'll bring her home, Salvatore," Carlo promised.

"Thanks." Parker cleared his throat several times. "I'll keep you apprised of tactical while you're in the air."

"Understood." Carlo ended the call and tossed the phone onto the passenger seat as he pulled into traffic. He was steady as he drove, which meant it was probably good he could drive like a madman. Even by Italian standards, he raced wildly through the streets.

He spent most of his career in one life-threatening situation after another. He was man enough to admit to himself and the new therapist that he enjoyed the excitement at times. Losing his parents so early in his life, he felt like he'd been forced to come to terms with his own mortality. That was one thing. Until Alessandra, though, he never felt like it was a problem. But more and more now, he was concerned about not returning from one of his assignments.

And when his work had put Alessandra's life in danger, he'd beaten himself up and been angry along with a whole whirlwind of other emotions. He was working on coming to terms with all of it.

But now, being faced with the threat that the love of his life was in the kind of danger that could mean she wouldn't return home ... Well, that wasn't an option. He was going to spend the rest of his life making sure they spent every free hour they could together. Building something sustainable and lovely. And he'd move mountains to convince her of that and make it happen.

He shifted into a higher gear and ran a red light, oblivious of the screams coming from open windows of honking cars.

His heartbeat quickened at the thought of Alessandra. She continued to dismiss him out of hand, but he meant what he'd told a complete stranger. He was going to marry her.

And the mandated therapy was helping. For the first few weeks Carlo had been silent. But then, one day, the therapist asked him if he ever thought he could be someone other than just the 'job'.

That shook Carlo, that simple question. Because before Alessandra, he accepted the fact that he was probably going to die in the field, so he never planned for being someone outside of it.

Now, he wanted more. He could see more. He might be able to live without the constant adrenaline rushes and highs and lows of putting his life on the line. He was definitely open to being a whole lot more than just his job.

However, now, he was grateful for the job that would help him keep his heart rate intact and his mind focused as he made the proper plans to save Alessandra.

Chapter Fifty-Four

"We need to go. It's been three days. Che cazzo." *What the fuck*, Carlo growled angrily at the phone that was on speaker and sitting in the middle of the table.

"Jesus, Moretti, you think I don't *know* it's been three days?" Parker's tin can voice hissed.

Five men stood around a table in the rundown apartment where they'd been meeting, looking over maps and devising a plan to save the doctors, using all the recent intel they'd received.

Thankfully, with the contacts Carlo and Parker had, they were able to round up two mercenaries looking for work and two CIA agents who happened to be nearby. Their contacts also helped them assemble the needed weapons and gear.

The past few days had been spent working out two aspects of the operation that caused the most concern.

The first was that there was only one road in and out of the area they were headed. And the road was 'owned and operated' by a warring militant faction in the area with a leader known as El Jefe. With continued luck on his side, Carlo had an old colleague who was able to make an introduction to El Jefe.

A lot hinged on the man allowing Carlo's team to travel the road. And El Jefe made it explicitly clear, that if Carlo wasn't in the car when the extraction of the women took place, then he might be nervous enough to alert his enemy of the attempted rescue and kill whoever *did* show up.

If that road wasn't an option, then the extraction team would have to hike with the women roughly twelve kilometers through dense jungle to a secondary road. Second and third options were always needed when planning, but without knowing the state of the women's health or well-being, it was a concern if they were required to walk that far.

The second problem was that they didn't have any reliable information as to exactly where the women were being held. The LiDAR had shown a throng of people milling around an area next to heat signatures where only a handful of people were. The obvious conclusion was that the women were treating patients. But it also meant that a daylight retrieval was a no-go.

However, the nighttime scans revealed several encampments, but there weren't any segregated heat signatures that would suggest it was the women.

Knowing of a few caves in the area and that the women must be kept near the camp, the team turned their attention to maps and information about the regional caves.

Parker voiced his concerns. "But the info we have on the caves in that area is old and undocumented."

"But it makes sense," said Ricardo, a short mercenary who was ex-special ops and who would be the driver. "Caves would be a good place to hide and keep them out of the elements. This particular group has been living in the jungle for thirty years."

"Which means they know the area better than we could ever hope to," Parker reasoned.

"But we have better tactical gear. A small number. And we're used to being invisible," shot Richards, a CIA agent who had been in Peru on vacation and answered Parker's call for help. Parker had worked with the man before, and Carlo was glad to be working with someone Parker verified was 'stalwart and trustworthy.'

Carlo slapped Richards on the back. "It's the best plan we have."

"Agent Salvatore," another special operator chimed in, "we have the gear needed to help the women if we end up hiking." It was the polite way of saying time was running out.

"The plan is sound," Carlo insisted again.

The other men verbalized their agreement.

"There are too many variables." Parker's uncertainty was grating on Carlo's nerves.

"Because it's your sister," Carlo reasoned. "Take a step back. You know variables are part of the job and you know this is as sound a plan as there is, considering the circumstances."

There was a pause before Parker said, "Talk me through it once more."

Carlo leaned over the table that had the layout of maps and marks of distances and code names for the various parts of the operation. "We leave at 2200. That gives us time to get to the checkpoint Milan."

"Milan." Parker scoffed at the names Carlo had assigned each checkpoint.

Richards laughed. "It's an Italian operation."

Carlo continued, "We arrive at zero dark thirty, drop off ALPHA Team -the extraction team- which consists of ALPHA One, Two and Three. It's five kilometers to the outskirts of where we know the controlling militia are. When they reach checkpoint Florence, ALPHA One will use the drone to heatmap the area. Then ALPHA One, Two and Three will have two hours to reach checkpoint Rome where the targets are being held."

Nods came from all the men as they made their own personal flowcharts of the checkpoints.

Carlo continued, "Once the targets are secured, everyone moves to checkpoint Naples."

"Jesus Christ." Parker hissed at the names, again showing his irritation.

Carlo had to hold back a laugh, if anyone knew this was a serious situation it was him; but in the initial ops planning, the 'hired' men joked about it being an Italian operation, so he figured why not lean into it.

"BRAVO Team consists of myself and the driver. After we drop ALPHA Team at location Milan; BRAVO team continues to checkpoint Calabria. Arriving at 0130. I'll make sure El Jefe allows us use of the road. However, if there are any problems, we'll radio the move to checkpoint Sicily."

"How long will ALPHA have to reach checkpoint Sicily?"

"Three hours." Carlo knew this was the part of the plan that was bothering Parker the most. If the shit hit the fan with El Jefe, then the women would have to hike fast and far, and if they were hurt, well, that was what the morphine and adrenaline shots were going to be for.

"ALPHA Team will take the northern route, it puts distance between them and all heat signatures detected the past few days. The fact that no one is expecting this is going to have the element of surprise fully on our side."

"And the terrain?" Parker asked.

Richards answered, "Nothing we haven't run into before; thick foliage, but flat and manageable if there are any wounded."

Carlo continued, "Once ALPHA calls in confirmation they've reached checkpoint Rome, BRAVO Team, with the help of El Jefe, clears the road and moves to checkpoint Naples."

"And your exit?" Parker asked.

"The road is rough, but it's there," Ricardo voiced. "El Jefe claims it's drivable, and current LiDAR imagery doesn't show any large debris on the road."

Everyone in the room knew what that meant, including Parker. It meant one hell of a bumpy ride as they raced like hell to get away from the faction that captured the women.

Carlo continued, "Once we're on the road, it's twenty-five kilometers to the LZ where we meet the helicopter, then we're straight and clear to Guyana from there."

"The helicopter only has a ten minute window," Parker said.

"We'll make it," Carlo asserted.

Parker was silent for a moment before saying, "Our contacts in Guyana have no problem allowing you entrance. Since this is not a Venezuelan government problem, but a guerrilla issue, there should be no resistance. There might be a few palms to be greased, but that's easy enough."

Carlo stated, "Then we're a go?" It was more of a statement than a question.

Parker didn't reply. Carlo leaned closer to the phone in the middle of the table. "Salvatore?" Carlo was going to pull the trigger on the operation with or without Parker's blessing, but he'd just as soon have it.

"It's a go," Parker finally said.

The rest of the team began to move then; as organized as they were, there were still several logistics for each of them to put into place so they could function as a well-oiled machine.

Carlo picked up the phone then, taking it off speaker. "Salvatore, I'll bring her home."

"Take care of yourself," Parker said, then hung up.

Chapter Fifty-Five

"What do you mean he's your ex-fiancé?" Maggie asked from where she was gripping the back of the driver's seat as the van they were all crowded into hit another pothole. "Jesus," she breathed.

One of the men who'd extracted them from the cave apologized. "I know it's uncomfortable ladies, but we are on a schedule and trying to keep you safe."

"Alex?" Maggie tried to get her attention again.

Alessandra was still dazed, they hadn't really slept the past few days nor had they eaten much. And now, she was standing in front of Carlo. She reached out and pressed her hand against his chest, covered in a bulletproof tactical vest, like the other men. He was really here.

"Parker sent you?"

"Of course, he needed the best." He brushed a strand of hair behind her ear. "And he said to tell you how glad he is that you took the tracker."

"What happens now?" Sabrina asked.

Carlo explained, "We'll meet a helicopter that will take us to Guyana. Then we can get you all home safe and sound."

There was a long pause as the women glanced at each other, finally Alessandra looked back at Carlo and shook her head. "We need to go back to the hospital."

"Amo ..." Carlo began.

"Don't," she hissed in reply to his use of the endearment. "The hospital needs us. That's why we came here in the first place."

Sabrina voiced her agreement. "We don't know what's happened since we were taken."

"Ladies," one of the men began, "the objective was to get you back to safety. And Guyana is much safer."

Maggie shook her head. "We can't go to Guyana. The hospital was understaffed and their supplies were exhausted when we got here. The three of us are all capable surgeons. And I don't think you understand the effect our absence has most likely caused. Even if it's just been a few days."

"Carlo," Alessandra leveled her gaze, "we have to go back."

"Orders?" asked the man who had been manning the radio.

Carlo looked between all the women and Alessandra thought if he really wanted to, he could order these men (who could out muscle the women on a normal day) to easily subdue them, since they were dead on their feet, and force them to safety.

But she had other plans.

"Carlo." She said his name sharply; she knew what he was thinking. "You did your job, now we just need to get back to ours. This was what we signed up for. This is what we do and we all took an oath to help when and where we could. And this is where we can be of the most help."

After several long moments of silence, punctuated only by the rattle and squeak of metal and crunch of dirt beneath the van, Carlo turned to the man next to him. "Richards, how much for four months?"

"I was on vacation." He raised an eyebrow as if that would factor into the question.

"Do you have the time?" Carlo asked

Richards shrugged. "Basic bodyguard? I could swing it. I already saw Machu Picchu, I don't think there was much else to do in Peru."

"Orders?" the man on the radio asked again.

"Please," Alessandra whispered.

She was grateful he was even taking her request into consideration. Lord only knew how pissed Parker was going to be when she contacted him to explain she was safe but heading back to the place she was originally abducted.

Although, she didn't hate the idea that Carlo was setting the women up with a bodyguard. Richards looked capable, it would be a nice insurance policy. Of course, she would have to figure out how she was going to pay the man back. There was no way she would ever allow Carlo to pay for the security.

"Continue. We still rendezvous," Carlo said.

"Carlo!" Alessandra yelled and at the same moment Sabrina and Maggie began arguing.

He held up his hand and tried to speak, but they continued their various arguments. "You don't understand." "They need so much help." "You can't punish all the people just because of the actions of a few."

"Basta!" *Stop,* Carlo screamed, surprising the women into silence and pulling a laugh from Richards.

"The helicopter is our only way out of this jungle. We'll change course once we're all on board."

"And you'll take us back to the hospital?" Alessandra asked.

"Yes." Carlo nodded.

Sabrina fell back against the edge of the van, exhausted, and Maggie began to cry. The van hit a large hole and threw Alessandra into Carlo's arms.

He steadied her, then nudged her chin up so he could look at her. She knew what he'd see: bloodshot eyes, a healing bruise on her temple, and a few scratches on her cheek.

"You're safe," he said.

"I'm tired." She pushed herself away from him as a tear of relief escaped. "The adrenaline is wearing off, it's a normal reaction."

"Lo so." *I know,* he gestured for her to sit down. "It's going to be a rough ride and we still have several kilometers left."

She sat next to Sabrina, holding herself in place. After a moment, she looked between the men who remained standing, holding onto belts fed through vents in the roof.

"Why didn't you get married?" Richards asked after a few miles.

Carlo looked over at Alessandra and before she could answer, said, "She needs time to figure out I'm the only man for her."

Chapter Fifty-Six

When Carlo mentioned a helicopter, Alessandra imagined the small, sleek air ambulance helicopters that served the hospital. Not the military grade monstrosity hovering above them. The pilot expertly landed the decommissioned black hawk, and as the wheels touched down, the ferocious propellers blew back the surrounding foliage. Carlo pointed and urged the women forward, screaming over the noise, "Andiamo!" *Let's go.*

Alessandra forced her feet to move forward. They followed the rescue team, ducking their heads the way the men in front of them did. Richards climbed in first and held out his hand to help the women aboard. They were pointed into the row of four seats in the back of the beast's belly. The man who had been driving the van was climbing into the co-pilot seat. Carlo and Richards sat in the seats facing the women, and the other two men sat back-to-back in seats that looked out each side of the helicopter.

The beast roared back into the sky as Carlo demonstrated how the seat belts worked. The women fumbled to copy him. Alessandra hated how her hands shook, but out of the corner of her eye, she saw her friends' hands did the same. The adrenaline and all the other heightened emotions were wearing them thin. Not to mention the men's continued high-alert phase, an almost tangible sign that they weren't out of trouble just yet.

Carlo and Richards pulled on a set of headsets that had been perched behind their seats, and gestured for the women to copy them.

"How we doing?" Richards asked, his voice sounding polluted by the noise. He gave a thumbs-up and raised his eyebrows. The women gave their own weak thumbs-up.

Carlo pulled out a glossy map and the women were privy to the discussion that began between the men, plotting a new landing spot and time frame. Between her exhaustion and the large amount of military code talk, Alessandra was having trouble following the thread of the conversation.

Maggie, sitting in the middle, reached for her friend's hands. The simple act that had brought them comfort in the cave the past few days, helped ease Alessandra's panic.

"Doctors," Carlo caught the women's attention and explained, "our original plan was to fly to Guyana. Now we're going to land at an airport south of San Brochero."

"There's an airport in San Brochero, we flew into it," Maggie said.

He gave an apologetic smile. "That airport is busy today with a few military demonstrations."

"Oh." The color drained from Maggie's face.

Alessandra squeezed her friend's hand and tried to sound positive. "We're okay."

Carlo nodded. "So we'll be about an hour's drive from San Brochero. It's a small airport, but we're not cleared for landing, and this kind of helicopter landing without warning is going to put a few people on edge. Once we land, five of us will exit quickly and the helicopter will take off."

"Then?" Sabrina asked.

"It's going to take some quick talking and money," Richards explained.

"We just need you to do what we say ..." Carlo leveled his gaze at Alessandra and smiled, "with no arguments."

She nodded her head.

They came in for a landing in the middle of the small runway surrounded by lush green vegetation and not much else.

Once the wheels touched down, Carlo and Richards helped the women unbuckle then climb down. Their feet barely on the tarmac, the five jogged out of the way of the powerful propellers; the black hawk rose and the men staying on board gave a wave of departure.

Alessandra glanced at the motley picture they made. The three women, dirty and bruised. Two large men in full tactical gear with rifles.

"How is this going to work?" she asked. When Carlo glanced at her, she shook her head. "Sorry. I'm just ... I know you'll work it out."

He winked at her as he scanned the area. The airport was a large, dilapidated red building topped with the letters Aeropureto. An ambulance, several luggage cars, and two military trucks sat next to the terminal. Next to that building was the three-story radio tower. Opposite the whole airport layout, was a huge yellowed building and outside, a fleet of military vehicles.

"Shit," he cursed under his breath.

"What does that mean?" Sabrina asked, following his gaze. When she saw all the military trucks and three men in uniforms lounging against the hood of one, eyeing the recently dropped-off passengers with interest, she added her own curse. "Fuck."

Alessandra offhandedly commented, "That's what it means."

"Head to the terminal," Carlo instructed. "Slowly."

Richards added, "Like we have all the time in the world and nothing's wrong." Both men slung their rifles onto their backs.

"Why didn't we get dropped off at the farthest end of the runway?" Maggie asked in a whisper.

"We wanted to be near the road." Carlo muttered another curse.

"Heads-up." Richards nodded toward two armed men from the airport headed their way.

Richards and Carlo held up their hands, telling the women to do the same.

"Cómo están." Richards called out the friendly greeting to the men while Carlo calmly asked the women, "Do any of you have identification on you that declares you are here on a goodwill mission?"

"I do," Sabrina said, surprised. "I forgot about it, I have my ID."

Carlo saw her move to get it out of her pocket. "No," he whispered harshly, stopping her. "Don't reach for anything until we explain the situation. Where is the ID?"

"My back pocket," Sabrina whispered.

"It's probably safe to say they will retrieve the ID themselves." Carlo gave the warning.

"And they'll be assholes about it." Richards added his own whispered opinion.

One of the frowning guards asked, "Qué estás haciendo aquí?" *What are you doing here?*

Richards continued his good-natured smile and easy conversation as if he was a long-lost friend of the guards. They were helping these surgeons return to San Brochero, where they'd been abducted while working a goodwill mission. This was the closest airport.

The small group stood in an awkward semi-circle. Richards continued to gesture toward the women again and again.

Finally, one of the guards aimed his gun at Richards while the other approached Sabrina.

He purposefully reached into all of her pockets, groping, like an asshole, until he found her ID. He studied it for a moment then took it over to his partner.

Richard continued to speak and Alessandra understood his pointed words when he suggested, if the men didn't give them any trouble, he could make it 'worth their while.'

A whispered, heated conversation between the guards ended when the man who fished out the ID threw it on the ground and walked away.

Richards stepped toward the man who stayed. Keeping his left hand up, he reached slowly into his right pocket and pulled out a small number of bills. He handed it over and the man nodded. "Bienvenido a Venezuela." He swept his hand for the group to follow the other guard.

Richards took the lead and Carlo motioned for the women to follow. They walked to the gate that separated the front of the terminal to the landing strip, the guard unlocked it and stood aside. When the group was through, he slammed the gate shut for good measure.

"We need to find a ride," Richards said.

"That's going to be tough," Carlo answered honestly. Alessandra watched his frown increase as he surveyed their surroundings.

"No taxis out here," Richards offered and then sighed. "We peaked their interest."

"Who?" Alessandra asked, following Richards' gaze. The men who'd been lounging by the truck had seen the interaction and were now headed their way.

"I've got cash." Richards shrugged.

"Want to stick around and see if they're the kind of guys who can be reasoned with?" Carlo asked.

"Ladies ..." Richards pointed to the terminal building, "keep walking calmly."

They did as instructed while Carlo took out his phone and the map.

"We need a ride," he said into the phone, then gave a set of coordinates. There was a long pause as they were finally ducked behind the building, Richards surveyed the area and pointed to the thick tree line beyond the road that pulled into the dead end of the airport drop-off.

Carlo nodded as he said, "Five. We're fully loaded and going to get looks."

"Ladies, when I say go, we're running for the tree line right over there." Richards pointed.

Carlo pulled out a wax pencil and made a mark. "We'll be there."

"Go." Richards said the word and began running, the women following, and Carlo bringing up the rear.

Alessandra held her arms up in front of her face as she barreled into the brush, her ankles slapped with overgrowth and she pushed aside the wispy trees that hadn't grown enough to be too problematic. Once they had gone several steps into the trees, Richards stopped the women and motioned for everyone to crouch down.

Alessandra glanced around and when she didn't see Carlo nearby, she started to stand, but Richards put a hand on her arm and gave a shake of his head, mouthing, "He's fine."

The tense moments ticked by, agonizingly slow.

When a rustle of leaves erupted in sound, Alessandra was sure the blood stopped pumping through her system.

Carlo crouched next to the group. "They're headed into the airport to look for us. If they don't find us, we'll find out how tenacious they're going to be in their search."

"How long until we rendezvous with our ride?" Richards asked.

"Thirty minutes."

"How far?" Richards asked.

"Far." Carlo looked at the women and assessed them quickly. "We have to get a little more than three kilometers in thirty minutes."

"Through this jungle area?" Alessandra asked.

Carlo nodded then added, "To the outskirts of the nearby city."

"Is it safe?" Maggie asked, her voice thick with emotion.

"No," Richards said honestly.

"Then we're wasting time," Sabrina said.

Methodically they pushed their way through the overgrown jungle, there was no time to be careful, the overall mood was haste. So that's what they made, with branches slapping arms and faces, the terrain wobbly at best, and Alessandra trying to hold tight to every last bit of energy and calm she possessed. When it began to rain, the torrential downpour continued to test her limits which she had been certain she'd reached two days prior. She hoped the adrenaline would boost her endurance.

They stumbled out of the jungle and into the town where a 'ride' was supposedly waiting.

"Take a breath," Carlo instructed, as he studied the map once more with Richards looking over his shoulder.

Carlo checked his watch. "We have eleven minutes to make it to the other side of town."

"Is everyone able to run?" Richards asked.

They began to jog through the sleepy town, down the paved roads crawling with patches of dried tar. The poverty of the town was evident in the wear and tear of the buildings, the buildup of moss on red tin roofs and sagging walls with cracks. But the mixture of yellow and orange painted homes set against the foliage-covered mountains that crawled up around the outskirts of the city, created a charming scene.

The rain continued, no longer a downpour, but it was hardly noticeable compared to the stitch in Alessandra's side and cramp in her leg.

Richards came to a church and continued right inside.

Their heavy breathing and the squeak of their wet shoes echoed off the vaulted ceiling.

Carlo checked his phone, keeping the door open a crack and watching outside.

Only a handful of seconds seemed to pass when Carlo grunted, "Here we go."

Outside there sat an old Toyota van. Carlo slid open the van's door and he along with the women climbed in as fast as they could, while Richards jumped into the front.

The driver took off just as Carlo was closing the door.

"El Jefe said you owe him a favor," the driver said.

Richards shook his head. "Tell El Jefe we appreciate the help, but we deal in cash, not favors." He pulled out another rubber banded sum of money and handed it over.

The man pulled the car over and made a quick call; Alessandra knew enough Spanish to understand he was asking this 'El Jefe' if he could accept money rather than a favor.

It must have been okay, because he smiled, called, "Es bueno," and put the car in drive.

"You know where we're going?" Carlo asked.

The man nodded, speaking in broken English. "It will take time. The military look for you."

"What?" Sabrina asked.

"We showed up unannounced in a black hawk, armed, with three women we claimed to be doctors," Richards said. "I'd follow us."

"We're being followed now?" Maggie asked.

"Not this car," the driver said, though he drove quickly. They had gone through two more small towns, on their way to San Brochero, when two military trucks parked at the edge of the third town came into view. The driver calmly pulled into a dirt road, and wound his way back to the town they'd just come from. He came to a gated driveway and honked twice. The gate automatically opened, and after he pulled in and around a slight corner, the high walls and now closed serrated gate hid the van.

"We wait for dark," he explained. "They give you food en la casa."

"Whose house is this?" Sabrina asked.

"Un amigo." The driver left it at that.

A woman welcomed them through the front door that led immediately into an enclosed atrium entryway. The walls were painted a bright yellow and native palms, ferns and colorful blooms surrounded the area. She gestured for the group to sit in the worn lawn chairs surrounding a table. Then she disappeared into the house beyond, bringing back bottles of water and a simple meal.

The doctors ate in silence, the air of a threat still stifling. After a few hours, once the sun set, the group was packed back into the van.

After an hour, Maggie glanced behind them; it was a rural road, so there were no lights.

"Are we safe?" Sabrina voiced Maggie's concern.

"Yes," Richards said.

"Are you sure?" Sabrina asked again.

He turned in his seat, looking in the back of the van. "I'm not the kind of guy who lies. You're okay, and we'll make sure you continue to be okay for the remainder of your work in Venezuela."

Sabrina nodded her head several times. Maggie tried to catch her breath but it came out in a sob. She wiped at her eyes and tried several deep breaths.

After two hours, the landscape was once again recognizable.

"We're almost there," Sabrina sighed.

San Brochero had a population of about three thousand. The position of the town near the Colombian border resulted in continual fighting. A lack of government funding brought about poverty and a division of the classes, the result of which meant that many of the younger population and those who had degrees were moving away in search of a better life. But Alessandra loved the people; they were robust, lively and passionate.

"How can you be so sure we'll be safe for the remainder?" Alessandra asked Carlo the question she'd been too nervous to ask since they'd convinced the men to take them back to the hospital.

"Because Richards and I will make sure of it," Carlo said.

"Richards and *you*?" Alessandra asked.

"Yes."

She began shaking her head no, but Carlo ignored her. He pulled out his phone, dialed, then handed it over to Alessandra.

She frowned at him until she put the phone to her ear and heard her brother's voice.

"Sono io." *It's me*, Alessandra said.

"O grazie a dio." *Thank God.* "Are you okay?"

"I'm fine." Her voice caught as she said the words, so she repeated, "I'm fine."

"It's been seven hours since Carlo was supposed to check in. What happened? Were there problems in Guyana?"

Alessandra cleared her throat. "We're not in Guyana."

"What? Where are you?"

"We're in Venezuela."

"What the hell do you mean you're still in Venezuela? What happened?" he asked angrily.

"I can't leave the hospital," she stated.

"The fuck you can't. Alessandra, you're coming home," he hissed.

"No, I'm not." She met his anger and it helped straighten her spine after everything she'd been through in the past few days. A good fight was just what she needed.

"I can't save you again. Do you know what kind of manpower, how many favors I had to call in, how many favors Carlo had to call in? Alessandra, I can't worry about you too."

"You don't have to worry. Carlo and another man are staying with us for the remainder of our time here. To protect us."

She made the mistake of looking at Carlo. He winked at her and she frowned in reply. *I'll deal with you in a minute*, she thought. At the same time she tried to push the problems aside that she knew would arise from being so close to him for the next three months.

Damnit.

"Voglio parlare con Carlo." *I want to talk to Carlo*, Parker said angrily.

She handed the phone to Carlo and it was her turn to wink at him as he faced her brother's wrath.

Chapter Fifty-Seven

"Gracias doctora, gracias." The patient Alessandra was finishing up with gripped her hands in thanks.

Alessandra smiled softly at the woman. "De nada." She turned to the nurse who was helping and instructed to give the woman some salve for the infection that had brought her to the hospital. She asked if there was any supply of penicillin and when the nurse answered in the negative, Alessandra tried not to let her annoyance show. "Then the salve should do most of the work. But perhaps we can prescribe some acetaminophen for the discomfort."

This time the nurse nodded.

Alessandra gently wrung herself from the woman's hands and left her to the nurse.

She rounded a corner and bumped into Maggie. "Alex! My god, I haven't seen you in three days." They'd made it back safely, had somehow found sleep, and were able to reorganize themselves and get back to work. The week since their return had flown by.

"How are you doing?" she asked, letting Maggie pull her in for a hug.

"Busy," Maggie sighed. "I know we're all busy, but I'm glad we came back. We're definitely needed."

Alessandra nodded in agreement.

"Now, I have about sixty seconds, tell me everything that's been going on." Maggie demanded.

"With my patients?"

"No. With that grunting, off-putting, attractive Carlo of yours." She winked.

"He's a friend." She waved the idea away. "There's nothing more."

Maggie snorted. "Well, that's not true."

"Maggie."

"He looks at you like–"

"I know," Alessandra muttered. She was tired of people telling her how he looked at her. Jessica, Cassie, Matteo, her mother ... she knew how he looked at her. And this time she had a heightened awareness of it because he hadn't *stopped* looking at her that way since he pulled her into the van.

At least he hadn't said anything that hadn't been work related. But the memory of the last time they saw each other, and the damn way she kept finding him *looking at her*, was driving her crazy. She didn't need another reminder.

"I wish I had someone who looked at me that way. That's all I'm saying." Maggie nodded. "And your time is up so I won't bother you about it anymore. I'm just grateful he and Richards stayed. It's nice to feel safe." The words were barely out when Maggie changed directions with an offhanded wave goodbye.

"Have a good shift," Alessandra called. Her own was finally over. She was glad for the rest she would be able to get, but returning to her room was tricky.

She, Sabrina and Maggie were always chaperoned by one of the two men. And one of those damn men was always lurking about, *looking* after Alessandra's well-being.

She turned into the waiting room of the hospital and found that off-putting, attractive Carlo. He was slouched in a chair, looking at nothing in particular, but his daunting presence had caused the five waiting patients to sit as far away from him as they could.

When she saw him for the first time in the van, tight black shirt, muscles straining against the short sleeves, dark green bulletproof vest, gun strapped to his side, and an earpiece crawling into his ear; he was the most frightening, glorious vision she'd ever laid eyes on.

Now, he sat wearing khaki pants and a loose gray button-down shirt. She knew, though, that there was a gun strapped to his waist and the earpiece was still present, so he and Richards could be in constant contact as they took turns patrolling the perimeter of the hospital.

The first order of business on the women's return (after a good night's sleep and a shower) was to talk with the hospital directors. Carlo and Richards offered their services as private security for the duration of the women's contracts.

The Chief of Medicine thanked the men but as the organization ran on a bare-bones budget, private security was not something they could even begin to afford.

Carlo stopped the man with his words. "It will be no cost to you. We feel the need to volunteer our time. And we're happy to supply you with the background information you might need on us."

When Carlo and Richards were cleared to help, they began implementing changes to the rundown security measures that were in place.

As stolen medication was one of the major problems the hospital suffered from, they replaced two of the flimsy medicine cabinets with narcotic safes.

On the second floor, they reinforced one of the large rooms with steel bulletproof doors, then installed locks on the inside and enough supplies to last forty-eight hours for the complete staff of eighteen and at least twenty patients. It was a panic room of sorts, a place to safely hide until help could arrive; should anyone come into the hospital to attempt more abductions.

Where the Chief of Medicine had been impressed with the amount of work the two men had gotten done so quickly, Alessandra was impressed at the number of contacts they both had.

She asked Carlo about it one night as he walked her back to the apartment she shared with Sabrina, Maggie, two other nurses from the program (and now Carlo and Richards). He shrugged and said, "It's cyclical. Someone needs help today, another one will need help down the line."

"But I thought Richards said you don't deal in favors?"

"We don't deal in favors with bad guys. With the good guys, it's always favors." He winked.

"Pronto?" *Ready?* Carlo asked, pulling Alessandra out of her thoughts.

She nodded and he stood for the walk back to the apartment.

Richards and Carlo had moved into the small four-bedroom apartment the women shared. It was a cramped space: one bathroom, four rooms with two twin size beds in each room, kitchen, tiny living room and a table with three chairs. But since the doctors worked opposing twelve-hour shifts, there were usually only two or three roommates home at a time, so a bed was always available for sleeping.

Carlo and Richards walked each of the women to and from work. They checked on them during various times of the day. The men were constantly changing their timing and paths, insisting that the women also switch up their movements as well. If another militant group was watching and wanted to take them hostage, they would be plotting movements and schedules. So it was better to keep them irregular. The rule even extended to the walk back to the apartment.

Today, Carlo led Alessandra across the small street in front of the hospital to where a taxi was waiting.

Since the apartment was only a seven-minute walk, she figured they were going to be taking a long drive this evening.

"Sabrina and Maggie are working tonight," she said.

He winked at Alessandra. "So are the nurses and Richards."

"That's not what I meant." She waved his innuendo away and yawned. "I'm starving. Since we're driving, can we find a place to eat?"

"What did you have in mind?"

She shrugged. "I'm not sure where we're going. Maybe you know someone who knows someone who knows a good place to eat." She hid her smile.

"Probably." He leaned forward and had a quiet conversation with the driver; the man grinned. "I know good eat place," he said in thick English.

With that, he put the car in gear and pulled onto the road.

"How many languages do you know?" she asked. Why hadn't she thought to ask him such a question before? Probably because the only times they went anywhere it had been in Italy.

"I only know three," he answered.

"Only?"

"*You* speak three languages," he said.

"How do you know that?"

"Italian, English and French," he said in way of an answer.

"I never told you I speak French."

"No, you didn't."

She didn't ask him to explain how he knew and instead said, "My Spanish is getting better every day."

"It is."

She gave into another yawn, stretched her arms, bent her head back and elbowed Carlo's shoulder as she breathed in deep and let out a wide 'ahh-yawww'.

"How was your day?" Carlo asked.

"Difficult."

He nodded as if he understood, and he probably did; he had watched the comings and goings and inner workings of the hospital for the past week.

"It's the same thing every day; shortages of various medications, and what we can get goes quickly; malaria, malnutrition; poor living conditions ..." She rolled her neck and stretched it as she talked. "We're out of penicillin again, but I think there should be a shipment arriving in a day or two. If it doesn't get intercepted."

Carlo reached behind her and began to knead her neck with his hand. She thought about telling him to stop, but it felt good. And she was too exhausted to fight or pretend it *didn't* feel good.

"I don't think I ever realized exactly how impactful your work is," Carlo admitted. "I knew it was important, but it's different seeing it firsthand."

A gentle rain began. The driver turned on the windshield wipers, cracked his window and turned on the poor excuse for a defroster. Alessandra was mesmerized by the wipers, soothed by the sound of the rain and Carlo's hand working the knots out of her shoulders and neck.

The driver had taken them around the outskirts of the city and was now crawling up the main road into the low foothills surrounding San Brochero.

"Was it the same, working in Kyrgyzstan?" Carlo asked.

She thought about not answering him, she wasn't opposed to talking about Kyrgyzstan. It was the circumstances that led to her decision to go that she was reluctant to talk about.

"It was different." She finally decided the bland answer was the best. "Kyrgyzstan was gorgeous. Mountainous, a nomadic lifestyle really, but unfortunately, a war-torn country." She smiled and sighed. "Most of their problems stem from those conflicts, but their biggest problem is tuberculosis."

"You've saved a lot of people in your career, haven't you?" It wasn't quite a statement or a question.

Alessandra shrugged. "I've tried."

He dropped his hand and it was several moments before he quietly whispered, "I've killed a lot of men."

Alessandra was taken aback by the confession. "We never talked about that." She pointed out the obvious. "I'd argue that self-defense was a big part of those deaths." It was her turn to make a statement that didn't need an answer, but he nodded anyway. "I think there's an argument for the line of work you've chosen and the fact that you choose to put yourself in harm's way."

He grunted in reply, looking out the front window.

Alessandra licked her lips. "How many people would you say you've saved?"

His head turned quickly with the comment, shock on his face.

Alessandra continued, "How many times have you gone into a dangerous situation and saved someone like me, Sabrina and Maggie? Like Jessica?"

He narrowed his gaze. "I don't know if that makes it right."

If there was more to say, he was cut off by the arrival at their destination.

The driver got out explaining that he might as well get himself some dinner too. He would wait for them until they were ready to go back to town, and Carlo could pay him at the end of the night. Then he gestured for the couple to go ahead of him.

Carlo took Alessandra's hand and they hurried up the wooden-planked walkway that led to a shack of a building with a glowing neon beer sign in each window beside the front door.

The more impoverished of San Brochero lived in shacks made from whatever debris they could find, creating a shantytown among the foothills. Alongside the makeshift homes, some of the more industrious had opened businesses.

San Brochero was big enough to house a mall, grocery stores and plenty of restaurants, *so there must be something pretty special about this place*, Alessandra mused.

She ran a hand through her hair, ridding it of the slight rain that had drizzled on her, as she took in the dilapidated room set with several tables, most of them full. An older woman, carrying food to one of the tables, smiled and called out a greeting, then gestured for them to sit anywhere they liked.

Carlo motioned to an empty table in the back of the room. "They have the best asado negro in the area," Carlo said as they sat.

"Ah, that was the whispered conversation with the driver."

"I told him to take us to a restaurant that had the best local dish."

The woman who greeted them brought two beers to the table. She was in her early seventies, short, her shoulders slightly hunched from age, but her eyes were alight and bright with mischief and life. She put a hand on Carlo's shoulder and commented about his size. "A man like this has a big appetite." She laughed and gave his bicep a squeeze. "I don't know if we have enough food."

The woman was contagious; just a moment in her presence and Alessandra felt comfortable and at peace.

"Dos especiales?" the woman asked, then gave another laugh. "But that's what everyone comes here for, the special."

"Sí, por favor," Carlo said.

She gave Alessandra's shoulder a squeeze as she walked away.

Alessandra took a long drink of the beer; she might have questioned the assumption if she hadn't been here long enough to know that the water wasn't always that reputable. So if someone wanted a cold drink at a bar or restaurant, a cerveza was the given choice.

She rolled the bottle between her hands. "You really *are* good at gathering intel."

"When you've been around as long as I have, you learn a few things," he said.

"Like what?"

"Like who to talk to in order to get information on local militia. Or, that on the first Friday of every month, the militia in the area receive a sort of welfare check and need to come to town to collect their money. That's when they purchase goods, make trouble in bars, and possibly abduct people that can help their cause."

Alessandra raised an eyebrow. "Tomorrow is the first Friday of the month."

"We have a plan in place," he reassured and continued his list of specialties. "I can also find out what the most recommended local cuisine is and who makes it the best."

"Hence ..." She gestured with her beer bottle around the building.

The proprietress brought over a small plate of food that looked like a mix between bread and a tortilla. She shook her head in wonder as she gazed at Carlo and in Spanish said, "Start with this. I need to start filling that stomach."

Carlo took a bite and grinned. "Es muy bueno."

The woman nodded. "Of course it is." She gestured for Alessandra to eat as well then called out a greeting to a family of four that walked in.

"You have a way with the ladies," she said before taking a bite. "It's like naan."

Carlo nodded, his head tilted to the side as he watched Alessandra. "What?"

"I was going to say something suggestive," he admitted, "but it's not right. So I'll just say thank you for coming to dinner with me tonight. This is nice."

"It is," she admitted. "Although, I think it's just the exhaustion that's keeping me from arguing with you."

"I think it's because some time has passed," he offered. But before either of them could contemplate that idea, the rest of the food was delivered.

Simple black beans and rice were served next to two healthy slices of seasoned meat. The older woman sighed and this time, she squeezed Alessandra's arm. "You have a good-looking man here."

Alessandra licked her lips and gingerly pieced together some of her broken Spanish. "He might look pretty, but he is ..." She frowned and asked Carlo, "How do you say high maintenance?"

He supplied the word and the older woman bent over laughing. She gave a rapid-fire reply and then waved to the food, ordered them to eat and left.

"I didn't catch all that."

Carlo studied his food as he muttered, "She said, he might be high maintenance but he looks like he could make up for it in bed."

Alessandra laughed as she watched the woman across the room. "No she didn't."

He held up his hands. "On my mother's life, that is exactly what she said."

Alessandra turned her attention to her meat, cut into it and took a bite. She thought her eyes might roll into the back of her head. "Oddio. E molto buono." *Oh God, it's so good.*

Carlo took a bite and nodded in agreement as he went about inhaling his own food.

Alessandra glanced at Carlo several times as they ate in appreciative silence. When she was full, and the beer had aided in relaxing her exhausted bones, she sat back and admitted, "You are quite a handsome man, Carlo Moretti."

Chapter Fifty-Eight

Carlo slowly lowered his fork.

From the moment he had her in his arms in the van, he'd been desperate for any sign that she was willing to give him a chance, that she might still find him more than a brute who ruins lives.

He hated that he couldn't be the face of her rescuer in the cave, but El Jefe was an untrusting, punchy man. When Carlo arrived at the agreed upon time and day, El Jefe had been reluctant to allow him use of the road. It took more soothing and money than anticipated.

But from the moment Ricardo and Carlo dropped ALPHA Team off, the guilt and worry picked at him. When the call came that Richards had the women, his anxiety only seemed to heighten as Parker's words swirled around him that Alessandra had gone to Venezuela because *she's so damn heartbroken, she didn't feel like she had any other choice.'*

And then he was helping her into the van and all his fears dissipated. Since then, he'd used every moment, every opportunity to prove to her what he was willing to do to make *them* work.

Now, her seemingly offhanded compliment elated him and froze him in place at the same time.

He weighed his options, should he return the compliment? Should he tell her how much he missed her? Should he apologize, for more things than a true man should ever have to apologize to the love of his life for? Should he tell her about a vision of a life together he had the past week that might fit both of their passions?

In the span of several heartbeats, a lifetime of thoughts came and went. In the end, he decided to give her space, fearing anything he said would shut her down.

"Thank you," she broke the silence, "for saving me."

Light poured through his whole body. "I always will." He whispered the truth.

He would save her a hundred times over if that was what he had to do in order to have her in his life. If his assigned Herculean tasks were to save her again and again to prove his love, he would.

"I wish …" Her words petered out as the old woman approached the table.

Carlo was half tempted to yell for the woman to leave so he could find out what it was that Alessandra wished. Instead, he took a deep breath and met the old woman's smile with his own.

"¿Cómo estuvo la cena?" *How was your meal?*

"Excelente," Carlo said, then added an Italian, "Buonissimo."

She patted him on the back and praised their empty plates as she bussed them, asking, "Would you like anything else?"

Alessandra hid a yawn and then admitted, "Just my bed. I'm exhausted."

The woman nodded. "Usted es una doctora muy ocupada." *You're a very busy doctor.*

"I'm sorry, have we met?" Alessandra asked.

"I've seen you at the hospital."

"Oh. I'm sorry, I see so many patients."

"It was my husband, you saw him for a rash, but he's doing much better now."

"Oh good, I'm so glad." She didn't think she would remember the husband if she saw him, either. The long days and vast number of patients caused the faces to run together.

"How much do we owe you?" Carlo asked.

"Nada." The woman waved her hands as if the offer offended her. "It's a pleasure to serve the doctor in our restaurant."

Carlo looked at Alessandra, wondering what they should do. She held out her hands to the woman. "Thank you. I'm going to tell everyone to come here for the special. And if you need anything, please come to the hospital and ask for me, I'm Doctor Salvatore."

Carlo pulled out a few bolivar, the Venezuela currency, and hid them under his glass bottle while Alessandra had the woman's attention.

The driver was in the car waiting for them. Even with the rain still coming down, he had his windows slightly open, and they could hear a female voice crooning over the crackle of his radio.

He asked after their meal as they settled themselves and beamed when Carlo said, "It was amazing. Thank you for the suggestion."

"It was really good," she reiterated as the driver pulled onto the dirt road that brought them here. "Since everyone is working tonight, does Richards need help?" she asked Carlo.

"Everything should be fine, but if you want to sleep at the hospital, I can go help him."

"God, no. I need a break from the hospital. I hate to say that. But I need a bed in a place that isn't a hospital."

"In that case, I stay with you and see to your safety."

Alessandra nodded and looked out the window, lost in thought. Carlo watched out the front windshield as the lights and colors from the city center lit up the horizon.

It didn't take long to arrive back at the apartment. Carlo didn't realize until the cab pulled up to the front of the building, just how tired he was too.

It would be good to get some rest, to recharge.

He paid the taxi driver and they jogged the slight distance in the rain to the covered door of the building. Alessandra was already fishing out her keys, so he pressed himself against the wall by the entry to wait when a memory flashed. He recalled another time, after a satisfying dinner, when they stood in front of her building while she looked for her keys. It had been raining then too.

They were all smiles and laughter that night. Lost in the early stages of love. Lost in the early stages of each other. They'd been desperate to get upstairs. Desperate to explore each other.

He stepped away from the wall and turned toward her. "Why did you leave?" He had felt so at ease around her lately, as if so much had been left behind them and they'd amicably taped themselves back into a friendship, that the question had a life of its own and thought this was the perfect time to slip out.

Alessandra turned slowly to look at Carlo. Her face paled, the ease replaced with anger.

He took a step back, out from the cover of the awning, into the rain. "What?" Her voice hitched on the whispered question.

What had he done?

Proving himself to her did not require questioning the past. Especially not the questions he could answer himself. He *knew* why she left him.

"I'm sorry," he quickly tried to amend.

"I don't want to talk about this."

"I know. I'm sorry." He took another step away from her.

She found the keys, put them in the lock and turned, but she didn't open the door. Her voice was low when she muttered, "There's a divide between us. It's too wide."

Still, she didn't open the door, but turned her head slightly and gave a sad smile.

"I took you for granted." It was time to truly apologize. Carlo touched her arm and tugged gently. She let go of the keys in the lock and turned her body so she was facing him. He dropped his hands, even though they burned to hold her, to touch her, to pull her to him. She was listening and that was enough. She didn't meet his gaze, her eyes stayed glued to his shoulder. He went on, "I never worked on our relationship, as many times as I begged you to let me try, I never did."

She visibly swallowed.

"I let you down, again and again. And when I put your life in danger, I disappeared. Of course you had to leave." His throat burned as he owned his flaws.

Alessandra reached out and touched his shoulder, but pulled her hand away as if it had been scorched.

"You're getting drenched," she said.

"I'm sorry I wasn't there for you."

She turned back to the door, but the second her hand touched the keys, she swung back to him. She opened her mouth and had to clear her throat several times before she said, "You left me long before I ever left you."

He nodded.

"I'd go two weeks, three weeks, two damn months and not receive one word from you. I had to work too. I had to look after patients and be at my very best for them and I couldn't do it." She pointed a finger at him.

"I was falling apart and you ... as long as you had a piece of ass that was there for you whenever you were around, you were fine."

"I never meant for it to be like that." She opened her mouth but before she could say anything he said, "You deserved so much better."

She turned back to the door, pushed it open slightly, and said, "I left to get away from the memories of you. They were everywhere."

"But–"

"Carlo." She hissed his name for him to stop.

He took her shoulders and turned her so she was facing him, he ran his wet hands down the length of her arms until he was holding her hands. "I haven't stopped thinking about you since I first met you. You have always been the first thing I think about when I wake up, the last thing I think about before I fall asleep, and if I'm lucky enough, you haunt my dreams."

"I waited and waited for you," she said softly, her eyes lowering. "For four weeks I waited, first in that damn hospital room and then in my apartment. The only person who showed up was your *partner*," she mocked. "Oh, and my damn bodyguard. They both told me how dangerous things were, and how, as soon as you could you'd come for me. But you didn't come, Carlo." When she finally met his gaze, the built-up anger and sorrow overflowed. "I waited and you never came and you never called."

"I have no excuse."

"No, you don't. I was stabbed, right outside my hospital. And you never showed up and as bad as all that was, the wound ... the doctor who saw to my surgery said I'll never be able to have kids now." She choked on the words and Carlo's foundation violently began to crumble.

"We never talked about kids–"

"Carlo, we never talked about *anything* important."

No amount of sorry or worthy actions to prove his love could correct any of this.

She continued, "I was all alone with such awful news and there was no real way to get in touch with you. I went home to my empty apartment and the life outside the hospital, a life with you, came crashing down around me. And I was left with the shadows and ashes. So I did the only thing I had the energy to do. I ran away to get over you." The tears fell uninhibited.

When she had been physically hurt because of his job, he thought distance was the best thing, to keep her safe. She was so strong, she never needed anyone, and he thought, even as she recovered, she wouldn't need him.

He'd been wrong about so many things.

"You were a ghost and if you had really wanted a life with me, if we were really going to get married, there would have been a way to get in touch with you when I needed you."

The floodgates of her pain and anger had opened, and the least he could do was take it all.

She pulled her hands away from him, and pushed open the door. She'd gone a few steps in the lobby when she turned to him, several steps behind her and said, "And I did your job for you, by the way."

He frowned at the sudden turn in the conversation.

"That self-defense stuff Cassie taught me kept me alive, and the knife that asshole used on me had fingerprints on it. The police were able to identify my attacker. Did you know that?"

He had no idea. His agency had never identified the man. He was presumed dead, but the body had never been recovered after it was 'lost' from the morgue. He'd overlooked the knife, failing her yet again.

Her voice quivered as she said, "The name they found on record was Paolo Costa. Otherwise known as–"

"Il Serpente," he whispered with wide eyes.

Chapter Fifty-Nine

Alessandra ripped the paper out of her notebook, wadded it into a ball and threw it across the room to join the other crumpled copies.

This shouldn't be that difficult.

But it was.

Her sunny kitchen mocked her, begging her to remember when Carlo sat in this very chair while she made pasta.

This, she thought, *this* was why she was leaving.

It wasn't running away. She wasn't a runner. She was steadfast and stalwart. Stoic and all the other crap her colleagues and review boards had said about her throughout her career.

But now, after everything, she needed to leave, she needed to mend her heart and spirit.

She'd waited longer than a person should, and she was no longer interested in excuses or talking it all out.

In fact, she didn't want to talk about anything. And she sure as hell didn't want to explain anything to the man who'd caused all of this.

And it wasn't like he'd done anything to check on her. He'd disappeared, abandoning her.

He didn't get any more chances.

Carlo,

We need to talk but I can't get in touch with you. I've tried your phone, Matteo and Luca. No one will give me answers or a different contact for you. I can't go on

like this. I'm volunteering to work with Doctors Without Borders. I am not certain how long I'll be gone. But I do know this, when I return, I think it best that we no longer see each other.
I do wish you well.
Be safe.
Alessandra

She ripped the page out, read through it again, then wadded it up and threw it across the room.

There were no right words for this. She didn't want to leave a note, but it was the very least she was willing to do.

She tried again.

Carlo,
I think it is time we both acknowledge we cannot build a relationship on absence. I'm going away for a while. I don't know when I'll return, but when I do, I don't wish to see you again.
-A

She read the note again and hated it, but she hated this one the least. So this was what she was going to leave in an envelope taped to her door, when Carlo finally came around.

This was all she could bring herself to do.

Chapter Sixty

Carlo and Alessandra walked quietly up the stairs to the shared first floor apartment.

He followed her at a distance, and she shook her head to dislodge the memories and manic feeling of frustration. She swore to herself that he never got to find out what she'd gone through. But he'd pushed her, so she used her words and the story to hurt him.

Her hands shook as she tried to open the lock. She should turn and demand he go back to the hospital or sleep outside the door.

She had no desire to go into an empty apartment with Carlo. Because she knew she would turn to him at some point. And she would look into his eyes again. And she would see the shock and horror and regret in them, and the way her words had the exact effect she wanted them to have as they thrust to the core of his being.

She knew how he felt. It was how she felt when the doctor came in and explained that the trauma to her abdomen was such that there were going to be a lot of pelvic adhesions, and most of the time, such damage caused infertility.

She waited then.

Waited for him to show up.

Waited for him to call.

Then she waited in her apartment when the tears had stopped.

And when she finally found a shred of herself; when she was finally able to piece herself back together, she decided to stop waiting and held fast to the first idea that came to her.

She contacted the team she befriended the first time she worked with Doctors Without Borders, and because of her expertise and previous work with the organization, they were able to get her an immediate assignment.

The timing was perfect.

Alessandra was done waiting.

Carlo watched her walk into the apartment, and before he knew what he was doing, he picked her up forcing her to wrap her arms around his neck.

Eyes wide she demanded, "Put me down. What the hell are you doing?"

He didn't answer, because he didn't have one. He was going on instinct now. He carried her into the room that was hers, feeling ridiculous now as he stood in the middle, dripping wet, holding her. But the last thing he wanted was to let her go.

She wiggled frantically in his arms, pushing at his chest, until he finally blinked and set her down.

"I'm sorry," he muttered.

She took several dramatic steps backward, an attempt to put distance between them, but misjudged how close her bed was and her knees buckled when they came in contact with the edge, the old mattress squeaking as she fell back, sitting on it.

Carlo ran his hands through his wet hair. He opened his mouth several times, but he couldn't find any words. He never thought about children when he'd proposed. He never thought about children as being something he lost when she left him.

Now the thought dislodged part of him. He clenched his jaw as his throat burned. His chest squeezed his ribs against his heart. He started shaking, unable to stop it, and when the first tear slipped down his face, he hung his head, as silent sobs tore his heart into pieces.

When she leaned forward and took his hand, it was his undoing. He fell to his knees in the middle of the small room.

Her hand on his shoulder urged him forward, to cover the slight distance that separated them. He rested his head on her lap, wrapped his arms around her waist and took solace in her whispered words and her hands as they gently smoothed his hair. Giving him the comfort he hadn't been able to give her.

"We did love each other." she whispered.

Chapter Sixty-One

R ome was hot and muggy. Most of the population fled the city during the month of August, opting for the cooler ocean fronts and higher mountain climates. Had it really been just last year when he and Alessandra joined the mass migration to Tuscany?

Now he was in the thick of a tricky situation, hot and miserable.

Sweat slid down his back as he walked down Alessandra's street, the sun scorched but he didn't care. He didn't believe Matteo when he'd told him that she'd left. Carlo had finally been able to text her, but she hadn't answered or checked her messages and when he called, the phone went directly to a message saying the number was no longer in service.

He convinced himself that she was possibly taking time off, hiding in her apartment. One thing he did know for sure, she was angry at him. Hell, he was angry with himself. But he was trying to keep her safe. Now if he could just get her to listen to him long enough to explain it. Maybe they could wash the slate clean and start over.

He studied his surroundings as he arrived at the front door of her apartment building; the streets were as tired and exhausted from the heat as he was, and there wasn't a soul in sight. He pulled out a few tools from his pocket and picked the lock. He wasn't going to call up to her apartment, he was just going to force his way in. He left the keys she'd given him in Pisa. Not sure why really, other than he liked the idea that he could hold the keys and know he had a home he was working on building one day.

He rolled his eyes as he stepped in the cool dark foyer, he couldn't pick her door lock; no, he *wouldn't* pick it. He'd just knock until she answered or sit in front of her door until she got home.

He took the stairs to calm himself. To take his time.

He rounded the corner and saw an envelope taped to the door, and as he got closer, saw that his name had been scribbled on the outside.

His heartbeat quickened and his hands shook as he pulled out the note.

Emotion obscured his vision as he read, so he had to try several times. When the words seeped in, he walked downstairs, the memories from the apartment and the words from the note following him. He put the paper back in the envelope and pocketed it.

When he pushed open the door the heat sent threatening fingers around his neck. He pulled on the front of his shirt as the world tilted a bit, he was dizzy and had to shake himself out of it.

This shouldn't have been a shock. He knew Matteo wasn't a liar but he'd held on to the pipe dream of finding her waiting for him.

His pride was hurt, but he couldn't blame her.

He'd get over this. What was a little break up? He'd been through hell and back in his life. He could deal with this.

He walked the city, unable to think of where to go, so he wasn't surprised when his feet carried him to the field office. It didn't take a lot of time or effort to find that her visa had been approved for a trip to Kyrgyzstan.

He sat in front of the computer for a long time, until he was brought out of his reprieve by a colleague who asked his opinion on something he was working on.

Carlo left the office, took a taxi to the airport and stood in the middle of the bustling entryway as he played out every argument for following her and every argument for leaving her alone.

In the end, he pulled out the note, ripped it up and tossed it into the nearest trash can. If this was what she wanted, then it was the least he could do for her.

Chapter Sixty-Two

Alessandra blinked her eyes open, they burned with the effort. That happened when she was exhausted and had been crying. She didn't move, but watched as the clouds, with a luminescent white and dark blue glow, drifted across the sky. She forgot to close the curtains. But maybe it was better this way.

She reached down and gently touched the warm hand that was wrapped just below her breasts. She traced the veins in Carlo's hands, gently so as not to wake him.

When they'd both shed the tears of regret from the past, exhaustion took over and they silently agreed to table any more conversation and took solace in each other's arms as they moved to cuddle together in the small bed.

Alessandra felt lighter this morning. Maybe because while she had bottled up the anger and heartache in an attempt to get over it, when she was pushed, it wasn't a fight that exploded between them, but finally Carlo's comprehension of what she'd gone through while waiting for him.

The buildup of pressure was released through Carlo's tears and silent sobs as he knelt before her, head in her lap, clutching her. And as she stroked his hair, she allowed her own tears to flow, as the void where she kept all the betrayal and anguish opened. It was the shared heartache that became the much needed balm.

Just before they fell asleep, his whispered words, "I am truly, truly sorry," were the offering of peace she needed.

Alessandra's eyes might have been swollen, and her body ached from the long hours at the hospital, but there was something else this morning.

Relief.

It was all gone, the anger and heartache she harbored in the quiet, lonely hours.

She took a deep breath and reveled in the tranquility.

"Ale." Carlo's deep, sleep laden voice tickled the back of her neck.

She linked her fingers with his. He leaned forward and kissed her neck.

"Are you okay?" he asked.

"I'm better."

His voice was thick when he said, "I'm so sorry."

She squeezed his hand. "Anch'io." *Me too.*

He buried his head in her hair and breathed her in. "Ti amo." *I love you,* his deep, muffled voice declared.

She loved him too. She had fought the emotion for so long and packed it away so strategically, when she opened her mouth to reply in kind, the words were still reluctant.

She rolled over, readjusting their position. The mattress gave annoyed grunts as Carlo lay on his back and she propped her body on top of his. He smiled as she gently brushed a kiss against his lips.

And the electric shock jump-started everything. The need was instantaneous.

She was desperate for him. The kiss deepened but she wanted more. She wanted his hands to roam and heat her skin. She pushed away from him and wiggled into a kneeling position so she could rid herself of her clothes.

Carlo followed her, sitting up but he stopped her hands as they gripped the bottom of her shirt. He didn't say anything but the message was clear, she didn't have to do this if she didn't want to.

She slapped his hand away, raising her eyebrow and allowing a smile to curve her lips. His eyes darkened with hunger and in a flash, he stood, pulled her to her feet and removed her clothes.

Alessandra missed this, the reverence he had for her body, the joy reflected in his eyes as he touched her, unable to get enough.

She reached out her hands to help him with his clothes and their hands tangled, their breathing shortened, they both laughed as they fought for control.

He pulled her into his arms and she let the breath of missing this rush out in a moan.

He kissed a frantic trail down the side of her neck, squeezed her waist in his grip and she splayed her hands across his chest. His skin burned, sizzling under her fingertips.

She pushed him until he was laying once more and she was on top of him.

She missed his rough, hot, skilled hands. She wanted more.

She wanted a lot more.

She wanted to tell him she loved him. She wanted to see what they could become as the fire drew them in and burned them. She wanted to see what happened when they both bent toward each other, when they were willing to give and take.

She wanted this passion that scorched and scared her. Hell, she might even want the arguments every now and again.

But the arguments always lead to pain.

As his hands groped, her thoughts got in the way. She was twisted up again, confused. "Wait, I'm sorry ... I can't."

Carlo stopped abruptly, letting her pull away and sit back. He propped himself up on his elbows and in a ragged breath said, "We don't have to do anything you don't want to do."

"I know." A tear slipped down her face and she growled, pushing it away.

"Do you want me to go?"

She shook her head and licked her lips. "No. I want you so much ..."

There was a soft rumble in his chest. "I think it's apparent how much I want you."

"You made so many promises before."

He sat up and adjusted so they could sit beside each other and took her hand as he said, "I did make a lot of promises, and I failed to keep them."

"Then what makes you think you won't fail this time?"

"I quit my job."

Alessandra's eyes widened. "What?" She turned toward him.

"I quit," Carlo repeated with a smile.

"When? Not for me. If you quit for me, you can't. Go back."

He laughed at the demand and explained, "I began the paperwork after I got shot. I figure four times in the line of duty is plenty."

But what did that mean? "What will you do?"

"I thought about taking my cousins up on their offer to get back into the family business." He shrugged. "I told you about them, the cousins, aunts and uncles who still run everything. I keep trying to give them my share of the business, but they insist on renting the land from me. It's mine whenever I want to go back."

She shook her head. "I don't think you'd like that life."

"No," he answered honestly, "I don't think so either."

"Do you miss your family? You've never really talked about them."

He shrugged. "I do miss them. But I've stayed away for so long ... I thought I was keeping them safe."

"Is that what you did? Did you stay away from me because you thought it would keep me safe?" She hadn't thought of it that way.

He nodded and she tisked at him, rolling her eyes. "Well it didn't work. And it probably isn't working for your family either."

"I suppose I need to figure out where to start over with them too."

"Were you going to try to start over with me?"

"I was, but luckily, you were kidnapped, giving me the perfect opportunity to weasel my way back into your life so I could try to prove how hard I was willing to work on a future with you."

"Hmph."

He brought her hand to his lips.

"What do you want from me, Carlo?"

He pressed her hand against his chest. "A chance. I think we were both playing at love the first time. I know I was. I didn't understand that making a relationship work takes a lot of compromise. Alessandra, I want whatever you're willing to give me." He smiled and licked his lips. "God knows I don't deserve to even be asking this of you, but I want a second chance."

Her heart was pounding frantically, could she do that?

"I can't give up being a doctor and I can't give it up for you," she said sadly, a catch in her throat.

"Then don't," he said matter-of-factly.

"We argue too much," she declared.

"Not really."

His question continued to hang in the air, but she didn't have a reply yet, so instead pointed, "Jessica said we challenge each other."

Carlo smiled. "You do challenge me."

"I don't know how we'll make this work."

"Well, you seem to enjoy volunteering for this organization in places that have little to no security," he said. "I have an idea how we can be together, how I can continue to work in the capacity where I thrive, and how you can too."

She gave a snort of laughter. "What, you're going to travel the world with me and be my bodyguard?"

He winked at her. "It sounds good doesn't it?"

The thought was interesting; she'd give him that.

"How will you make money?" she asked, curious.

"I was thinking about starting a non-profit organization for retired men who haven't quite taken to retirement. Men who still need a dash of adventure every now and then and think protecting doctors and strengthening hospital security in third world countries sounds like fun." He sat up then and took both of Alessandra's hands in his. "I made some calls and there is even an interest in funding from AISE, and I know several veteran organizations that would help support this kind of work."

She was stunned. When did he have time to come up with all of this?

"Ale, I'm not leaving you this time. When it's time to leave here, we'll go home to Rome and I'll spend time setting this organization up and running it from there. Normal business hours."

The idea had merit, she knew there were several locations that Doctors Without Borders had trouble staffing because of the security risks.

"It's interesting," she said as scenarios of waking up with him each morning, not worrying about him each day, and walking hand in hand through Rome to a little café near the Pantheon, fluttered through her vision.

"I'll admit, if you hadn't insisted on coming back here and your brother hadn't called me, I don't know that I would have come up with the idea."

"What if … you want kids?" she whispered.

"We never talked about kids."

"No, we never did."

"I'm thirty-eight Alessandra."

"So am I." She frowned.

"I never envisioned marrying anyone. Not until you came along. Children were definitely not in my future picture, but if you want kids, I'll give you a dozen."

Alessandra pulled her legs up and hugged her knees. "I told you what the doctors said …"

He waved the comment away with a 'pish'. "You told me once that the body takes time to heal and a doctor's best guess isn't always what comes to fruition. And there are a hundred ways to have kids. If you want kids, we'll get some."

She snorted out a laugh. "Carlo, you can't just scoop up kids off the street and start a family."

"Well, not exactly like that, but sure we can."

"What if you resent me? What if quitting your job wasn't the right move?" she asked.

"Alessandra," he blew out his breath and scrubbed his face, "maybe you need to stop telling me how I'm going to feel and allow me to make a life with you. The way I see it, I'm pretty sure my life would finally begin if you give me a chance." His voice was deep with emotion.

Alessandra never thought she'd hear the love of her life tell her that life began with her. Maybe it was her own worries she continued to project on to Carlo, that saw love as an ending. As a tether to something unwanted.

But she wanted him, he wanted her. There either had to be a beginning or an ending. And she needed to decide. It wasn't fair to either of them to not have some definitive decisions made.

"I'm scared," she confessed.

"I don't think this would be any fun if we weren't." He smiled and cupped her face in his hands. "But how many wise men have declared being scared of something was the first step to doing something truly great?"

"Compromise and a willingness to bend a bit?" she pondered.

"I'm willing," he said fiercely.

Her voice was a whisper when she admitted, "I won't be able to take it if you hurt me again."

"But could you take it if we figured this out and loved each other? If we found a way to live together and work together? Could you take it if the passion we have in this bed spilled over into the rest of our lives? I know you're scared, amo. But maybe the possibilities outweigh the fears."

She shook her head and looked at him, amazed. "Who are you?"

"A man in love."

She took a deep breath, and it felt so good she followed it with a few more before she finally whispered, "A second chance?"

He nodded, his eyes searching hers. "Please."

"You said you failed each of the promises you ever made to me."

"Ale–"

"Carlo, you promised my brother you'd save me, and you followed through with that one. I think we can build on that." Her voice shook as she laid her vulnerability before him. "I love you enough to give you a second chance."

She barely finished talking before his lips were on hers once again, sealing his promises.

Chapter Sixty-Three

Carlo adjusted the collar of his shirt for the sixth time, stood up and began to pace once again.

What the hell was he doing?

He scared men. He physically intimidated people just by walking down the street. He watched as some people's eyes darted uncomfortably, hell, he even watched as women took their wide-eyed fill, sensing their animalistic stirrings just by the way they looked at him.

Being intimidating was a big part of the job. So why the hell did he feel like he was about to unravel as he sat in front of her hospital?

Because he already made good on his promise to Salvatore and kept her safe for eight days and eight glorious nights. She told him goodbye in no uncertain terms, and he went back to Pisa, unable to get back to his old life. And like a lovesick moron, he went to his boss and begged for time off so he could jump on the earliest train and run to the siren that called to him.

And here he was. She didn't know he was coming, and he didn't even call and ask after her schedule.

So now he had four more hours to wait. He could have gone around the corner and had a coffee. He could have walked off all the excess nervous energy. Instead, he decided to sit on the bench outside the front of the hospital and wait. He could wait for her as long as he needed.

With each passing hour, he imagined a way she would sneak past him. But he could see her car in the parking lot from this vantage point. She would come for her car sometime.

He rubbed his hands together as he paced. He should have called her.

Hell, maybe he should call Jessica. This was her fault after all. She was the one who got in his head.

One night in Alessandra's apartment, after dinner, while Parker was in the living room on the phone and his sister did dishes, Carlo sat with Jessica on the balcony.

"I couldn't figure it out," Jessica said.

"Figure what out?"

"What kind of woman you'd like." She gave Carlo an exhausted smile.

"What?"

"All those women at all those parties." She referred to the parties her ex-fiancé had forced her to go to in Florence, while she waited for the CIA to get her out of harm's way. "They were so beautiful and you never even *looked* at one. You never even let your eyes follow one woman. Do you know, I actually thought you might be gay?"

"Is there something wrong with that?"

"No, if you were, that would be fine. I'd set you up with my friend John." She studied Carlo for a minute. "Oh my God, you two would make such a cute couple."

"Then better give me his number."

She laughed. "But your eyes follow her."

"Who?"

Jessica shook her head. "Alex. I've only known her for a few days and she's amazing. I know you already see it."

"Jessica," Carlo sighed, "she fights me on everything."

"You wouldn't respect her if she didn't." Jessica yawned and attempted to stretch but the wounds that had been inflicted on her screamed in pain as she tried, causing her to wince. "I think I need to go back to bed."

Carlo stood and picked Jessica up. She wrapped her arms around his neck and tried not to wince again.

"Could you do something for me?" she asked.

"I'm at your service."

"When all this is over, don't be your normal stiff, dickhead self. Come back here and ask Alessandra out on a real date."

"I'll have to ask the good doctor what medications you're taking that are making you rant like a crazy person," he muttered.

"Carlo, I see how you two look at each other." She gently patted the side of his face. "You need to come back for her."

"Why?" he asked.

"Because you can't stop looking at her." She snuggled into his arms and was asleep by the time he reached the room she was staying in.

That was why he could place all the blame for this ridiculous attempt, for these ridiculous emotions, squarely and completely on the shoulders of Jessica Dodd.

He stretched his neck from side to side. "So here I am, like a fool."

A nervous fool.

He sat down and rested his elbows on his knees, rubbed his face with his hands.

What the hell was he doing? He wondered for the hundredth time. The anticipation was going to be his undoing.

Then he saw her, walking out a side exit, heading toward the parking lot. His throat tightened and something squeezed in his stomach. She looked amazing. And he laughingly understood what the phrase 'a sight for sore eyes' meant.

He took long strides to keep up with her, but he also stayed in her blind spot, just out of view. He studied her; she still wore her lab coat, her hair was pushed back under a headband and she was carrying her shoulder bag, heavy with work.

He had to clear his throat twice before he could find his voice. "Doctor Salvatore." He said her name from where he stood a few feet away.

She looked up at him and froze in place. "Carlo?" She scanned the area around her. "Is everything okay?"

"Yeah. Yes. Everything is fine. I just ..."

She raised her eyebrows, waiting for him to explain what he was doing there.

"I couldn't stop thinking about you."

"Carlo."

"We can't let this go. It's bigger than both of us."

"I thought we agreed to just let it be what it was, a little affair."

"Have you thought about me at all?" he asked. She bit her lower lip and he smiled. "Let me take you out. On a real date."

"Tonight?" she asked, confused.

"Tonight, tomorrow night, a week from now. I really don't care when, as long as you say yes."

"This isn't a good idea."

He continued talking about the date. "If I'm going to be honest, I would prefer taking you out tonight. Just to talk with you. To spend time with you."

She put her bag in the car, then turned her attention toward him. "Then what?"

He stuffed his hands inside his pockets. He didn't have a plan. He didn't have a car. He didn't have a place to stay. When he asked for the time off, the only thing he'd thought through was going to Rome. Beyond that, he had nothing.

And you've worked most of your life as an intelligence officer? Real intelligent.

"I need you." He whispered the confession, and because being near her was killing him, he crossed the slight space that separated them, and before she could lecture him about why this was a bad idea, he captured her lips in a kiss.

After a brief moment, she tilted her head to deepen the dizzying kiss and slipped her hands around his neck.

His hands clenched the fabric at her waist and pulled her against him, and as she clung to him, every doubt he had eased from his body.

With a grunt, he let go of her clothes, wrapped his arms around her waist and lifted her so he could have better access to her mouth. She instinctively wrapped her legs around his waist. His hands slowly moved to her tantalizing ass, holding her in place.

She gave a shocked moan when he squeezed slightly, but then he pressed her against the car, using it for leverage, as his tongue swept through her mouth.

A loud cough and insistent clearing of a throat behind them broke Carlo's concentration. He glanced angrily behind him, just as Alessandra caught a view of who was interrupting them. She slapped at his arms to release her, and as she smoothed her clothes out she nodded to the doctor who'd interrupted.

"Doctor Martelli." She touched a hand to her hair.

"Doctor Salvatore?" The older doctor frowned as he held out a purse toward her. "You forgot this."

She looked at the purse and blinked several times.

"Thank you," Carlo offered and took the purse for her.

"Oh, yes. Yes, thank you. I had my keys in my pocket and had so many other things on my mind I completely forgot." Alessandra stumbled over the explanation.

The doctor assessed Carlo and nodded his head. "I see that."

"Thank you, Doctor," she said as Carlo handed her the purse. "Have a good night."

The doctor walked away but took several backwards glances toward Carlo and Alessandra.

"Can I take you to dinner?" Carlo asked.

"They don't see me as human." She sighed. "It's my own fault. I tend to keep people at arm's length. He's going to have so much fun telling everyone what he just saw." Carlo reached out and cupped the side of her cheek, she instinctively leaned into his hand. "And who he saw me doing it with." She smiled up at him.

That smile was his undoing, his home, his peace, and his storm all wrapped into one. "Don't worry, I don't think anyone will believe him."

Alessandra pulled away from Carlo. "Take me to dinner. Where's your car?"

"I took the train and metro. Walked the rest of the way."

She shook her head. "Get in."

When they were in the car, she asked, "Where are you taking me to dinner?"

"Did I mention I needed to see you so desperately, I came with no plan in mind, other than to ask you out?" He took her hand and brushed a kiss along her knuckles. "I don't care where we go, as long as I'm with you."

"Hmph." She laughed.

"La Pergola." He suggested the restaurant that had been declared the most romantic in Rome.

"I'm not dressed for La Pergola." Alessandra gestured to her clothes.

"I'll take you there tomorrow night then," he decided. "Tonight, I just want to be with you."

"We're going to fight," Alessandra said as she pulled her hand away. She started the car and began to drive.

"Probably."

"Our schedules are very different, and you don't even work in the same city as me."

"That's going to make it an interesting relationship," he countered.

"This is never going to work," she stated.

"Let's go to that little trattoria near your house."

"Carlo ..."

"I have a good feeling about all this." He fumbled with the radio until he found a soft, romantic song.

"You have a good feeling." She laughed.

"Amo." He caught her hand again when she came to a stoplight, pulling her attention to him. "Even if it takes us the rest of our lives to figure this out, I think it just might be a pretty great adventure."

She shook her head, eyes sparkling. The cars behind them erupted in honking when the light turned green and she didn't immediately start driving. She ignored the noise, reaching over to pull Carlo to her, and gave him a quick kiss. She pulled away, her eyes searching his, then with a sigh, continued to drive.

"Where are you staying?" She asked.

"With you," he said as he draped his arm around the back of her headrest.

"You're going to be trouble."

"Who knows, maybe it'll be worth it," Carlo replied.

Notes

Thank you so much for reading *Worth the Trouble*. I hope you enjoyed the time you spent with Carlo and Alessandra. Like an early reviewer said, "This book feels like catching up with old friends."

One of the things I like to do is to give my readers some fun book trivia. So without further ado ...

1. The Ospedale San Raffaele is a fictional hospital. But since Saint Raphael is known as the patron saint of the sick, and I grew up Catholic (as you may or may not have caught on to, as there are a few undercurrents of Catholicism in my books) I leaned into the saint and name.

2. For that matter San Brochero is a fictional town, but I named after the Catholic Saint San Brochero; who is the Patron Saint of the Province of Córdoba in Venezuela.

3. When my sister, who is an ex-pat living in Florence, was pregnant; her in-laws thrust quite a few (amazing) old, Italian wives' tales on her shoulders. Among them was that if a woman had bad indigestion, it meant the baby would be born with a lot of hair. Also, eating a big slab of meat helped you stay healthy during your pregnancy. And, she should stay away far away from wind. It seems wind is really bad when you are pregnant in Italy. A pregnant woman standing in front of a fan or an open window with a breeze ... get out your holy water and get that pregnant woman away from the wind! (It's a whole thing.)

4. The kitchen in the villa where the Dodd family visited with the Salvatores: The large table that sat at least 16, it isn't something from my imagination. When my sister was married, 22 family members descended upon the Tuscan countryside for the event and we all stayed in the same large farmhouse, which was broken up into three levels and 10-ish

rooms. The kitchen table there was huge and amazing. This photo of all of us eating together (and giving a heartfelt 'cin cin') is one of my favorite memories and pictures.

5. The Macchiato- oh, let's talk about the macchiato my friends. Starbucks stole the name and changed it completely and it's a problem. The word Macchiato comes from the Italian verb: *macchiare*, which means "to stain". The traditional (real) macchiato is a shot of espresso that is 'stained' or 'marked' with a hit of steamed milk. That's it. That's the glory of it.

6. Giovanni Donato, who works for Rome's Archeological Ruin and Excavation Team, is not some random character I threw in for the hell of it. We're going to meet him again! And sure you aren't that invested in him just yet. But trust me, you will be! Find him in my book *La Bella Luna*.

7. I lost my grandma, Rose Marie, during the final editing of this book. She was 94 years young. An amazing woman who lived a fabulous life. In her own words (via her will), she said, "I have lived a great life and love you all so much." She was of Italian descent (that's where I get it from), and I was lucky enough to go to Italy twice with her. I got to sit next to her in a gondola, walk with her in the Vatican, throw a coin in the Trevi fountain in Rome with her ... all the while she marveled about 'what her people had done.' Knowing she was on the decline during the final edit,

made me quite reminiscent and I ended up adding her throughout the book in little ways. (The Trattoria Rosa, is one example). I added her to this book for myself I suppose. So her memory would continue through something I'd created

Hey Grandma, look what *my* people helped me do!

Acknowledgements

A big thanks to **Biggs**, whose military expertise helped me plan a seemingly plausible extraction of Alessandra from her kidnappers.

Thank you to **Jessica and Cami** at <u>Soul Self Defense</u> for letting me take a few classes so the women I write, when faced with difficult situations, can continue to be badass in very believable ways.

Krista Harper at <u>Happily Ever After Required</u>. Her work was two-fold this book! She's an amazing book coach, and as a former nurse, she helped guide me so that Matteo and Carlo didn't *unreasonably* bleed out and could *reasonably* be saved.

A.M. Rasmussen. You know I love the works of art you create for my book covers, right? You know how amazing you are, right? For those who are getting to know me at this point, when I started on this road of self-publishing, I had a vision of what I wanted my covers to look like; as a purveyor of world travel, and a writer who talks about sense of place *a lot*, I wanted covers that were reminiscent of retro travel posters. A.M. Rasmussen has hit the nail on the head each and every time.

Ariane Kimlinger. I've said it before, she's my Grammatical Guru. She's also one hell of an editor and friend. When I set out to self-publish, I knew I would need a good editor. I ended up with a great one. (Side note: When you read an indie book, if you find one or two spelling mistakes or none at all, please think about that for a moment. There are only two of us doing all the heavy lifting when it comes to the words on the page. These books run about 94k words. That means Ariane is 150% amazing for making me look as good as I do!)

Michele who is the final reader of my books before they are published. You are amazing. I can't thank you enough.

TIRAA (The Independent Romance Author Association), an amazing group of writers who continue to inspire and motivate me! Come check us out if you're an established writer who would like support or you're just getting started.

To the early readers and continual cheerleaders who always comment "I can't wait til the next book" (even when the book they just read hasn't been released yet!) … thank you thank you thank you for the endless support.

And last but not least, although I didn't know anything about Doctors Without Borders when I began writing this book, I have found it is a pretty amazing, wonderful and brilliant organization: We provide independent, impartial medical humanitarian assistance to the people who need it most. Doctors Without Borders/Médecins Sans Frontières (MSF) cares for people affected by conflict, disease outbreaks, natural and human-made disasters, and exclusion from health care in more than 70 countries.

My family and friends, you know how much I love and appreciate you, right?

And you, my dear reader, thank you for taking a chance on this book. If you like reading the fun behind the scenes stuff and want to be notified about my upcoming releases and other information you won't find anywhere else, why not sign up for my Newsletter?!

You can find the sign-up at nicolesharpwrites.com

Chapter 1

It was almost time.

Cassandra Dodd's breathing was jagged and shallow.

Every few seconds, she'd gulp as deep a breath as she could to inflate her lungs, in the hopes it would settle her nervous system.

It didn't work.

She glanced at her phone again: one minute.

She began to cough, a mingled result of her damned nerves, erratic wheezing, and stupid aridness of her mouth. She rolled her eyes at the rising of emotions pressing against her chest. No one could truly ready someone else for moments like this, no matter how many detailed conversations. And no one ever mentioned that such overwhelming emotions could render a woman unable to create saliva. The thought turned the cough into a barked laugh.

Another glance at the time; any second now.

Cassie attempted another deep cleansing breath in through her nose, but the abrupt exhale of hot air was an exercise in breathlessness that overpowered the attempted calm.

Her irregular heartbeat was in charge now.

The faint squeak of floorboards, just outside the door, electrified every last nerve her body housed; she flung the front door open and blew out the name 'Benji' as she greedily soaked in the vision of the man standing before her: bearded; tired rings around his eyes; rumpled polo, untucked yet still hugging his well-toned frame; jeans, and black and white Adidas. Every inch of the man's entire six foot three frame was wonderfully, ridiculously sexy.

His fatigued features brightened at the sight of Cassie and his own greeting was an incoherent mixture of a groan and garbled "hey" as he dropped the duffle bag he carried and reached for her in the same instant she reached for him.

They crashed into each other, desperate to make up for the last three weeks of lost time. Lips and hands fumbled as they claimed territory they'd been parted from for far too long. They were animals, moaning and clawing at each other.

"Oh my God," a laugh called, "get a room."

Cassie reluctantly pulled away and turned to stare daggers at her sister, Jessica, who had chosen that precise moment to walk by and disrupt the heated display.

Cassie took in her sister's appearance; dishwater blonde hair pulled into a loose bun, wearing a T-shirt and yoga pants on a frame that stood a fraction shorter than her own five nine. She was mildly irritated at how 'at home' Jessica looked. "I have a room," Cassie grumbled, "In fact, we have an entire apartment. Maybe *you* should get out of our apartment."

"I can't. *Our* place is being fumigated." Jessica's blue eyes sparkled as she mocked Cassie's anger.

Agent Benjamin Stills–Benji to his girlfriend; Stills to the rest of the world–moved his bag just inside the apartment, used his foot to close the door, then urged Cassie's attention back to him.

When she met his amber gaze, the fog of frustration dissipated as his fingers splayed across her hips, then moved up to her waist and pulled her closer so she could feel the heat radiating off him. He winked and finally uttered the greeting she so needed, his voice low and velvety, "Hey Dodd."

Saying her last name, which had become an alluring endearment over the past two years, melted her against him and refocused her. "I missed you," she sighed.

He leaned his forehead against hers and breathed her in as she wrapped her arms around his waist. Abruptly, she stepped away and held his face gently in her hands. Stills raised an eyebrow as she turned his head slowly to the right and then left, narrowing her gaze in a study of his face.

"What are we doing?"

"Seeing if you're hurt." Cassie was searching for cuts or bruises, or any other signs. Satisfied with his face, she pulled his hands from around her and studied the knuckles; no bruising or cuts.

"I think I'd tell you if I'd been hurt."

"Would you?" She slipped her hands under his shirt and spread them across his muscular chest, watching his face for a reaction that might give away any serious injury. His eyes darkened with the attention, but there was no sharp intake of breath. She continued her tactile search, slipping her hands around his powerful back and shoulders, running them along the broad span.

"Is there something else I can help you with?" Stills didn't disapprove of having her hands all over him.

"Are you okay?" Finished with the upper part of his body, she crouched, apparently in an effort to continue searching his lower extremities for wounds. Stills crouched down, mirroring her attempt, and gripped her hands in his. "That's enough," he said gently.

She sprang into a standing position, pulling him up with her; worried eyes searching his. "Did something happen to your legs?"

"Dodd ..." He nodded across the room. "I'd prefer that intimate part of my pat-down to happen without your sister present."

"But you're okay?"

"I'm okay," he promised.

Cassie squinted as she tried to ascertain exactly what he'd been through with by examining his bloodshot eyes.

For the past three weeks Stills had been on the longest assignment he'd been given in the last two years. But if Cassie was certain about anything when it came to this man; he was careful, calculating and damn good at his job. He didn't work in the field often, and the few times it couldn't be avoided had only been assignments lasting two or three days. This trip couldn't be helped and Cassie found herself in the precarious position of trusting his judgment and intuition while going about her day-to-day life, then having to ward off unfounded worries late at night.

She ran her fingers along his chin. "I really like the beard."

"Oh yeah?"

She lowered her voice as she admitted, "I have a few itches I think will benefit *tremendously* from it."

"Do you want me to leave?" Jessica called from the sofa where she was dramatically turning up the sound on the TV.

Cassie's eyes widened before she turned all her attention toward her sister. "Yes." She put her hands on her hips, "You and your *husband* should leave."

"He's not my husband."

"You're getting married in four months." Cassie waved exhaustedly. "And you never got divorced from your Vegas wedding, so on paper, you're still married."

"It's not the same." Jessica muttered her lame defense.

"Yes. It is. And you know what else? You and your husband bought a house together. So you should go back to your *home*."

Jessica rolled her eyes. "I *want* to, but we *can't*."

"Just tell the fumigator to ... fuck off," Cassie insisted.

"Cassie, the house is still tented and it's not my fault everything is taking longer than anticipated. And we would have stayed with Mom and Dad, but Mom's the one who found the two for one coupon in the first place."

Cassie opened her mouth but before she could continue, Jessica added, "And *you're* the one who said it was fine if we stayed here." She pointed while mocking the invitation Cassie had given— "It'll be nice to have company while Benji's away."

"And *you* said you would only be here for *three* days." Cassie pointed back. "It's been ten. *Ten* days!"

"We'd stay in a hotel, but we just bought a house!" Jessica bit back to her older sister. "We need to save money."

Stills laughed and tugged on Cassie's arm, propelling her back to him. He slowly lowered his lips to hers, whispering when he was a mere fraction away, "If she gets uncomfortable, she can leave the room."

"I thought you said you didn't want to do anything intimate in front of my sister."

"Well ..."

Just then the door flung open and slammed into Stills' side, parting him from Cassie, and forcing her back a few steps.

"Dammit!" Stills growled.

The offender, Jessica's non-husband, Parker Salvatore, glanced a disheveled sandy blond head around the door. "Shit, sorry man."

Cassie rolled her eyes, shrugging as she mumbled, "Welcome home, Benji."

TO
CONTINUE
Reading

Go to:

NicoleSharpWrites.com

Legend has it that Nicole Sharp was born to hippies during an ice storm in Stone Mountain, Georgia. While confirmation of said events cannot be agreed upon, one fact is for certain, it was a Tuesday.

By age twelve, Nicole was sure of two things: 1) She wanted to be a writer and 2) She wanted to travel. She begged her parents to allow her to voyage alone to exotic lands. They permitted her to go from California to Boise, Idaho to visit a great-grandmother.

After muddling through her college years, Nicole graduated with a Bachelors in History (think Greeks and Romans). Why not study English if she wanted to be a writer? There were better stories in history class.

Nicole is Italian. According to Ancestry.com it's a rather low percentage, but she feels she is at least 51% Italian. She's visited the homeland a handful of times, studied the language and loves the Italian cappuccino.

Nicole's first concert was to see the bluegrass group The Seldom Scene when she was a fifteen-year-old, thanks to her parent's bluegrass phase. However, she never admits it, and instead tells everyone that They Might Be Giants, whom she saw in college, was her first real concert.

Her first car was a yellow Chevy Celebrity and her favorite job was working as a docent at a museum in an old Colorado mining town. She has written extensively about both.

Visit NicoleSharpWrites.com for more entertainment.

www.ingramcontent.com/pod-product-compliance
Lightning Source LLC
Chambersburg PA
CBHW020337010826
48970CB00012B/1472